Splatoon™

VOL. 2

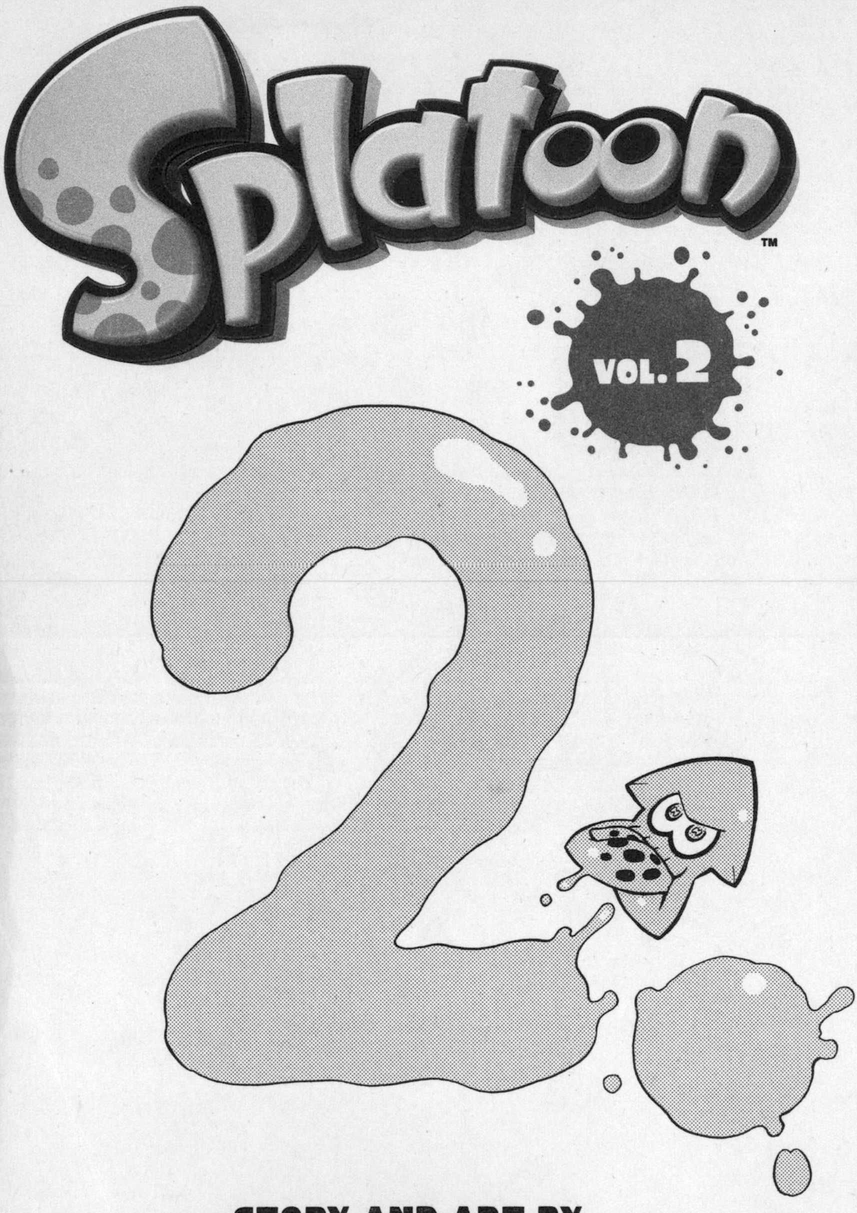

STORY AND ART BY

Sankichi Hinodeya

CONTENTS

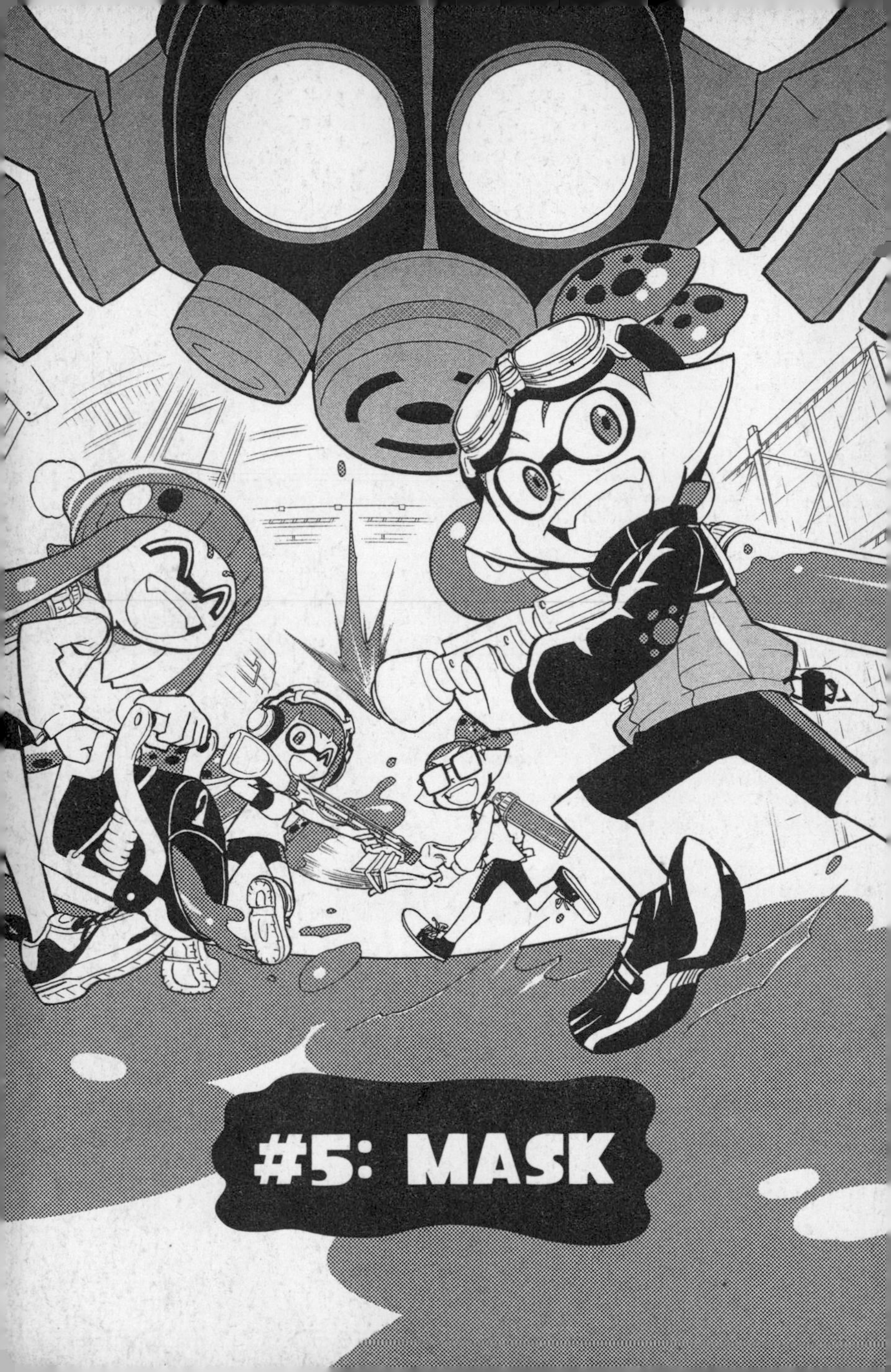
#5: MASK

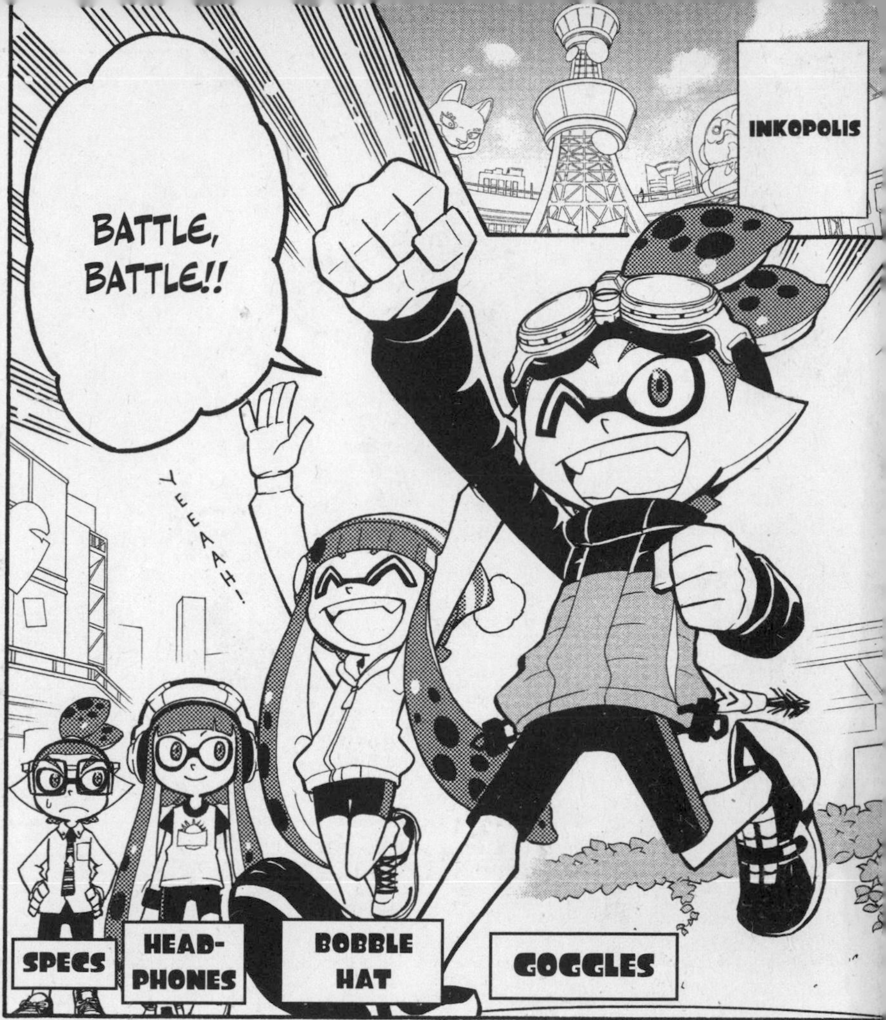
INKOPOLIS
BATTLE, BATTLE!!
YEEEAAAH!
GOGGLES
BOBBLE HAT
HEAD-PHONES
SPECS

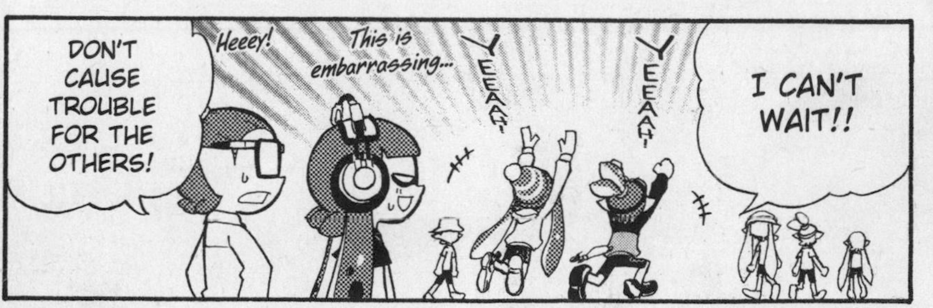
I CAN'T WAIT!!
YEEEAAH!
YEEEAAH!
This is embarrassing...
Heeey!
DON'T CAUSE TROUBLE FOR THE OTHERS!

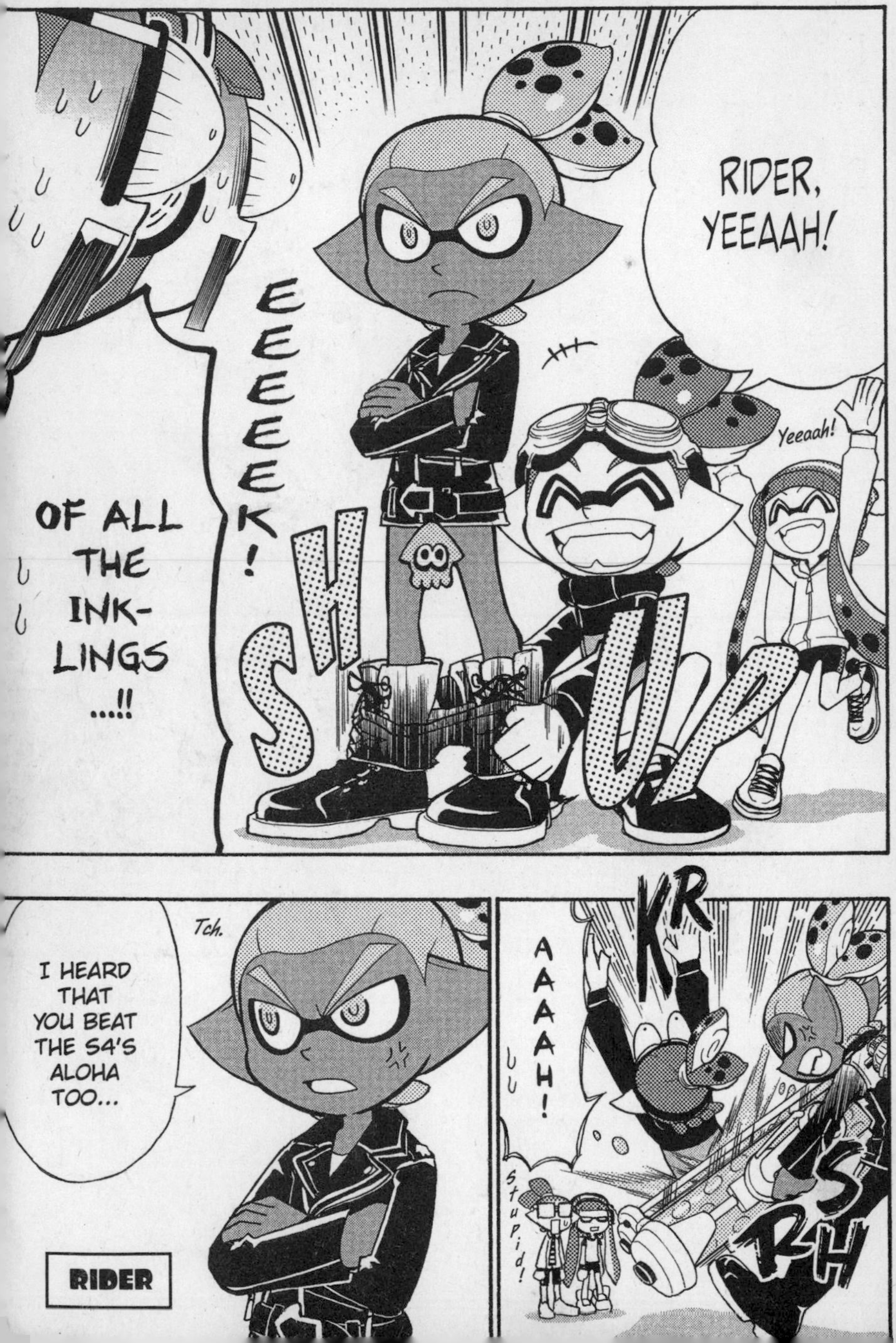
RIDER, YEEEAAH!
Yeeaah!
EEEEEEK!
OF ALL THE INK-LINGS ...!!
KR
AAAAH!
Stupid!
Tch.
I HEARD THAT YOU BEAT THE S4'S ALOHA TOO...
RIDER

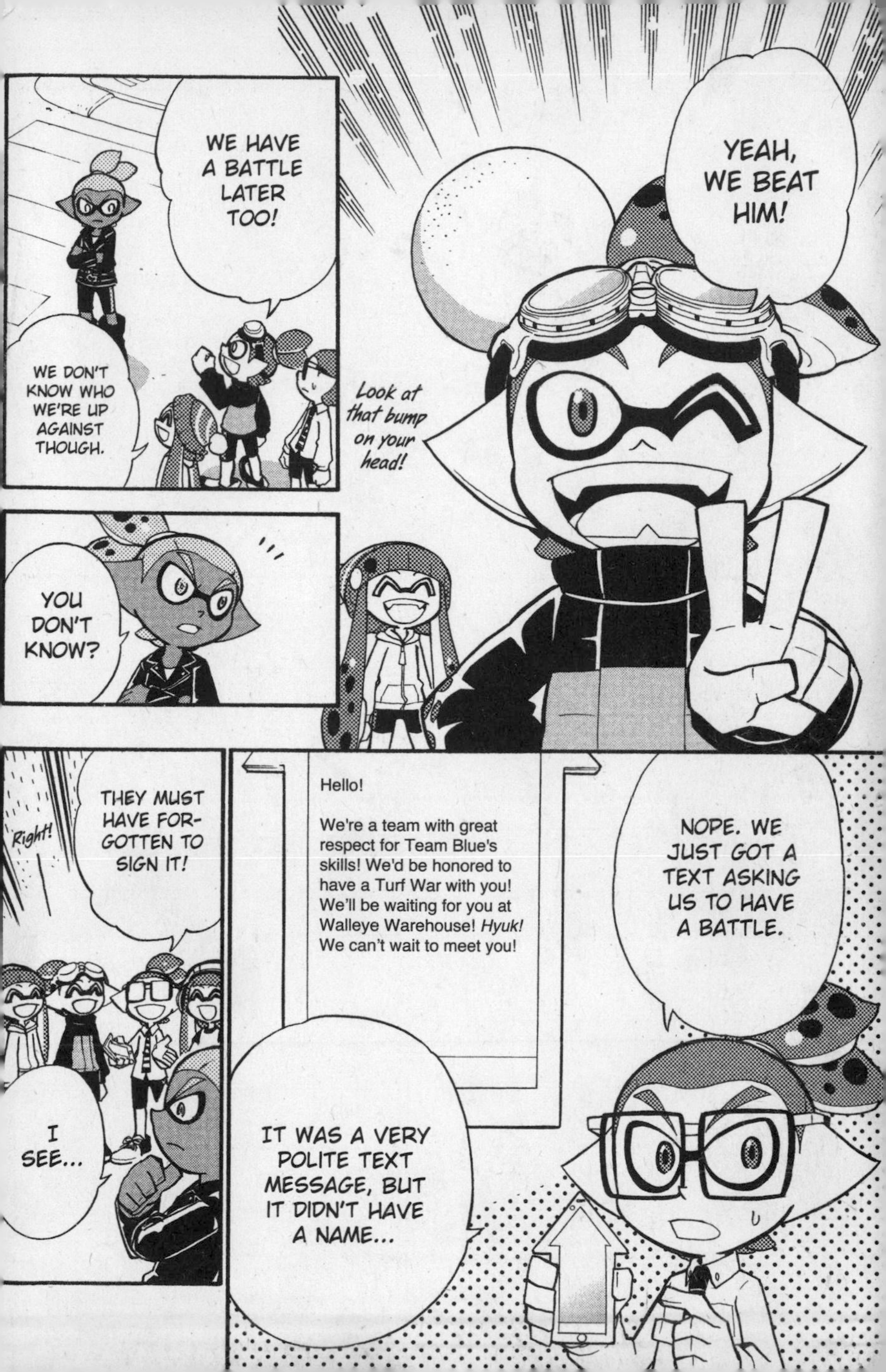

YEAH, WE BEAT HIM!
Look at that bump on your head!
WE HAVE A BATTLE LATER TOO!
WE DON'T KNOW WHO WE'RE UP AGAINST THOUGH.
YOU DON'T KNOW?
NOPE. WE JUST GOT A TEXT ASKING US TO HAVE A BATTLE.
Hello!
We're a team with great respect for Team Blue's skills! We'd be honored to have a Turf War with you! We'll be waiting for you at Walleye Warehouse! *Hyuk!* We can't wait to meet you!
IT WAS A VERY POLITE TEXT MESSAGE, BUT IT DIDN'T HAVE A NAME...
THEY MUST HAVE FOR-GOTTEN TO SIGN IT!
Right!
I SEE...

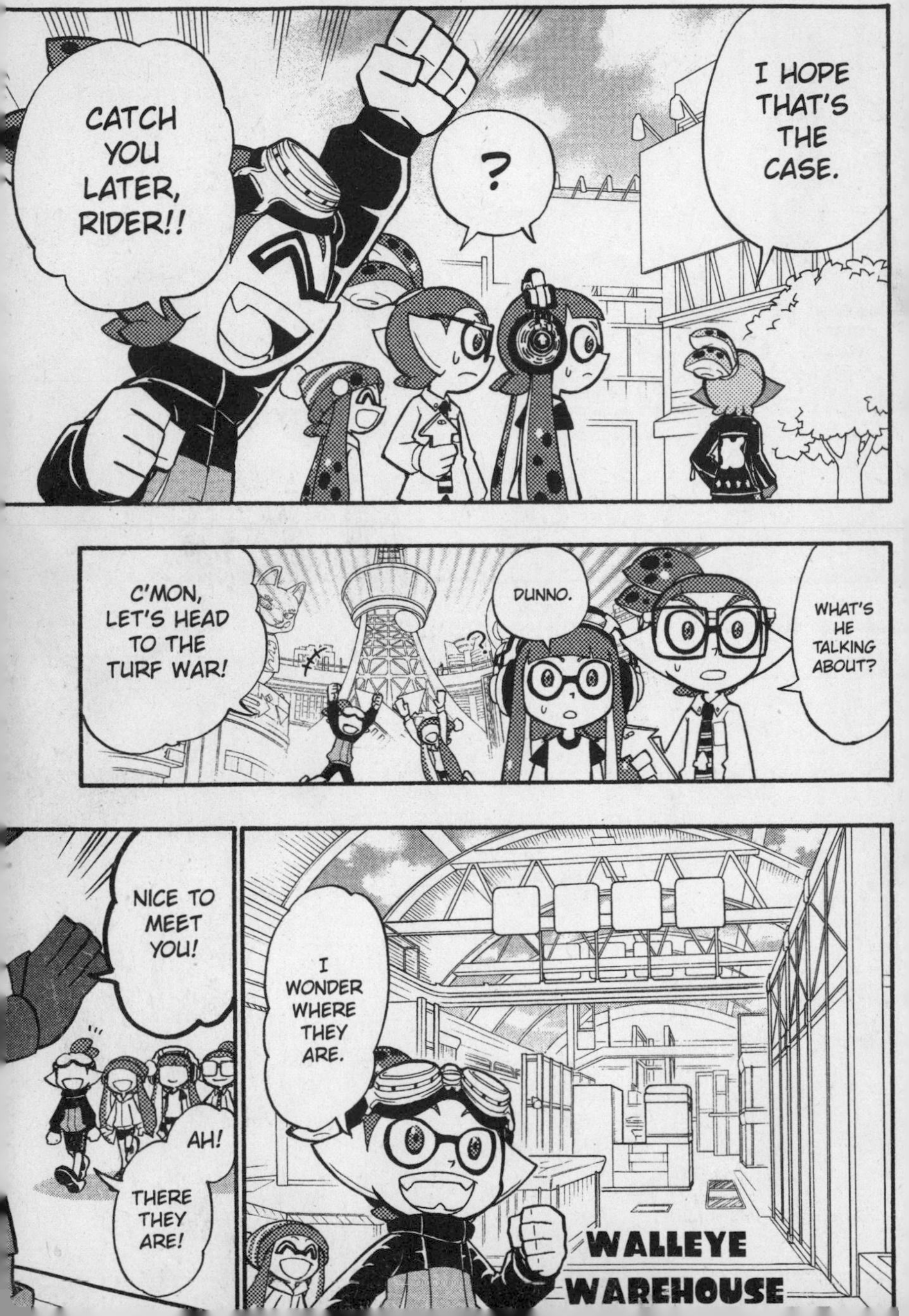
I HOPE THAT'S THE CASE.
?
CATCH YOU LATER, RIDER!!
WHAT'S HE TALKING ABOUT?
DUNNO.
C'MON, LET'S HEAD TO THE TURF WAR!
I WONDER WHERE THEY ARE.
WALLEYE WAREHOUSE
AH!
THERE THEY ARE!
NICE TO MEET YOU!

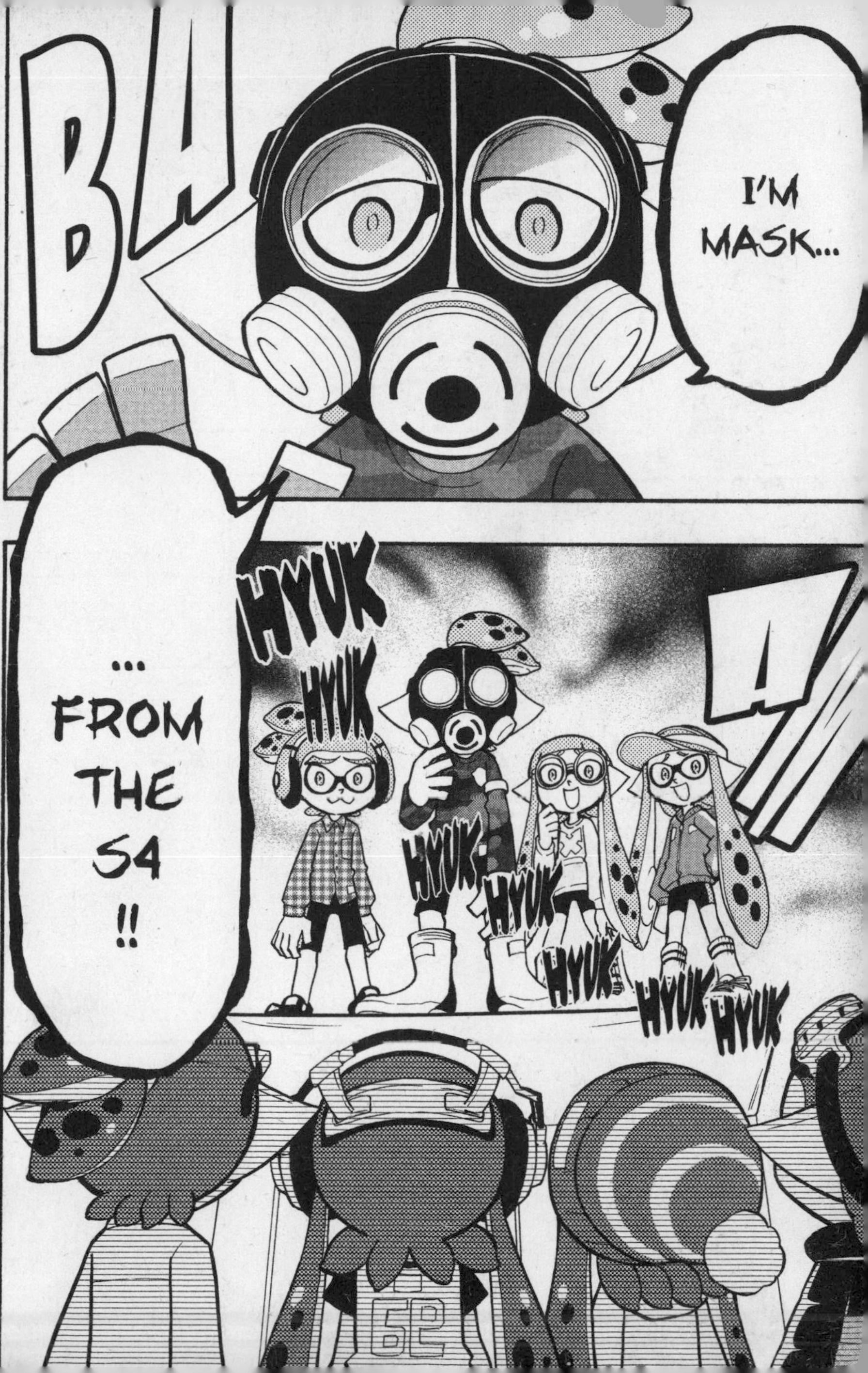
I'M MASK...
BA
!
... FROM THE S4 !!
HYUK HYUK
HYUK HYUK
HYUK HYUK
HYUK HYUK

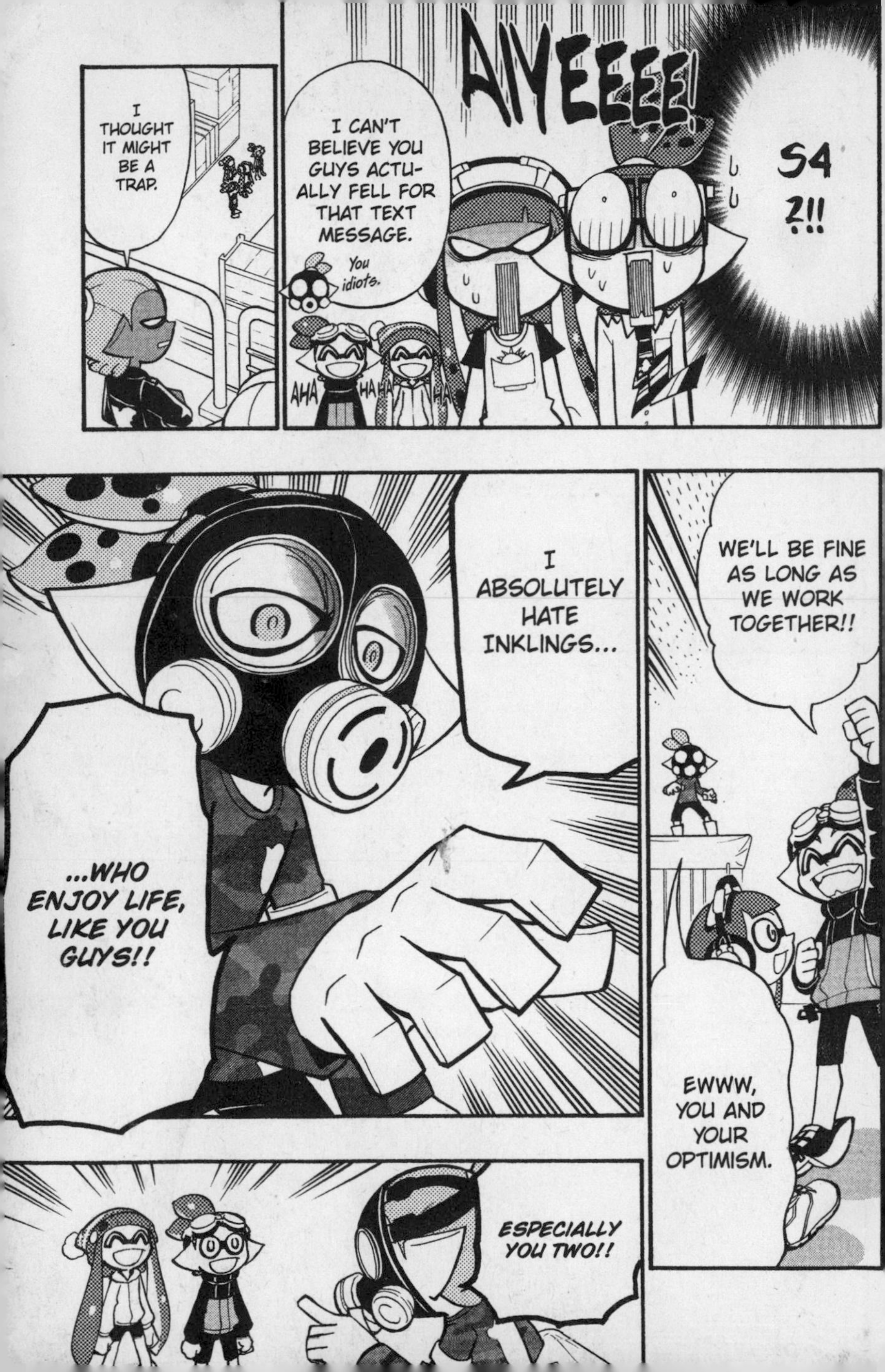
S4 ?!!
AIYEEEE!
I CAN'T BELIEVE YOU GUYS ACTUALLY FELL FOR THAT TEXT MESSAGE.
You idiots.
HA HA
AHA HAHA
I THOUGHT IT MIGHT BE A TRAP.
WE'LL BE FINE AS LONG AS WE WORK TOGETHER!!
EWWW, YOU AND YOUR OPTIMISM.
I ABSOLUTELY HATE INKLINGS...
...WHO ENJOY LIFE, LIKE YOU GUYS!!
ESPECIALLY YOU TWO!!

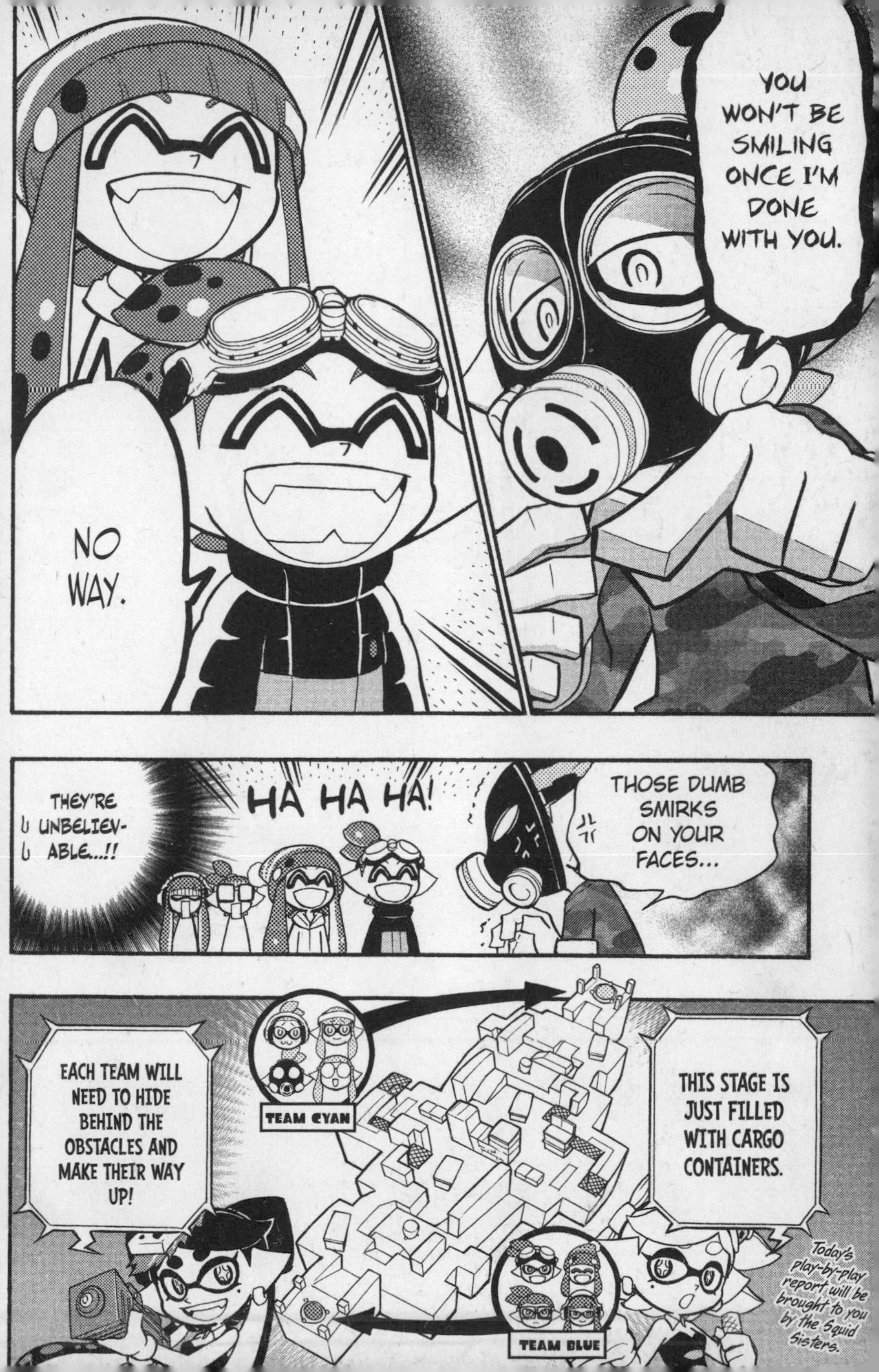
YOU WON'T BE SMILING ONCE I'M DONE WITH YOU.
NO WAY.
THOSE DUMB SMIRKS ON YOUR FACES...
HA HA HA!
THEY'RE UNBELIEV-ABLE...!!
THIS STAGE IS JUST FILLED WITH CARGO CONTAINERS.
Today's play-by-play report will be brought to you by the Squid Sisters.
TEAM CYAN
TEAM BLUE
EACH TEAM WILL NEED TO HIDE BEHIND THE OBSTACLES AND MAKE THEIR WAY UP!

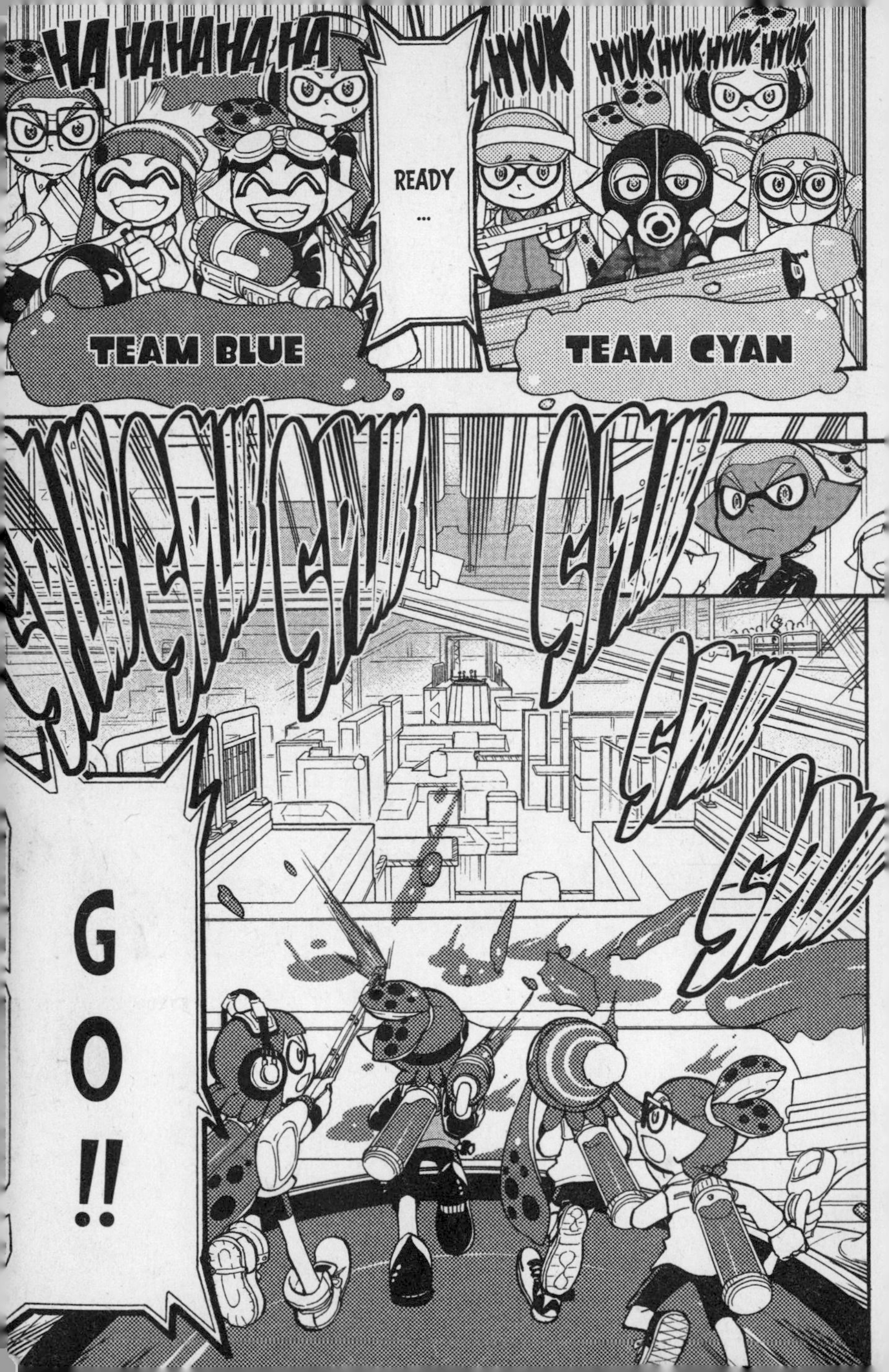
HYUK HYUK HYUK HYUK HYUK
TEAM CYAN
READY
...
HA HA HA HA HA HA
TEAM BLUE
GO!!

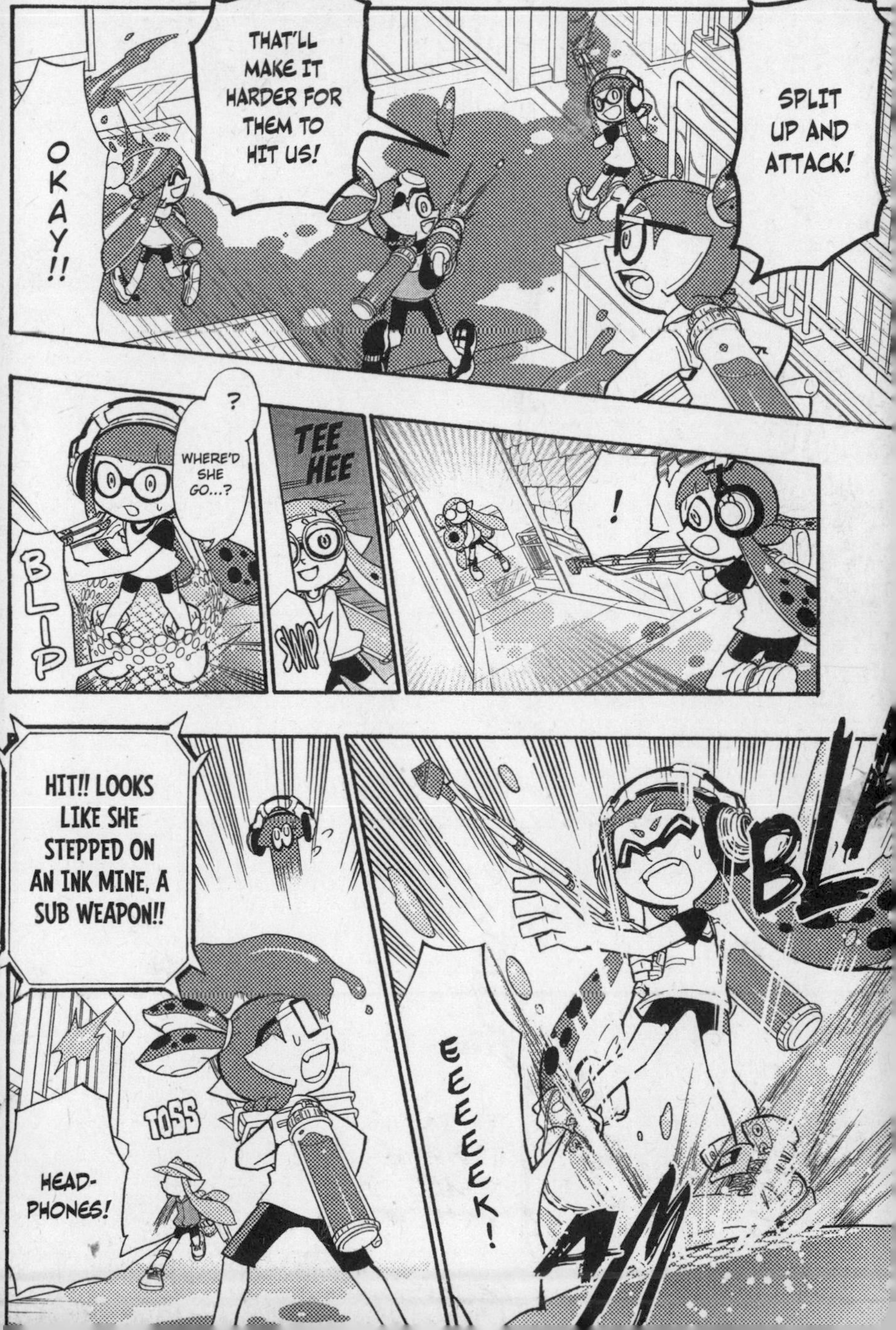
SPLIT UP AND ATTACK!
THAT'LL MAKE IT HARDER FOR THEM TO HIT US!
OKAY!!
!
TEE HEE
SWP
?
WHERE'D SHE GO...?
BLIP
EEEEEEK!
HIT!! LOOKS LIKE SHE STEPPED ON AN INK MINE, A SUB WEAPON!!
TOSS
HEAD-PHONES!

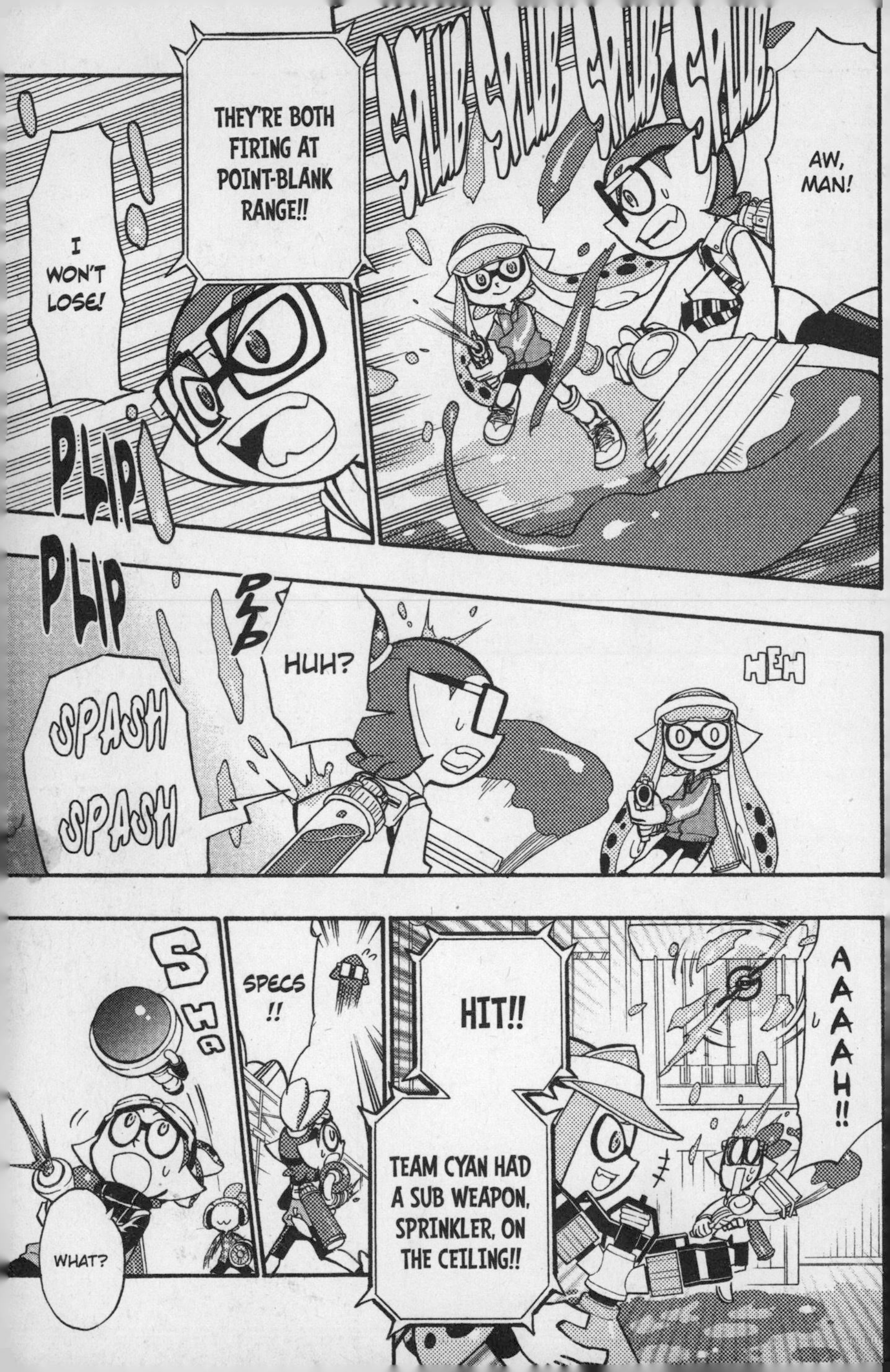
AW, MAN!
SPLUB SPLUB SPLUB SPLUB
THEY'RE BOTH FIRING AT POINT-BLANK RANGE!!
I WON'T LOSE!
PLIP
PLIP
HEH
HUH?
PLIP
SPASH
SPASH
AAAAH!!
HIT!!
TEAM CYAN HAD A SUB WEAPON, SPRINKLER, ON THE CEILING!!
SPECS!!
SHA
WHAT?

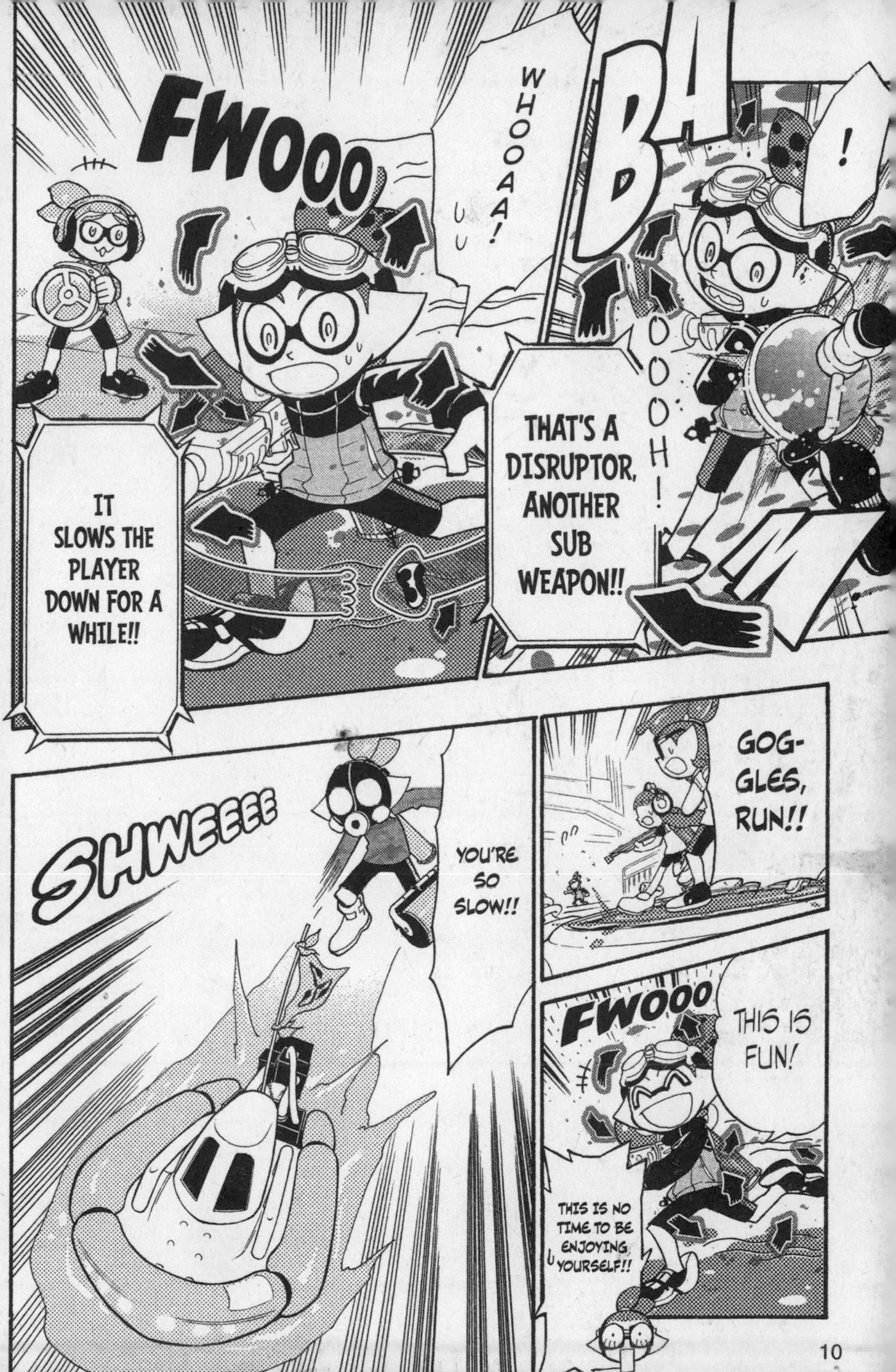
BA
!
M
OOOOH!
THAT'S A DISRUPTOR, ANOTHER SUB WEAPON!!
WHOOAA!
FWOOO
IT SLOWS THE PLAYER DOWN FOR A WHILE!!
GOG-GLES, RUN!!
FWOOO
THIS IS FUN!
THIS IS NO TIME TO BE ENJOYING YOURSELF!!
SHWEEEE
YOU'RE SO SLOW!!

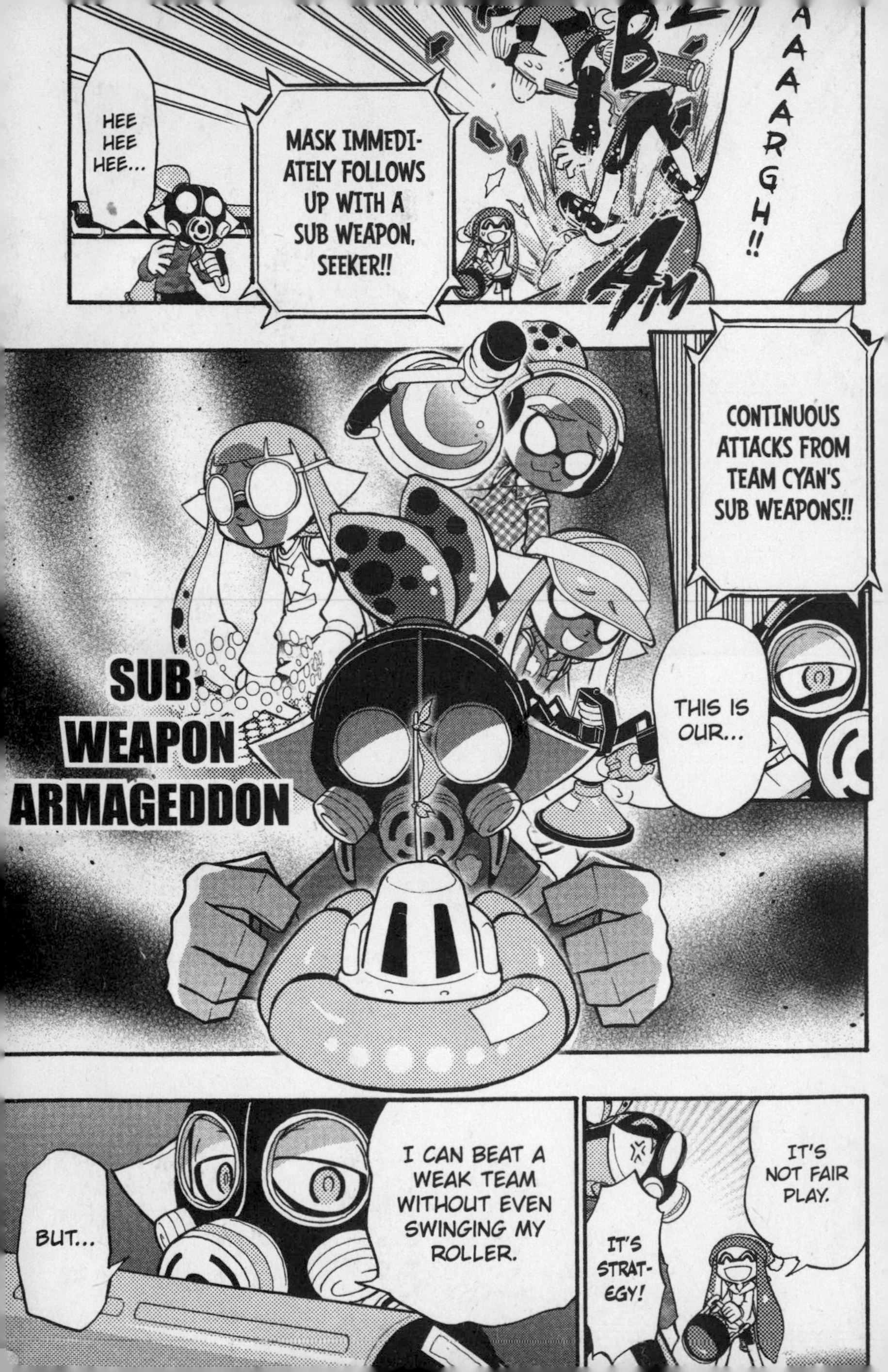
AAAARGH!!
BAM
MASK IMMEDIATELY FOLLOWS UP WITH A SUB WEAPON, SEEKER!!
HEE HEE HEE...
CONTINUOUS ATTACKS FROM TEAM CYAN'S SUB WEAPONS!!
THIS IS OUR...
SUB-WEAPON ARMAGEDDON
IT'S NOT FAIR PLAY.
IT'S STRATEGY!
I CAN BEAT A WEAK TEAM WITHOUT EVEN SWINGING MY ROLLER.
BUT...

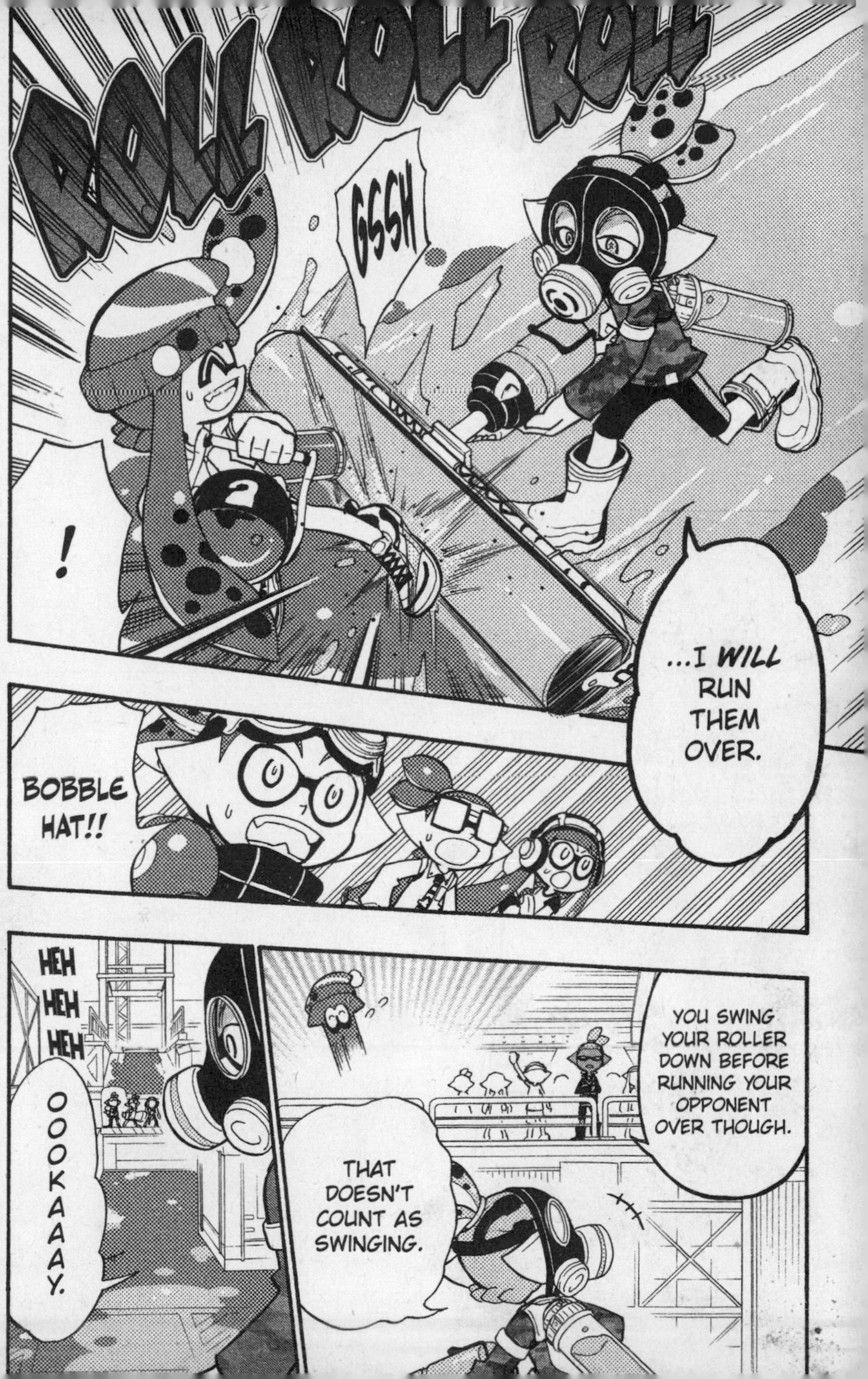
ROLL ROLL ROLL
GSSH
...I WILL RUN THEM OVER.
!
BOBBLE HAT!!
YOU SWING YOUR ROLLER DOWN BEFORE RUNNING YOUR OPPONENT OVER THOUGH.
THAT DOESN'T COUNT AS SWINGING.
HEH HEH HEH
OOOKAAAY.

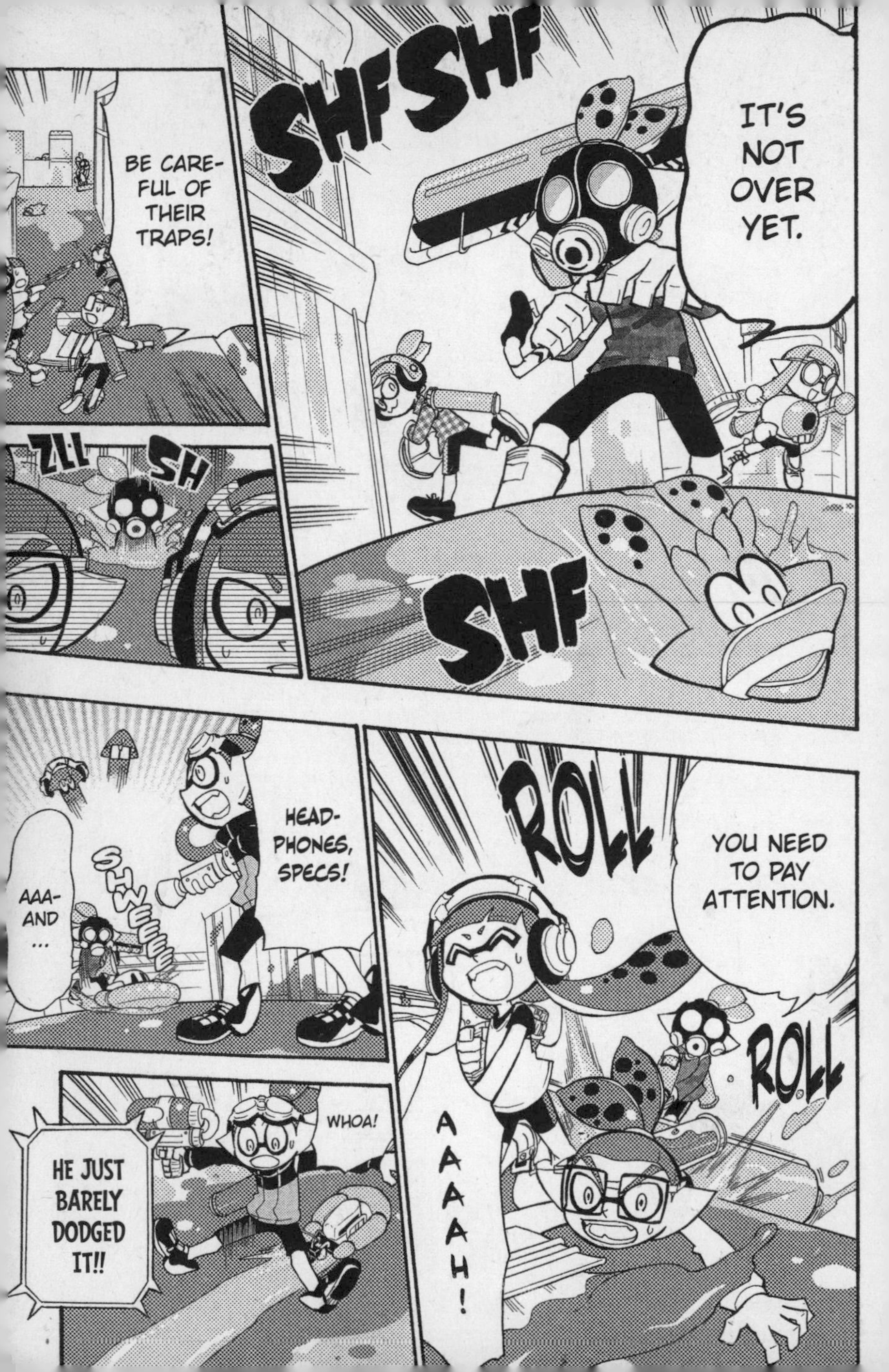
IT'S NOT OVER YET.
SHFSHF
SHF
BE CARE-FUL OF THEIR TRAPS!
SH
YOU NEED TO PAY ATTENTION.
ROLL
ROLL
AAAAH!
HEAD-PHONES, SPECS!
SHWEEE
AAA-AND ...
WHOA!
HE JUST BARELY DODGED IT!!

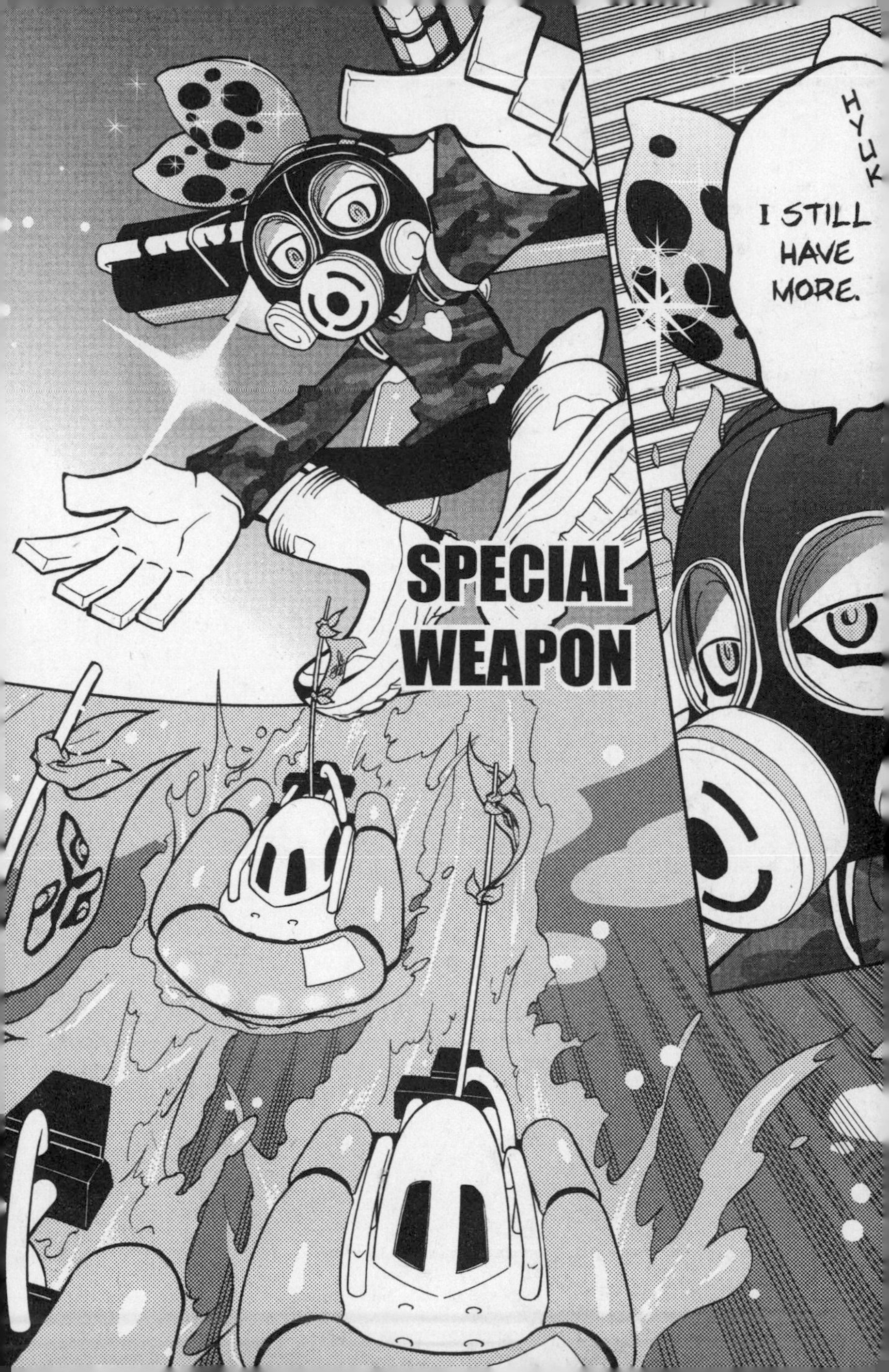
HYUK
I STILL HAVE MORE.
SPECIAL WEAPON

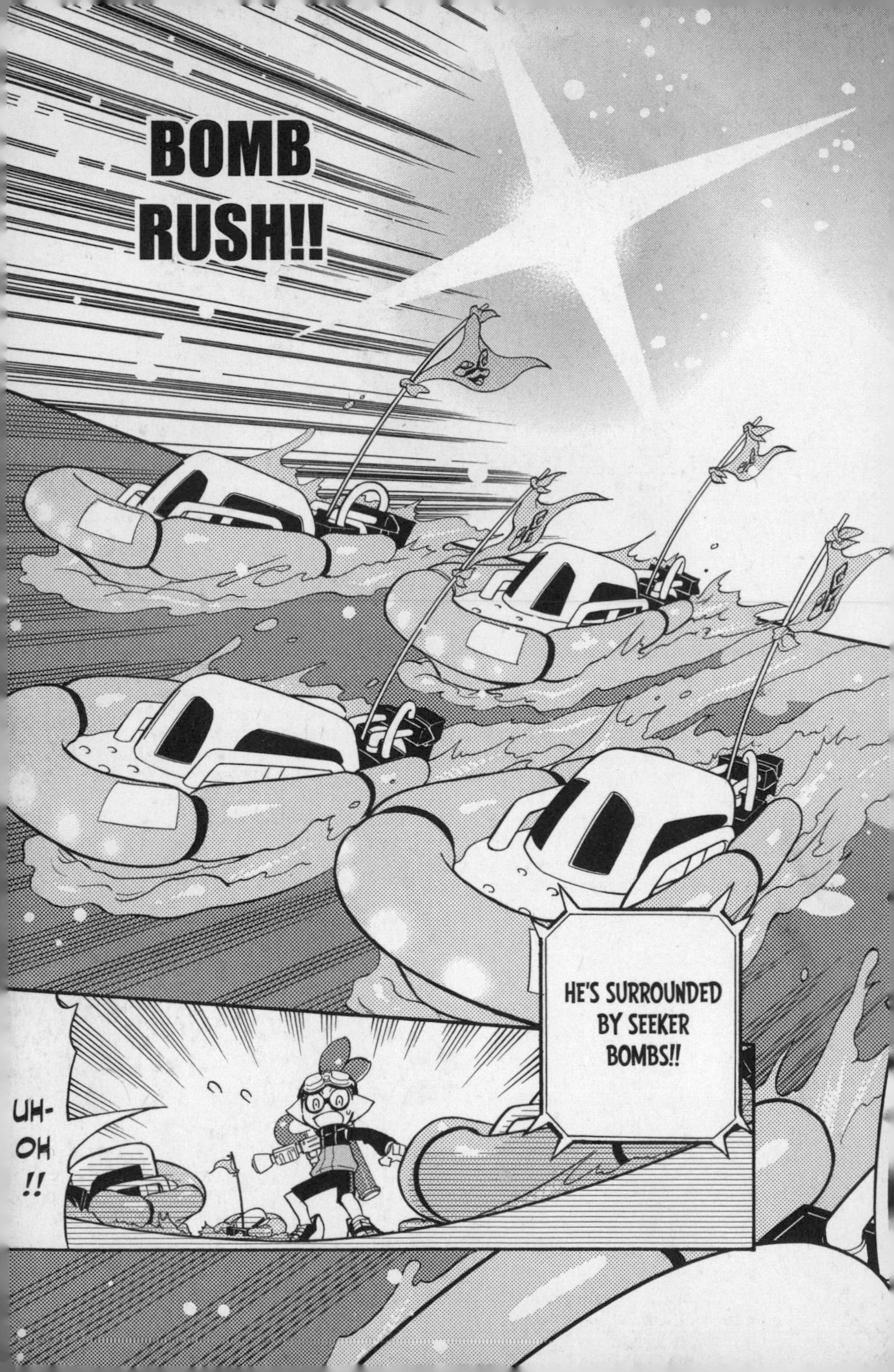
BOMB RUSH!!
HE'S SURROUNDED BY SEEKER BOMBS!!
UH-OH!!

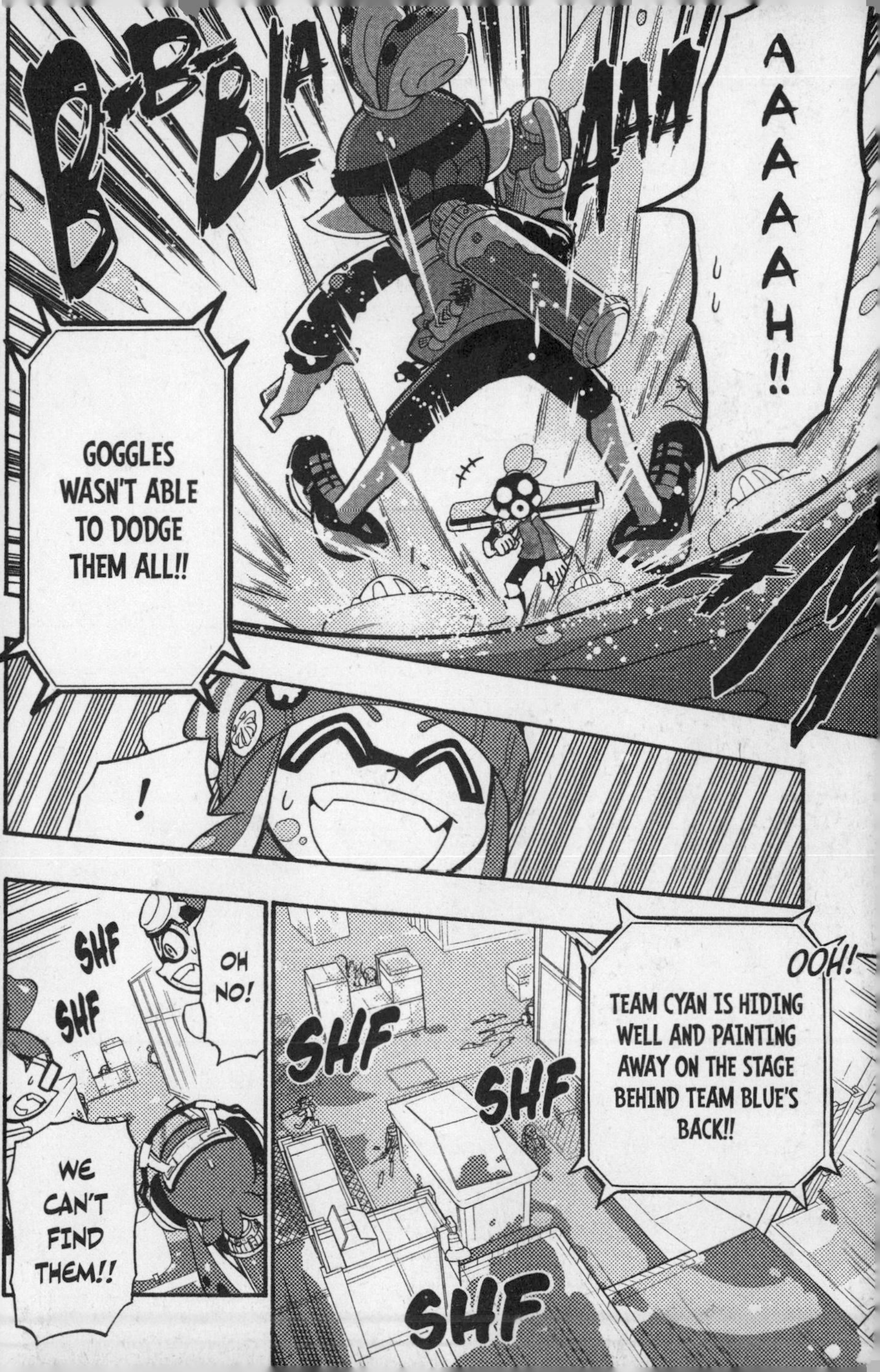
AAAAAH!!
B-B-BLAAAA
GOGGLES WASN'T ABLE TO DODGE THEM ALL!!
!
OOH!
TEAM CYAN IS HIDING WELL AND PAINTING AWAY ON THE STAGE BEHIND TEAM BLUE'S BACK!!
SHF
SHF
SHF
SHF
SHF
OH NO!
WE CAN'T FIND THEM!!

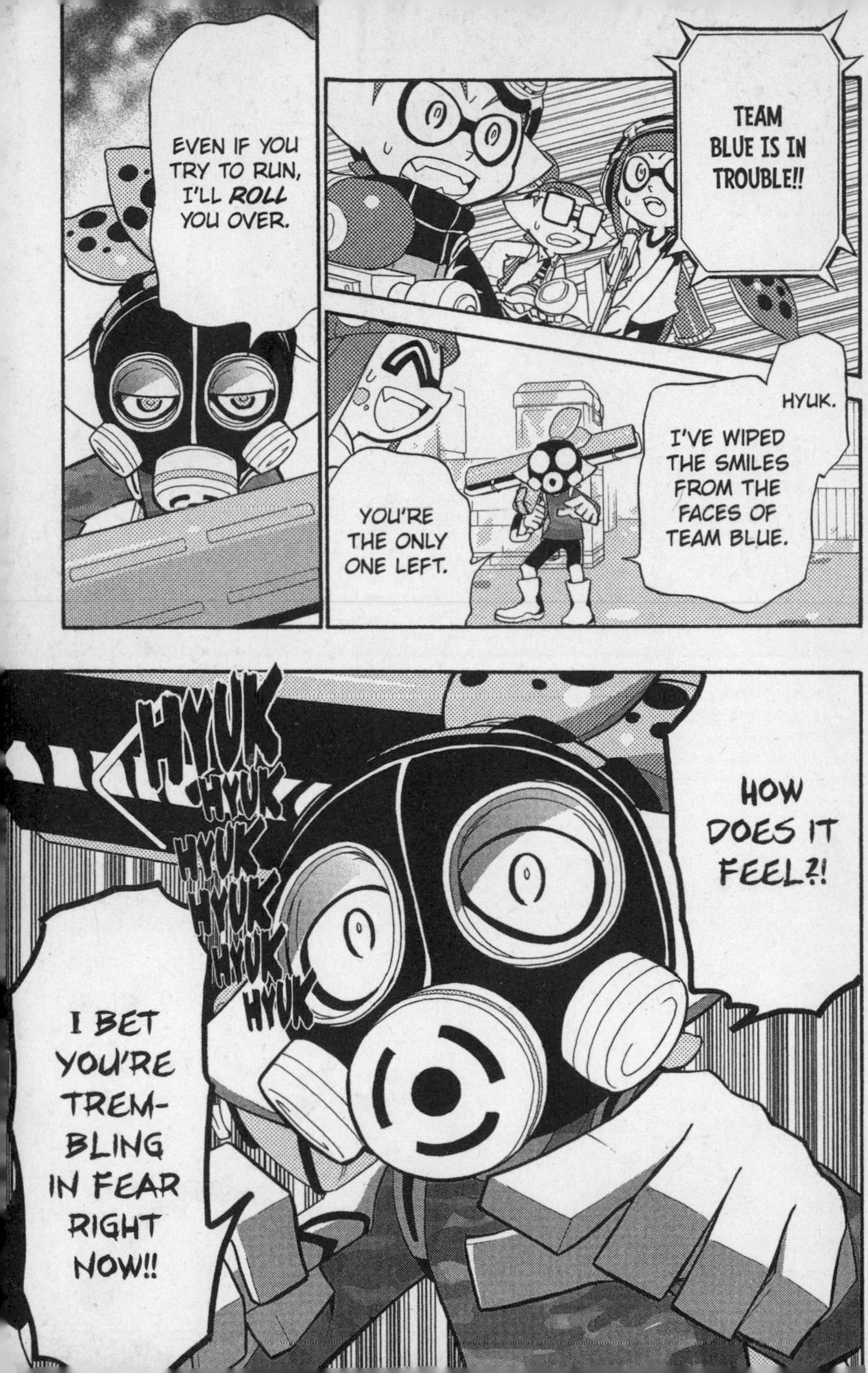
TEAM BLUE IS IN TROUBLE!!
HYUK.
I'VE WIPED THE SMILES FROM THE FACES OF TEAM BLUE.
YOU'RE THE ONLY ONE LEFT.
EVEN IF YOU TRY TO RUN, I'LL *ROLL* YOU OVER.
HOW DOES IT FEEL?!
HYUK HYUK HYUK HYUK HYUK HYUK
I BET YOU'RE TREM-BLING IN FEAR RIGHT NOW!!

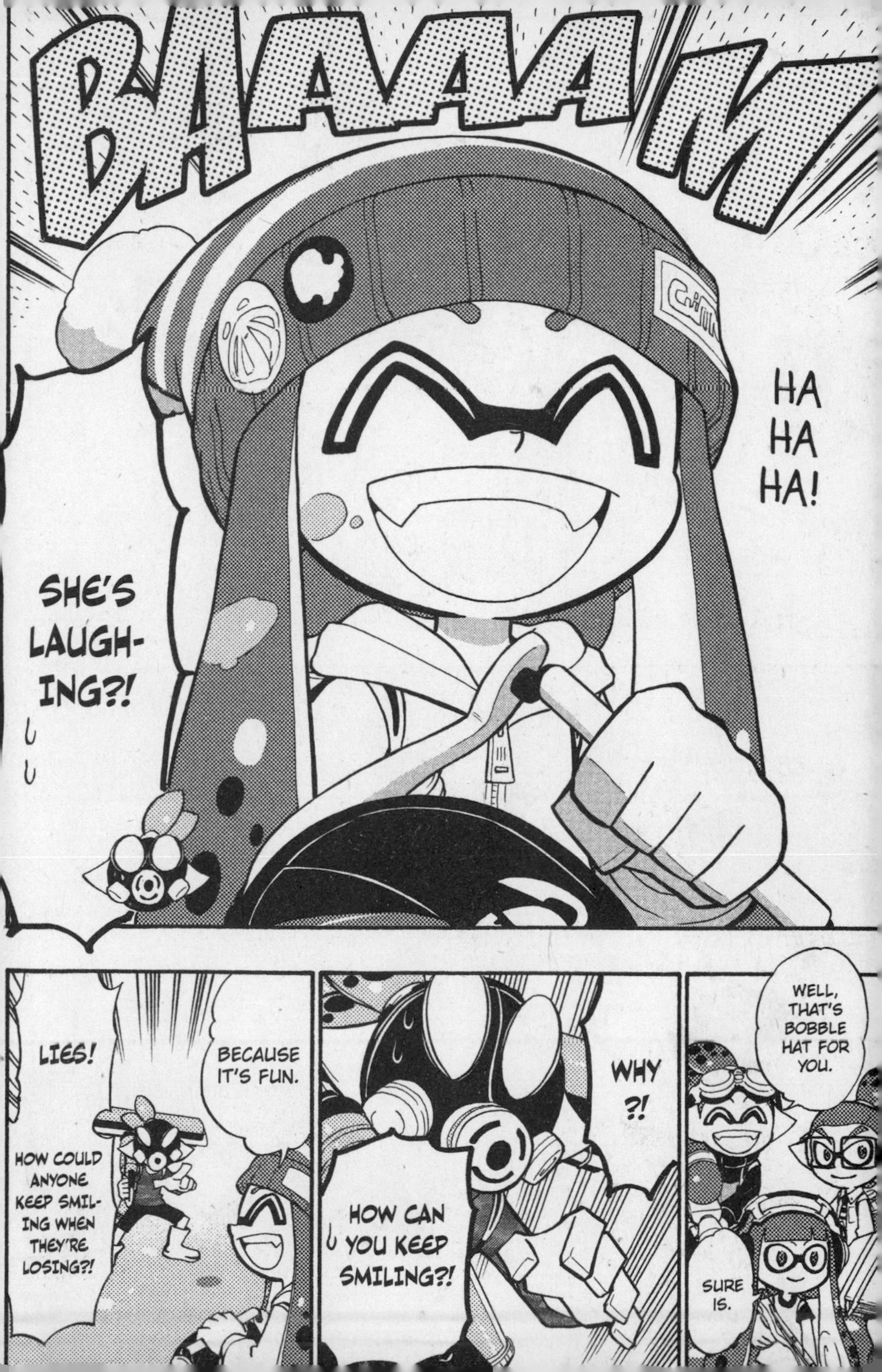
BAAAAM
HA HA HA!
SHE'S LAUGHING?!
WELL, THAT'S BOBBLE HAT FOR YOU.
SURE IS.
WHY?!
HOW CAN YOU KEEP SMILING?!
BECAUSE IT'S FUN.
LIES!
HOW COULD ANYONE KEEP SMILING WHEN THEY'RE LOSING?!

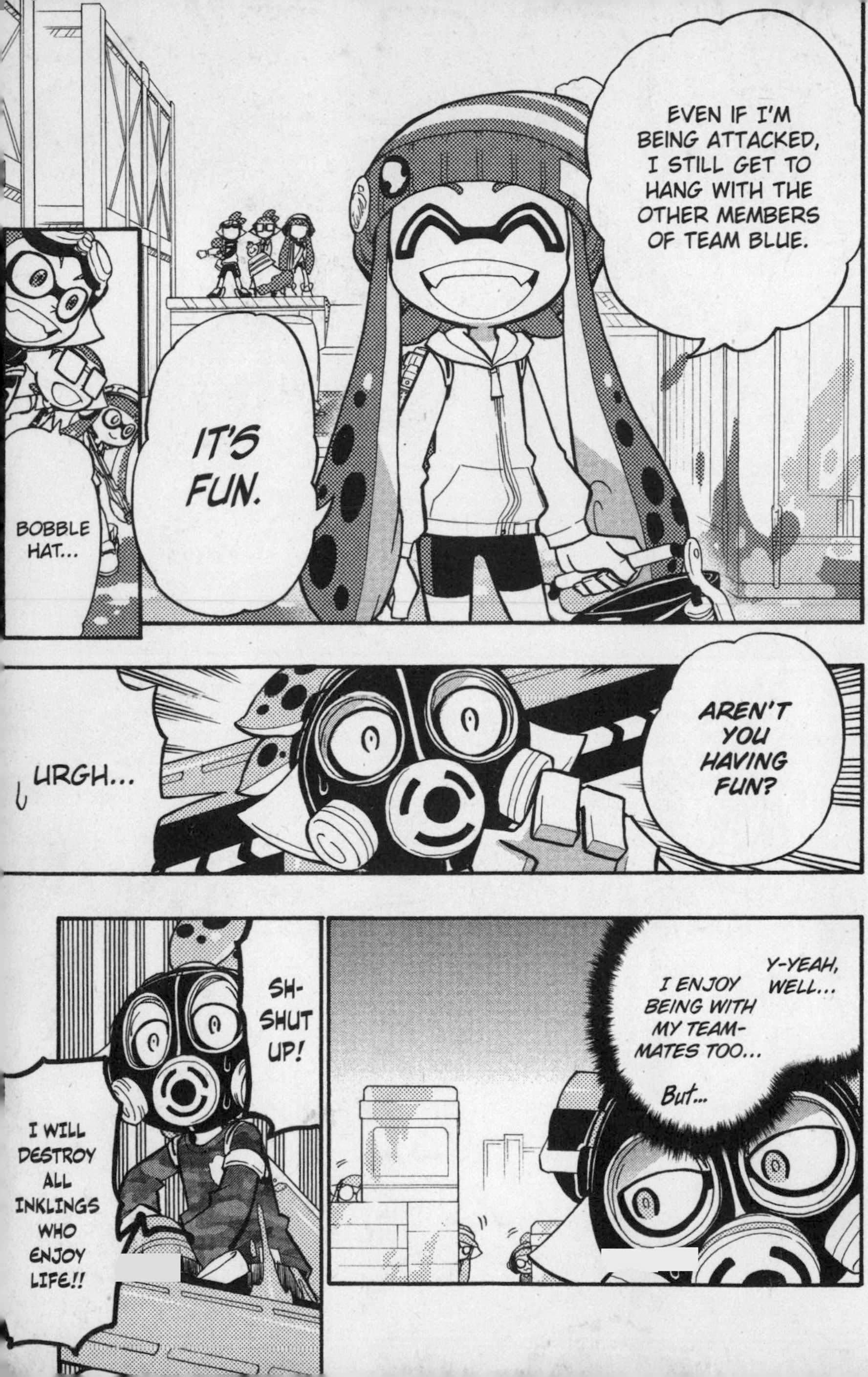
EVEN IF I'M BEING ATTACKED, I STILL GET TO HANG WITH THE OTHER MEMBERS OF TEAM BLUE.
IT'S FUN.
BOBBLE HAT...
AREN'T YOU HAVING FUN?
URGH...
Y-YEAH, WELL...
I ENJOY BEING WITH MY TEAM-MATES TOO...
But...
SH-SHUT UP!
I WILL DESTROY ALL INKLINGS WHO ENJOY LIFE!!

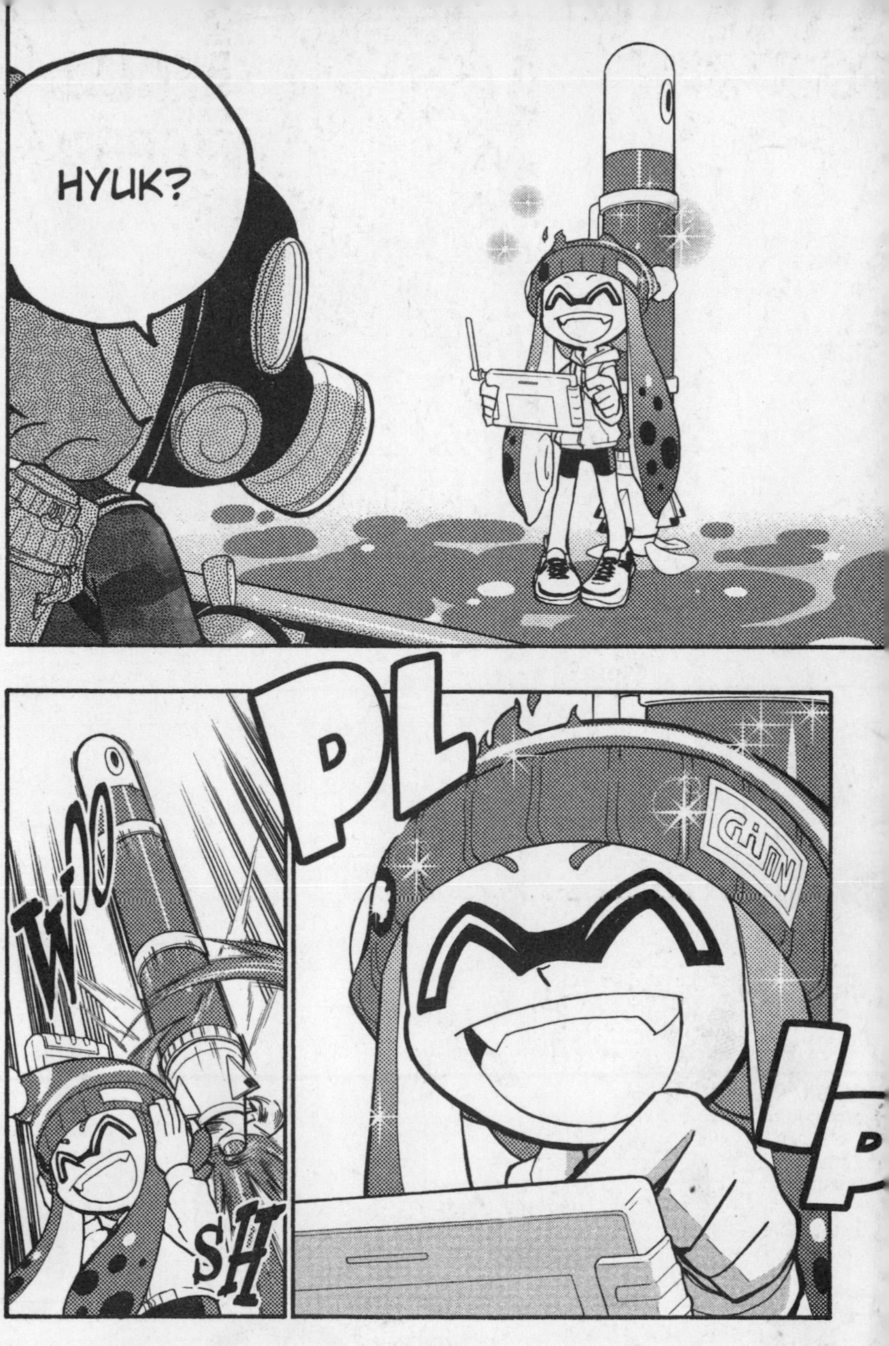
HYUK?
PL
IP
WOO
SH

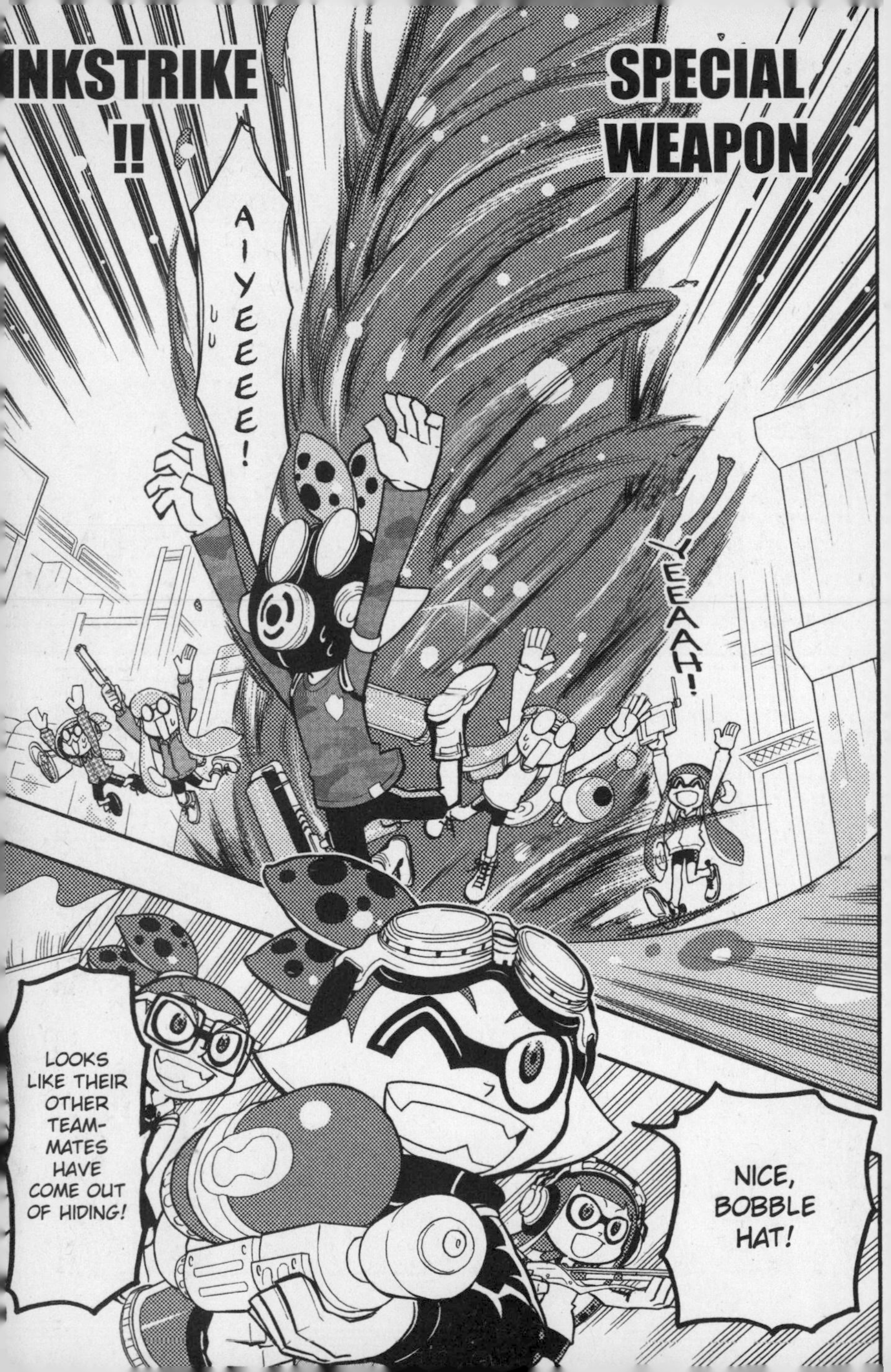
SPECIAL WEAPON
INKSTRIKE!!
AIYEEEE!
YEEAAH!
NICE, BOBBLE HAT!
LOOKS LIKE THEIR OTHER TEAM-MATES HAVE COME OUT OF HIDING!

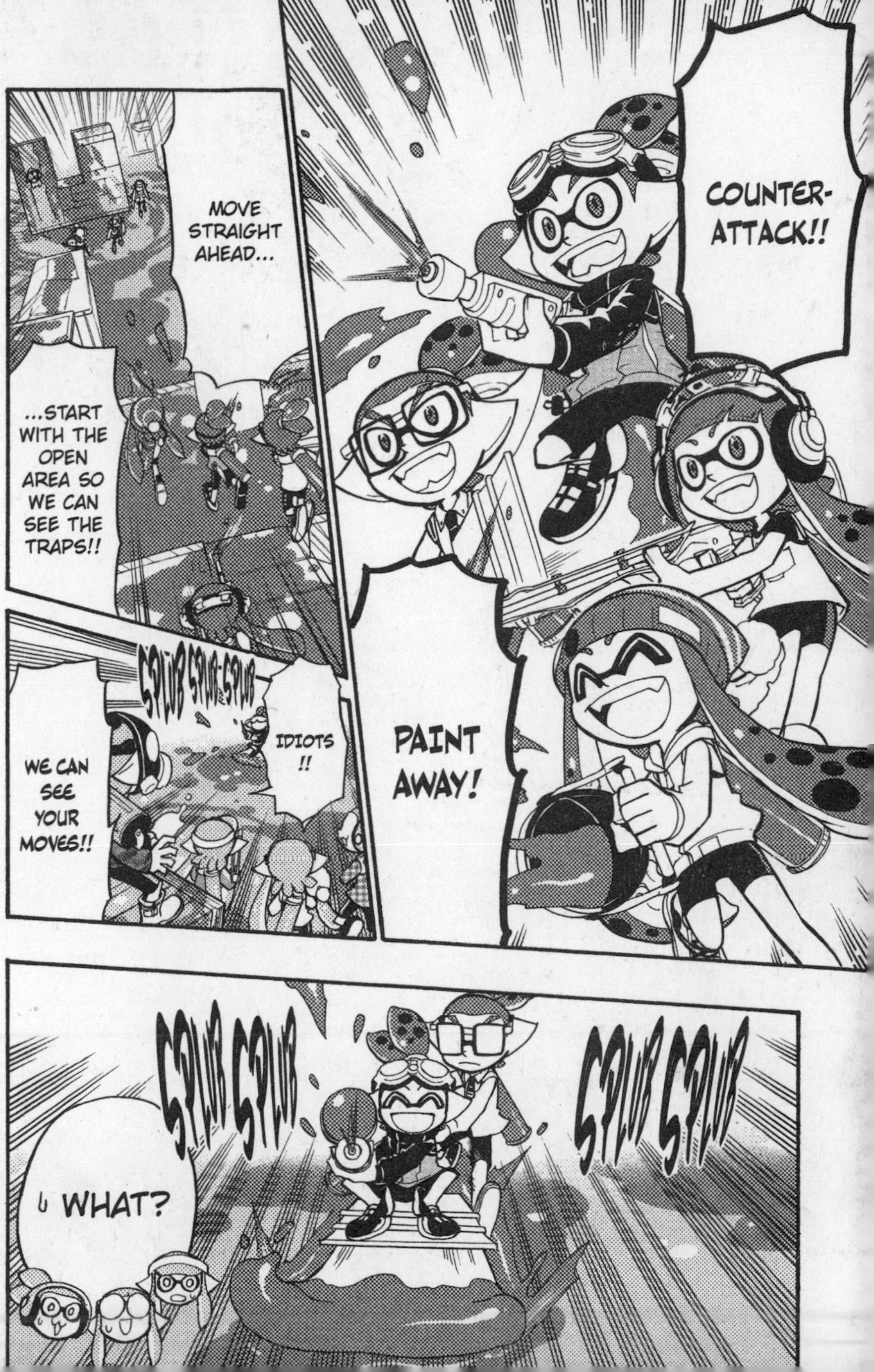
COUNTER-ATTACK!!
PAINT AWAY!
MOVE STRAIGHT AHEAD...
...START WITH THE OPEN AREA SO WE CAN SEE THE TRAPS!!
SPLUB SPLUB-SPLUB
IDIOTS!!
WE CAN SEE YOUR MOVES!!
SPLUB SPLUB
SPLUB SPLUB
WHAT?

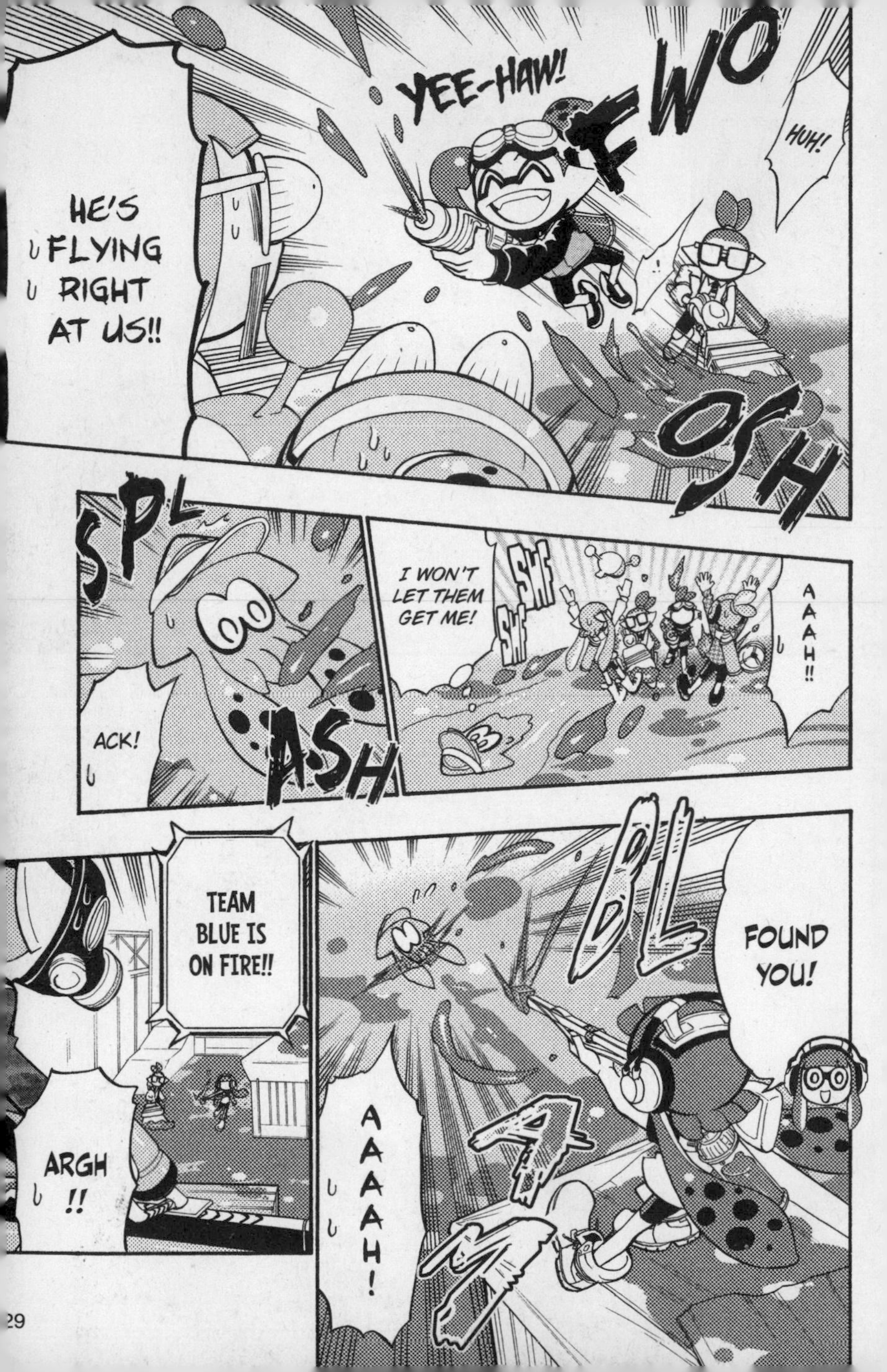
HUH!
FWO
YEE-HAW!
OSH
HE'S FLYING RIGHT AT US!!
AAAAH!!
I WON'T LET THEM GET ME!
SHF
SHF
SHF
SPL
ASH
ACK!
FOUND YOU!
AAAAH!
TEAM BLUE IS ON FIRE!!
ARGH!!

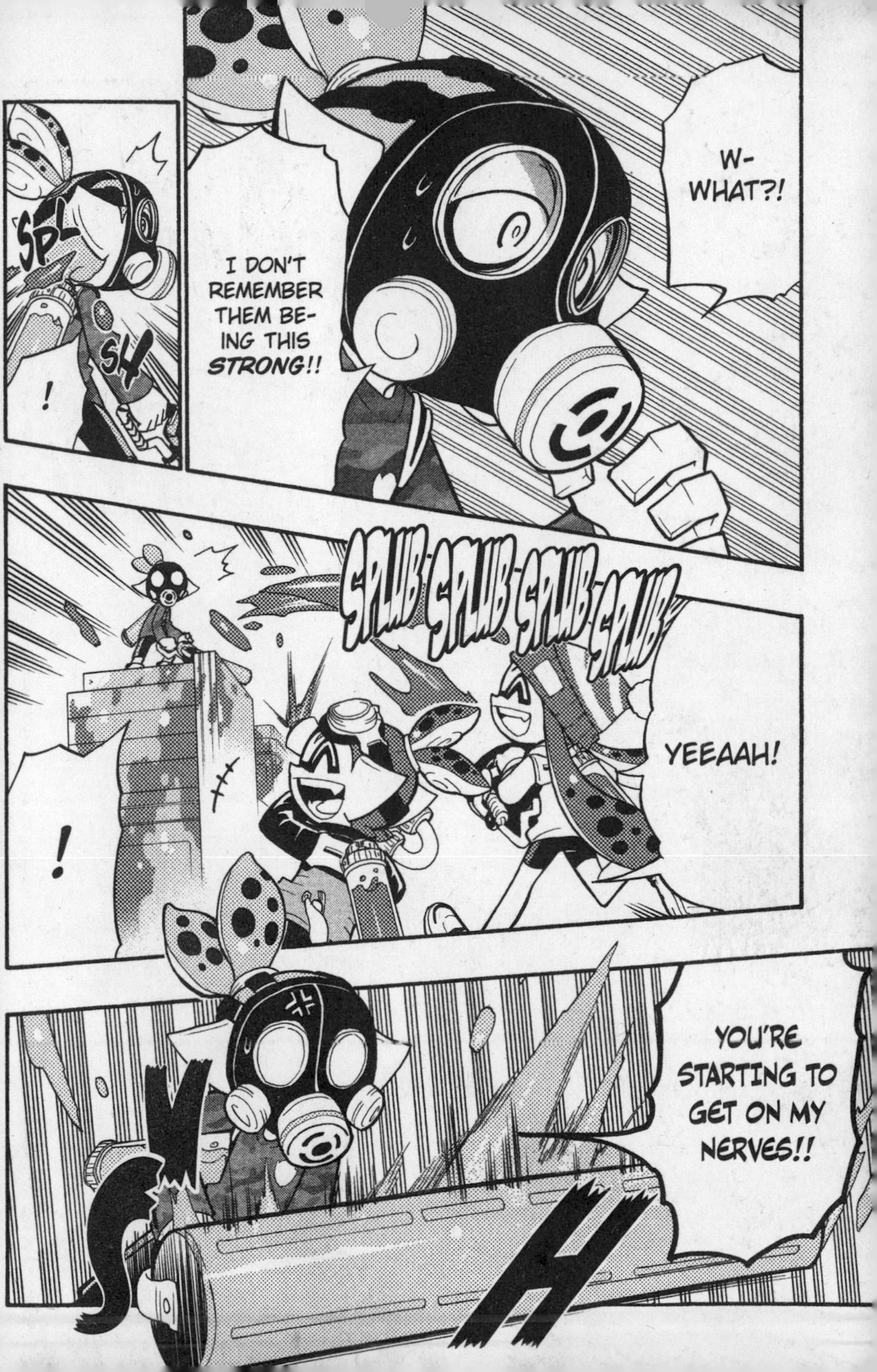
W-
WHAT?!
I DON'T REMEMBER THEM BE-ING THIS *STRONG*!!
SPL
SH
!
SPLUB-SPLUB-SPLUB-SPLUB
YEEAAH!
!
YOU'RE STARTING TO GET ON MY NERVES!!

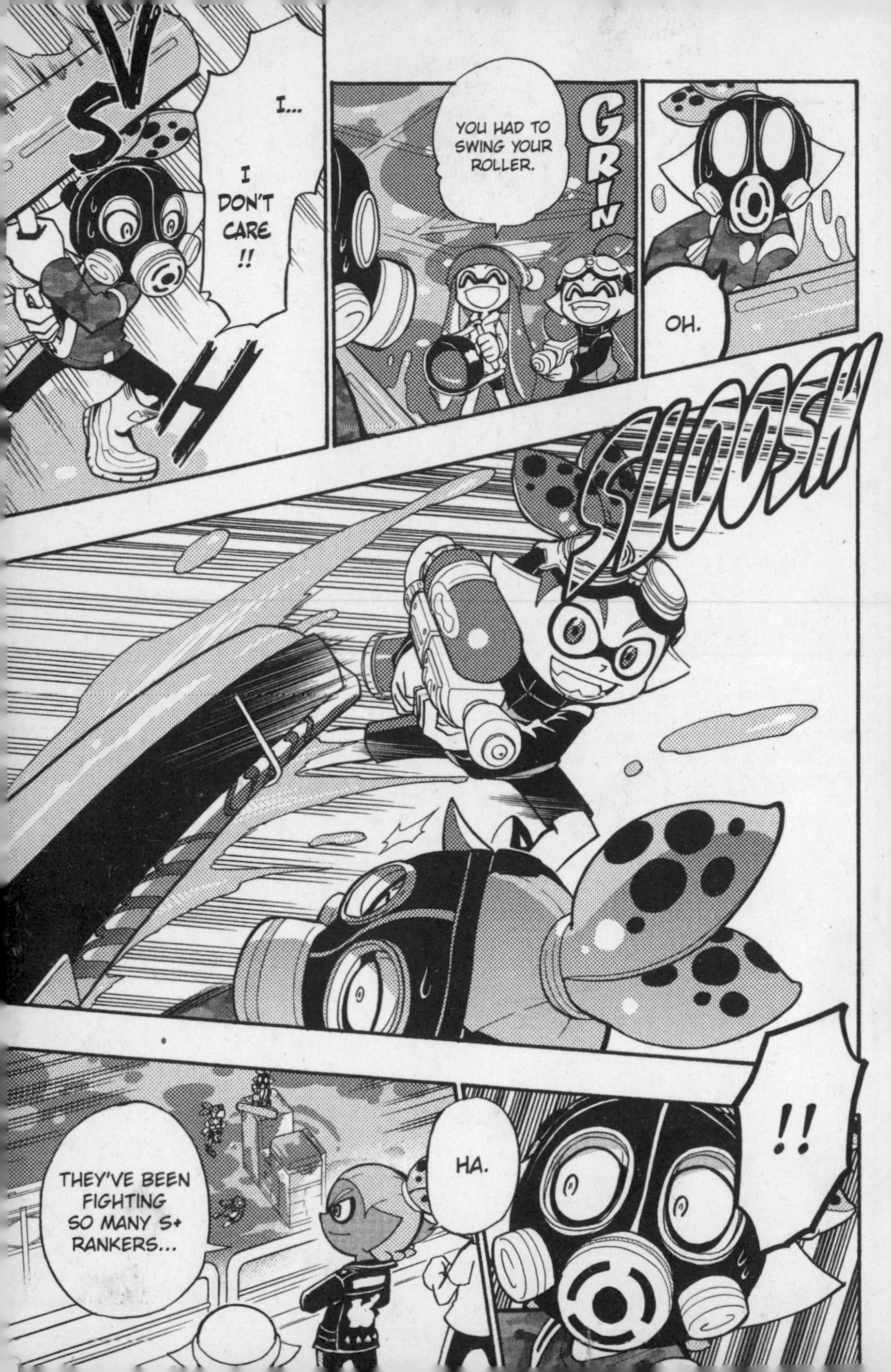
OH.
GRIN
YOU HAD TO SWING YOUR ROLLER.
I...
I DON'T CARE!!
SLOOSH
!!
HA.
THEY'VE BEEN FIGHTING SO MANY S+ RANKERS...

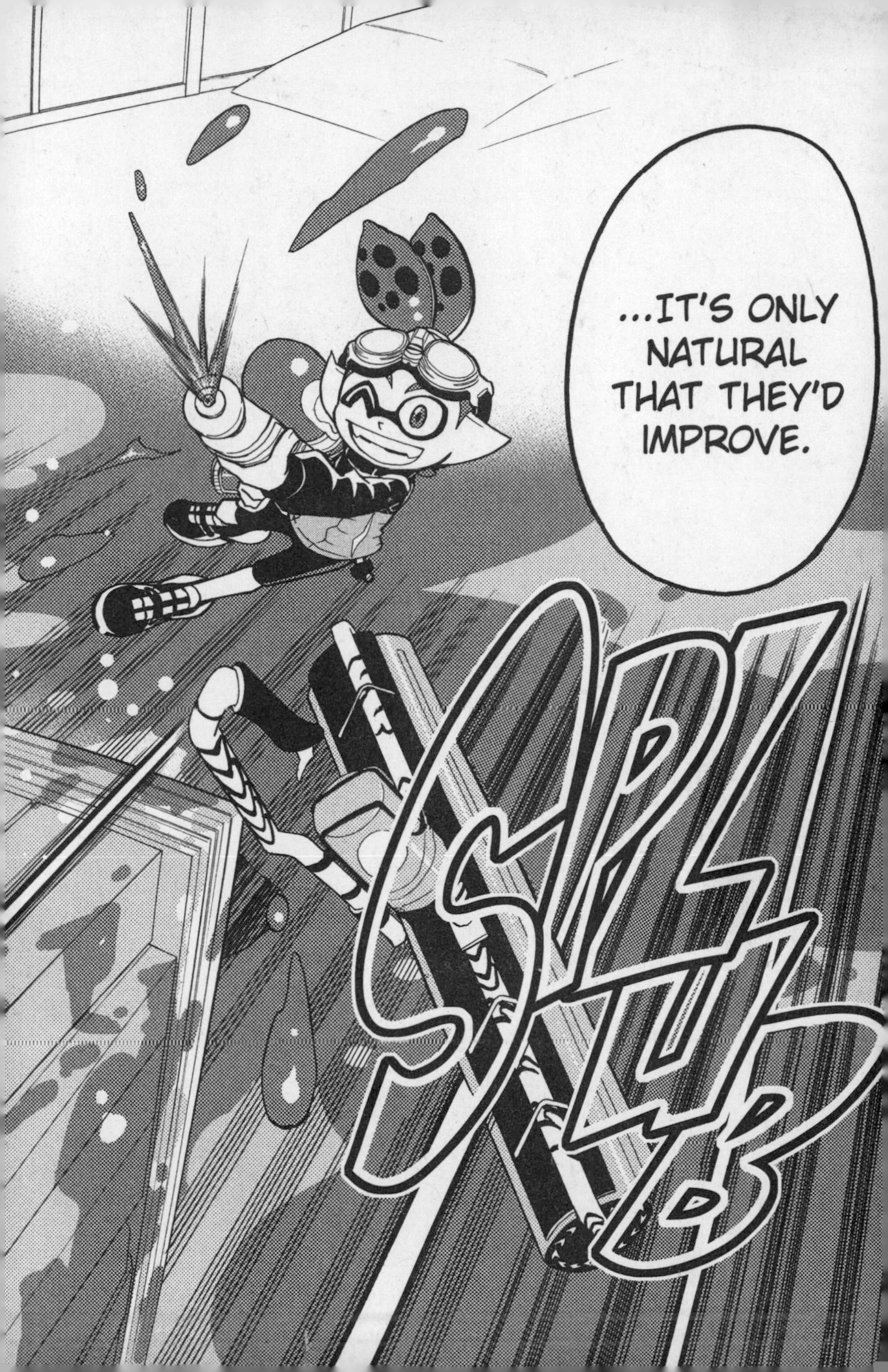
...IT'S ONLY NATURAL THAT THEY'D IMPROVE.

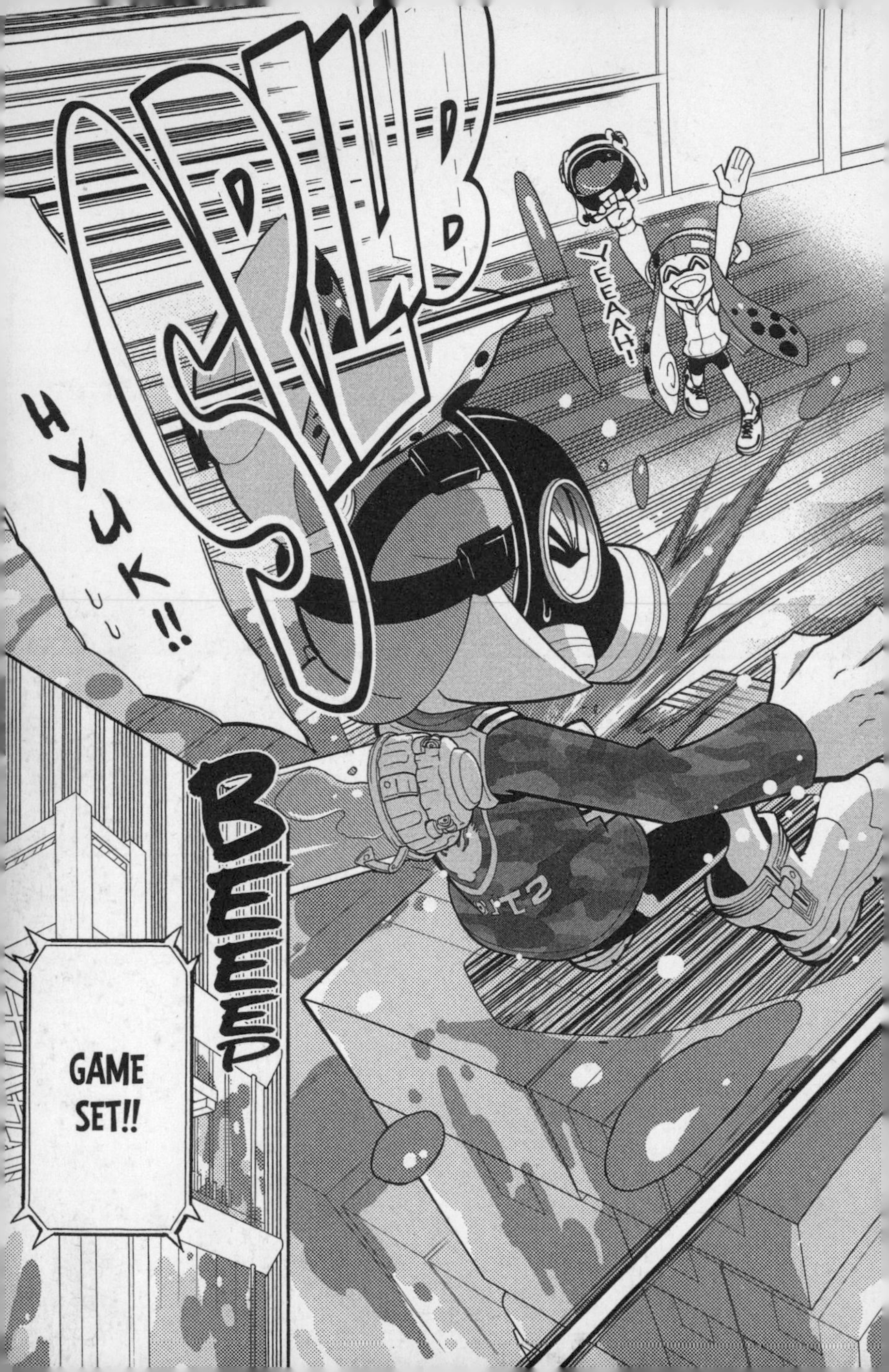
YEEAAH!
HYUK!!
BEEEP
GAME SET!!

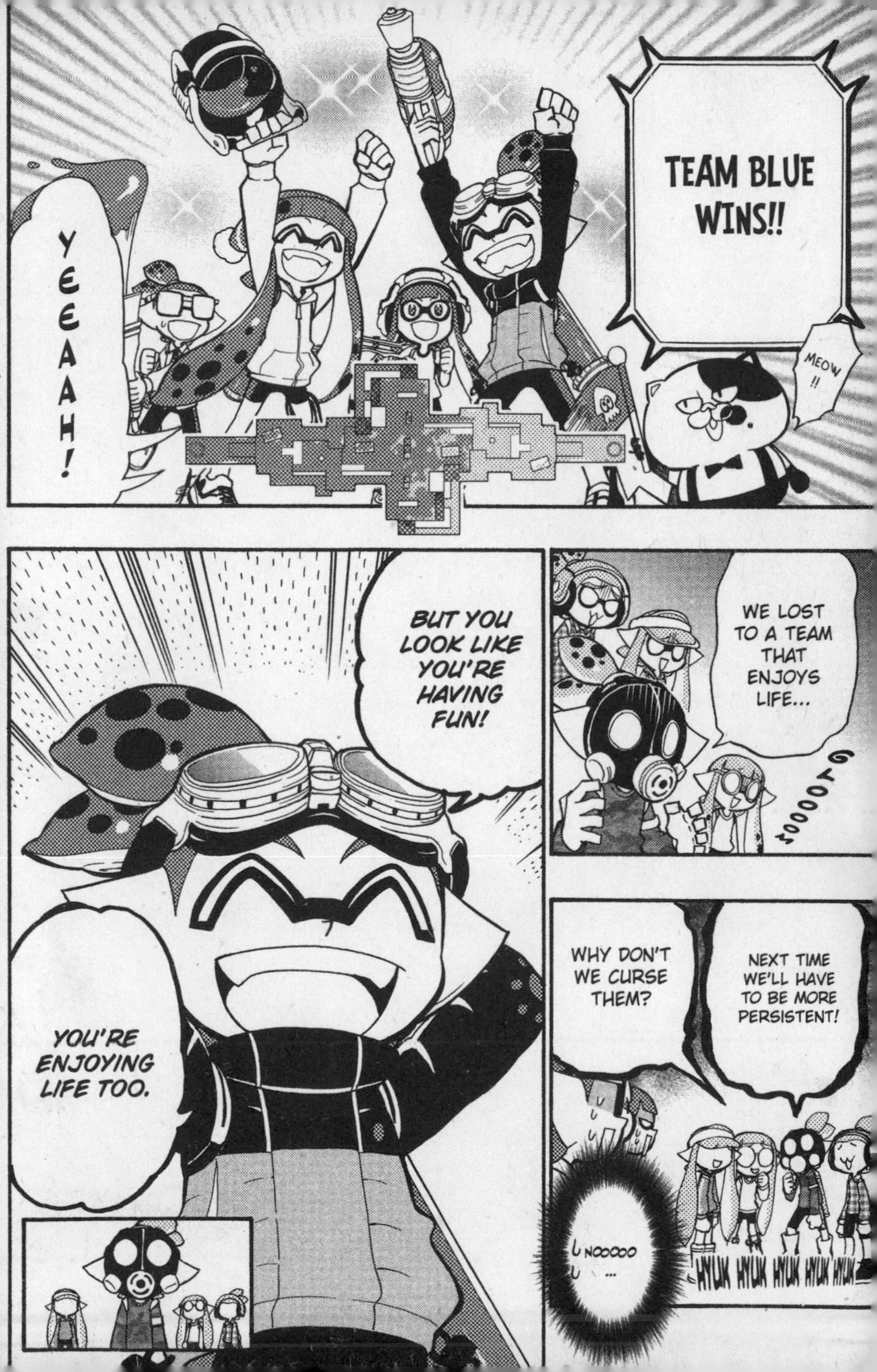
TEAM BLUE WINS!!
MEOW!!
YEEAAAH!
WE LOST TO A TEAM THAT ENJOYS LIFE...
GLOOOOM
NEXT TIME WE'LL HAVE TO BE MORE PERSISTENT!
WHY DON'T WE CURSE THEM?
NOOOOO...
HYUK HYUK HYUK HYUK HYUK
BUT YOU LOOK LIKE YOU'RE HAVING FUN!
YOU'RE ENJOYING LIFE TOO.

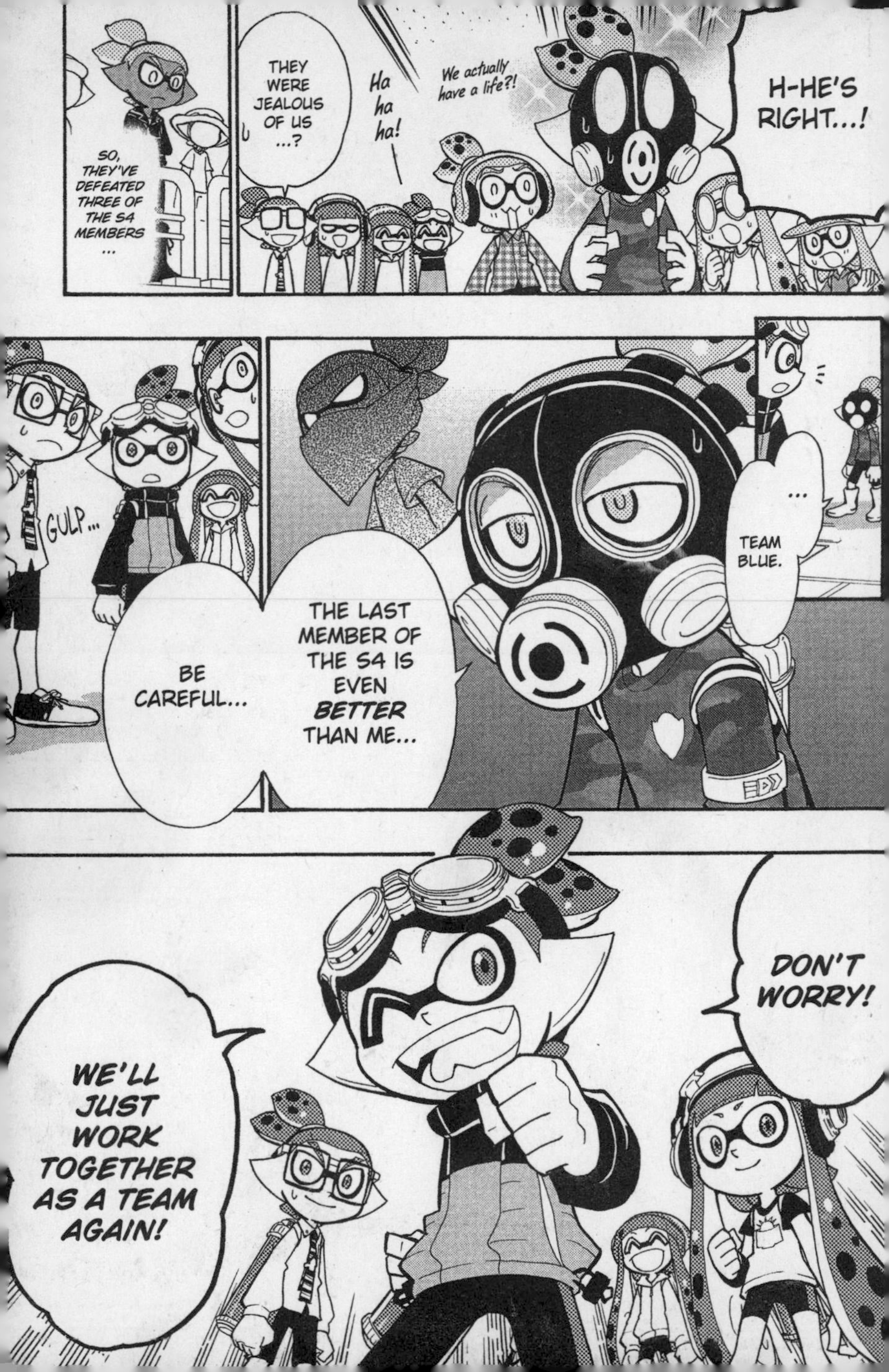
H-HE'S RIGHT...!
We actually have a life?!
Ha ha ha!
THEY WERE JEALOUS OF US ...?
SO, THEY'VE DEFEATED THREE OF THE S4 MEMBERS ...
...
TEAM BLUE.
THE LAST MEMBER OF THE S4 IS EVEN BETTER THAN ME...
BE CAREFUL...
GULP...
DON'T WORRY!
WE'LL JUST WORK TOGETHER AS A TEAM AGAIN!

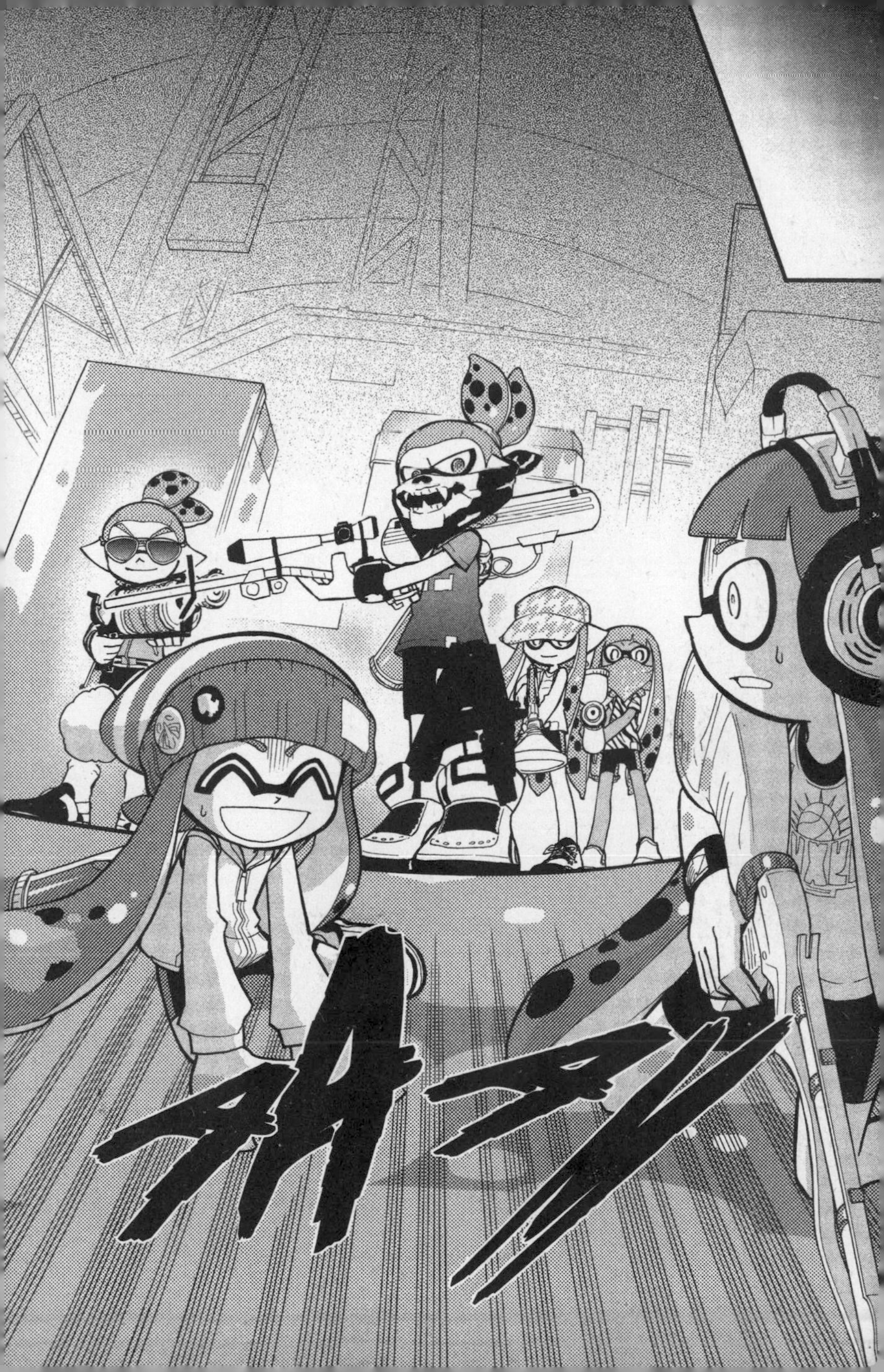

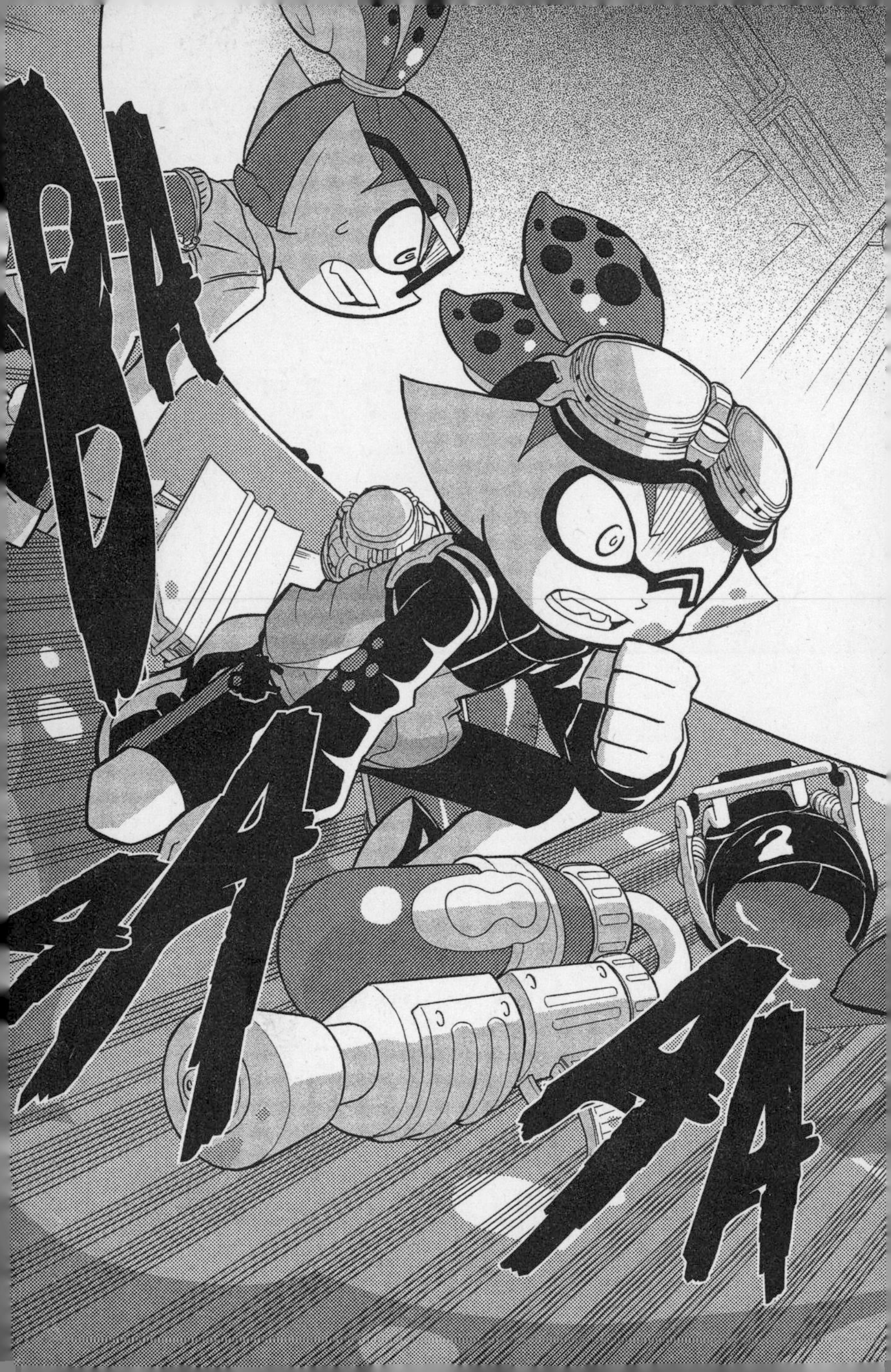
BAAAAA

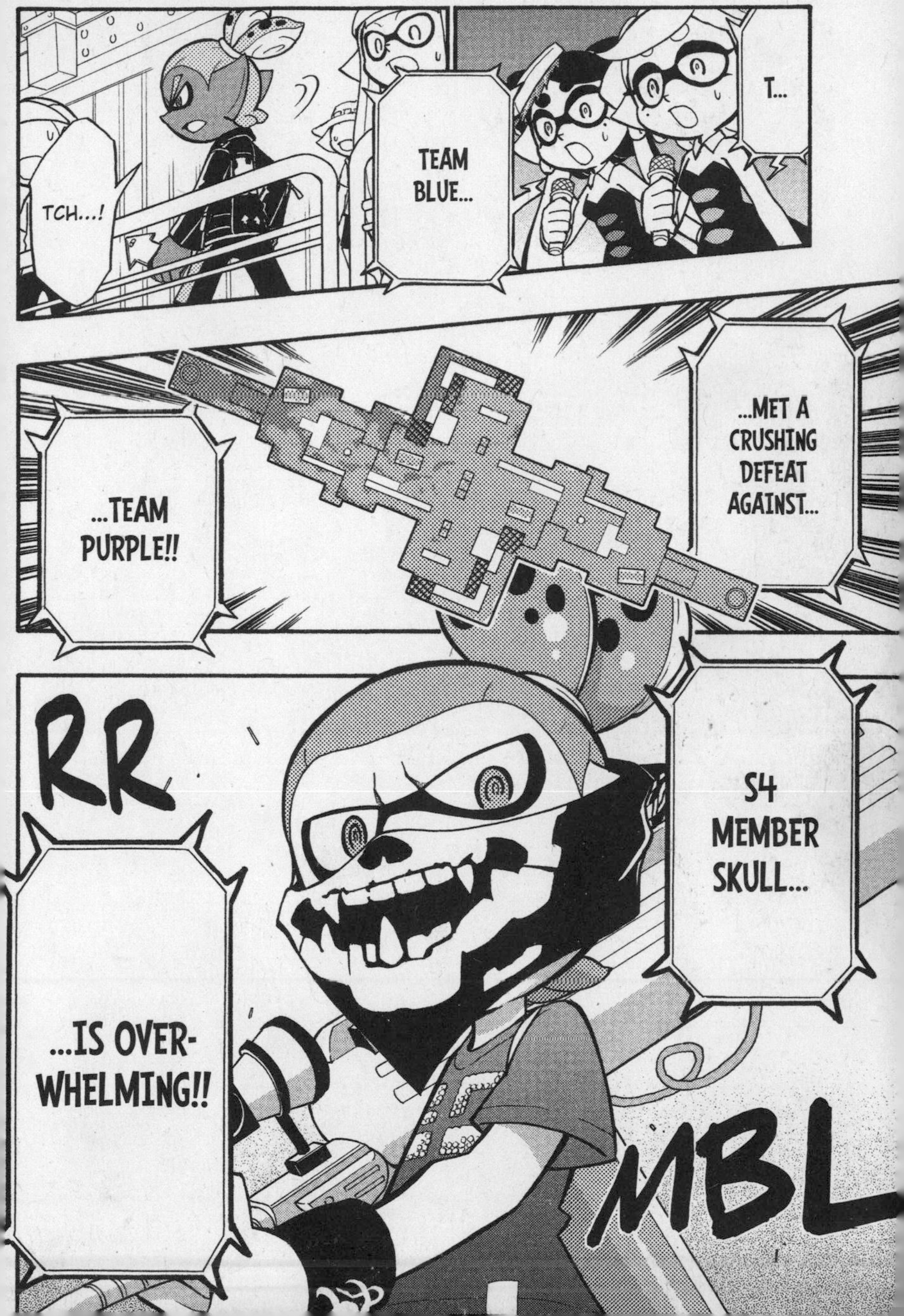
T...
TEAM BLUE...
TCH...!
...MET A CRUSHING DEFEAT AGAINST...
...TEAM PURPLE!!
S4 MEMBER SKULL...
RR
...IS OVER-WHELMING!!
MBL

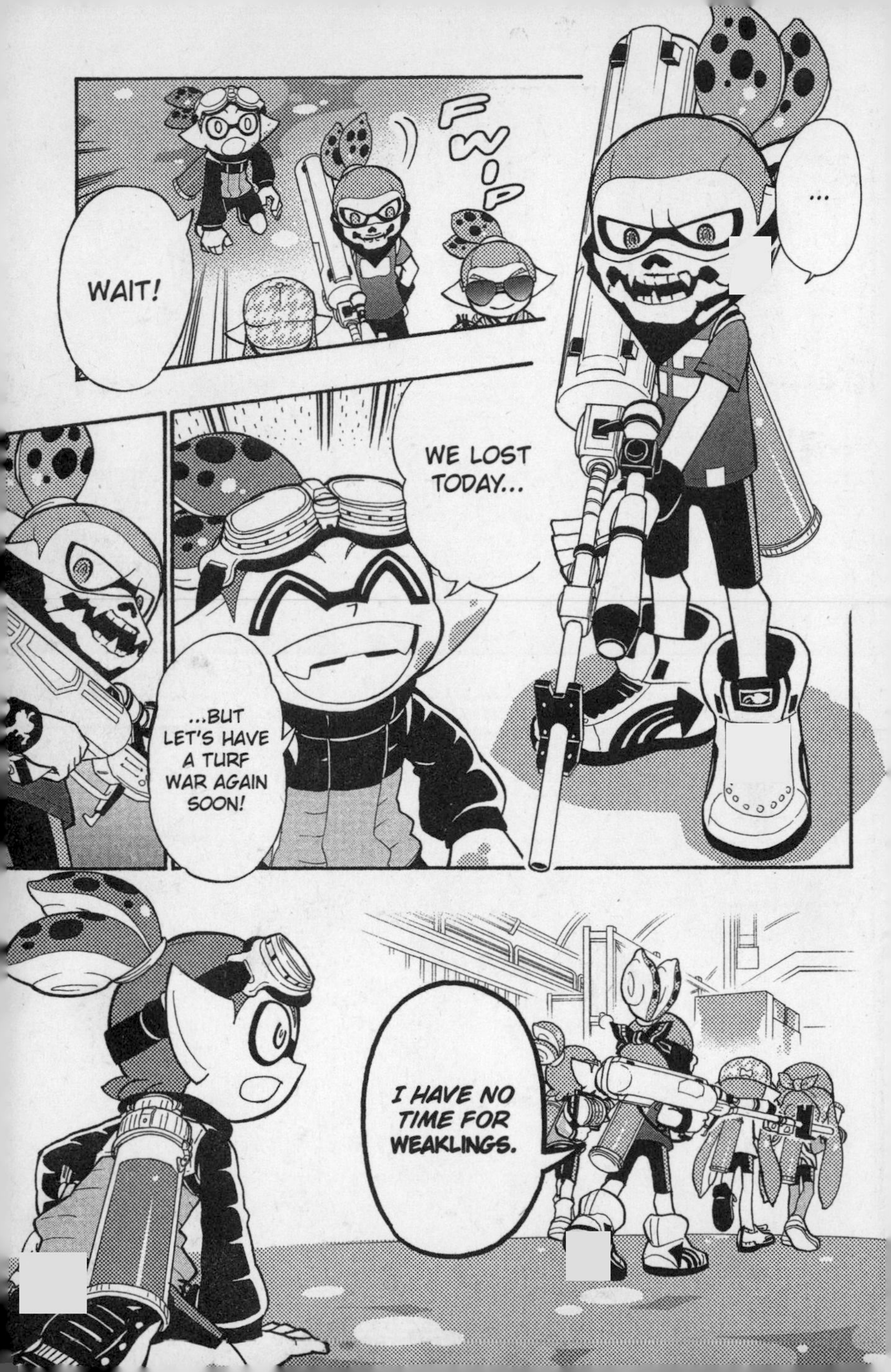
FWIP
WAIT!
...
WE LOST TODAY...
...BUT LET'S HAVE A TURF WAR AGAIN SOON!
I HAVE NO TIME FOR WEAKLINGS.

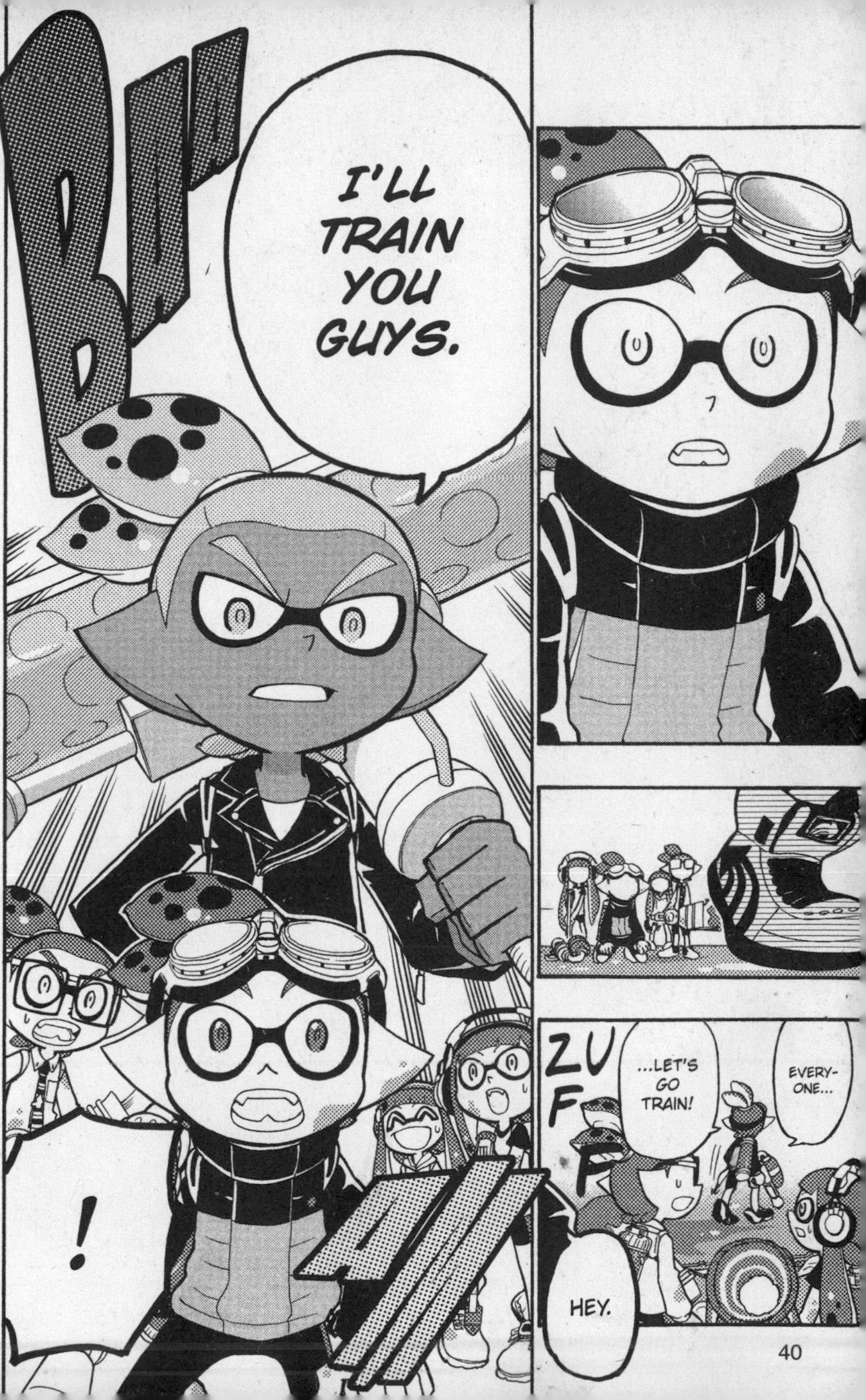
EVERY-ONE...
...LET'S GO TRAIN!
ZUFF
HEY.
I'LL TRAIN YOU GUYS.
!

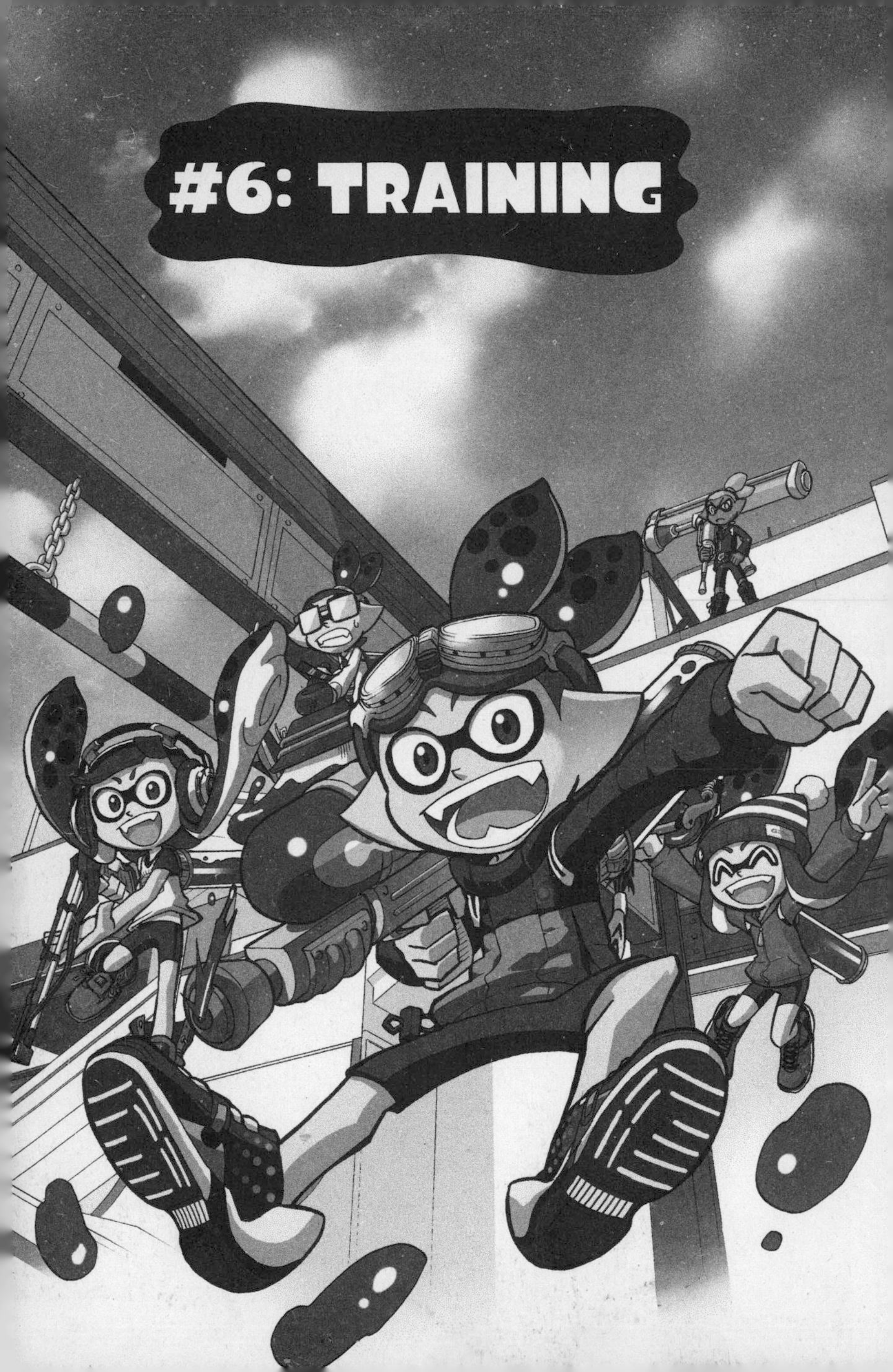
#6: TRAINING

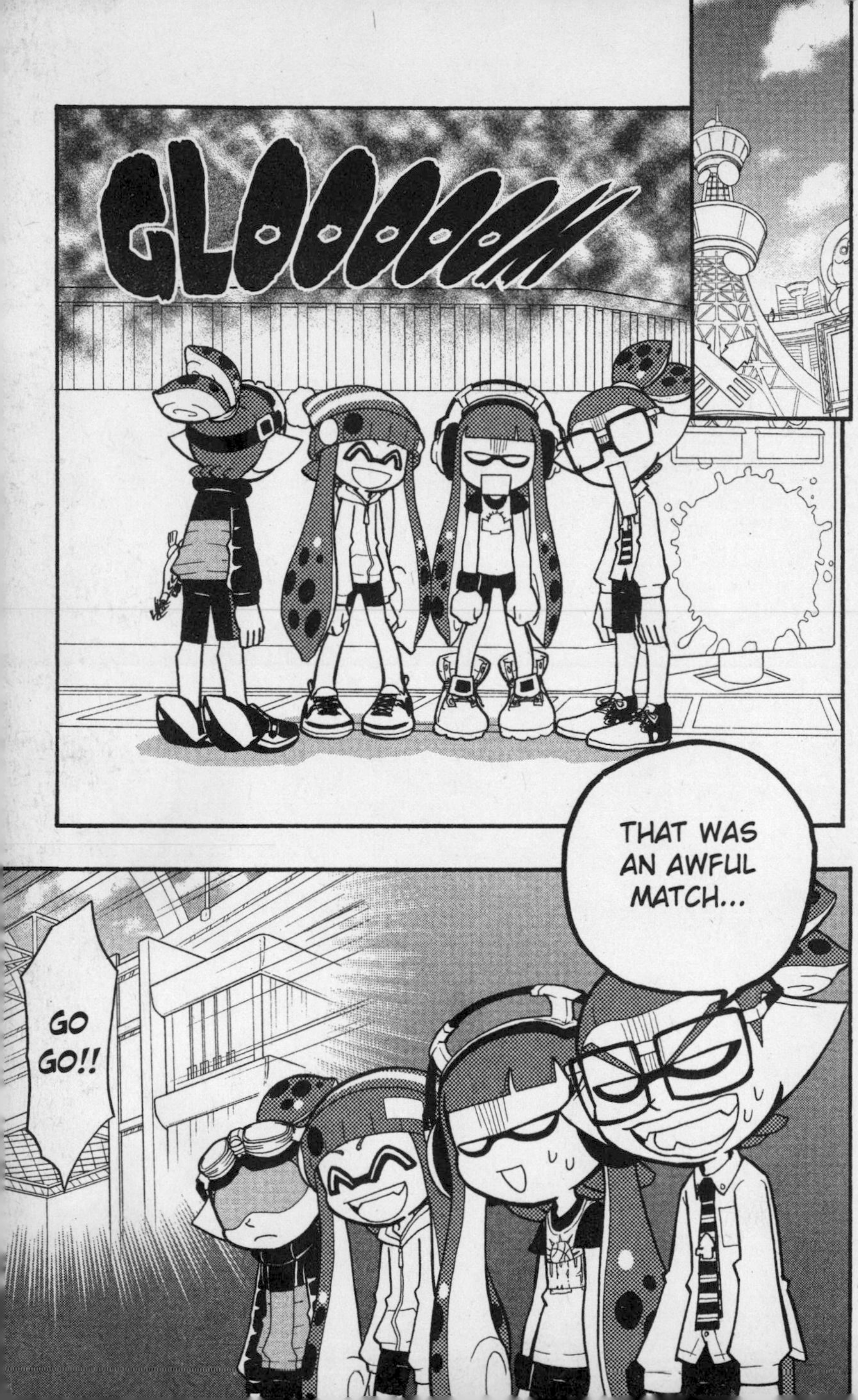
GLOOOOOM
THAT WAS AN AWFUL MATCH...
GO GO!!

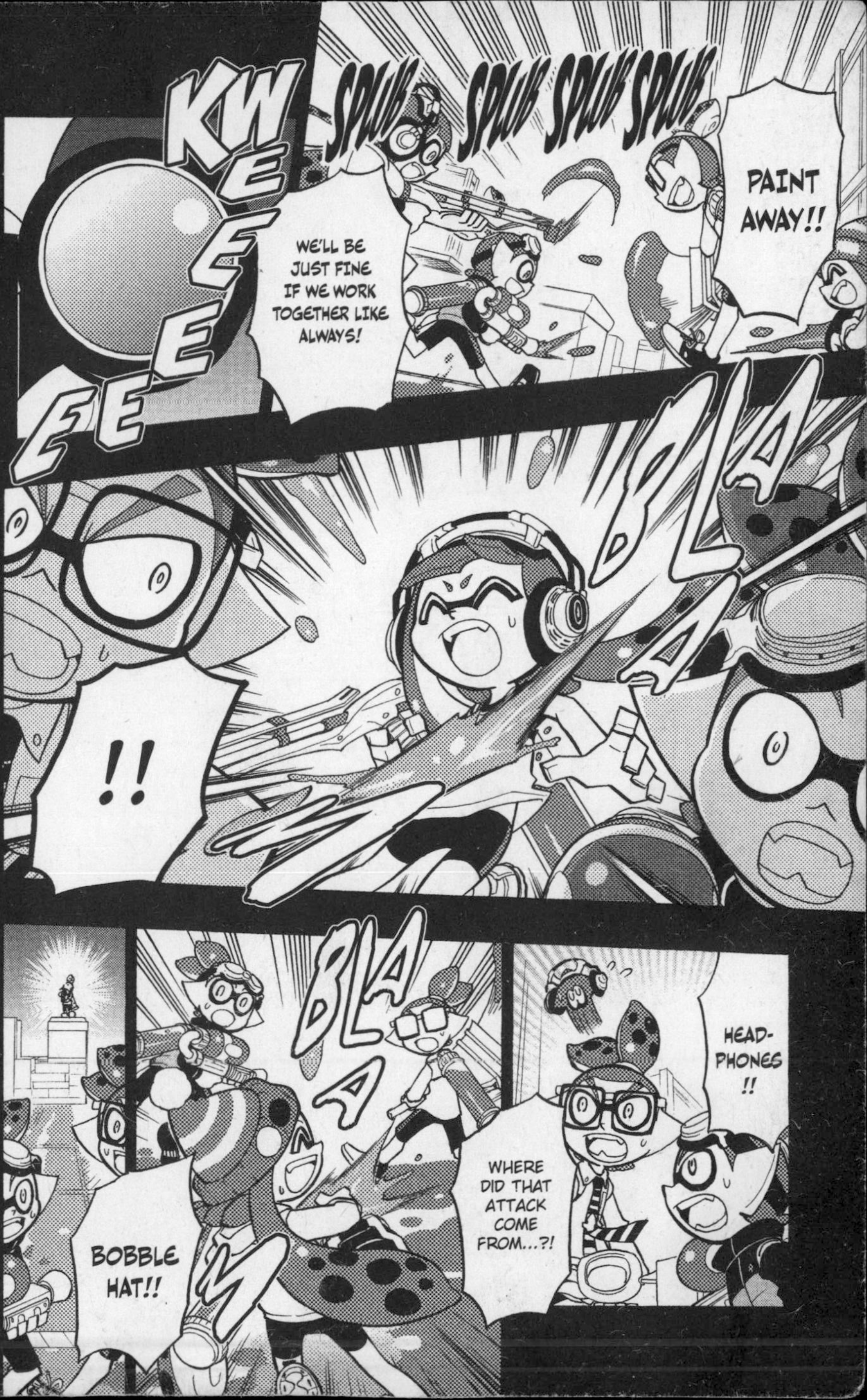
SPLUB SPLUB SPLUB SPLUB
PAINT AWAY!!
WE'LL BE JUST FINE IF WE WORK TOGETHER LIKE ALWAYS!
KWEEEEE
BLAA
!!
HEAD-PHONES!!
WHERE DID THAT ATTACK COME FROM...?!
BLAA
BOBBLE HAT!!

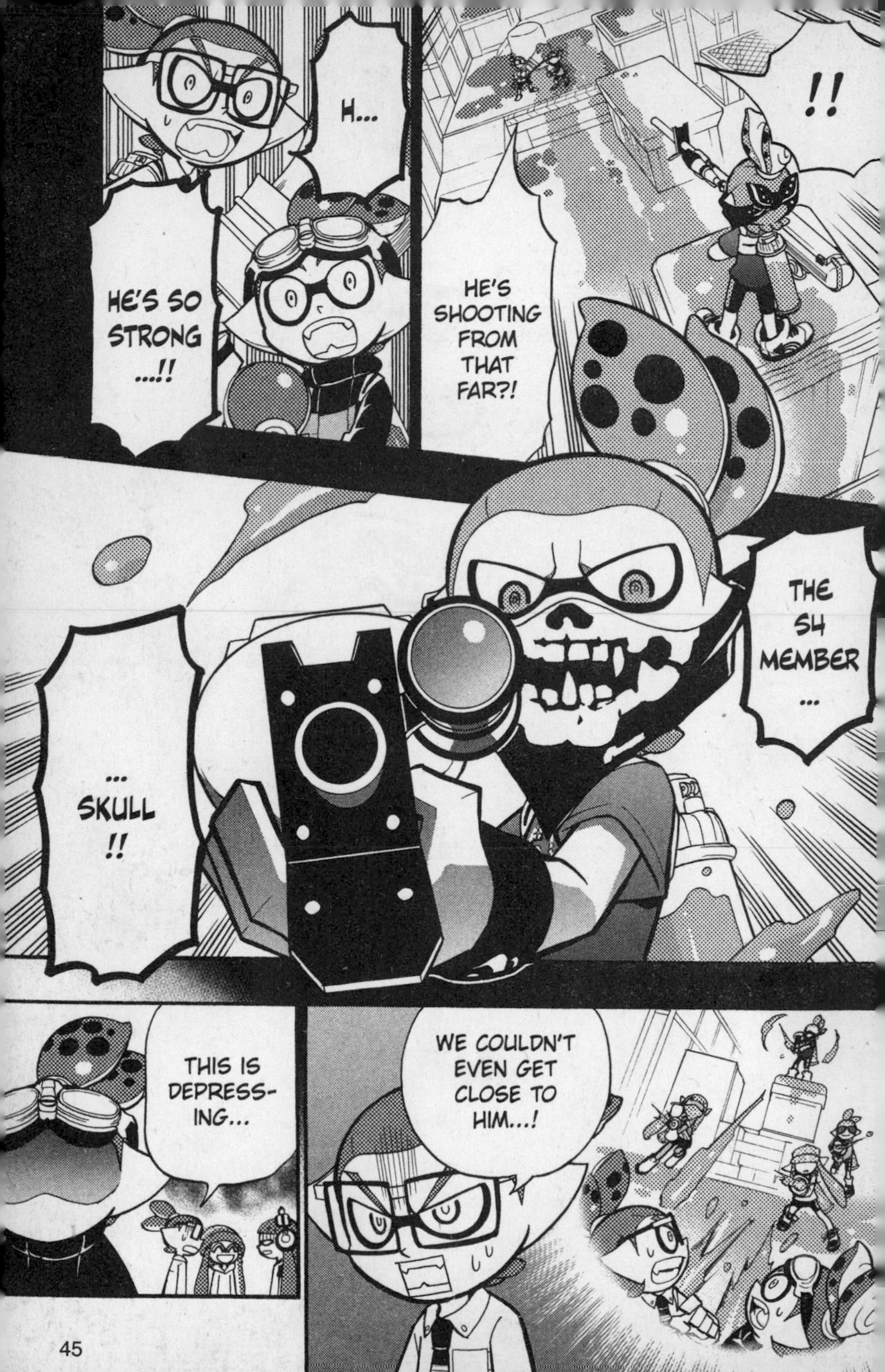
!!
HE'S SHOOTING FROM THAT FAR?!
H...
HE'S SO STRONG ...!!
THE S4 MEMBER ...
... SKULL !!
WE COULDN'T EVEN GET CLOSE TO HIM...!
THIS IS DEPRESS-ING...

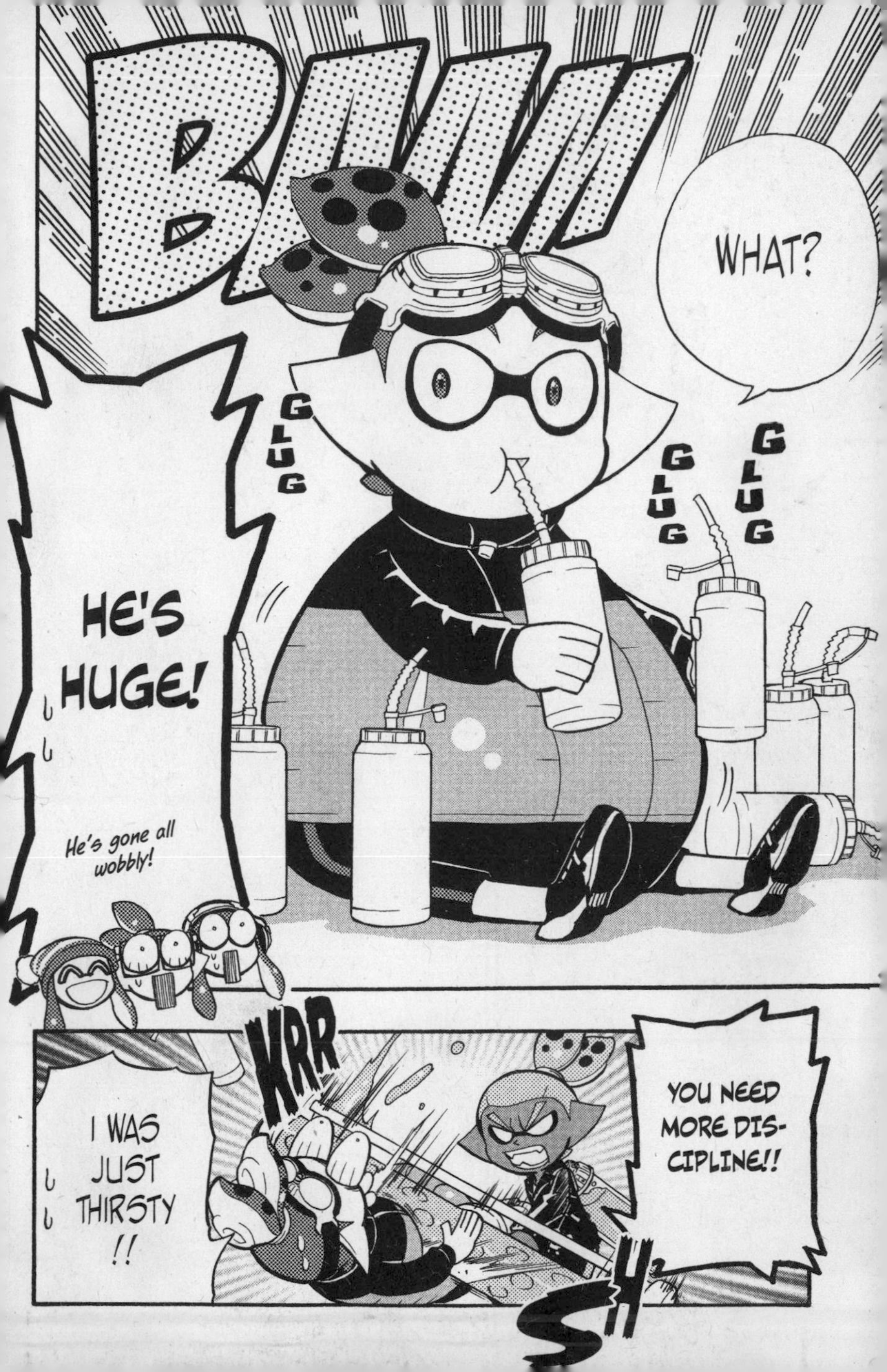
BAM
WHAT?
GLUG
GLUG
GLUG
HE'S HUGE!
He's gone all wobbly!
KRR
YOU NEED MORE DIS-CIPLINE!!
I WAS JUST THIRSTY!!
SH

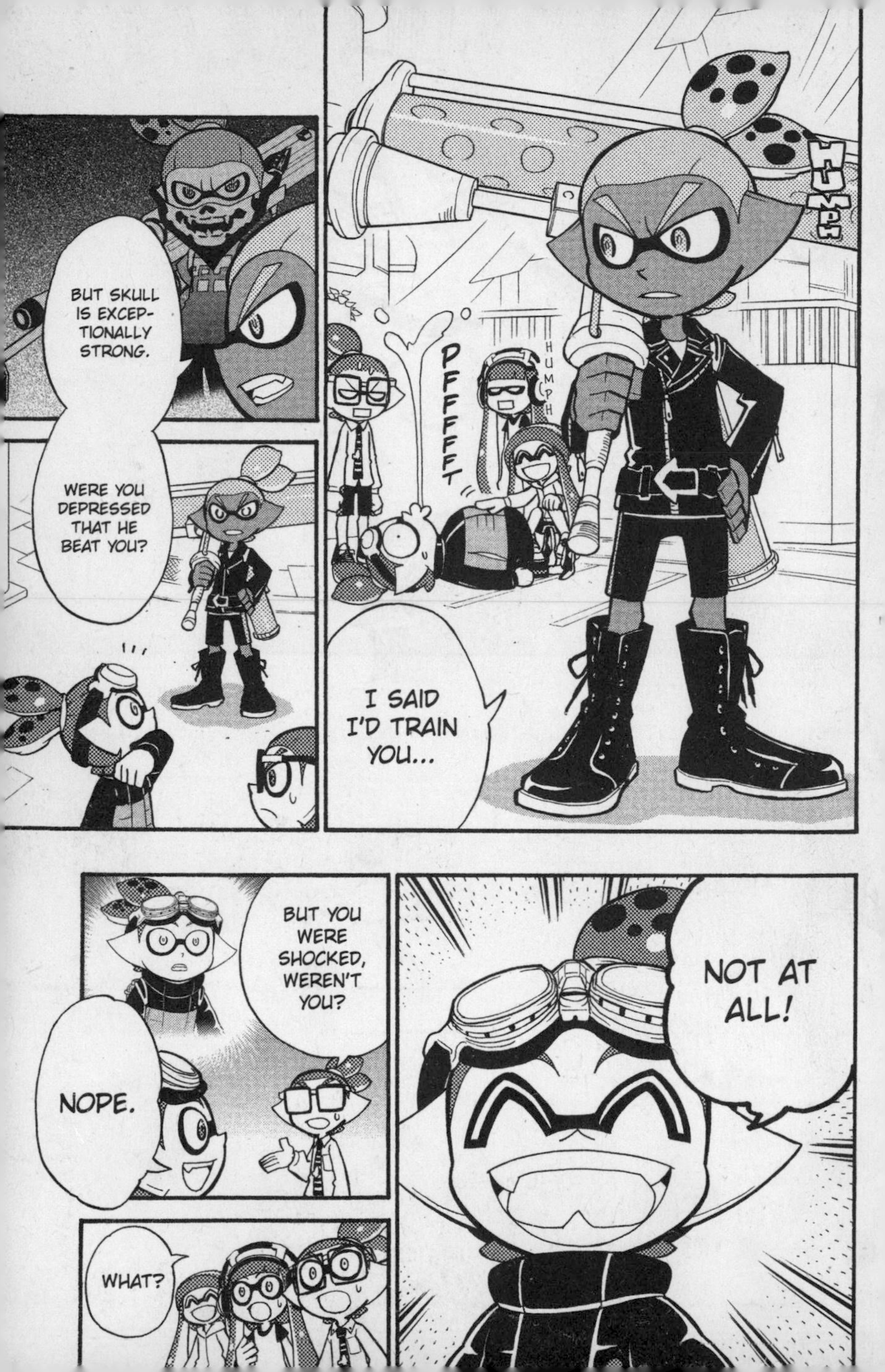
HUMPH
PFFFFFT
HUMPH
I SAID I'D TRAIN YOU...
BUT SKULL IS EXCEPTIONALLY STRONG.
WERE YOU DEPRESSED THAT HE BEAT YOU?
NOT AT ALL!
BUT YOU WERE SHOCKED, WEREN'T YOU?
NOPE.
WHAT?

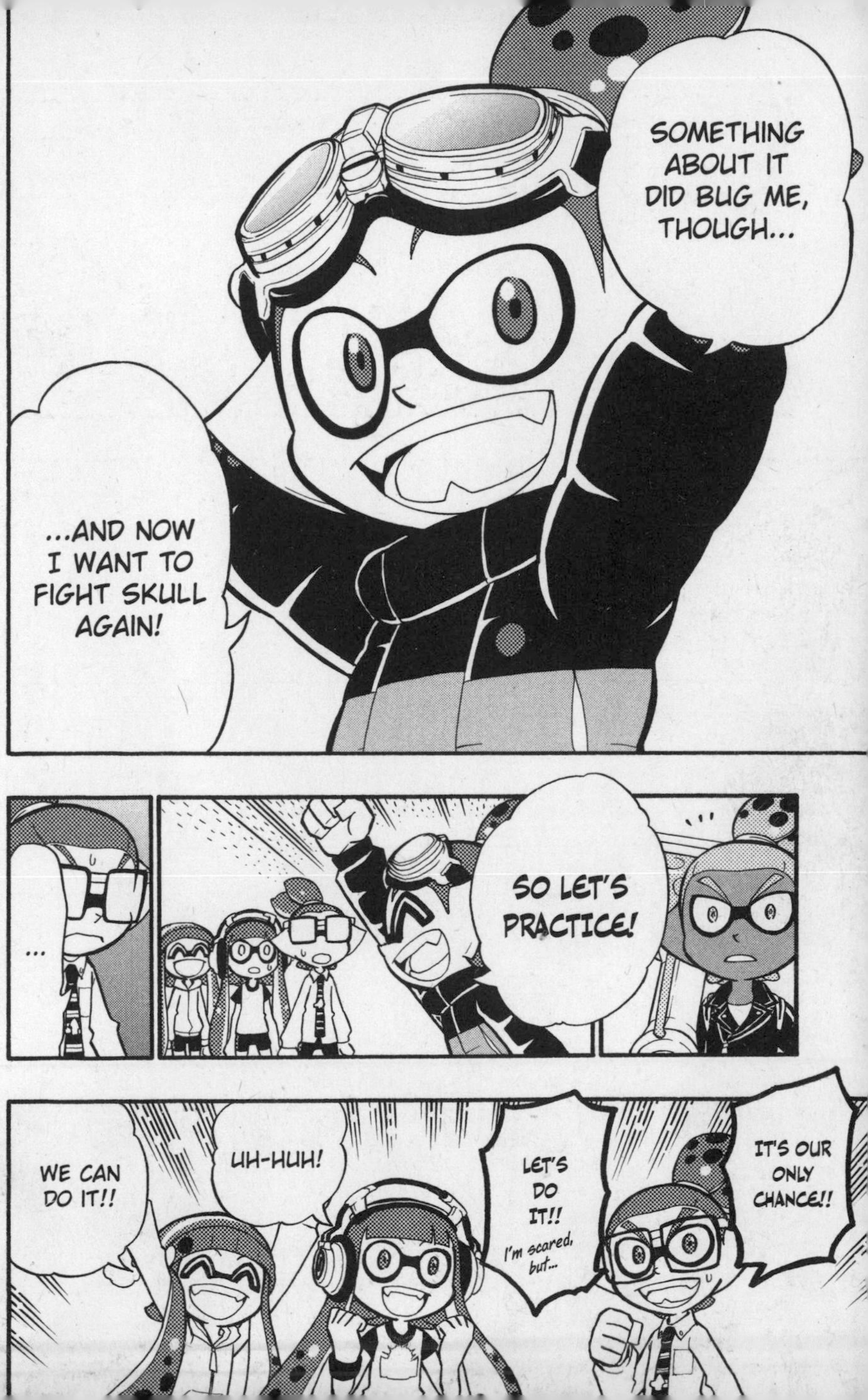
SOMETHING ABOUT IT DID BUG ME, THOUGH...
...AND NOW I WANT TO FIGHT SKULL AGAIN!
SO LET'S PRACTICE!
...
IT'S OUR ONLY CHANCE!!
LET'S DO IT!!
I'm scared, but...
UH-HUH!
WE CAN DO IT!!

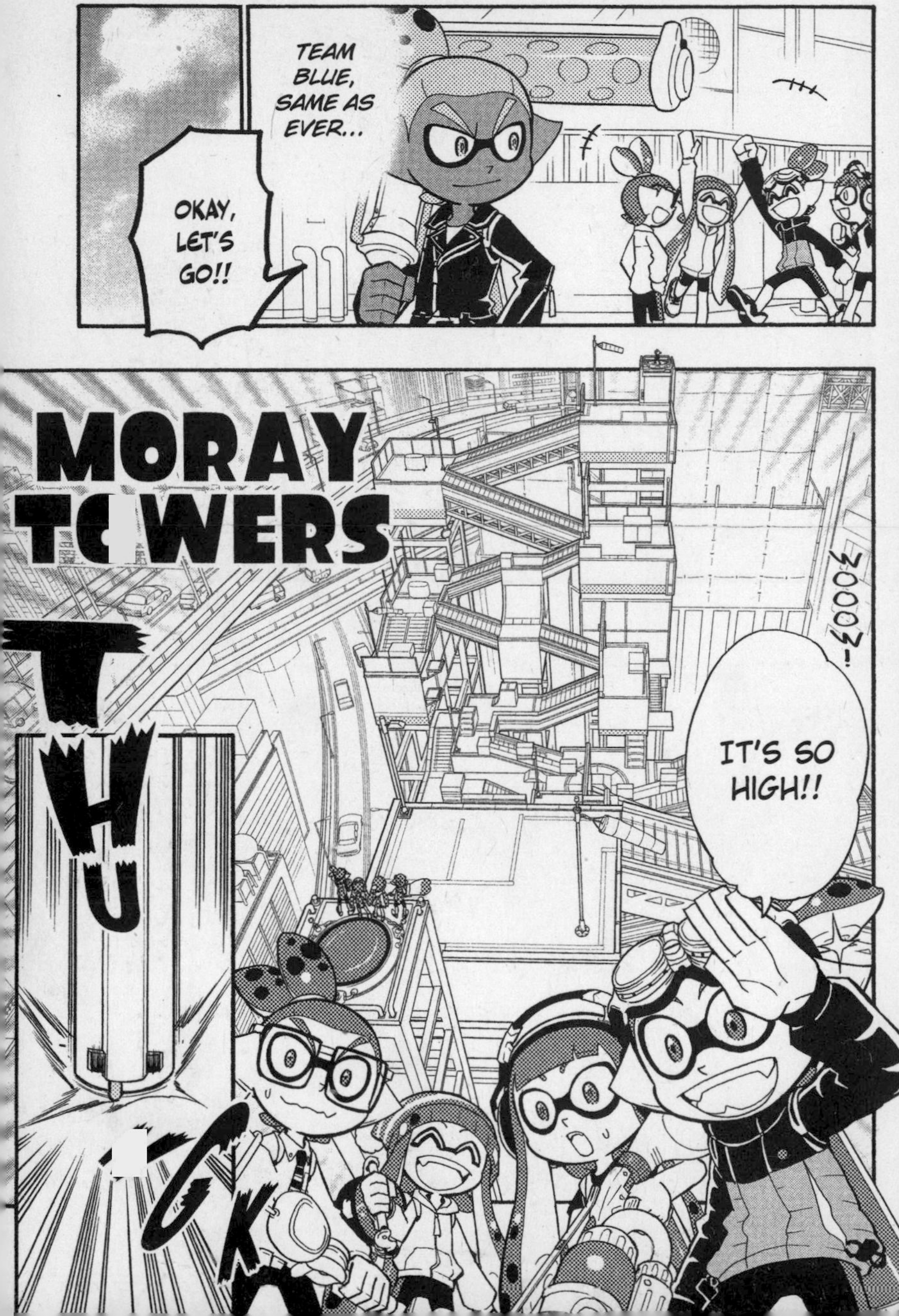
TEAM BLUE, SAME AS EVER...
OKAY, LET'S GO!!
MORAY TOWERS
WOOOW!
IT'S SO HIGH!!

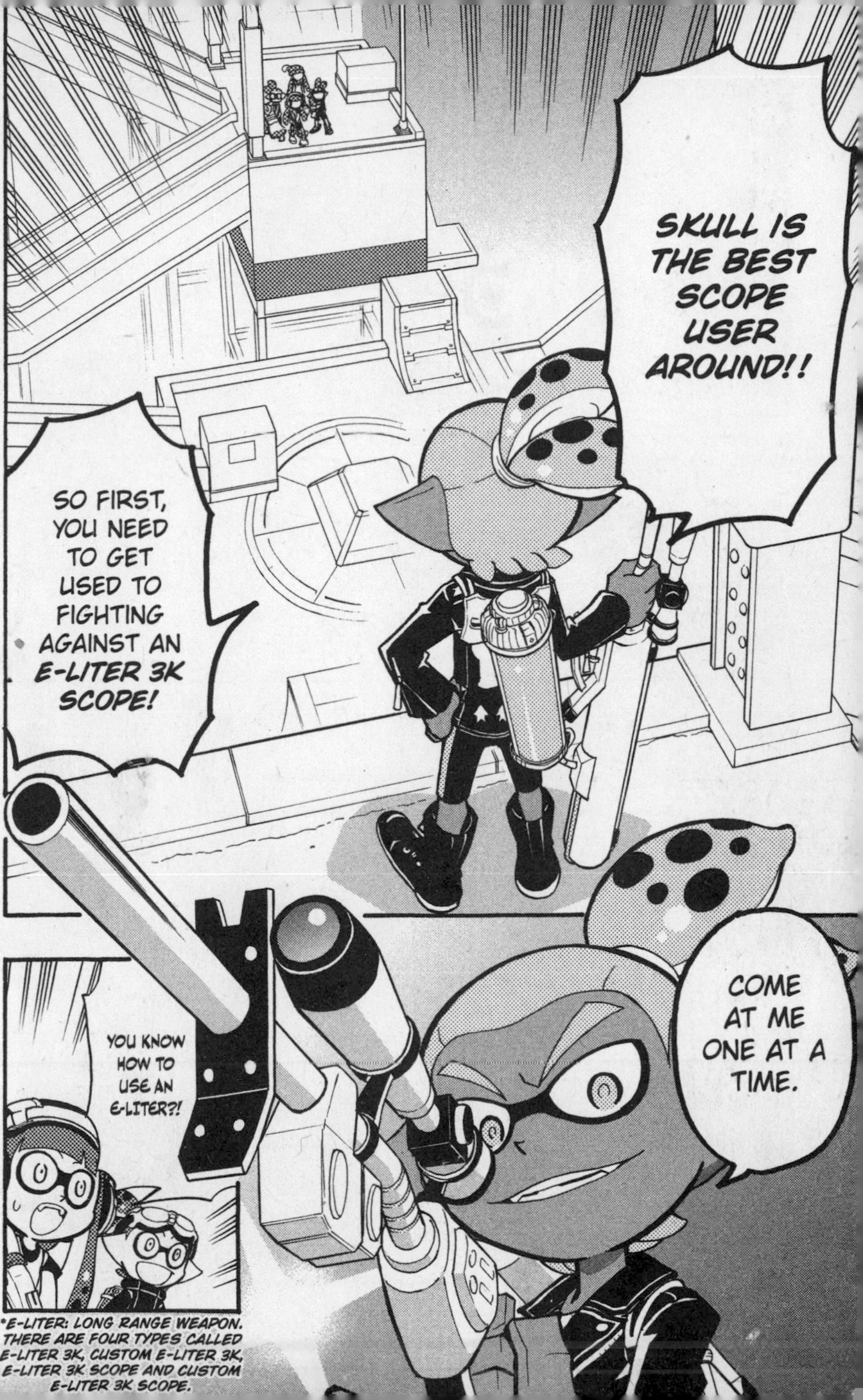
SKULL IS THE BEST SCOPE USER AROUND!!
SO FIRST, YOU NEED TO GET USED TO FIGHTING AGAINST AN *E-LITER 3K SCOPE!*
COME AT ME ONE AT A TIME.
YOU KNOW HOW TO USE AN E-LITER?!
*E-LITER: LONG RANGE WEAPON. THERE ARE FOUR TYPES CALLED E-LITER 3K, CUSTOM E-LITER 3K, E-LITER 3K SCOPE AND CUSTOM E-LITER 3K SCOPE.

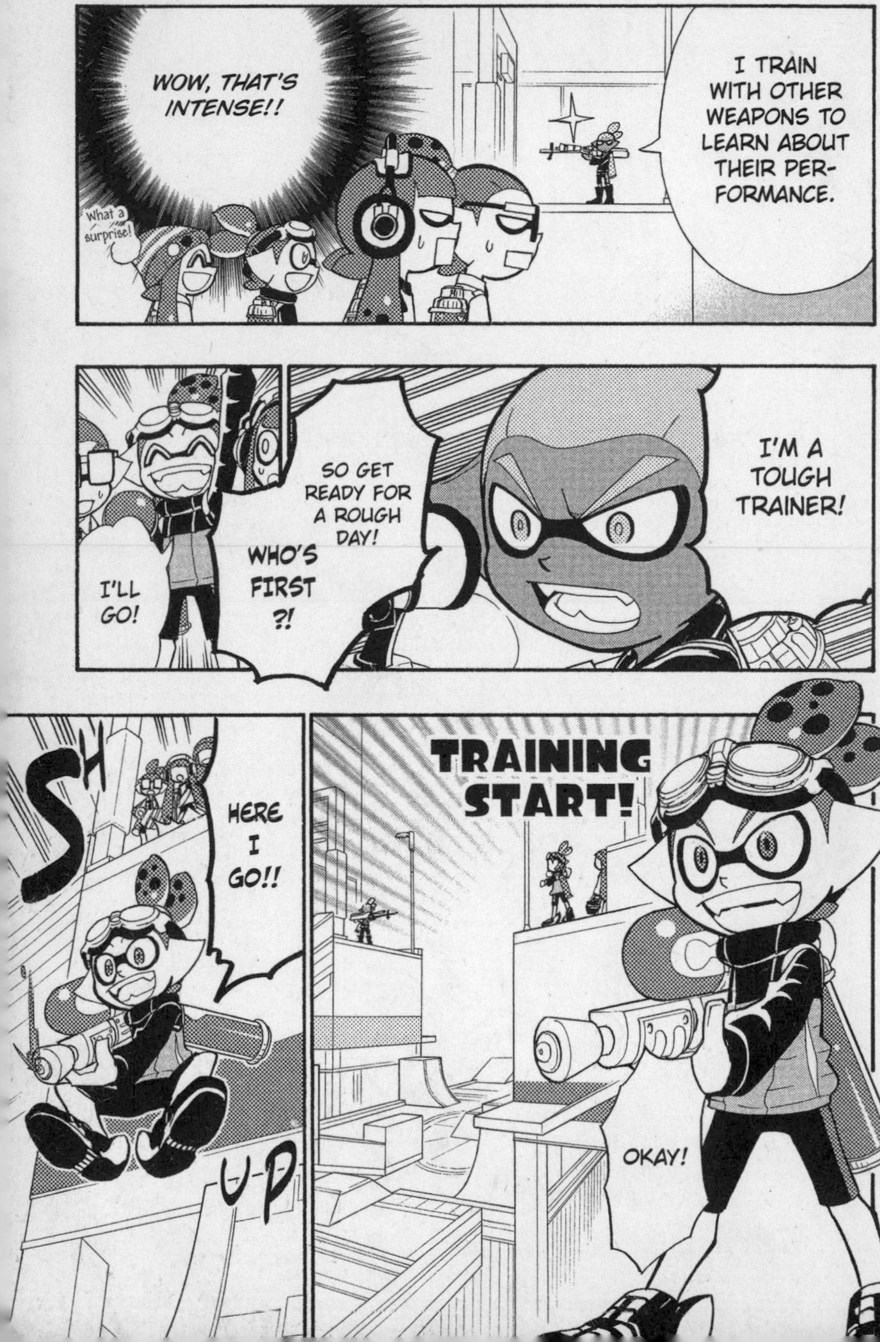
I TRAIN WITH OTHER WEAPONS TO LEARN ABOUT THEIR PER-FORMANCE.
WOW, THAT'S INTENSE!!
What a surprise!
I'M A TOUGH TRAINER!
SO GET READY FOR A ROUGH DAY!
WHO'S FIRST ?!
I'LL GO!
TRAINING START!
OKAY!
SH
HERE I GO!!
U-P

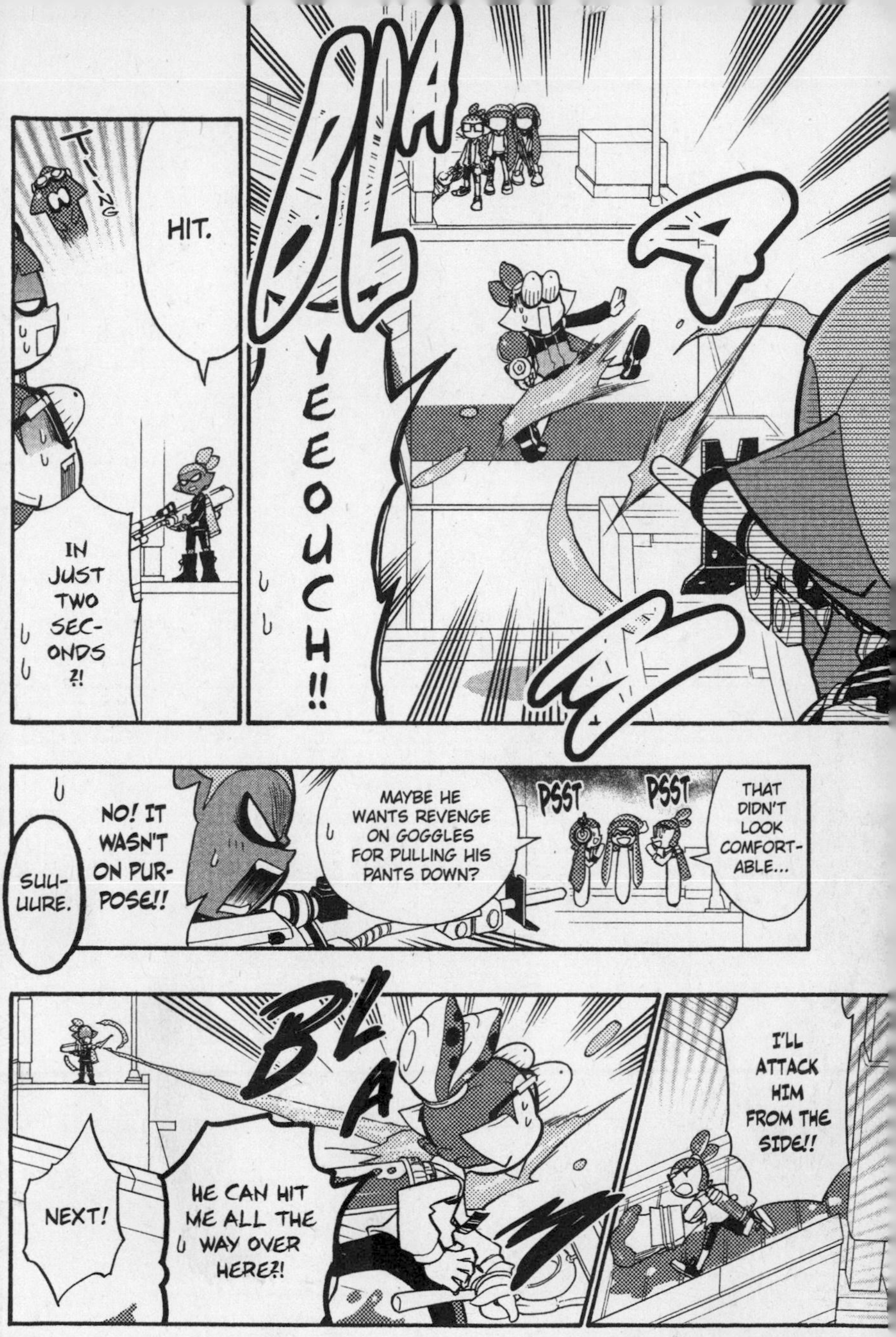
YEEEOUCH!!
TIIING
HIT.
IN JUST TWO SEC- ONDS ?!
THAT DIDN'T LOOK COMFORT- ABLE...
PSST
PSST
MAYBE HE WANTS REVENGE ON GOGGLES FOR PULLING HIS PANTS DOWN?
NO! IT WASN'T ON PUR- POSE!!
SUU- UURE.
I'LL ATTACK HIM FROM THE SIDE!!
BLAM
HE CAN HIT ME ALL THE WAY OVER HERE?!
NEXT!

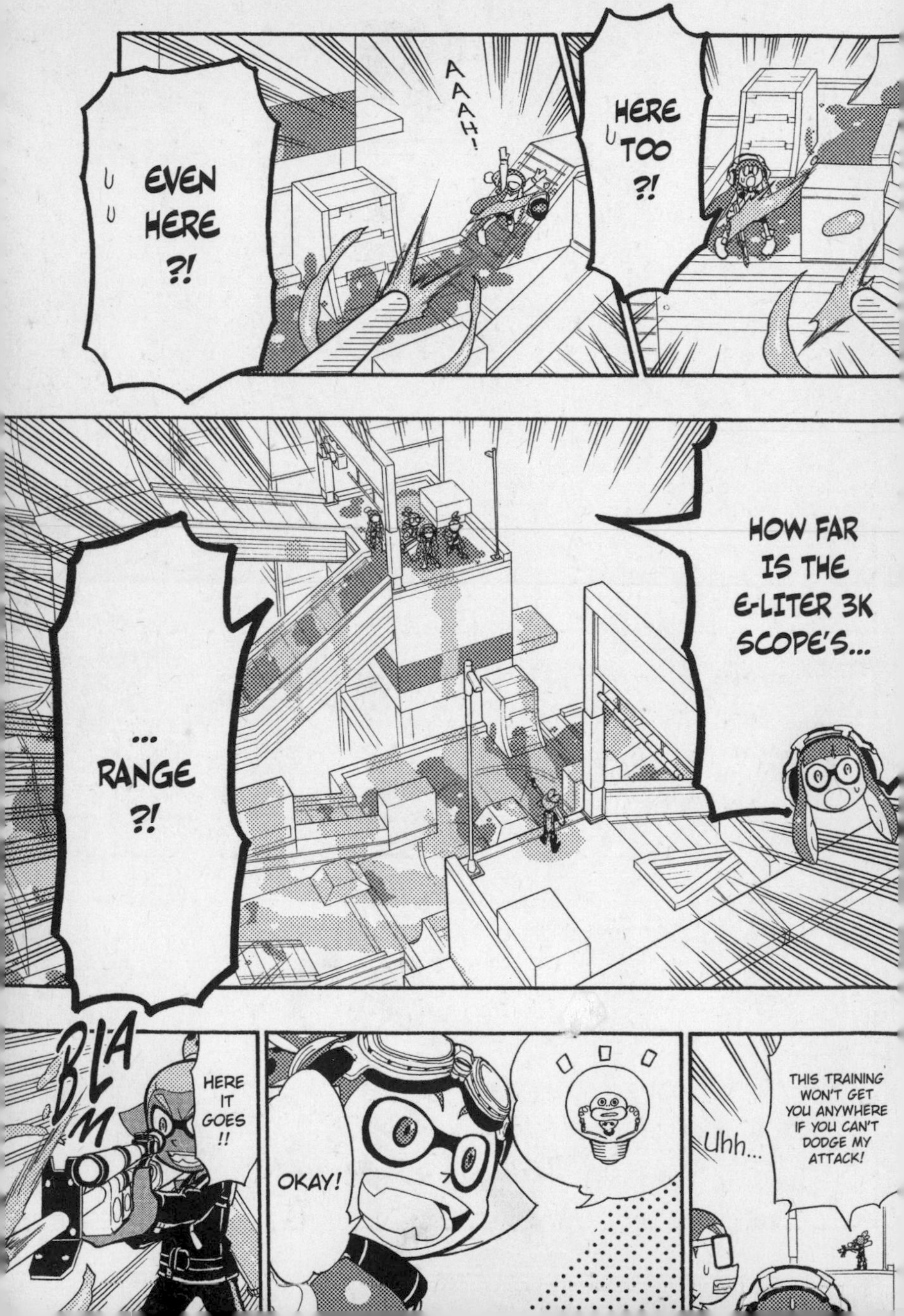
HERE TOO ?!
AAAH!
EVEN HERE ?!
HOW FAR IS THE E-LITER 3K SCOPE'S...
... RANGE ?!
THIS TRAINING WON'T GET YOU ANYWHERE IF YOU CAN'T DODGE MY ATTACK!
Uhh...
OKAY!
HERE IT GOES !!
BLAM

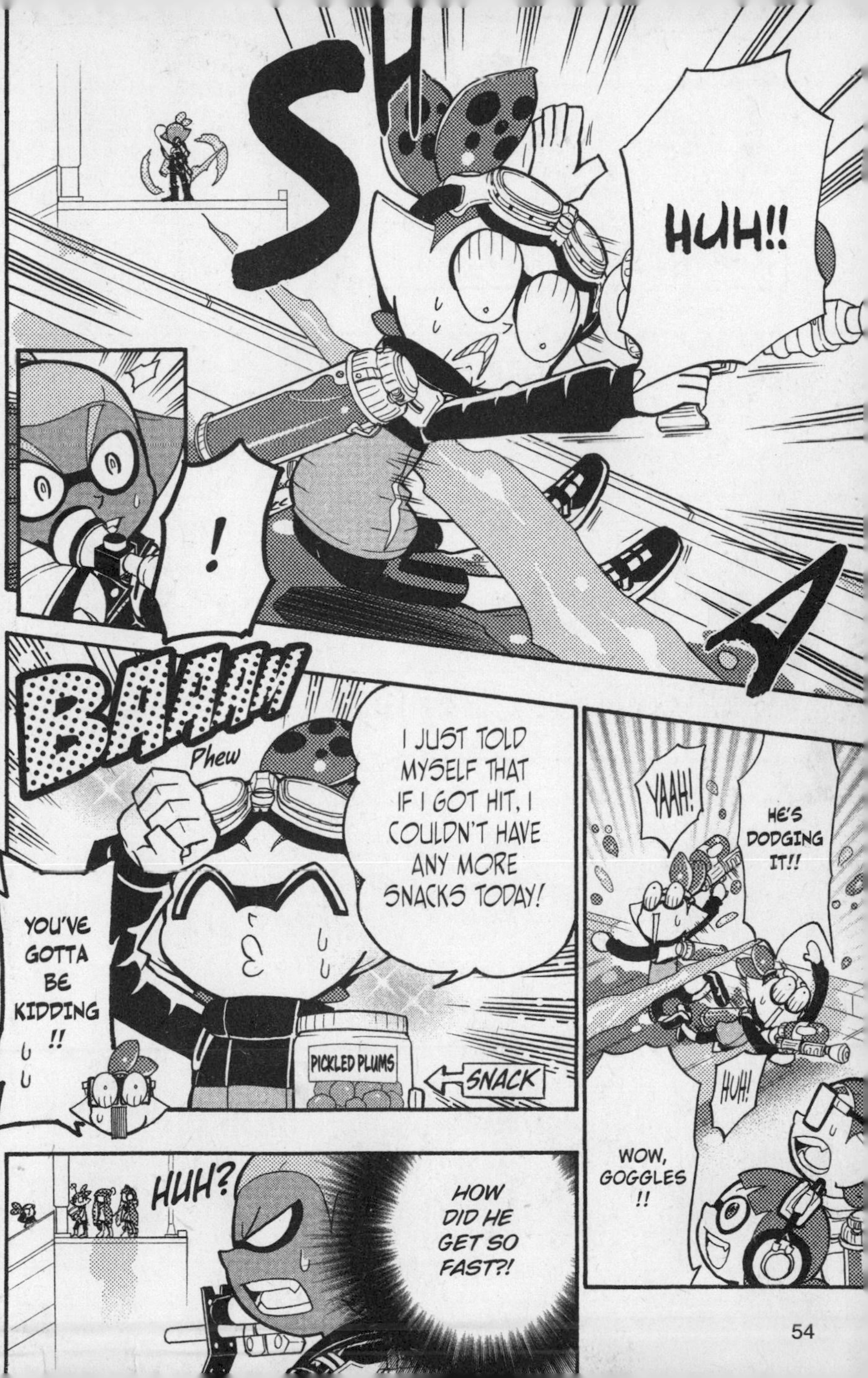
HUH!!
!
YAAH!
HE'S DODGING IT!!
HUH!
WOW, GOGGLES!!
Phew
I JUST TOLD MYSELF THAT IF I GOT HIT, I COULDN'T HAVE ANY MORE SNACKS TODAY!
SNACK
PICKLED PLUMS
YOU'VE GOTTA BE KIDDING!!
HUH?
HOW DID HE GET SO FAST?!

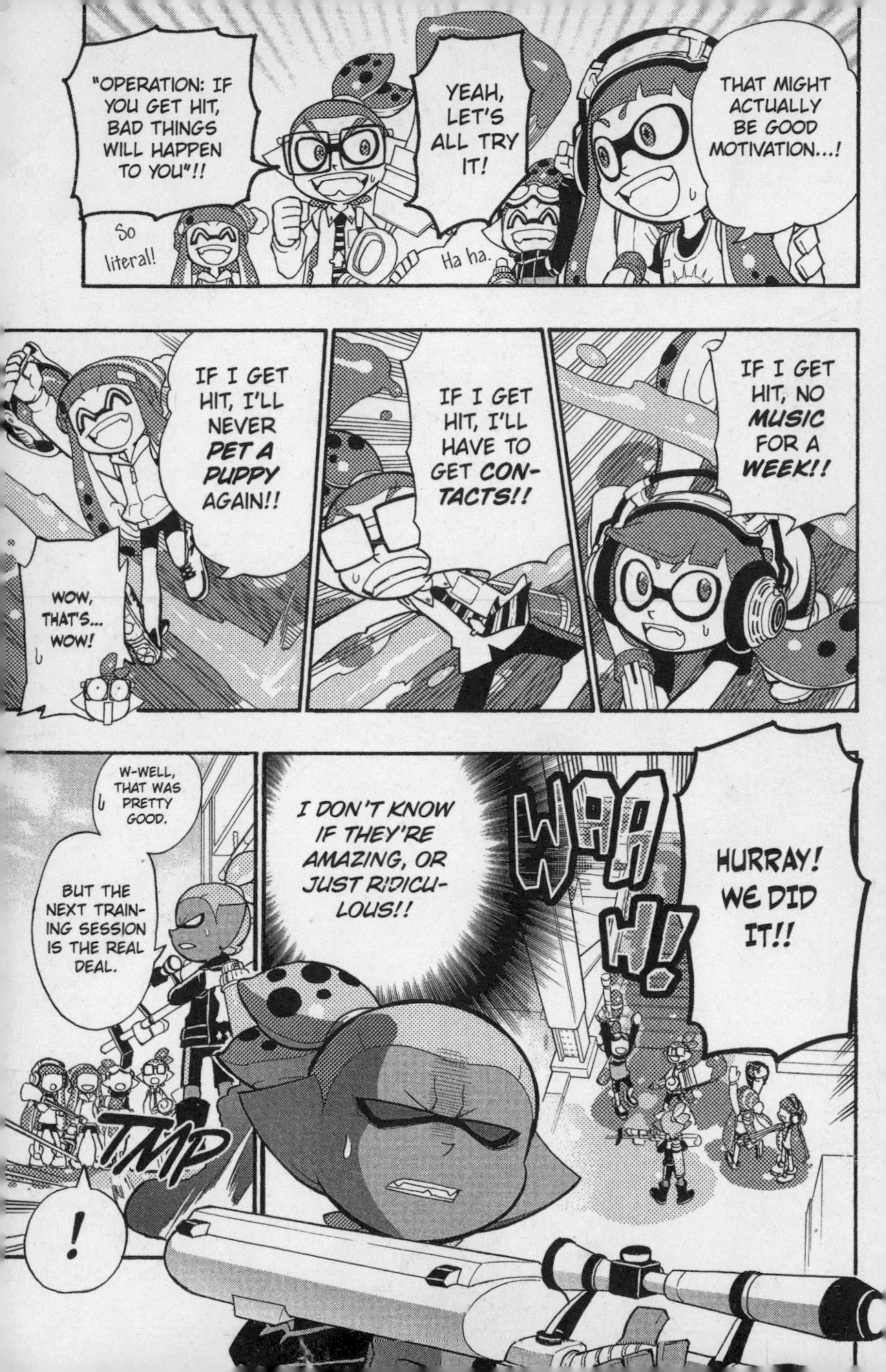
THAT MIGHT ACTUALLY BE GOOD MOTIVATION...!
YEAH, LET'S ALL TRY IT!
"OPERATION: IF YOU GET HIT, BAD THINGS WILL HAPPEN TO YOU"!!
Ha ha.
So literal!
IF I GET HIT, NO MUSIC FOR A WEEK!!
IF I GET HIT, I'LL HAVE TO GET CONTACTS!!
IF I GET HIT, I'LL NEVER PET A PUPPY AGAIN!!
WOW, THAT'S... WOW!
HURRAY! WE DID IT!!
WAAH!
I DON'T KNOW IF THEY'RE AMAZING, OR JUST RIDICULOUS!!
W-WELL, THAT WAS PRETTY GOOD.
BUT THE NEXT TRAINING SESSION IS THE REAL DEAL.
TMP
!

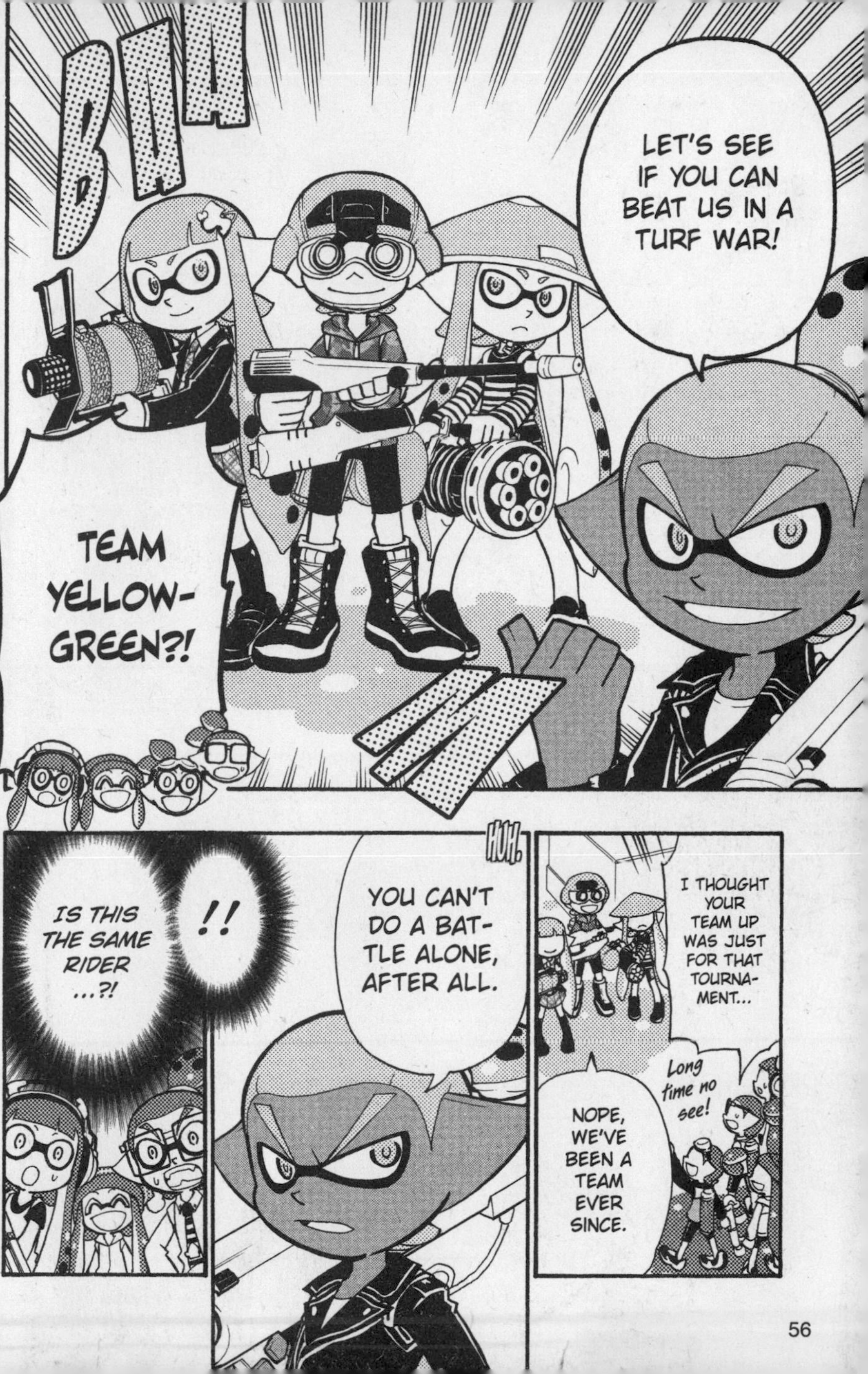
BAA
LET'S SEE IF YOU CAN BEAT US IN A TURF WAR!
TEAM YELLOW-GREEN?!
I THOUGHT YOUR TEAM UP WAS JUST FOR THAT TOURNAMENT...
Long time no see!
NOPE, WE'VE BEEN A TEAM EVER SINCE.
HUH.
YOU CAN'T DO A BATTLE ALONE, AFTER ALL.
!!
IS THIS THE SAME RIDER ...?!

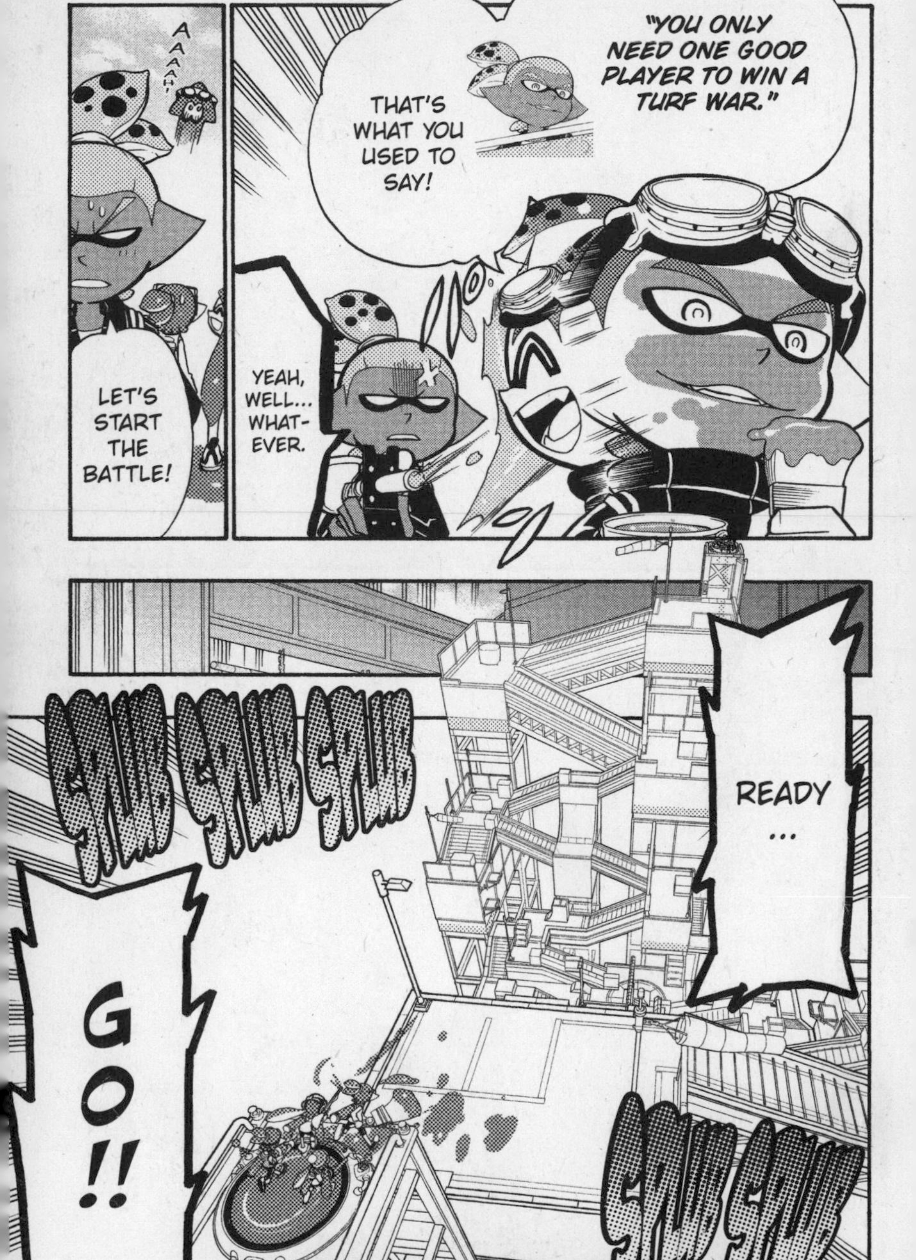
"YOU ONLY NEED ONE GOOD PLAYER TO WIN A TURF WAR."
THAT'S WHAT YOU USED TO SAY!
YEAH, WELL... WHATEVER.
AAAAH
LET'S START THE BATTLE!
READY ...
GO!!

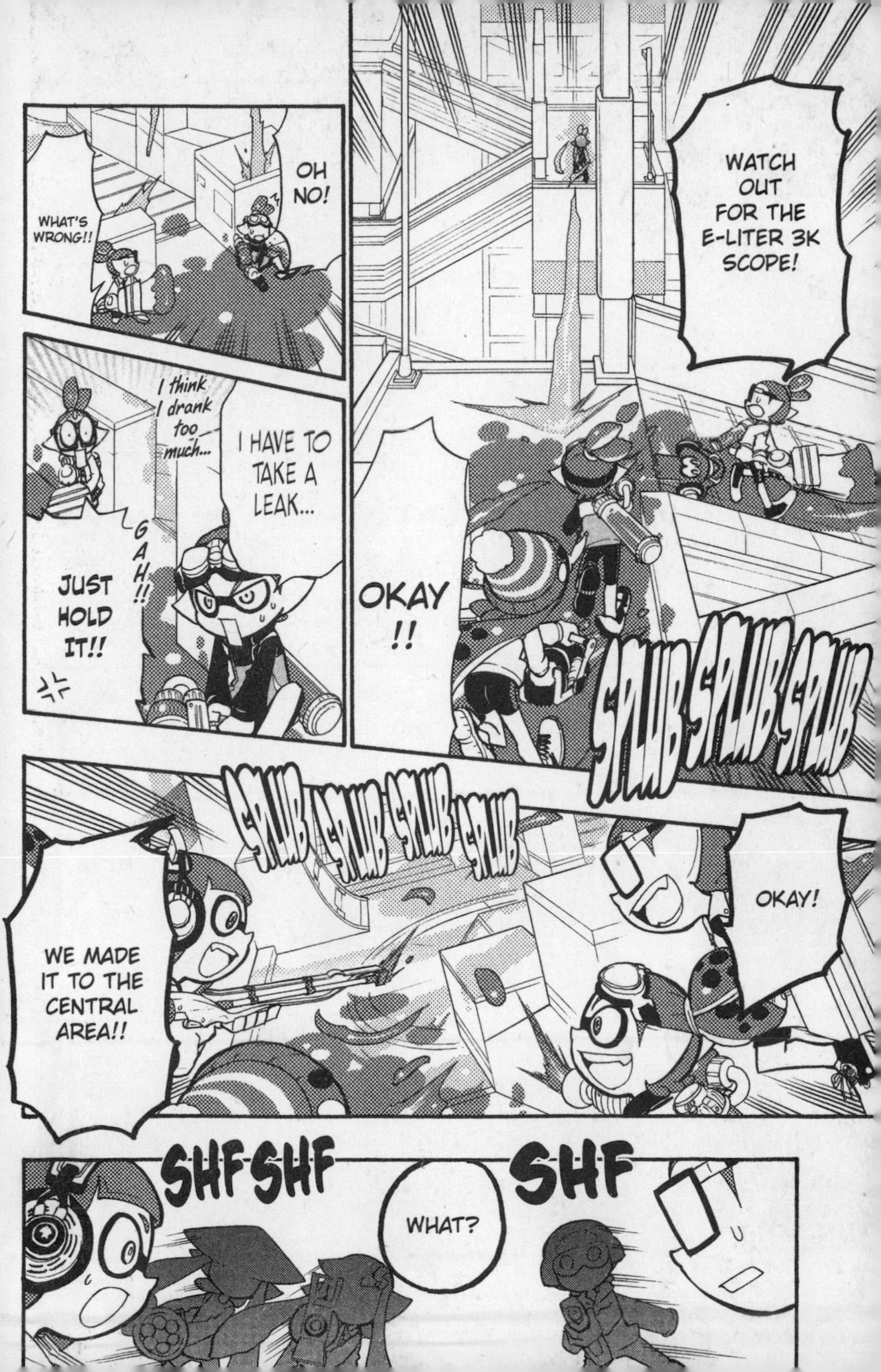
WATCH OUT FOR THE E-LITER 3K SCOPE!
OKAY!!
SPLUB SPLUB SPLUB
OH NO!
WHAT'S WRONG!!
I HAVE TO TAKE A LEAK...
I think I drank too much...
GAH!!
JUST HOLD IT!!
SPLUB SPLUB SPLUB SPLUB
OKAY!
WE MADE IT TO THE CENTRAL AREA!!
SHF
WHAT?
SHF SHF

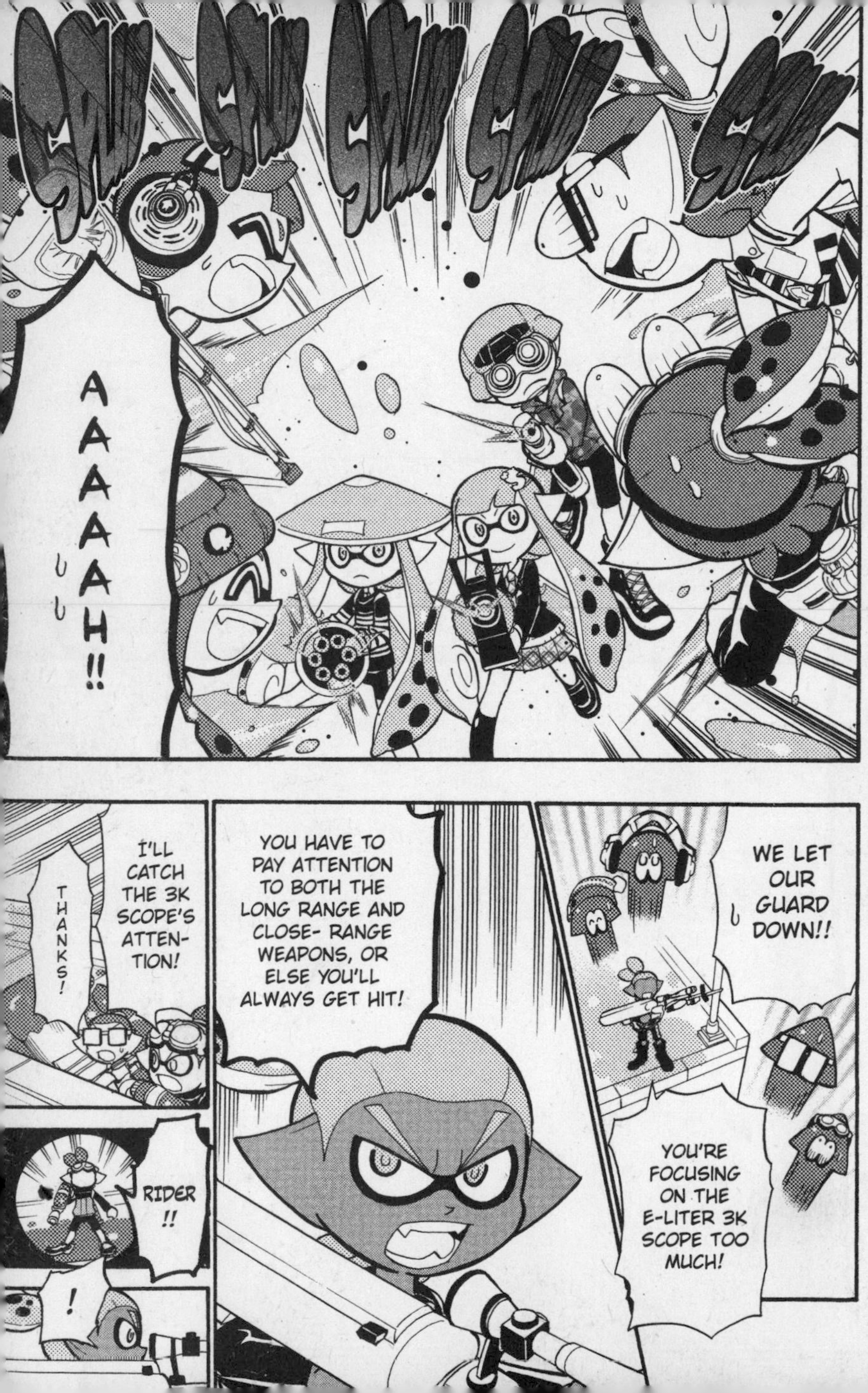
AAAAAH!!
WE LET OUR GUARD DOWN!!
YOU'RE FOCUSING ON THE E-LITER 3K SCOPE TOO MUCH!
YOU HAVE TO PAY ATTENTION TO BOTH THE LONG RANGE AND CLOSE- RANGE WEAPONS, OR ELSE YOU'LL ALWAYS GET HIT!
I'LL CATCH THE 3K SCOPE'S ATTEN- TION!
THANKS!
RIDER!!
!

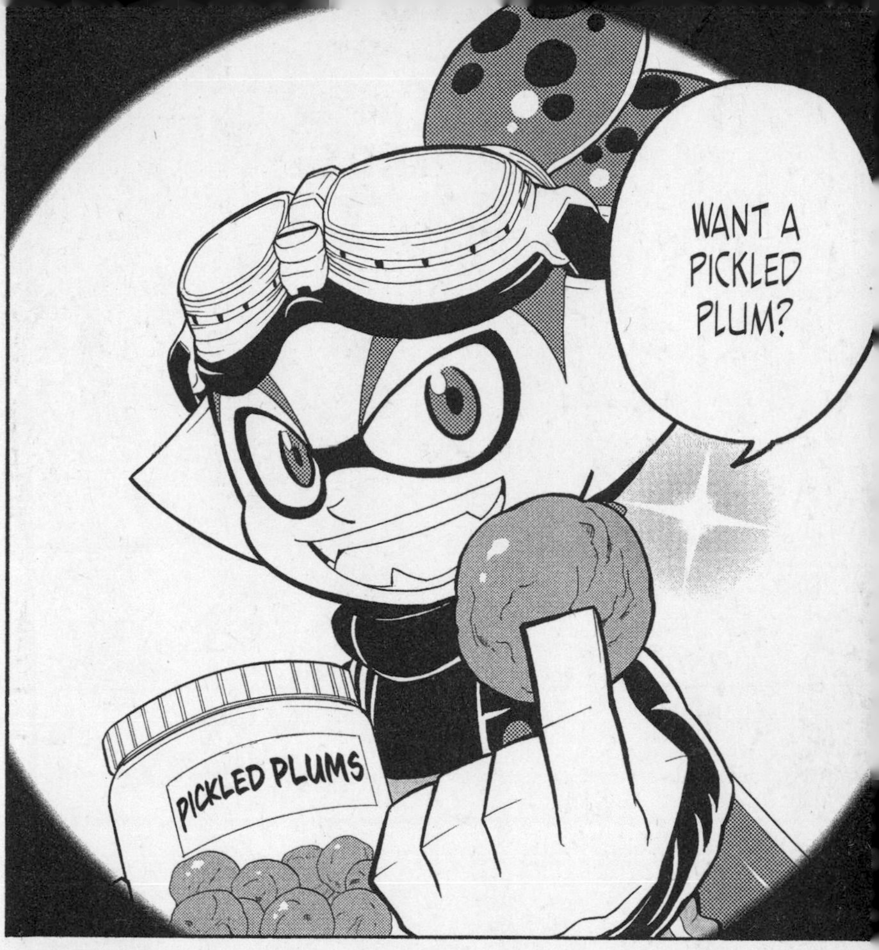
WANT A PICKLED PLUM?
PICKLED PLUMS

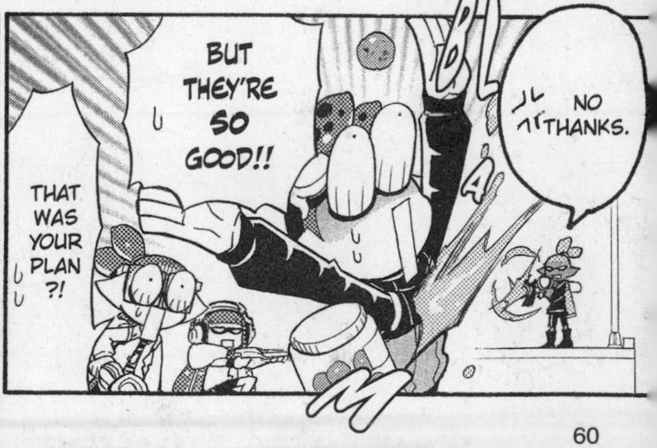
NO THANKS.
BLAM
BUT THEY'RE SO GOOD!!
THAT WAS YOUR PLAN?!

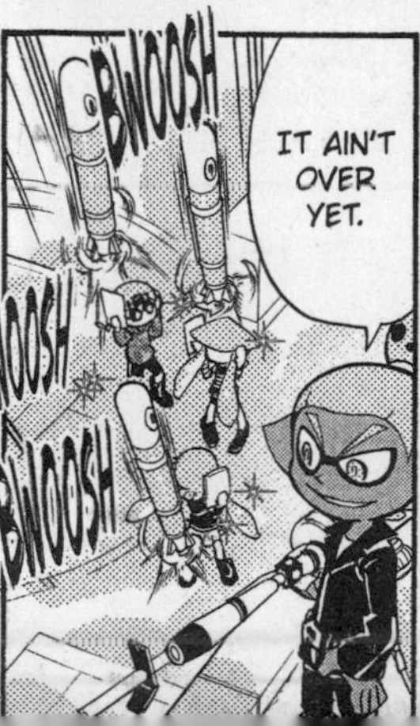
BWOOSH
IT AIN'T OVER YET.
BWOOSH
BWOOSH
BWOOSH

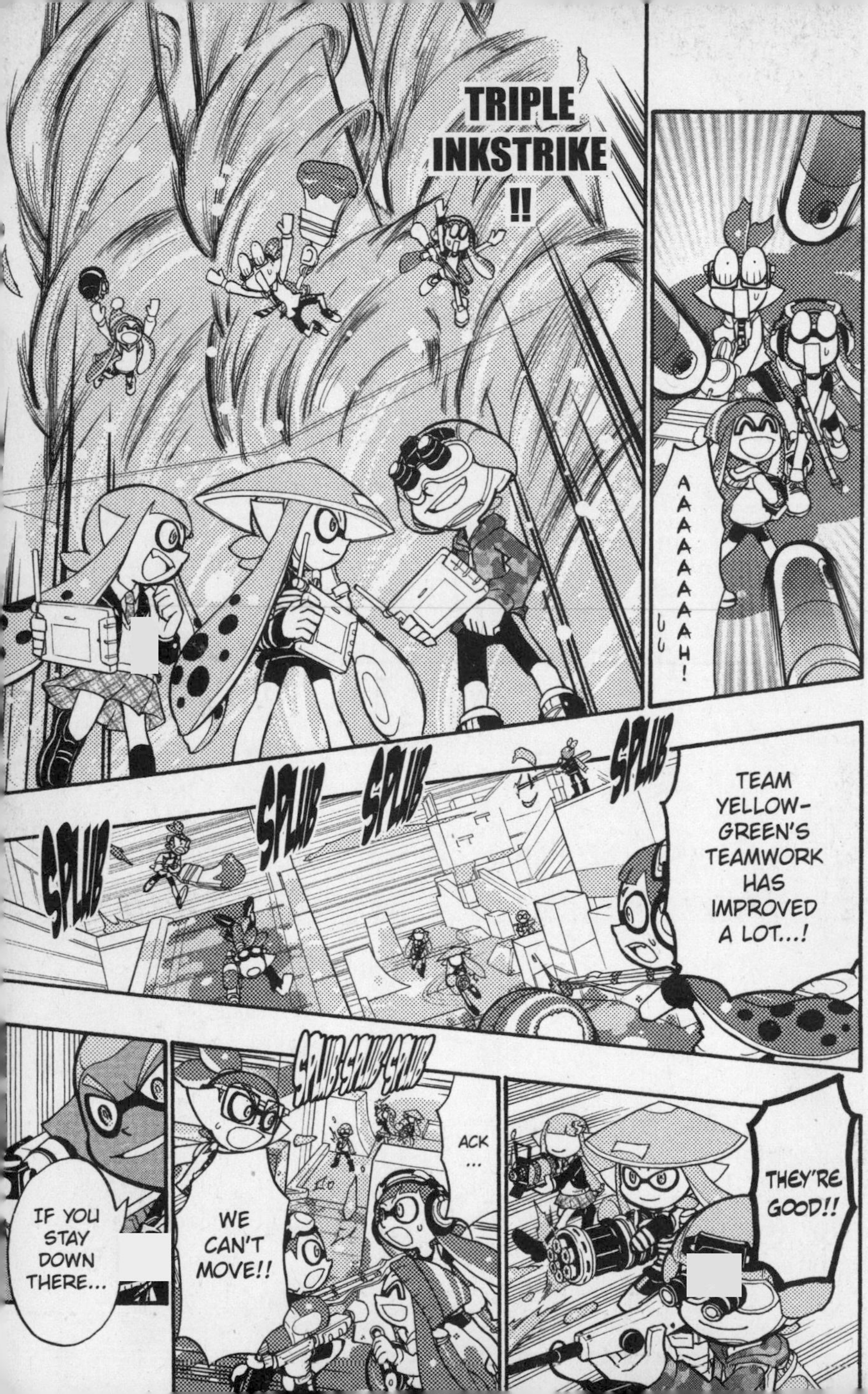

AAAAAAAAH!
TRIPLE INKSTRIKE!!
SPLUB
SPLUB
SPLUB
SPLUB
TEAM YELLOW-GREEN'S TEAMWORK HAS IMPROVED A LOT...!
THEY'RE GOOD!!
SPLUB SPLUB SPLUB
ACK...
WE CAN'T MOVE!!
IF YOU STAY DOWN THERE...

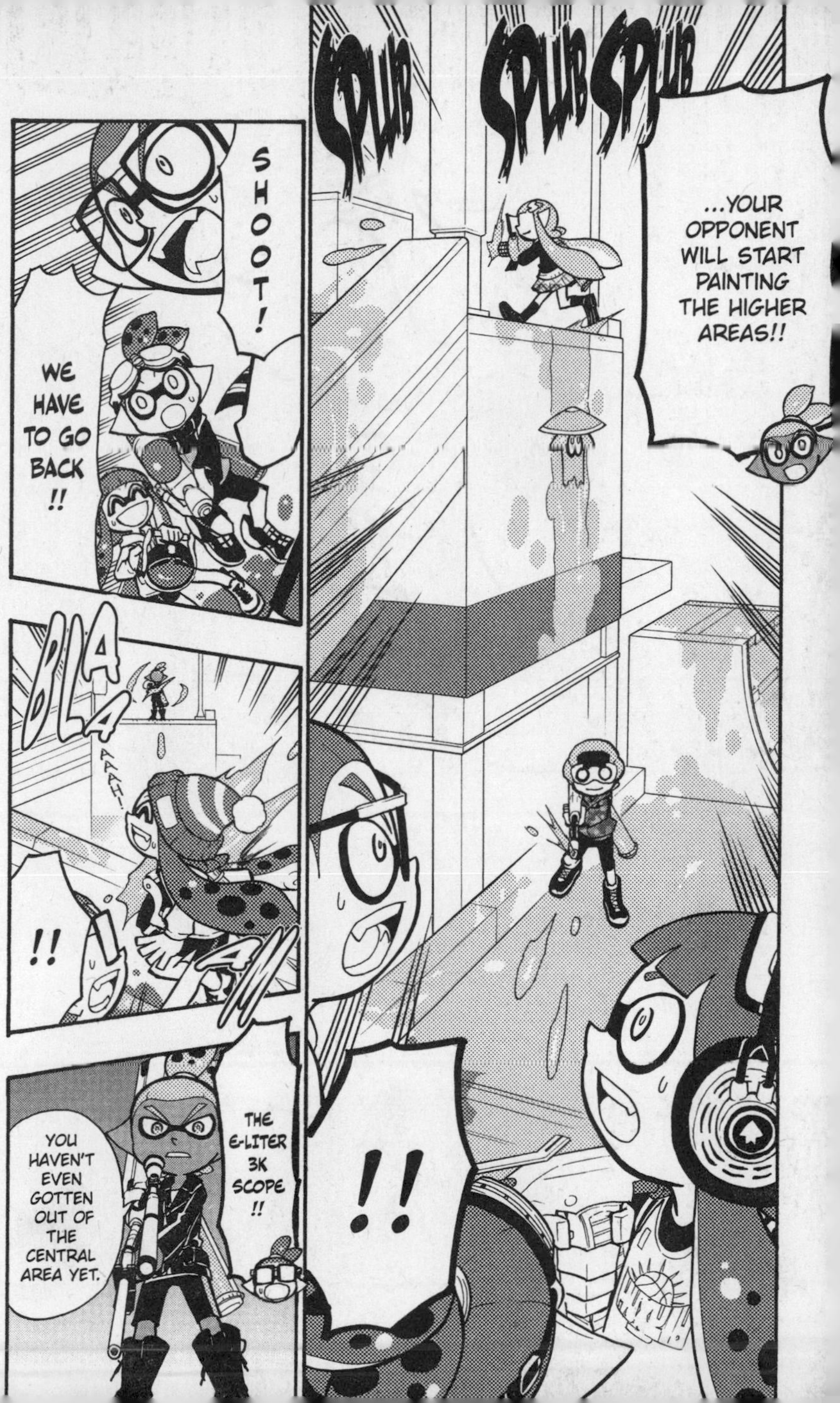
SPLUB SPLUB SPLUB
...YOUR OPPONENT WILL START PAINTING THE HIGHER AREAS!!
!!
SHOOT!
WE HAVE TO GO BACK!!
BLA BLA
AAAH!
!!
THE E-LITER 3K SCOPE!!
YOU HAVEN'T EVEN GOTTEN OUT OF THE CENTRAL AREA YET.

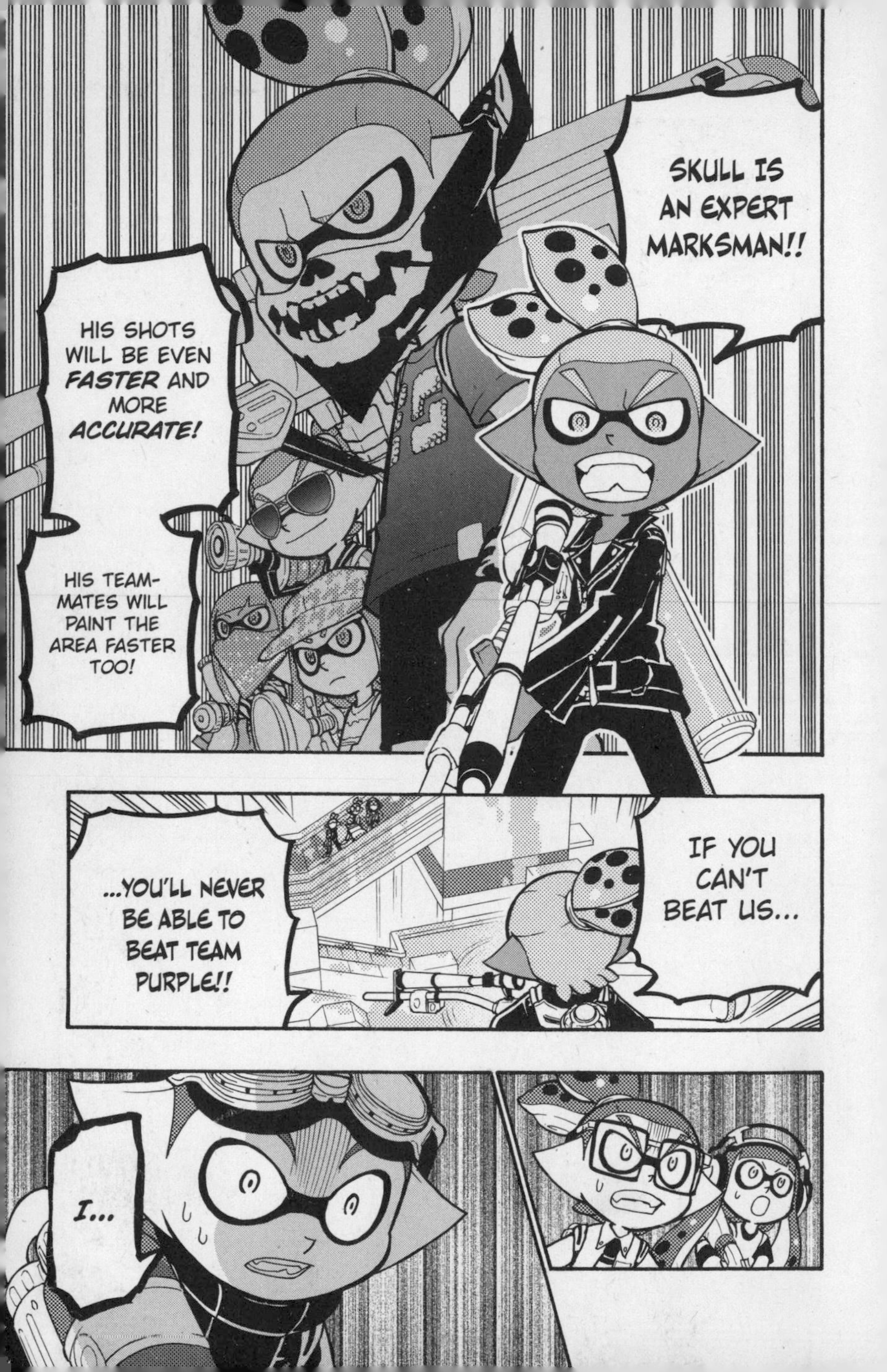
SKULL IS AN EXPERT MARKSMAN!!
HIS SHOTS WILL BE EVEN FASTER AND MORE ACCURATE!
HIS TEAM-MATES WILL PAINT THE AREA FASTER TOO!
IF YOU CAN'T BEAT US...
...YOU'LL NEVER BE ABLE TO BEAT TEAM PURPLE!!
I...

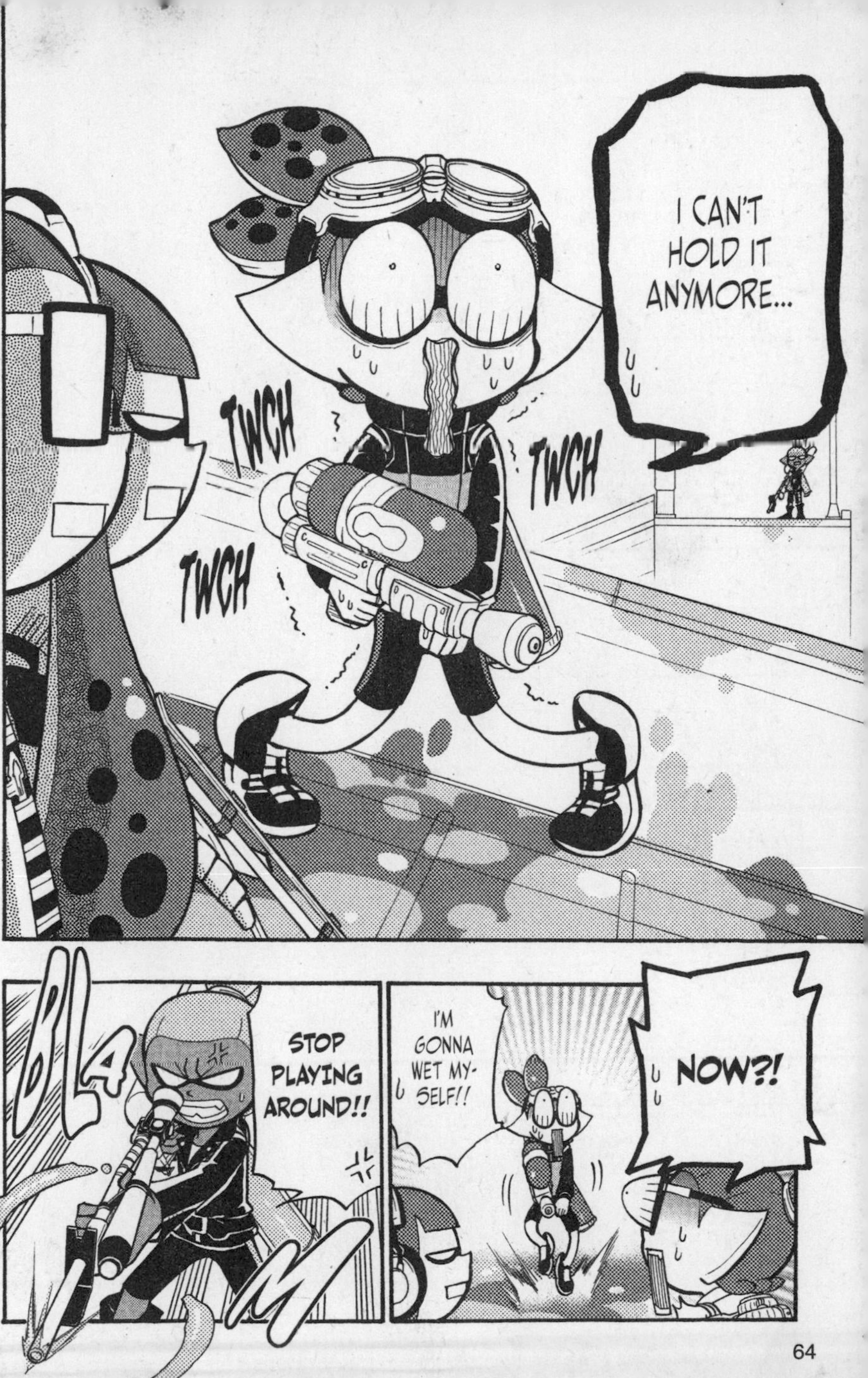
I CAN'T HOLD IT ANYMORE...
TWCH
TWCH
TWCH
NOW?!
I'M GONNA WET MY-SELF!!
STOP PLAYING AROUND!!
BLAM

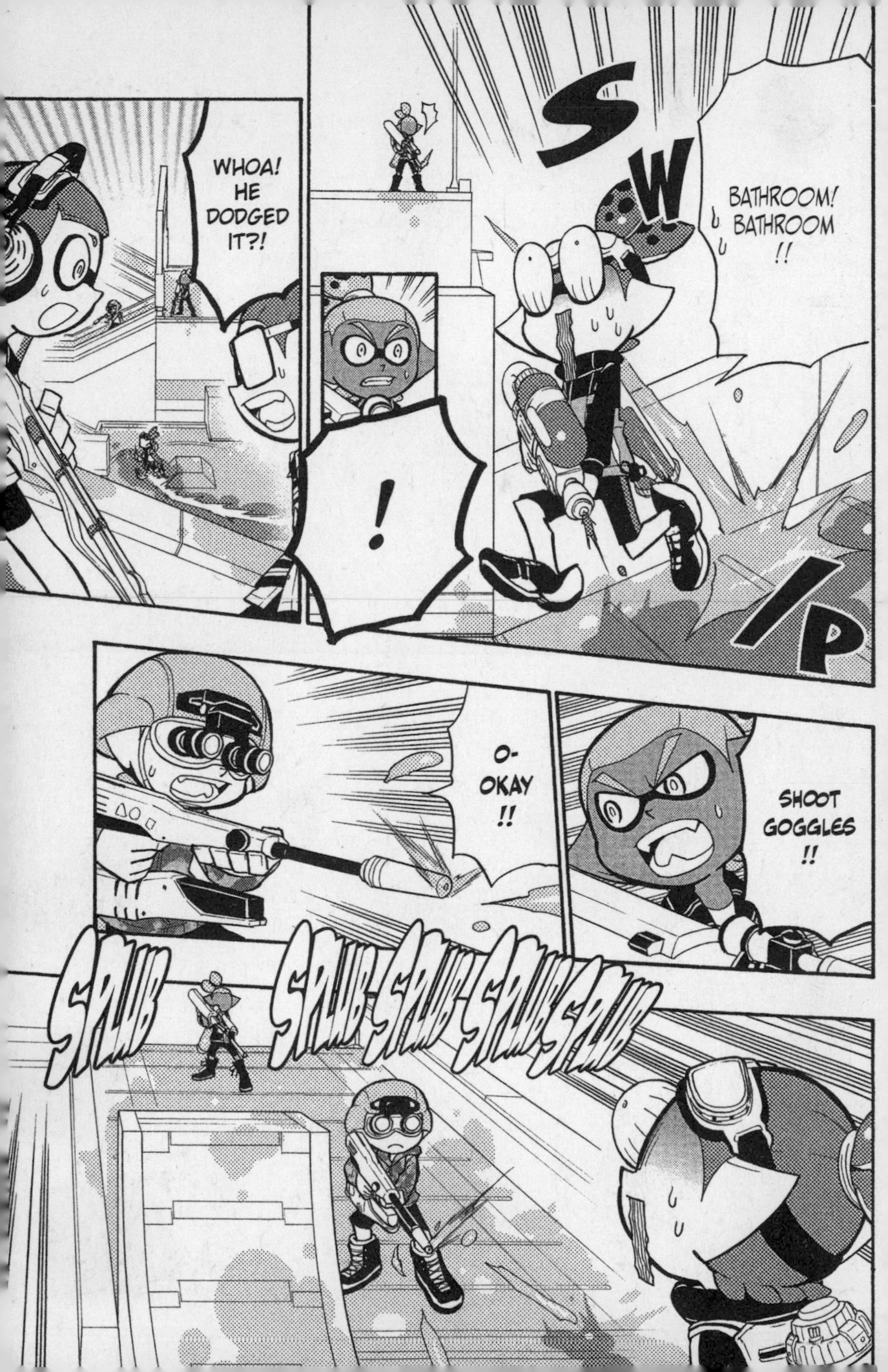
SWIP
BATHROOM! BATHROOM !!
!
WHOA! HE DODGED IT?!
SHOOT GOGGLES !!
O-OKAY !!
SPLUB
SPLUB-SPLUB-SPLUB-SPLUB

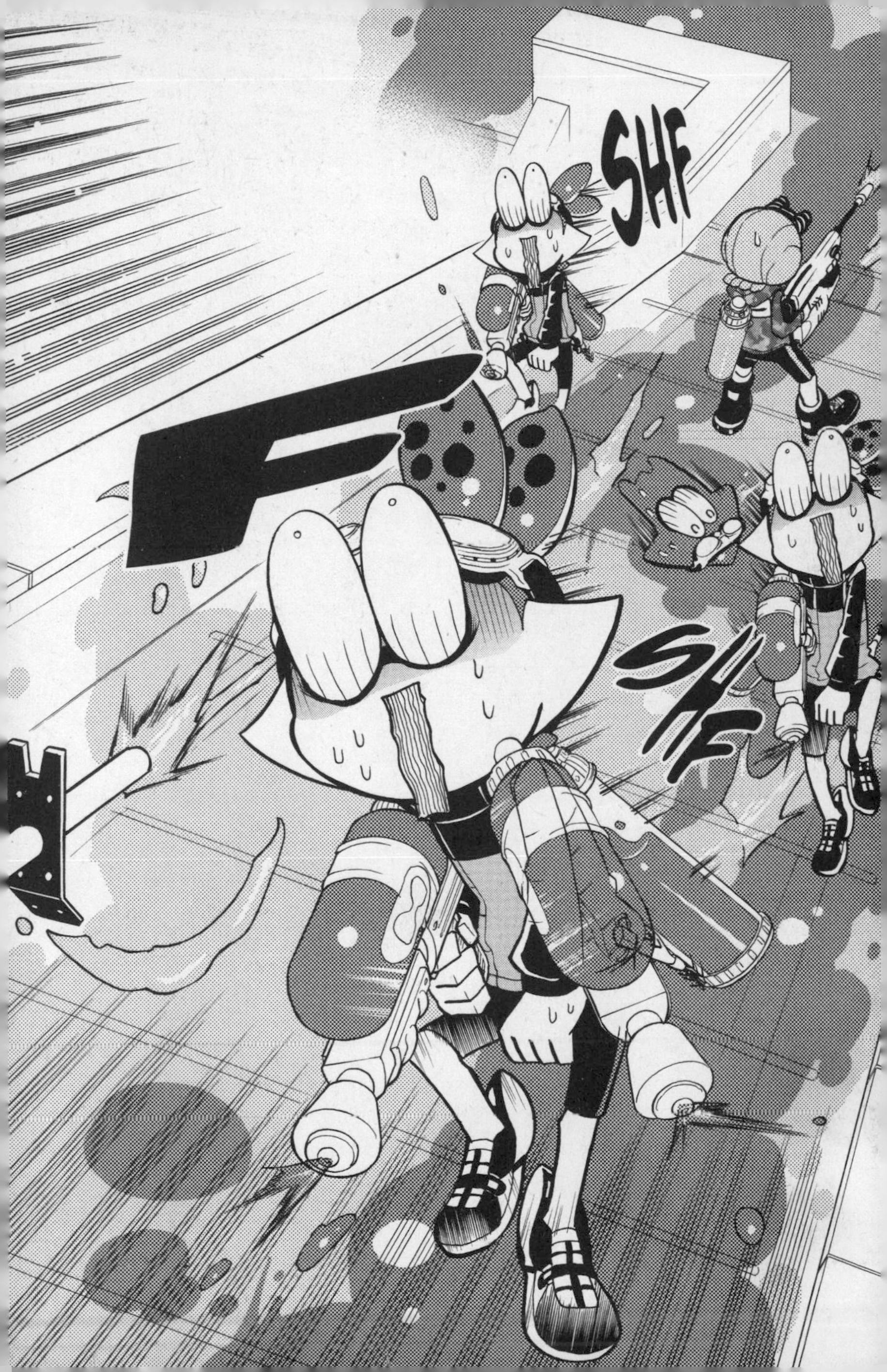
SHF
SHF

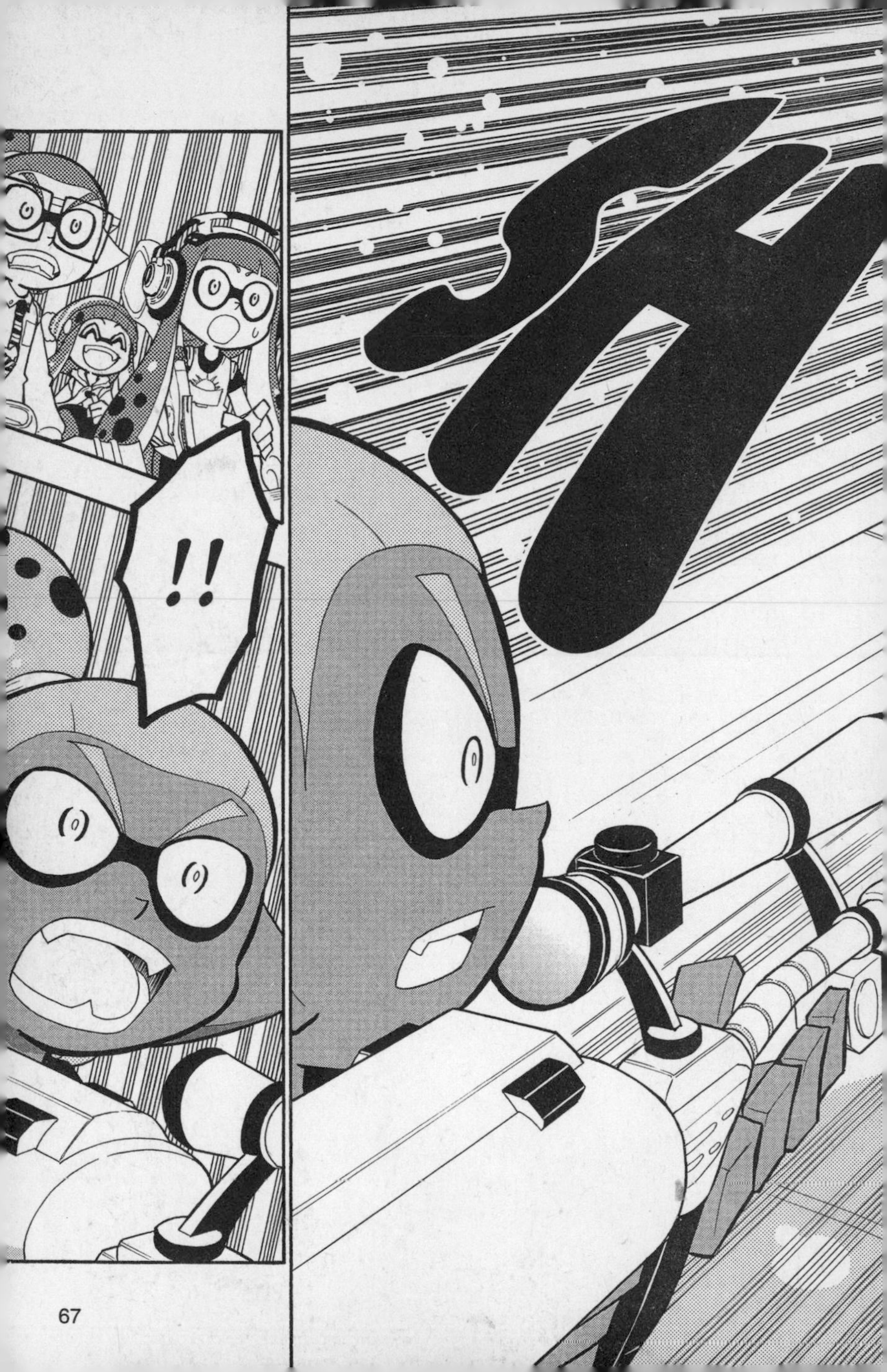
!!

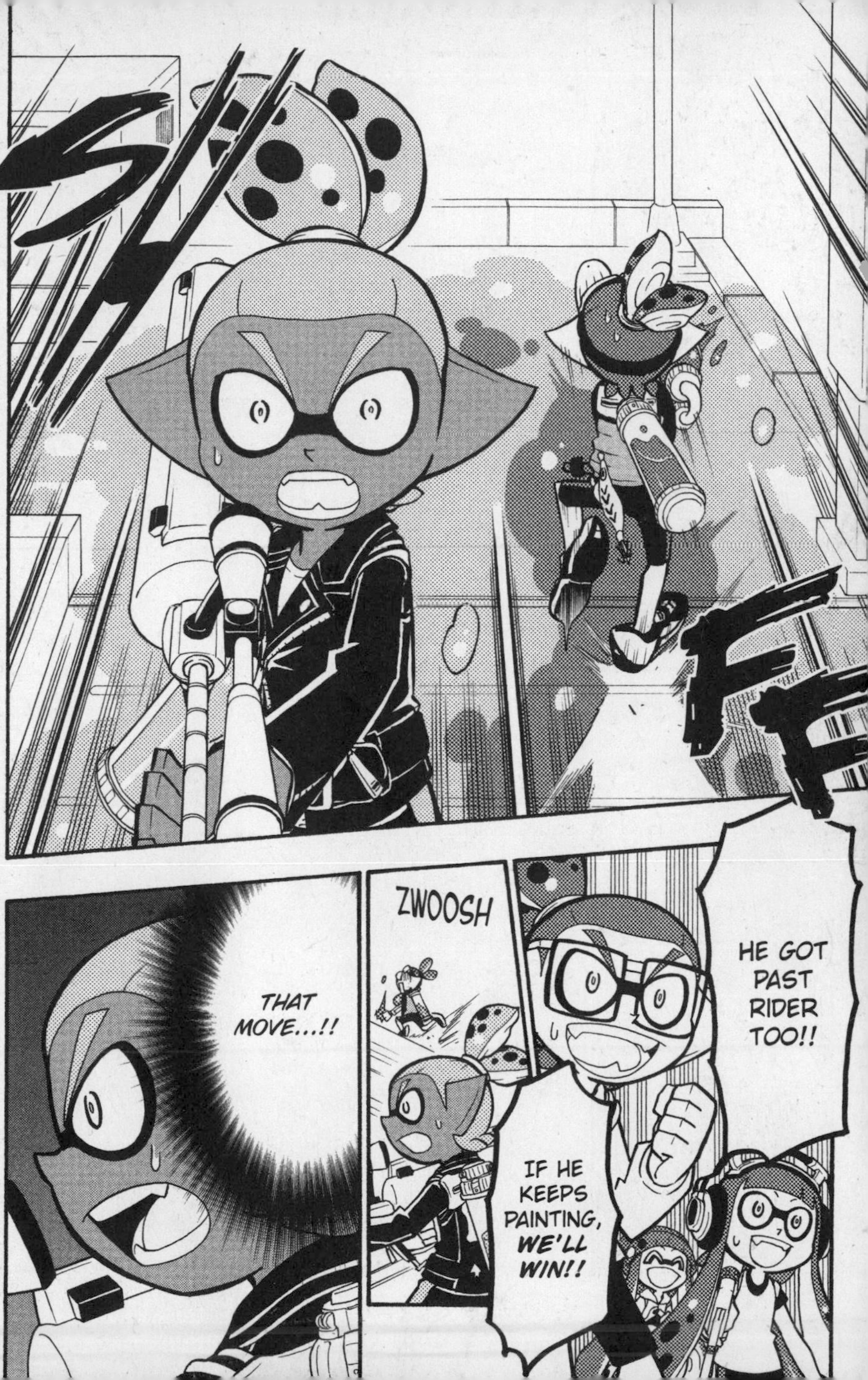
HE GOT PAST RIDER TOO!!
IF HE KEEPS PAINTING, WE'LL WIN!!
ZWOOSH
THAT MOVE...!!

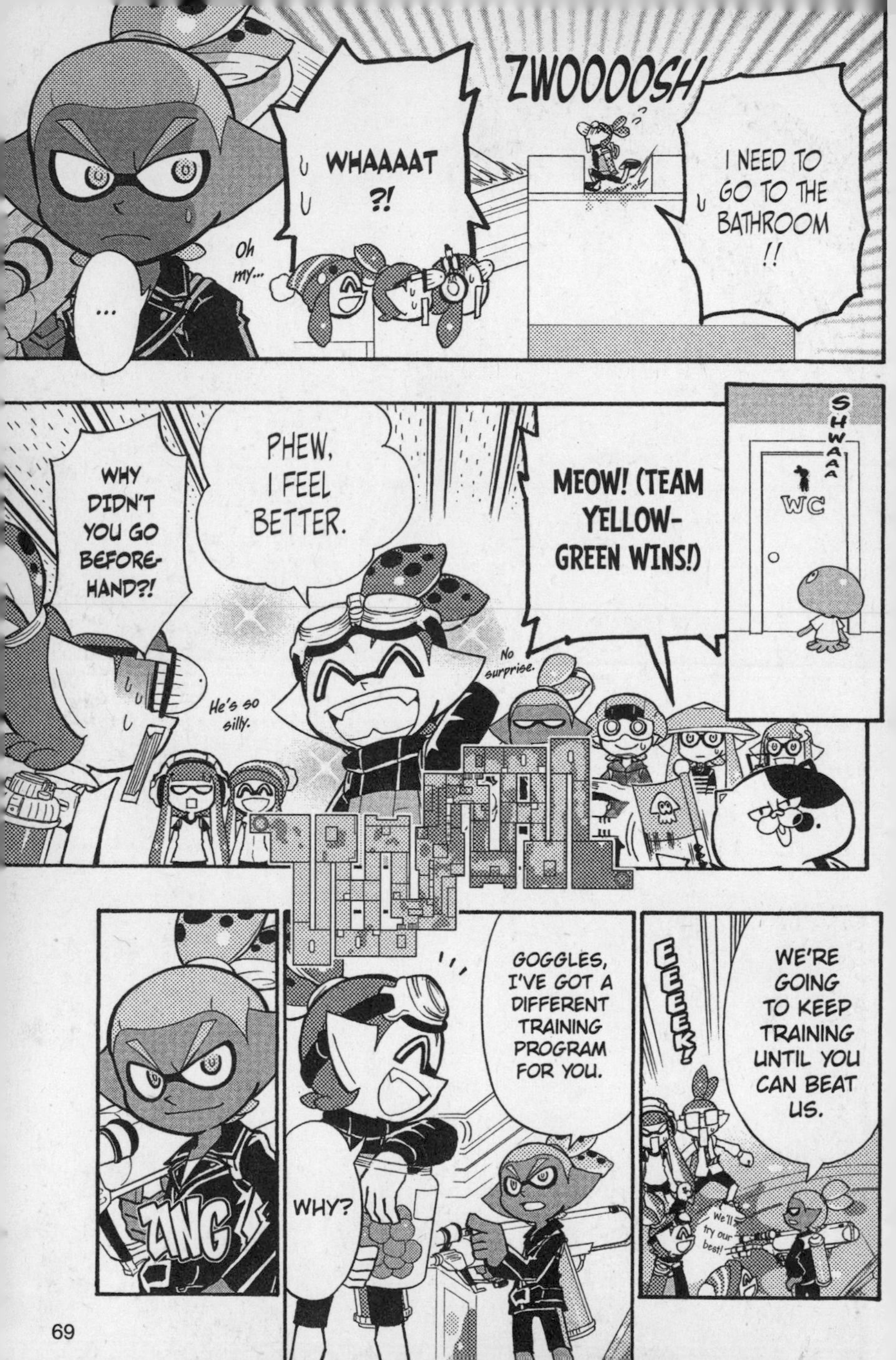
ZWOOOOSH
I NEED TO GO TO THE BATHROOM !!
WHAAAAT ?!
Oh my...
...
SHWAAA
WC
MEOW! (TEAM YELLOW-GREEN WINS!)
No surprise.
PHEW, I FEEL BETTER.
WHY DIDN'T YOU GO BEFOREHAND?!
He's so silly.
WE'RE GOING TO KEEP TRAINING UNTIL YOU CAN BEAT US.
EEEEK!
We'll try our best!
GOGGLES, I'VE GOT A DIFFERENT TRAINING PROGRAM FOR YOU.
WHY?
ZING

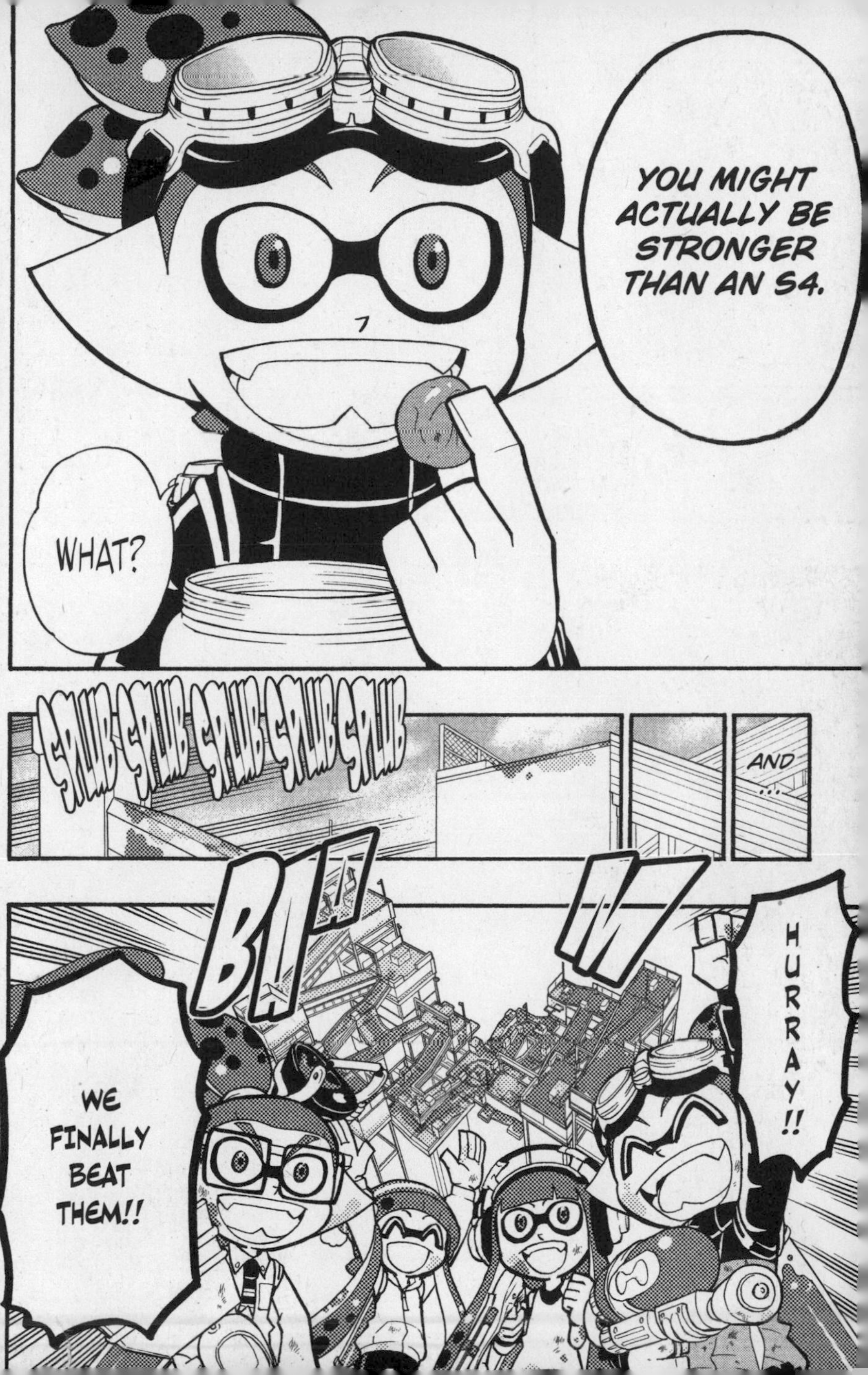
YOU MIGHT ACTUALLY BE STRONGER THAN AN S4.
WHAT?
AND ...
SPLUB SPLUB SPLUB SPLUB SPLUB
HURRAY!!
WE FINALLY BEAT THEM!!

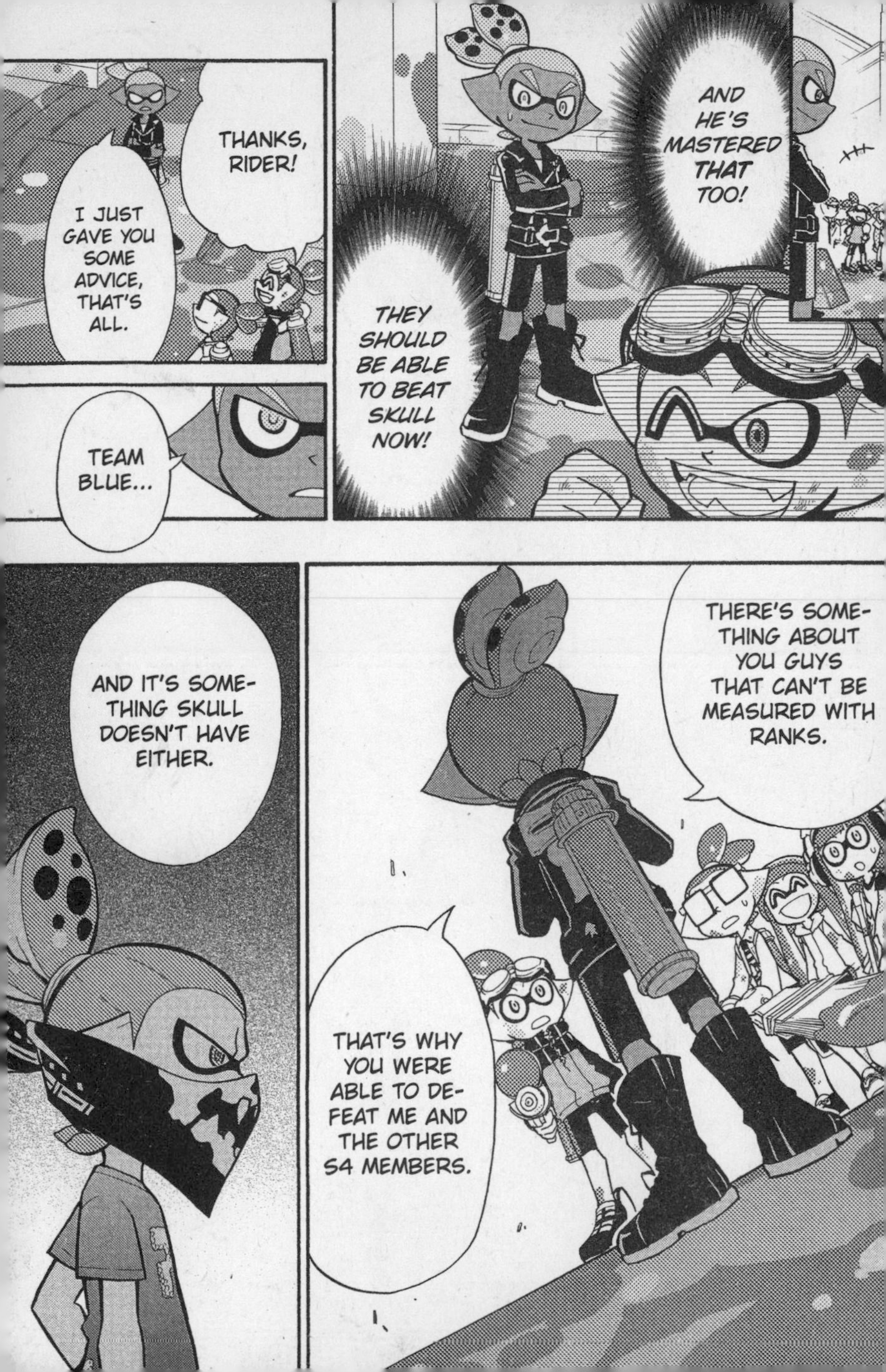
AND HE'S MASTERED THAT TOO!
THEY SHOULD BE ABLE TO BEAT SKULL NOW!
THANKS, RIDER!
I JUST GAVE YOU SOME ADVICE, THAT'S ALL.
TEAM BLUE...
THERE'S SOME-THING ABOUT YOU GUYS THAT CAN'T BE MEASURED WITH RANKS.
THAT'S WHY YOU WERE ABLE TO DE-FEAT ME AND THE OTHER S4 MEMBERS.
AND IT'S SOME-THING SKULL DOESN'T HAVE EITHER.

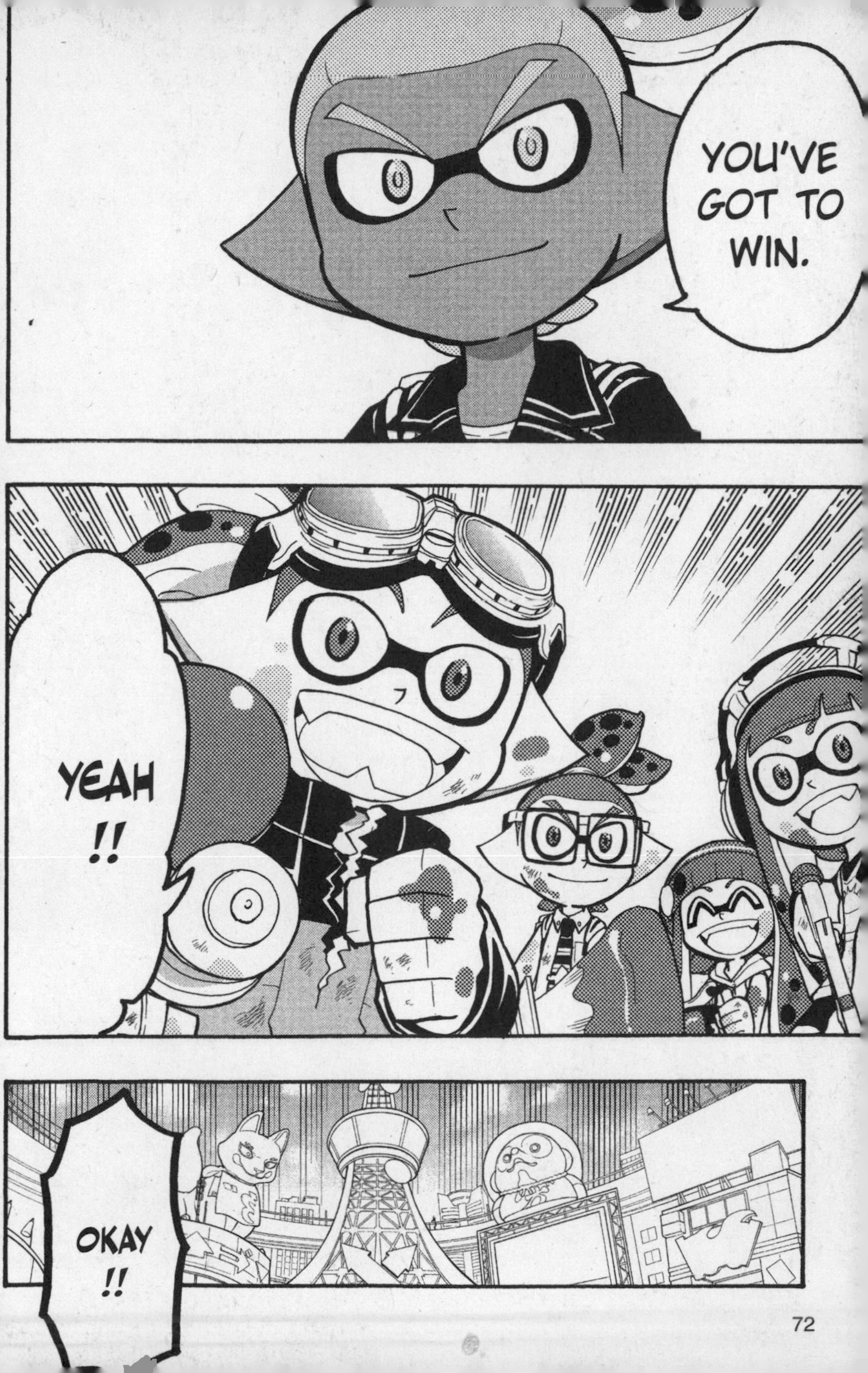
YOU'VE GOT TO WIN.
YEAH !!
OKAY !!

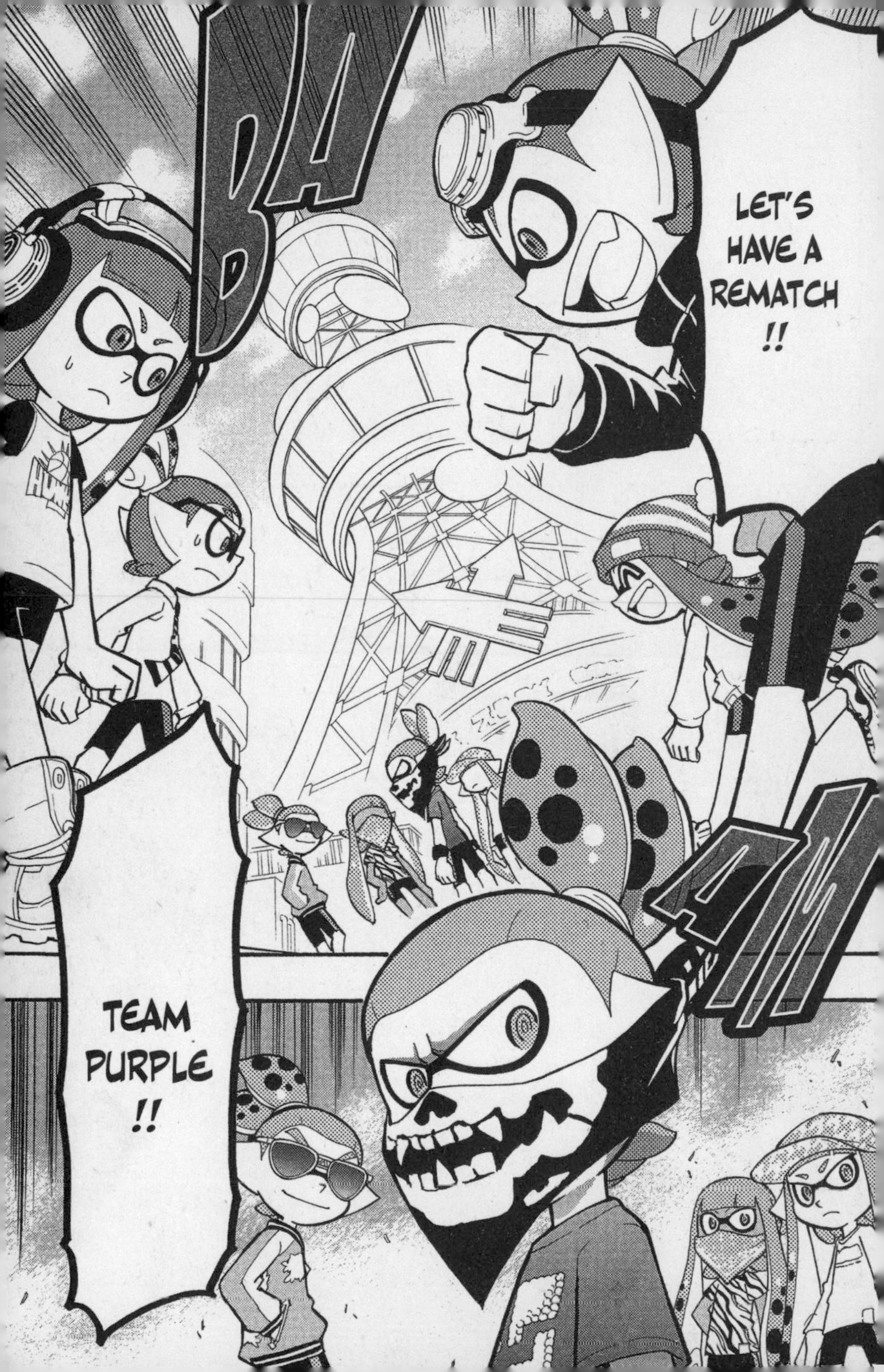
LET'S HAVE A REMATCH !!
TEAM PURPLE !!

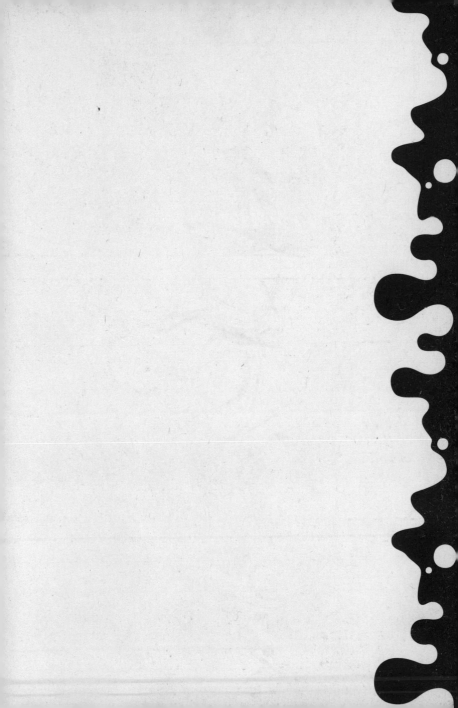

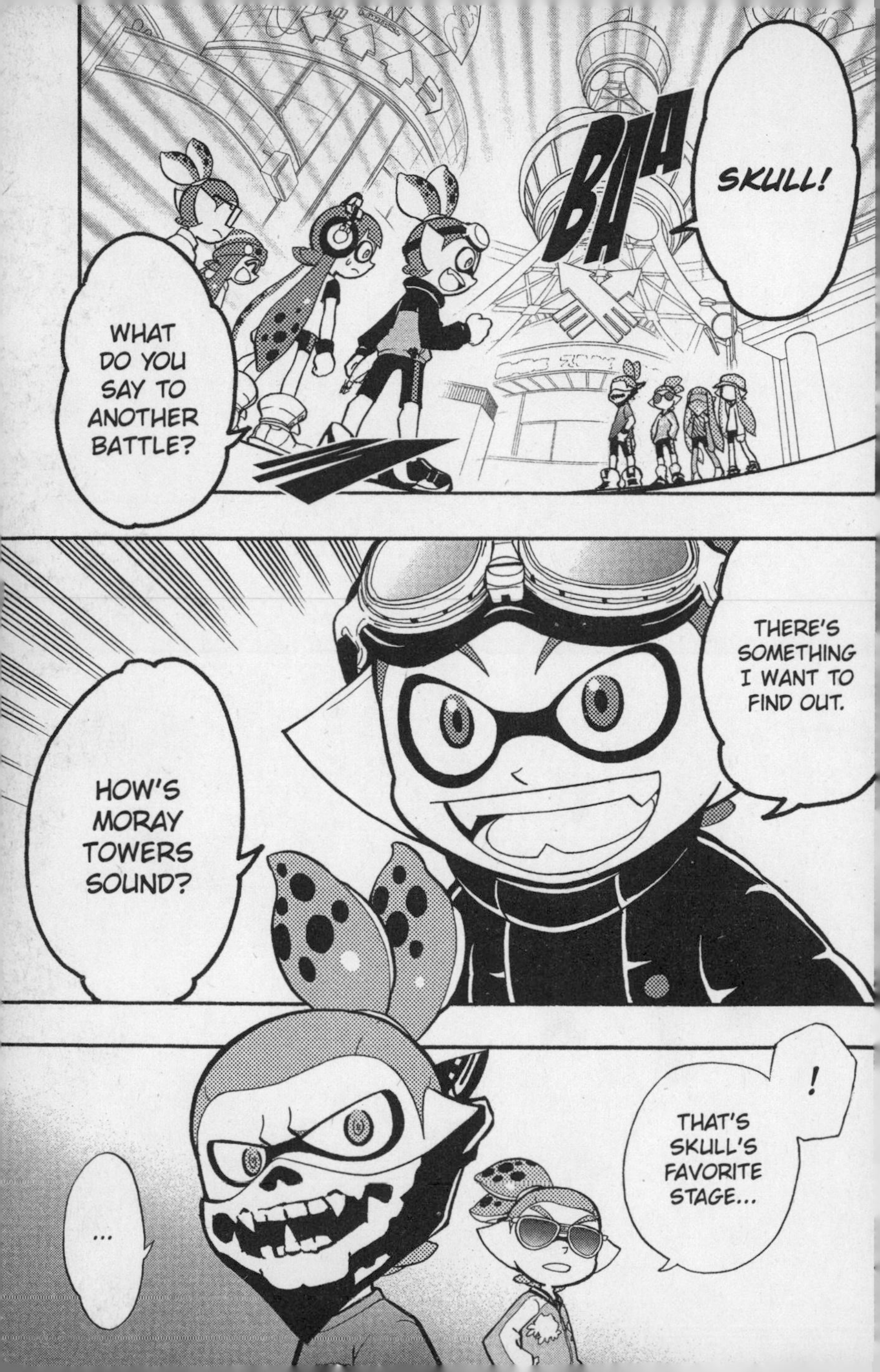
BAA
SKULL!
WHAT DO YOU SAY TO ANOTHER BATTLE?
THERE'S SOMETHING I WANT TO FIND OUT.
HOW'S MORAY TOWERS SOUND?
!
THAT'S SKULL'S FAVORITE STAGE...
...

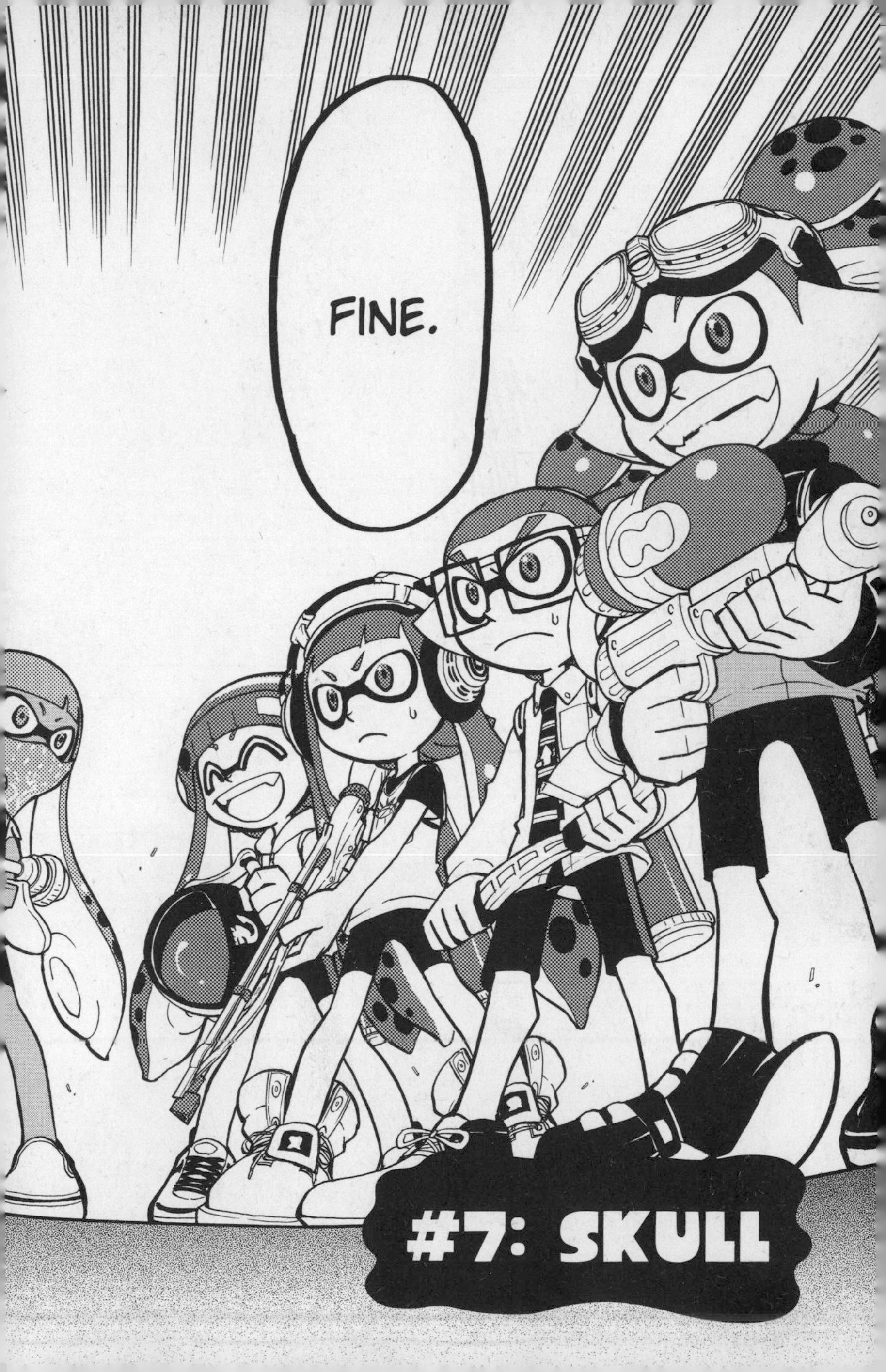
FINE.
#7: SKULL

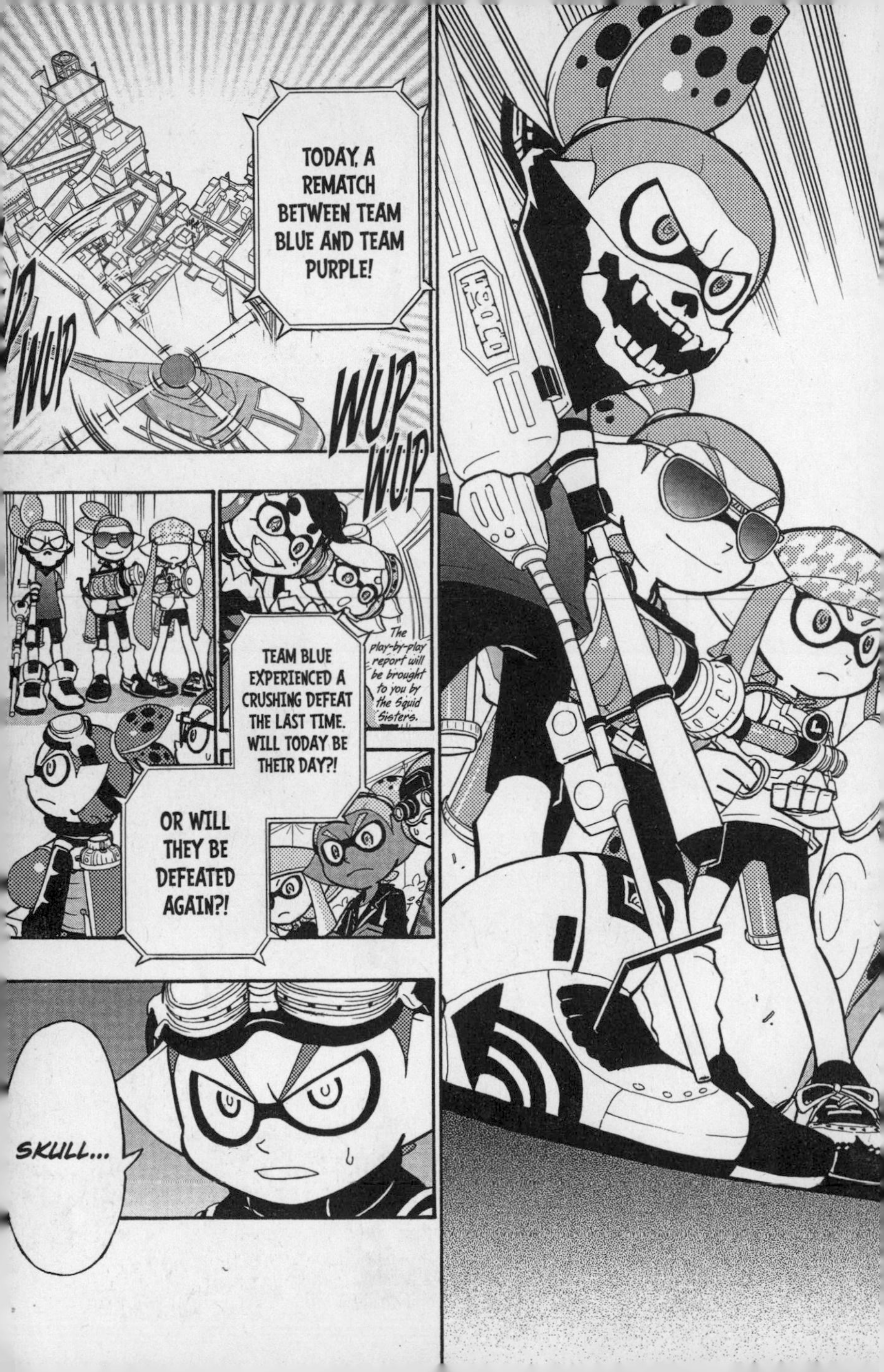
TODAY, A REMATCH BETWEEN TEAM BLUE AND TEAM PURPLE!
WUP WUP
WUP WUP
The play-by-play report will be brought to you by the Squid Sisters.
TEAM BLUE EXPERIENCED A CRUSHING DEFEAT THE LAST TIME. WILL TODAY BE THEIR DAY?!
OR WILL THEY BE DEFEATED AGAIN?!
SKULL...

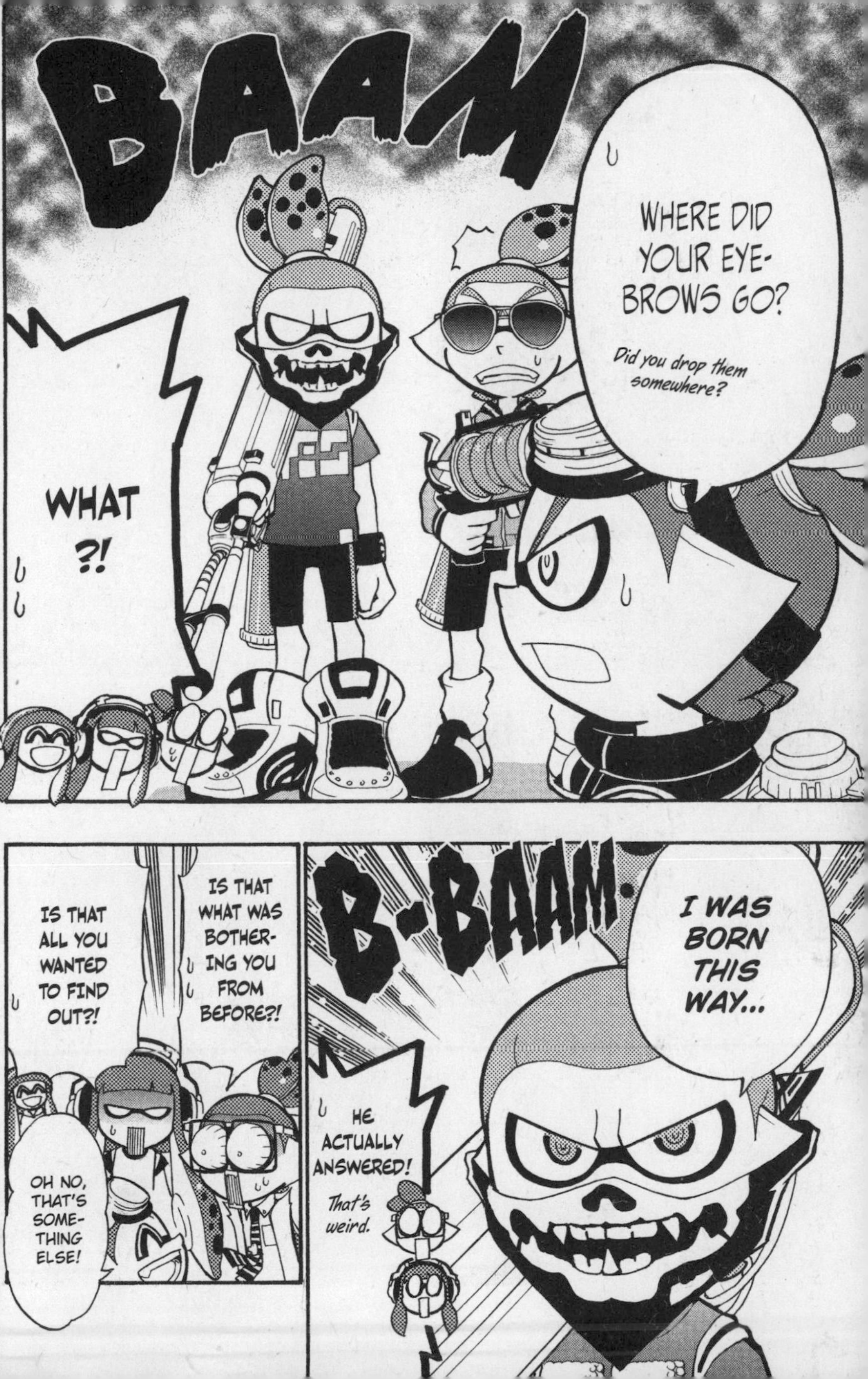
WHERE DID YOUR EYE-BROWS GO?
Did you drop them somewhere?
BAAM
WHAT ?!
I WAS BORN THIS WAY...
B-BAAM
HE ACTUALLY ANSWERED!
That's weird.
IS THAT WHAT WAS BOTHER-ING YOU FROM BEFORE?!
IS THAT ALL YOU WANTED TO FIND OUT?!
OH NO, THAT'S SOME-THING ELSE!

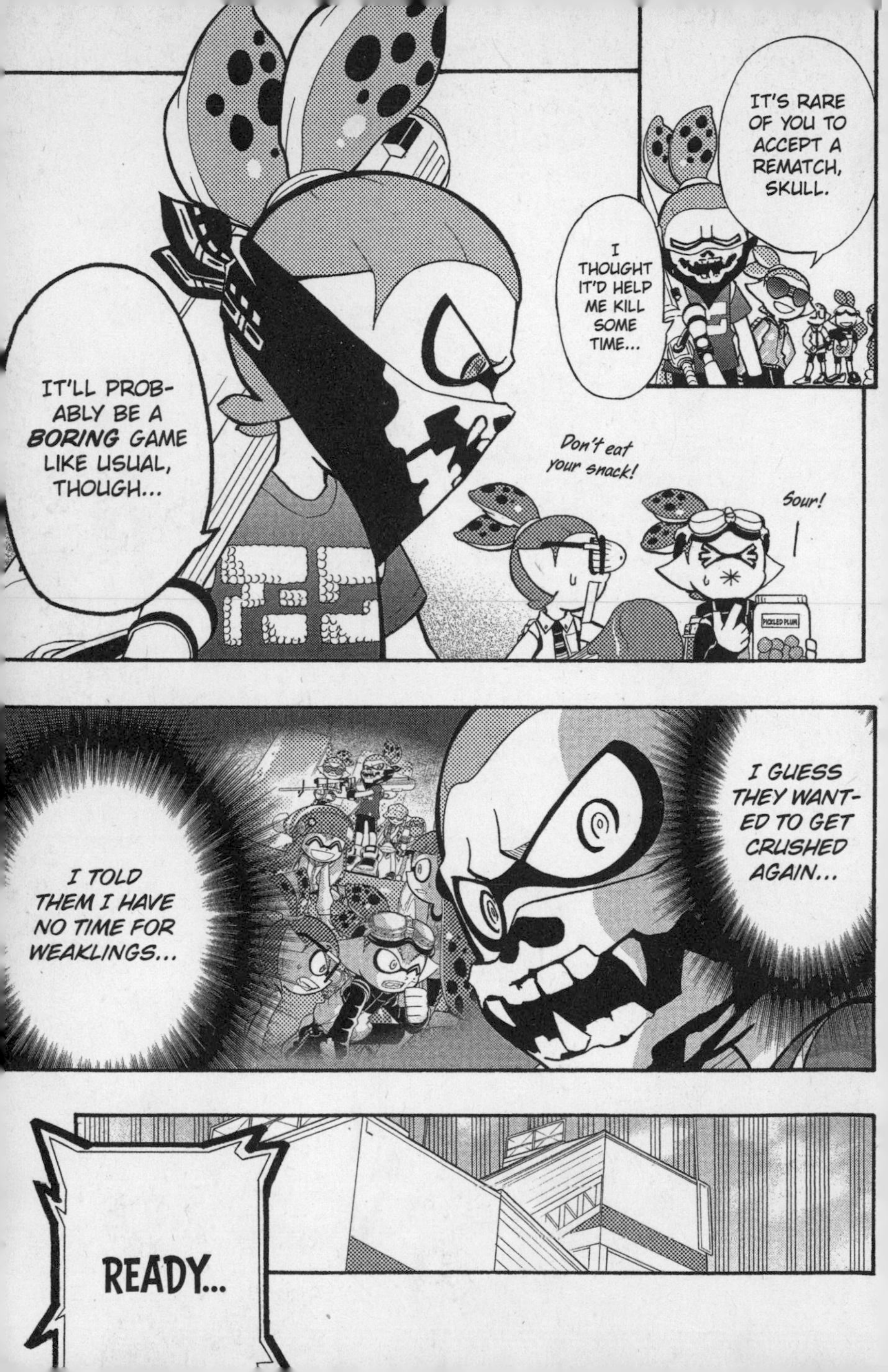
IT'S RARE OF YOU TO ACCEPT A REMATCH, SKULL.
I THOUGHT IT'D HELP ME KILL SOME TIME...
Don't eat your snack!
Sour!
PICKLED PLUM
IT'LL PROB-ABLY BE A BORING GAME LIKE USUAL, THOUGH...
I GUESS THEY WANT-ED TO GET CRUSHED AGAIN...
I TOLD THEM I HAVE NO TIME FOR WEAKLINGS...
READY...

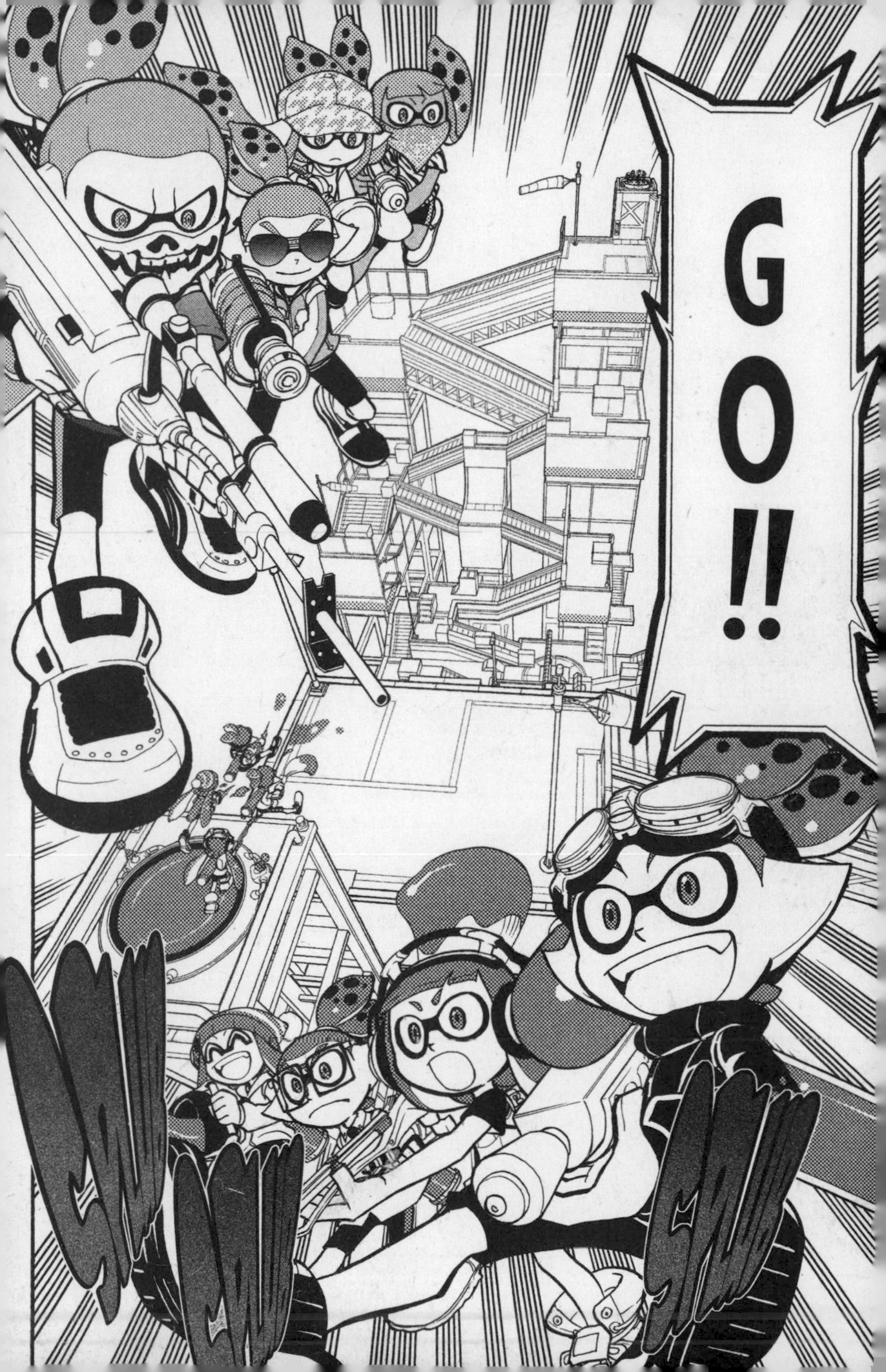
GO!!

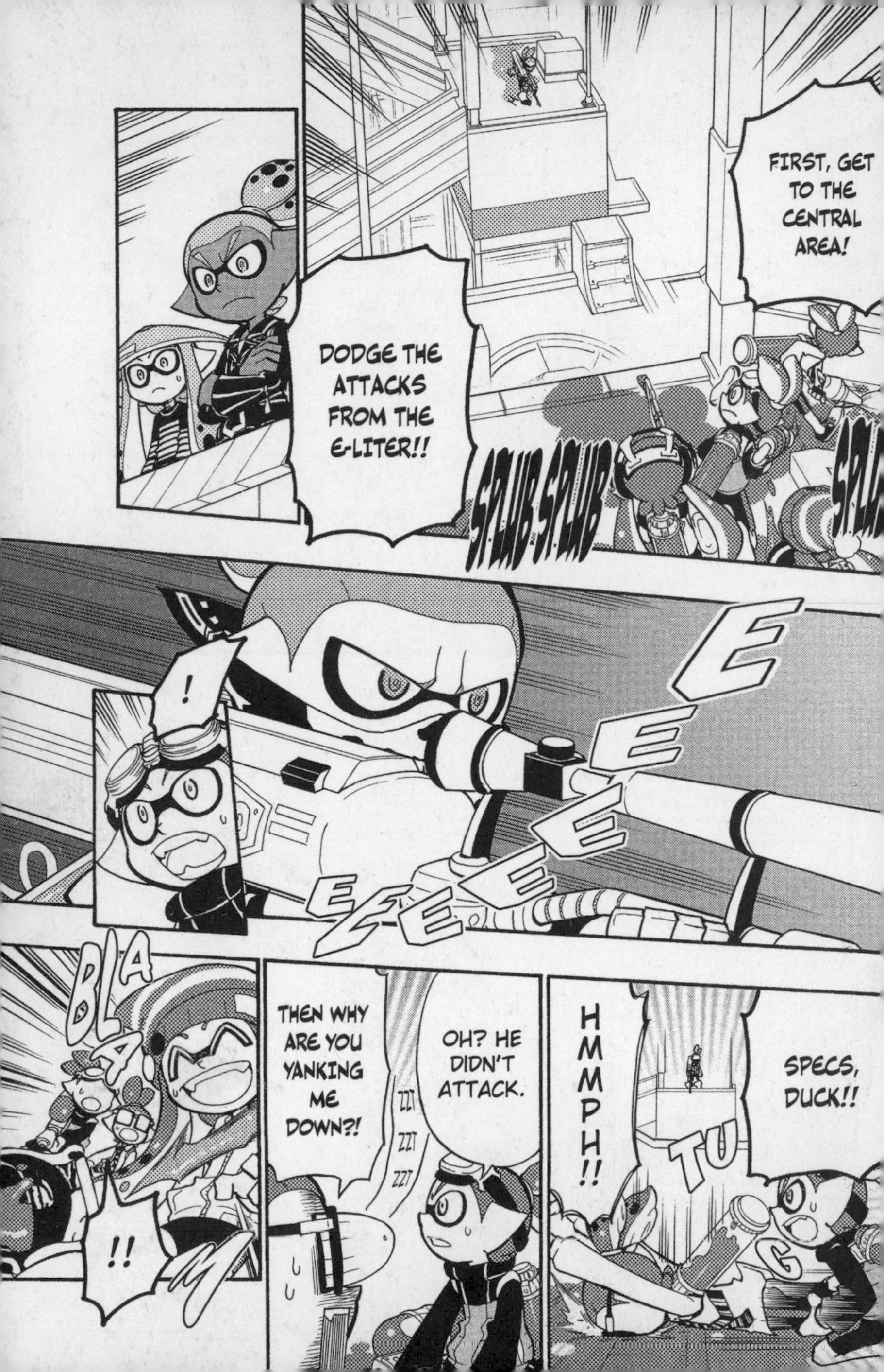
FIRST, GET TO THE CENTRAL AREA!
DODGE THE ATTACKS FROM THE E-LITER!!
SPLUB SPLUB
SPLUB
EEEEEEE
!
SPECS, DUCK!!
TUG
HMMPH!!
OH? HE DIDN'T ATTACK.
ZZT ZZT ZZT
THEN WHY ARE YOU YANKING ME DOWN?!
BLA BLA
!!
M

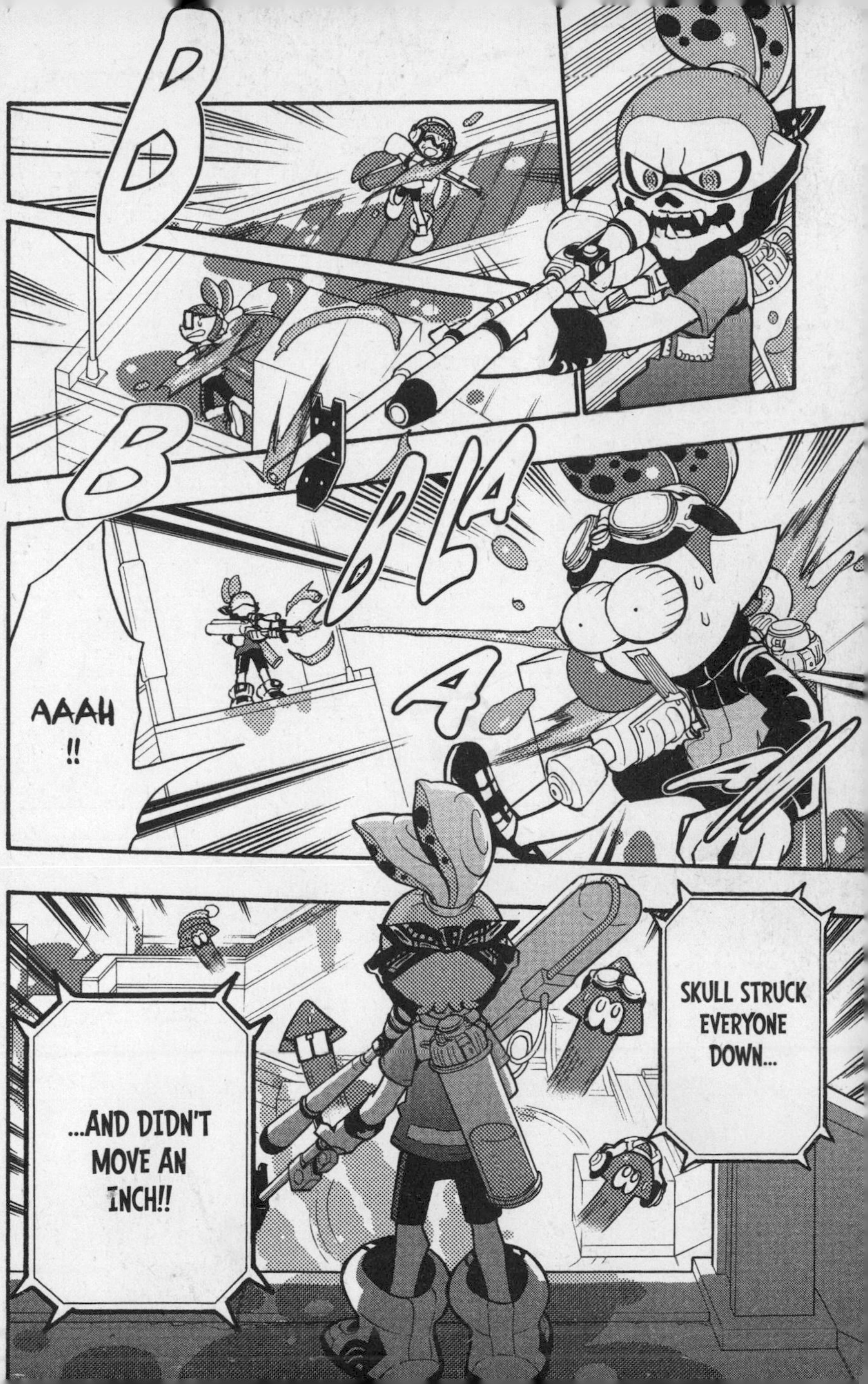
B
B
BLA
A
AAAH !!
SKULL STRUCK EVERYONE DOWN...
...AND DIDN'T MOVE AN INCH!!

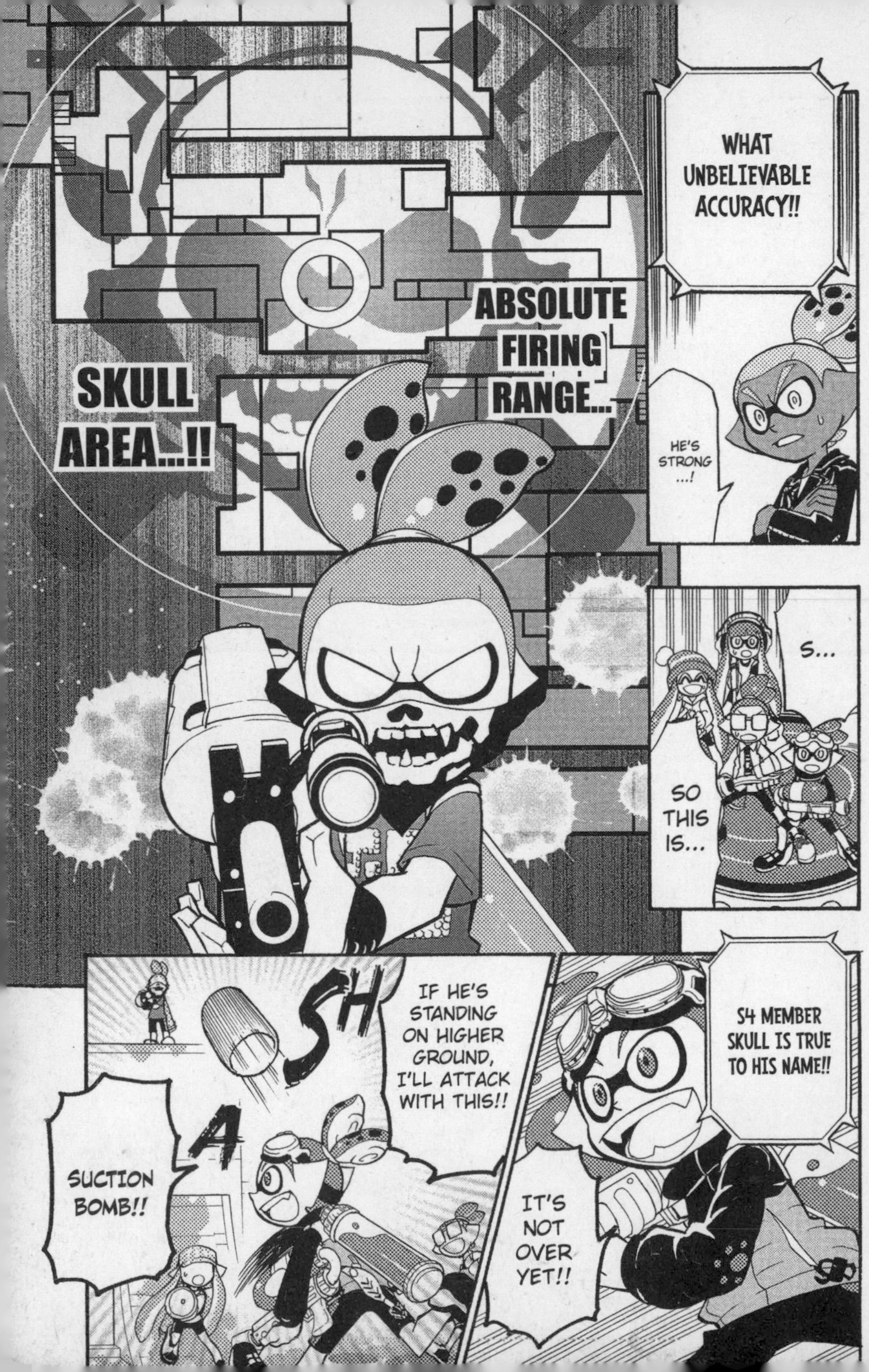

WHAT UNBELIEVABLE ACCURACY!!
HE'S STRONG ...!
S...
SO THIS IS...
ABSOLUTE FIRING RANGE...
SKULL AREA...!!
S4 MEMBER SKULL IS TRUE TO HIS NAME!!
IT'S NOT OVER YET!!
IF HE'S STANDING ON HIGHER GROUND, I'LL ATTACK WITH THIS!!
SH
A
SUCTION BOMB!!

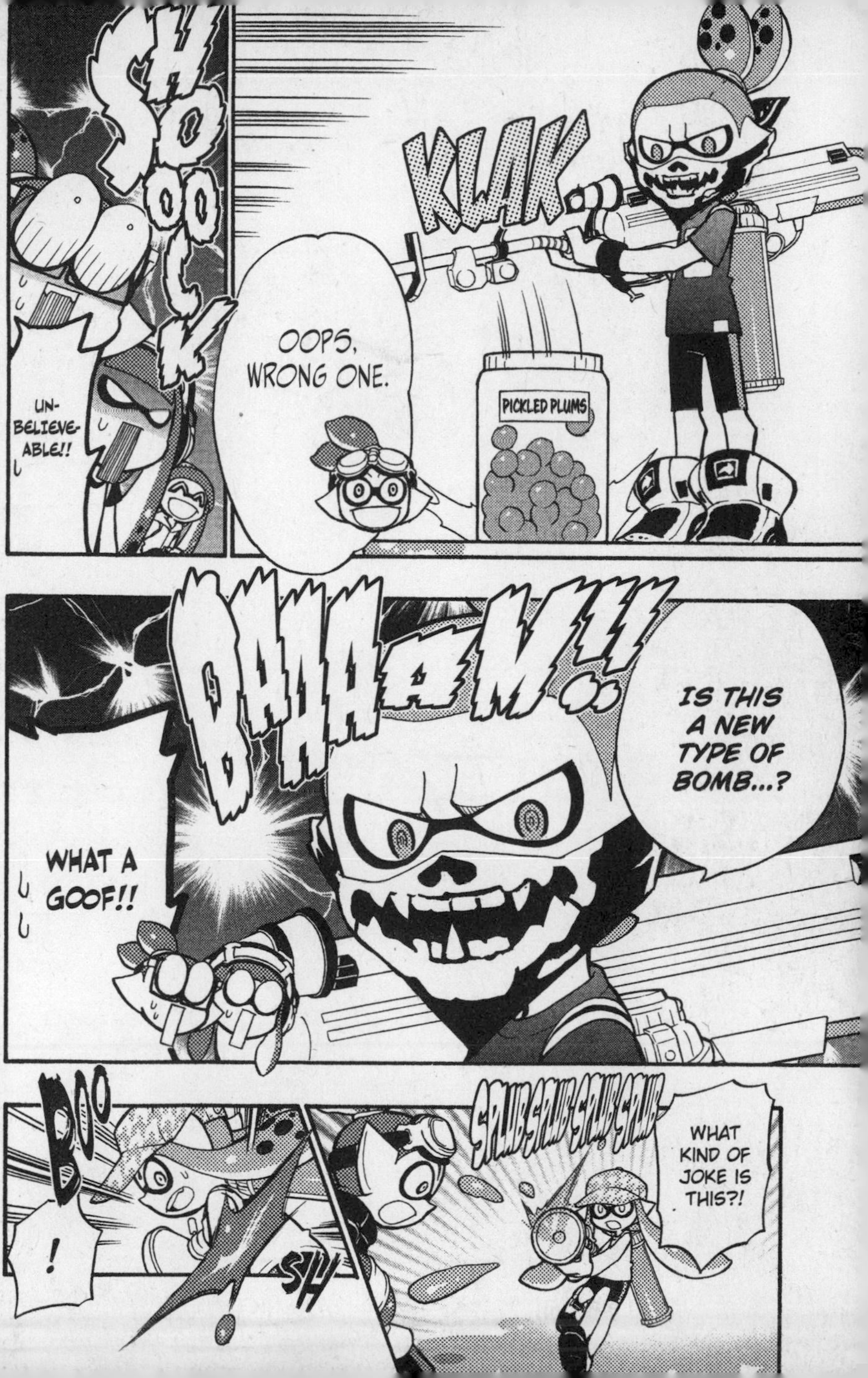
KLAK
OOPS, WRONG ONE.
PICKLED PLUMS
SHOOOCK
UN-BELIEVE-ABLE!!
BAAAM!!
IS THIS A NEW TYPE OF BOMB...?
WHAT A GOOF!!
SPLUB SPLUB SPLUB SPLUB
WHAT KIND OF JOKE IS THIS?!
SH
BOO
!

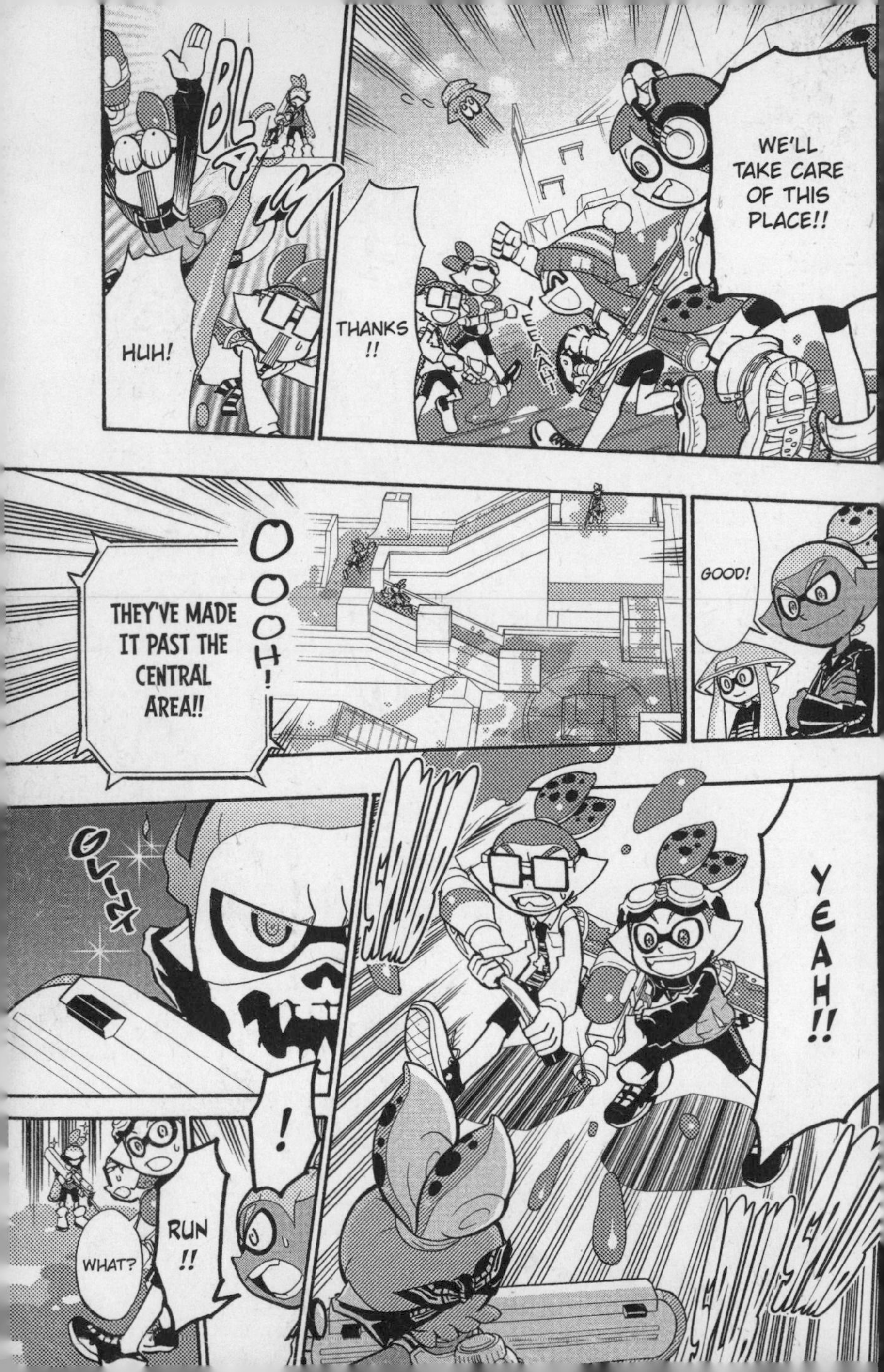
WE'LL TAKE CARE OF THIS PLACE!!
YEEAAH!
THANKS !!
BLAM
HUH!
GOOD!
OOOOH!
THEY'VE MADE IT PAST THE CENTRAL AREA!!
YEAH!!
!
RUN !!
WHAT?

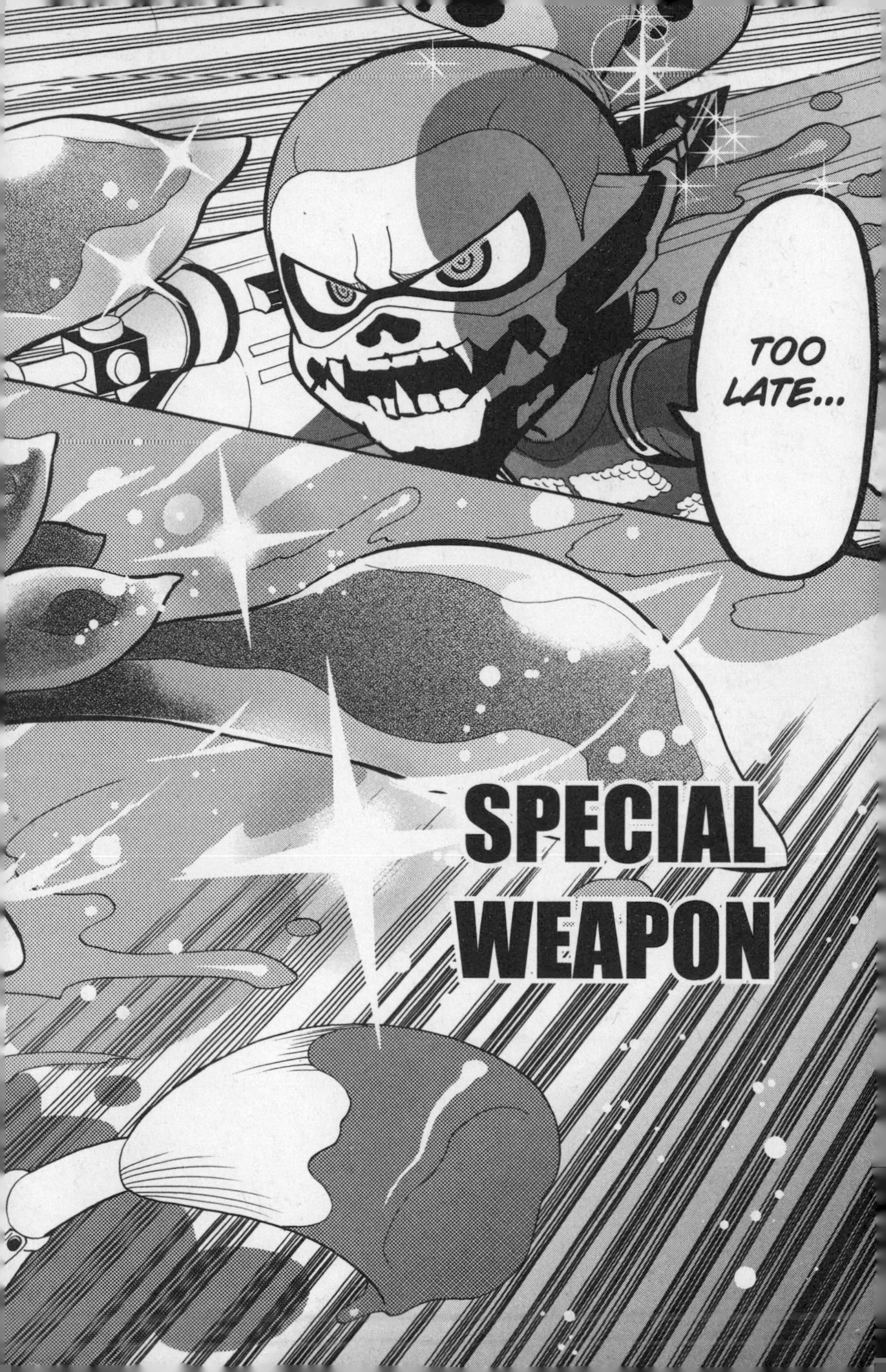
TOO LATE...
SPECIAL WEAPON

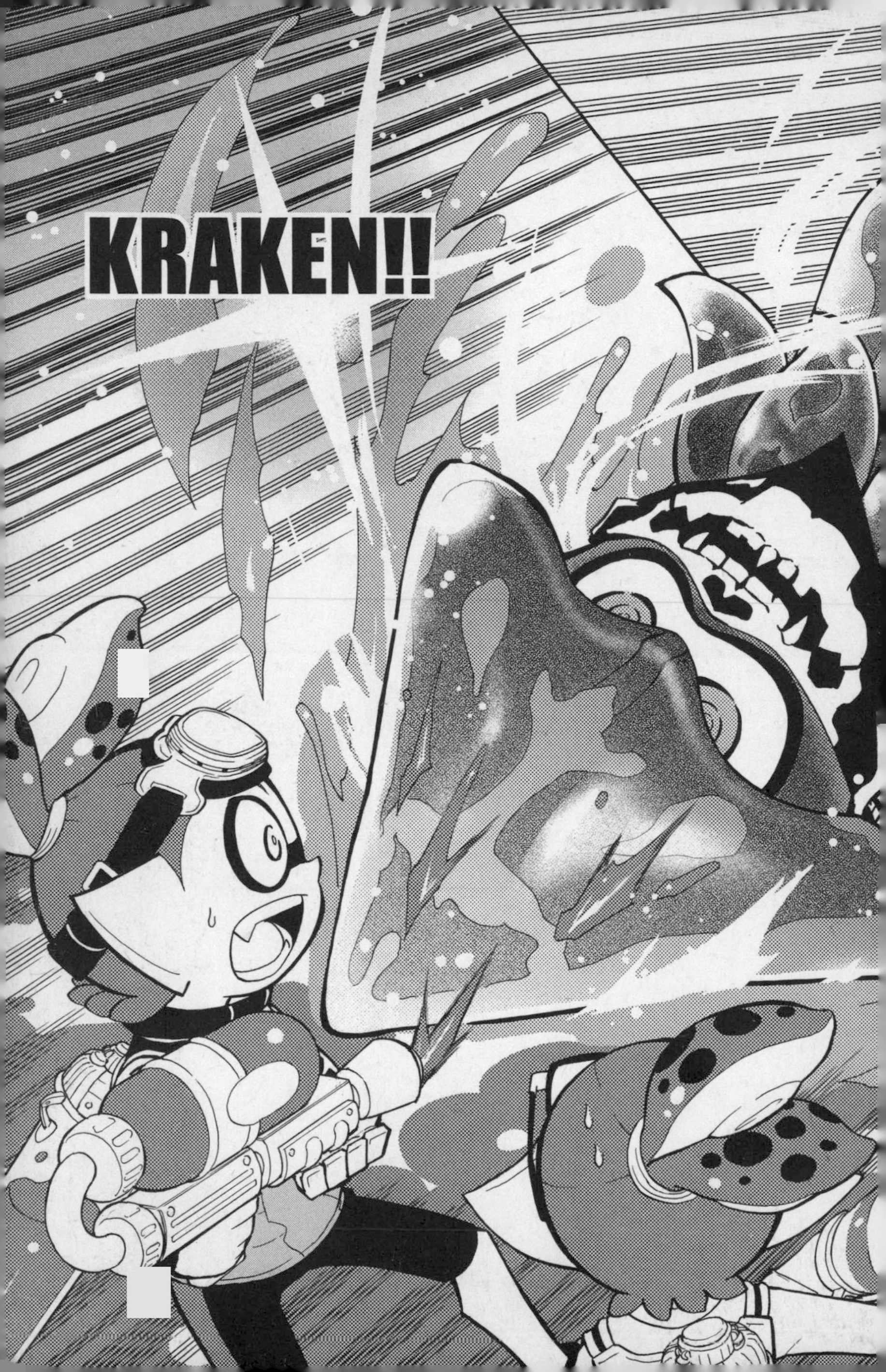
KRAKEN!!

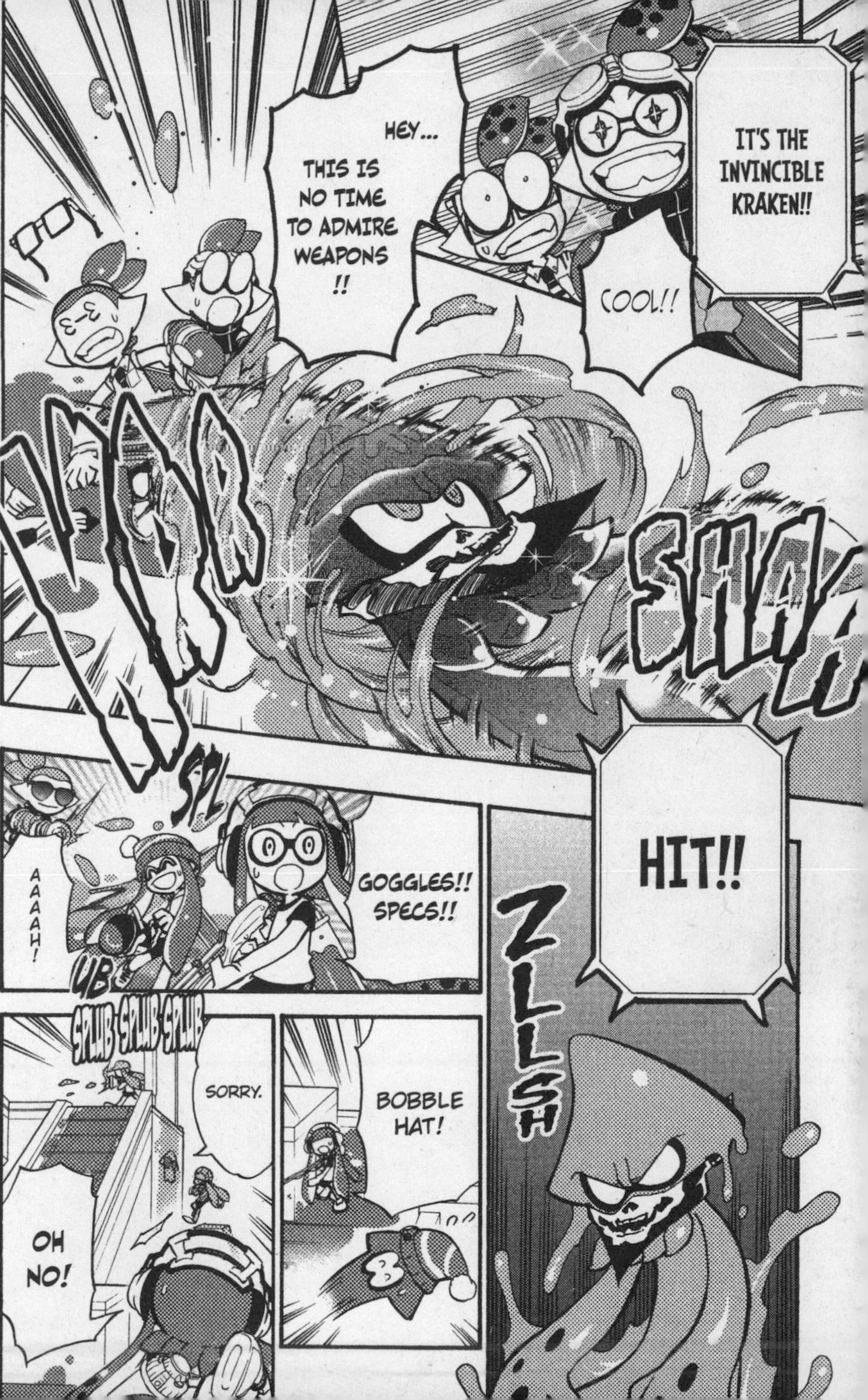
IT'S THE INVINCIBLE KRAKEN!!
COOL!!
HEY...
THIS IS NO TIME TO ADMIRE WEAPONS !!
HIT!!
ZLLSH
GOGGLES!! SPECS!!
SPL
AAAAH!
SPLUB SPLUB SPLUB
BOBBLE HAT!
SORRY.
OH NO!

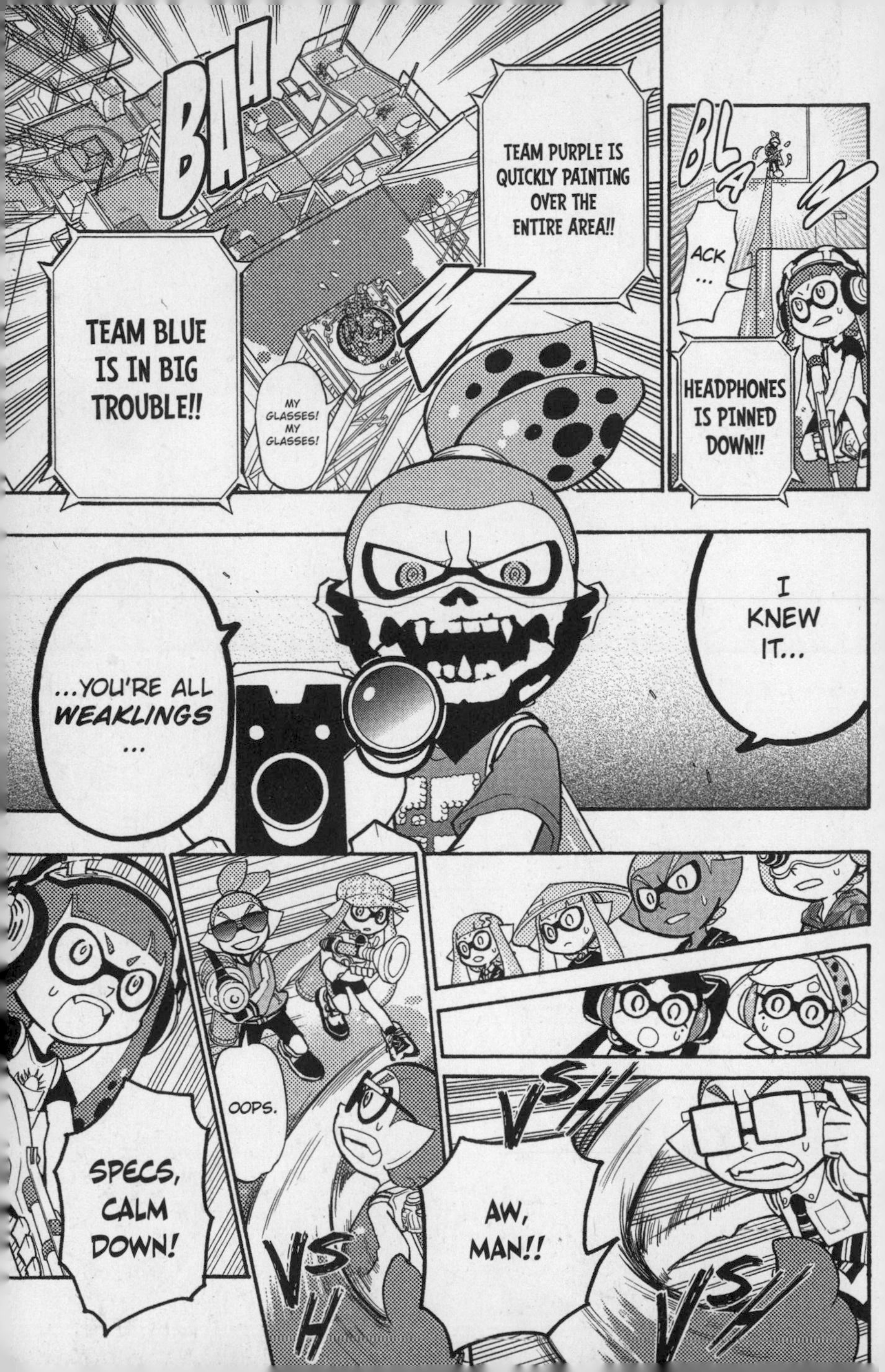
BLAM
ACK ...
HEADPHONES IS PINNED DOWN!!
TEAM PURPLE IS QUICKLY PAINTING OVER THE ENTIRE AREA!!
BAA
TEAM BLUE IS IN BIG TROUBLE!!
MY GLASSES! MY GLASSES!
I KNEW IT...
...YOU'RE ALL *WEAKLINGS* ...
VSH
AW, MAN!!
VSH
VSH
OOPS.
SPECS, CALM DOWN!

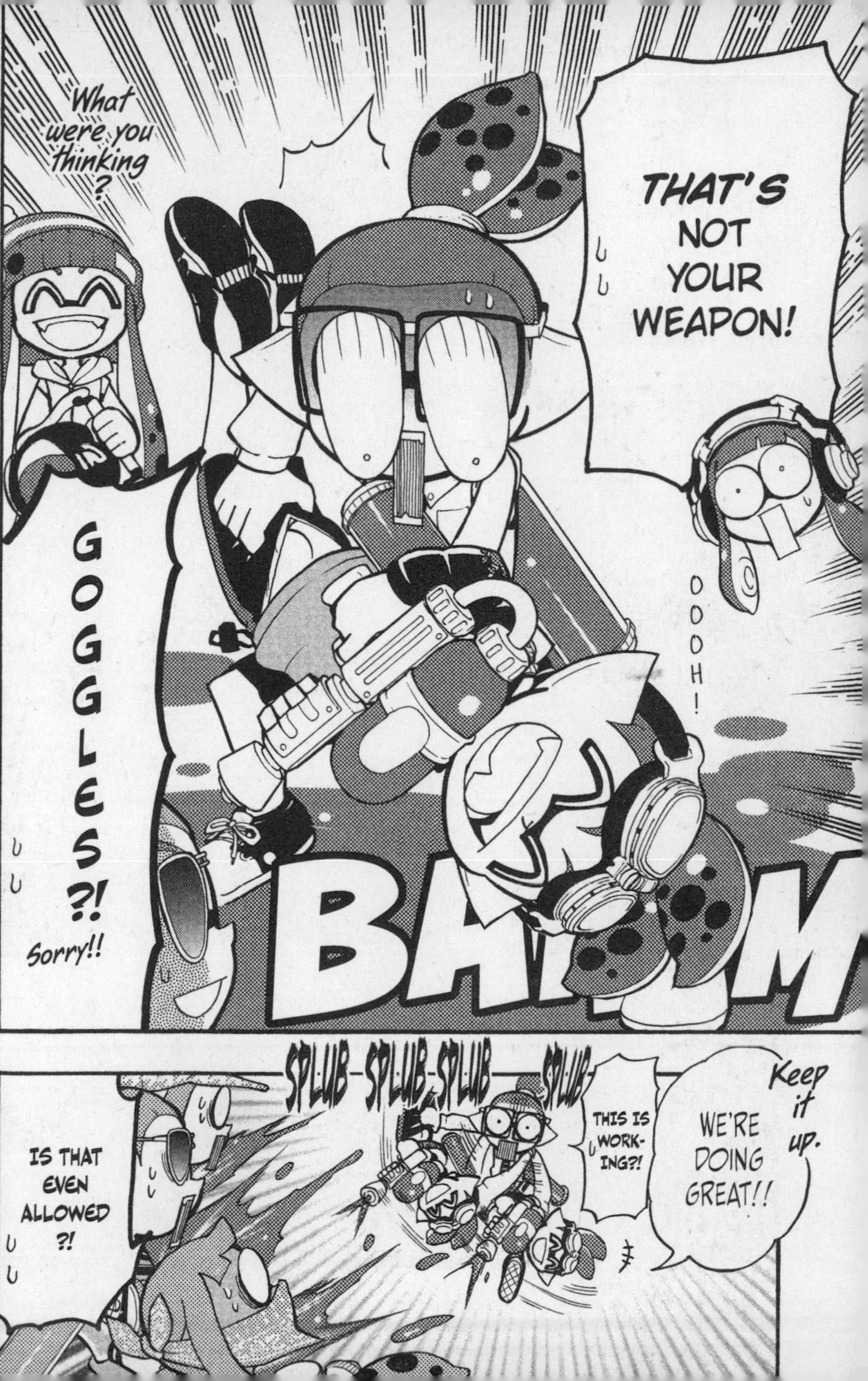
THAT'S NOT YOUR WEAPON!
OOOH!
What were you thinking?
GOGGLES?!
Sorry!!
BAM
SPLUB-SPLUB-SPLUB-SPLUB
Keep it up.
WE'RE DOING GREAT!!
THIS IS WORKING?!
IS THAT EVEN ALLOWED?!

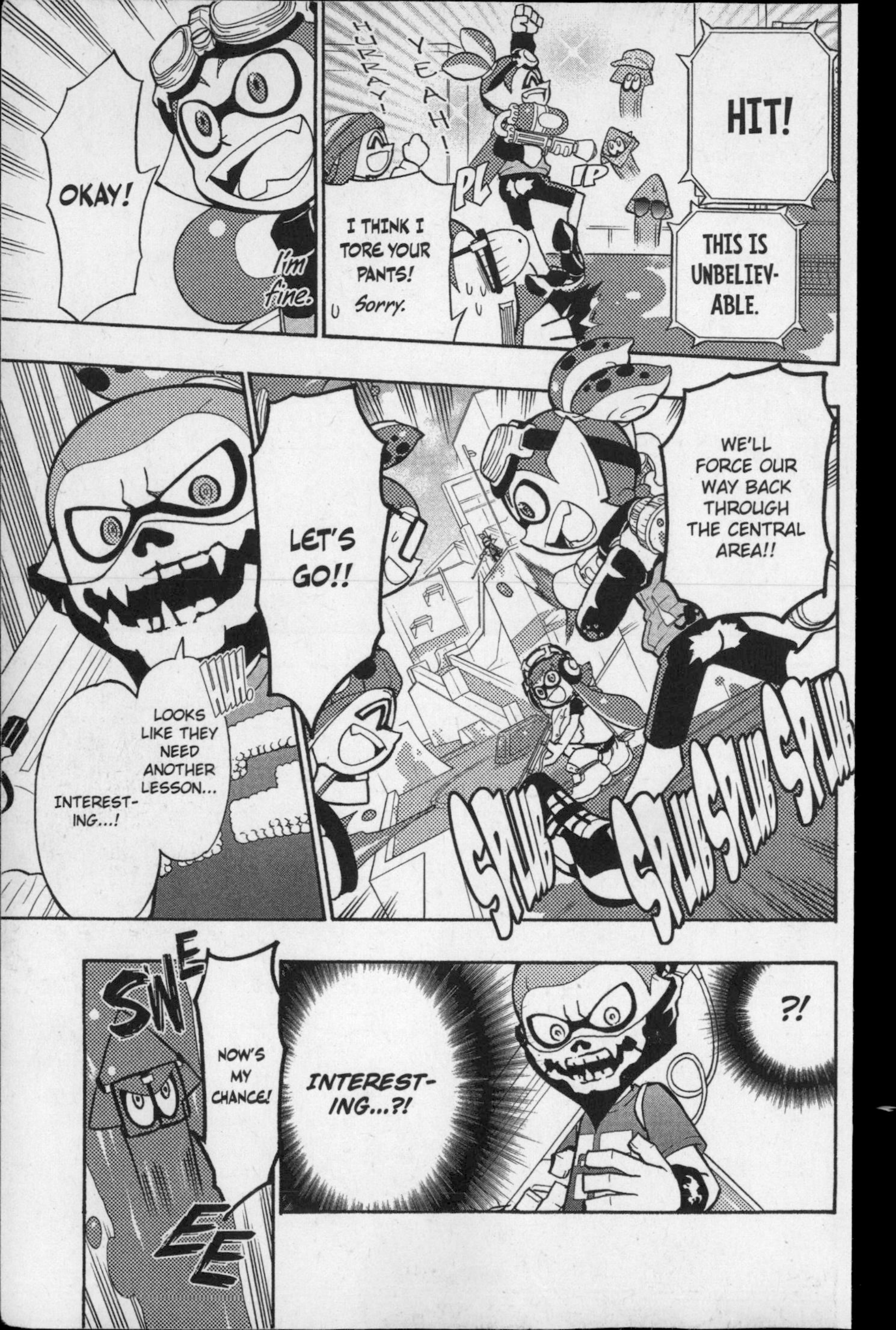
HIT!
THIS IS UNBELIEV-ABLE.
YEAH!
HURRAY!
PLIP
I THINK I TORE YOUR PANTS!
Sorry.
OKAY!
I'm fine.
WE'LL FORCE OUR WAY BACK THROUGH THE CENTRAL AREA!!
LET'S GO!!
SPLUB SPLUB SPLUB SPLUB
HUH.
LOOKS LIKE THEY NEED ANOTHER LESSON...
INTEREST-ING...!
?!
INTEREST-ING...?!
SWEEE
NOW'S MY CHANCE!

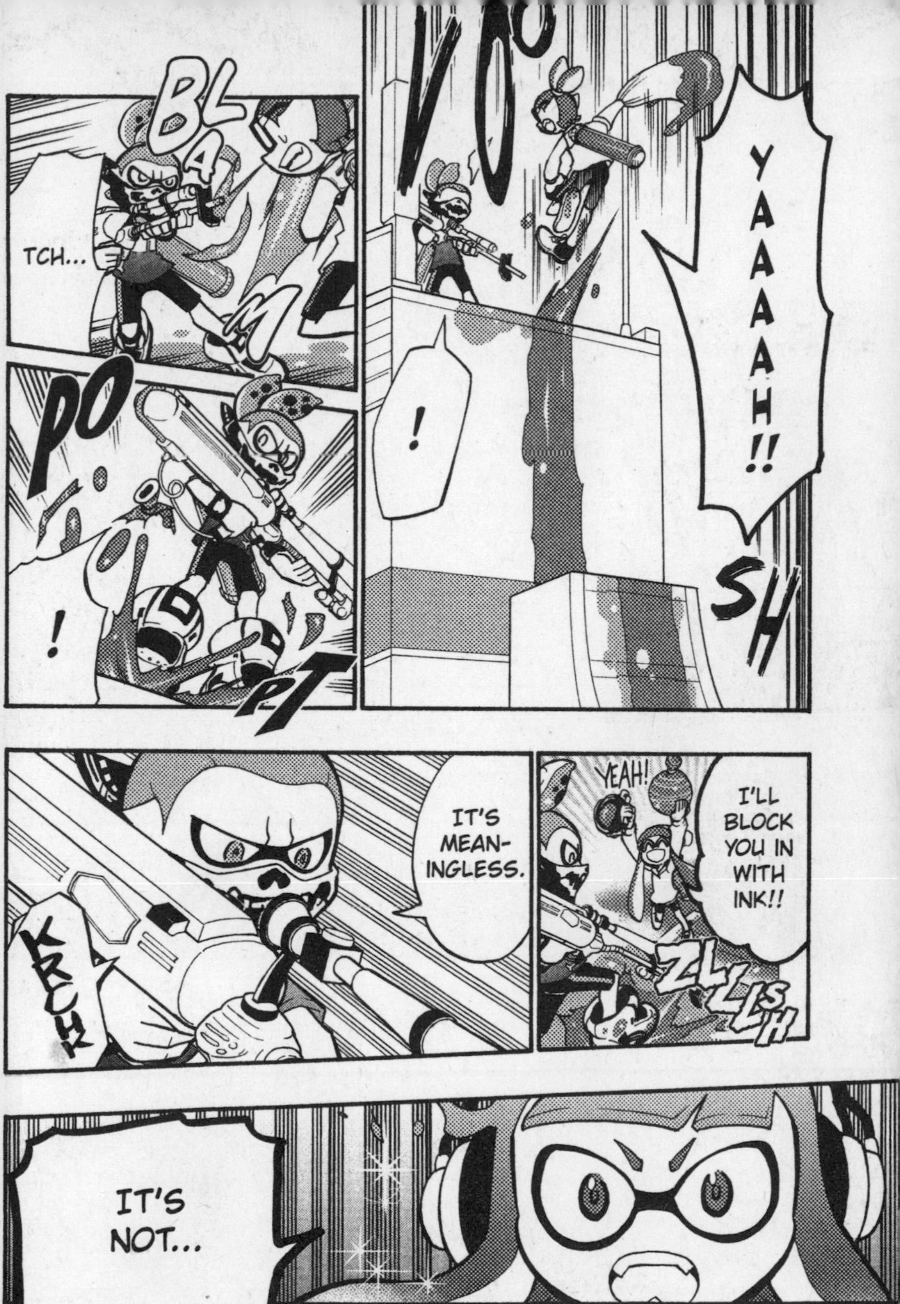
YAAAAH!!
VOO
SH
!
BLAM
TCH...
POP
!
PT
YEAH!
I'LL BLOCK YOU IN WITH INK!!
ZLLSLH
IT'S MEAN-INGLESS.
KRCHK
IT'S NOT...

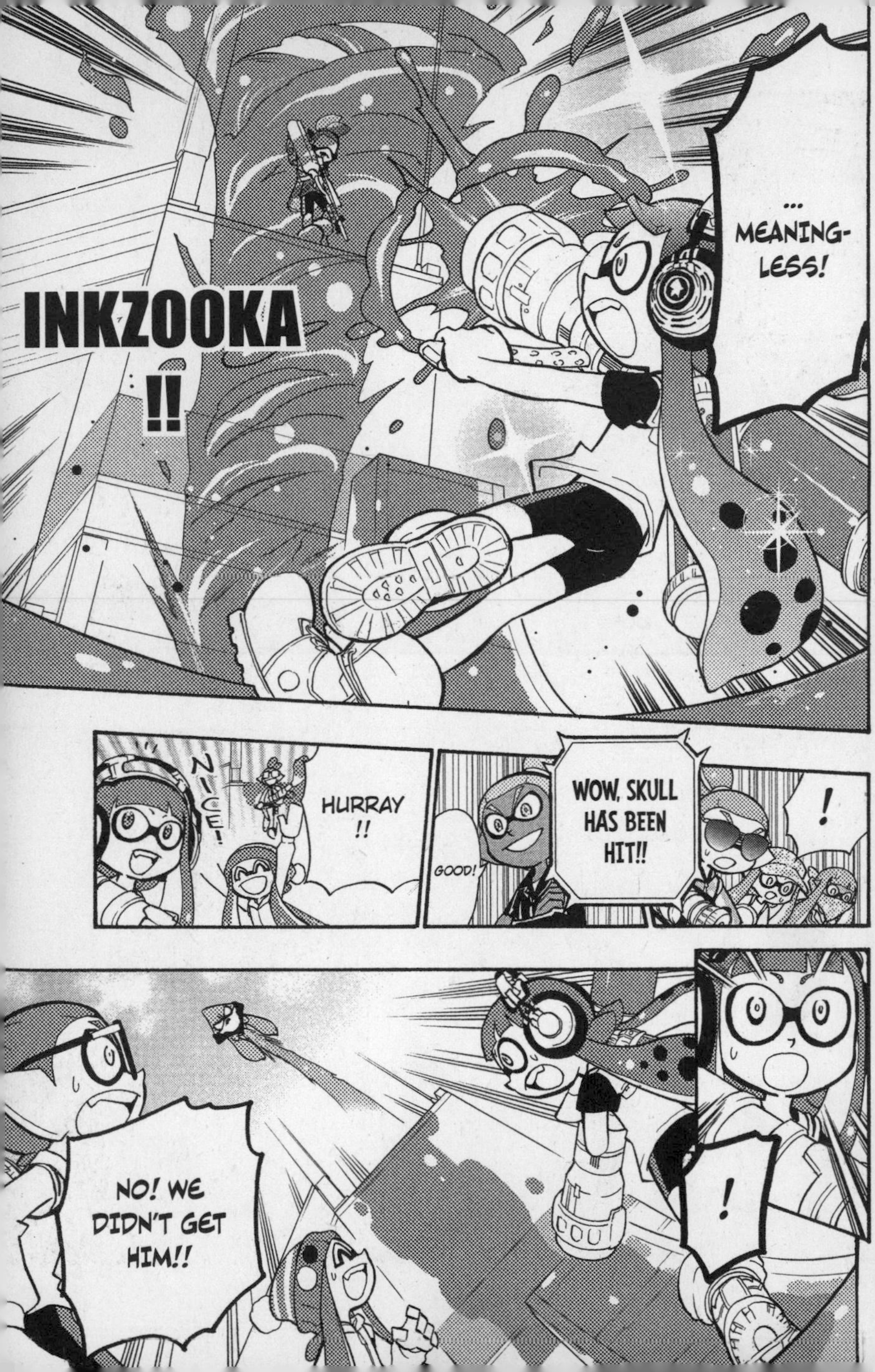
...MEANING-LESS!
INKZOOKA !!
!
WOW, SKULL HAS BEEN HIT!!
GOOD!
HURRAY !!
NICE!
!
NO! WE DIDN'T GET HIM!!

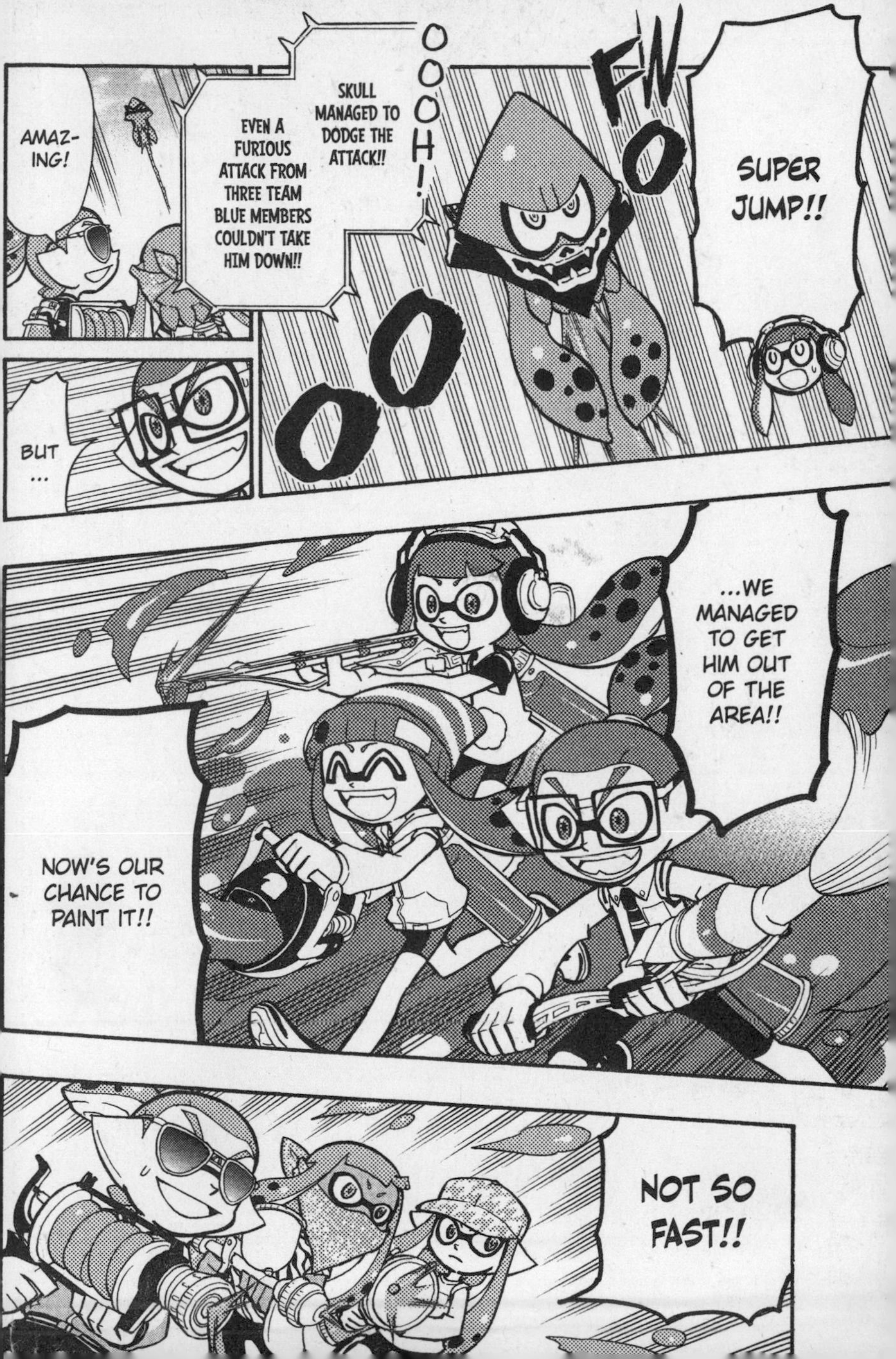
SUPER JUMP!!
FWOOOO
OOOOH!
SKULL MANAGED TO DODGE THE ATTACK!!
EVEN A FURIOUS ATTACK FROM THREE TEAM BLUE MEMBERS COULDN'T TAKE HIM DOWN!!
AMAZ-ING!
BUT ...
...WE MANAGED TO GET HIM OUT OF THE AREA!!
NOW'S OUR CHANCE TO PAINT IT!!
NOT SO FAST!!

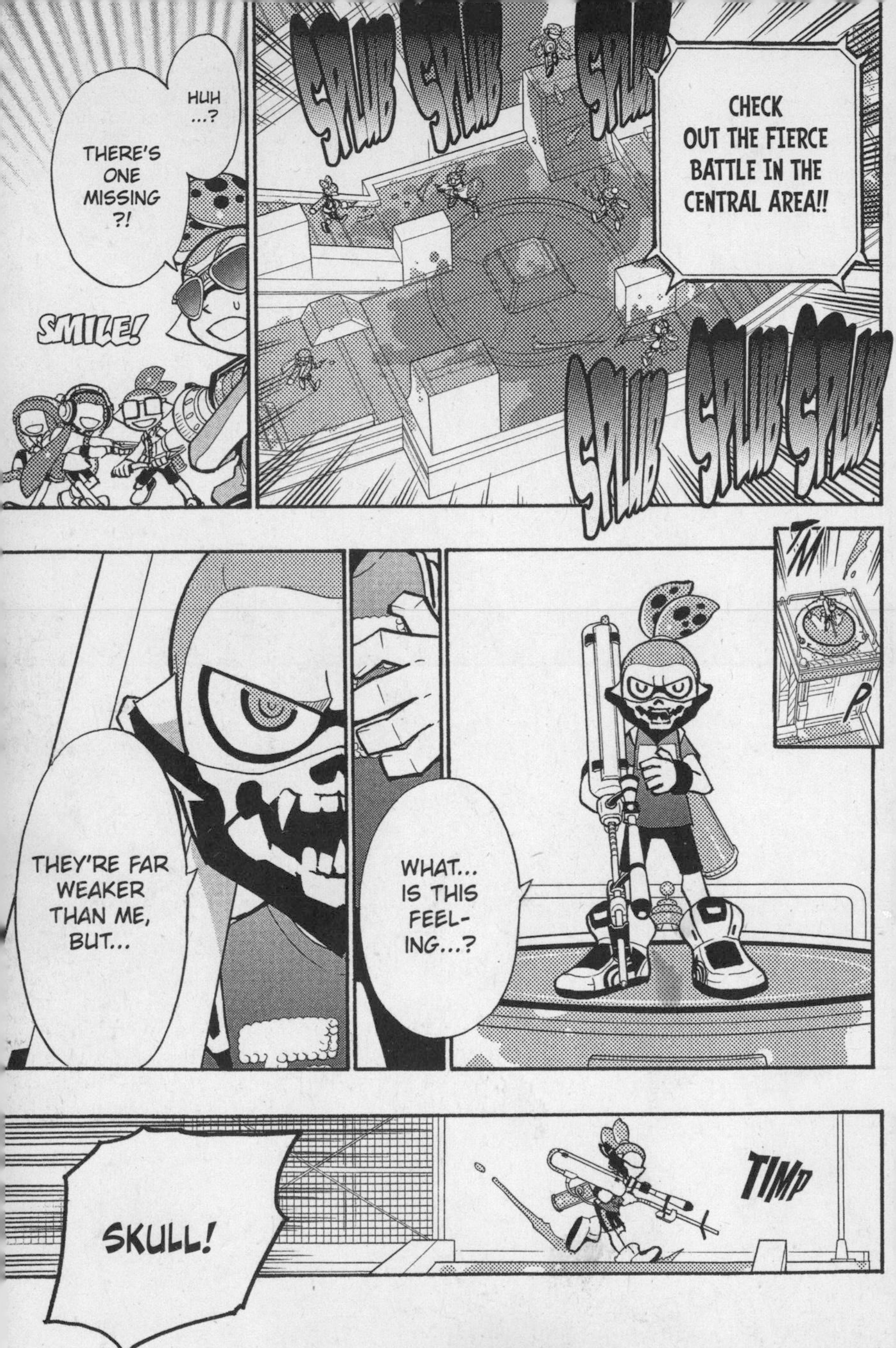
CHECK OUT THE FIERCE BATTLE IN THE CENTRAL AREA!!
HUH ...?
THERE'S ONE MISSING ?!
SMILE!
WHAT... IS THIS FEEL-ING...?
THEY'RE FAR WEAKER THAN ME, BUT...
TIMP
SKULL!

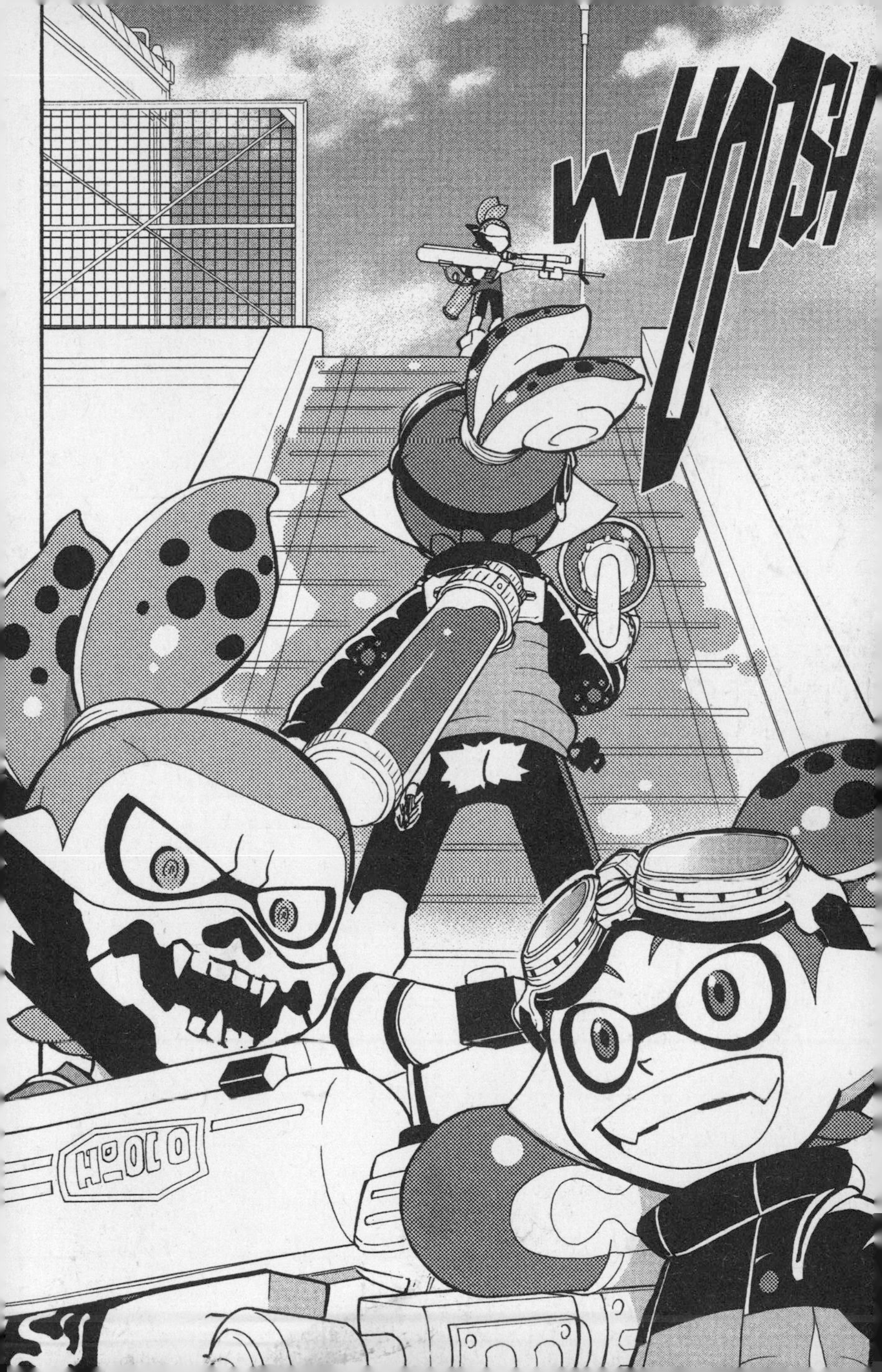
WHOOSH

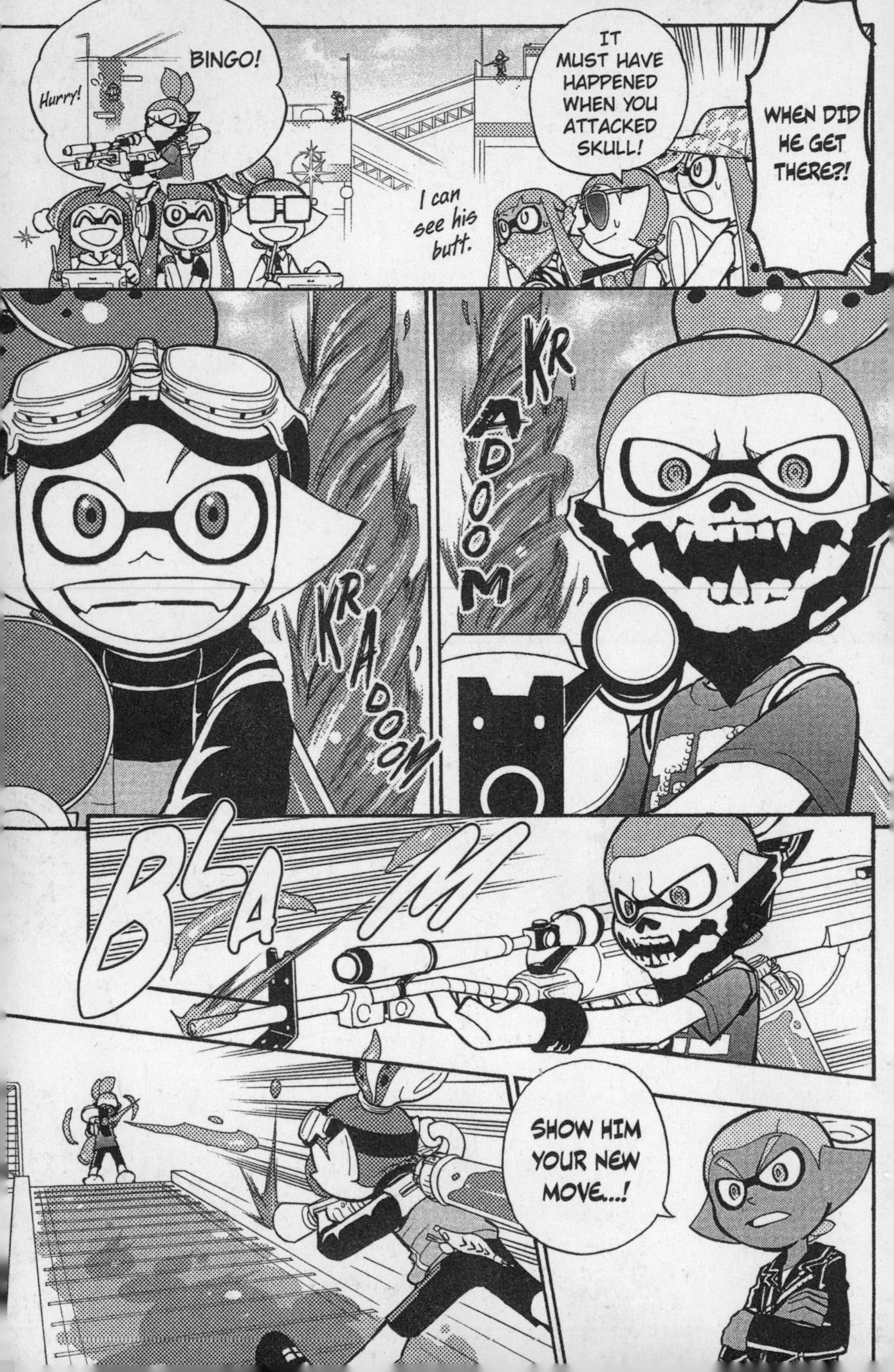
WHEN DID HE GET THERE?!
IT MUST HAVE HAPPENED WHEN YOU ATTACKED SKULL!
I can see his butt.
BINGO!
Hurry!
KRADOOM
KRADOOM
BLAM
SHOW HIM YOUR NEW MOVE...!

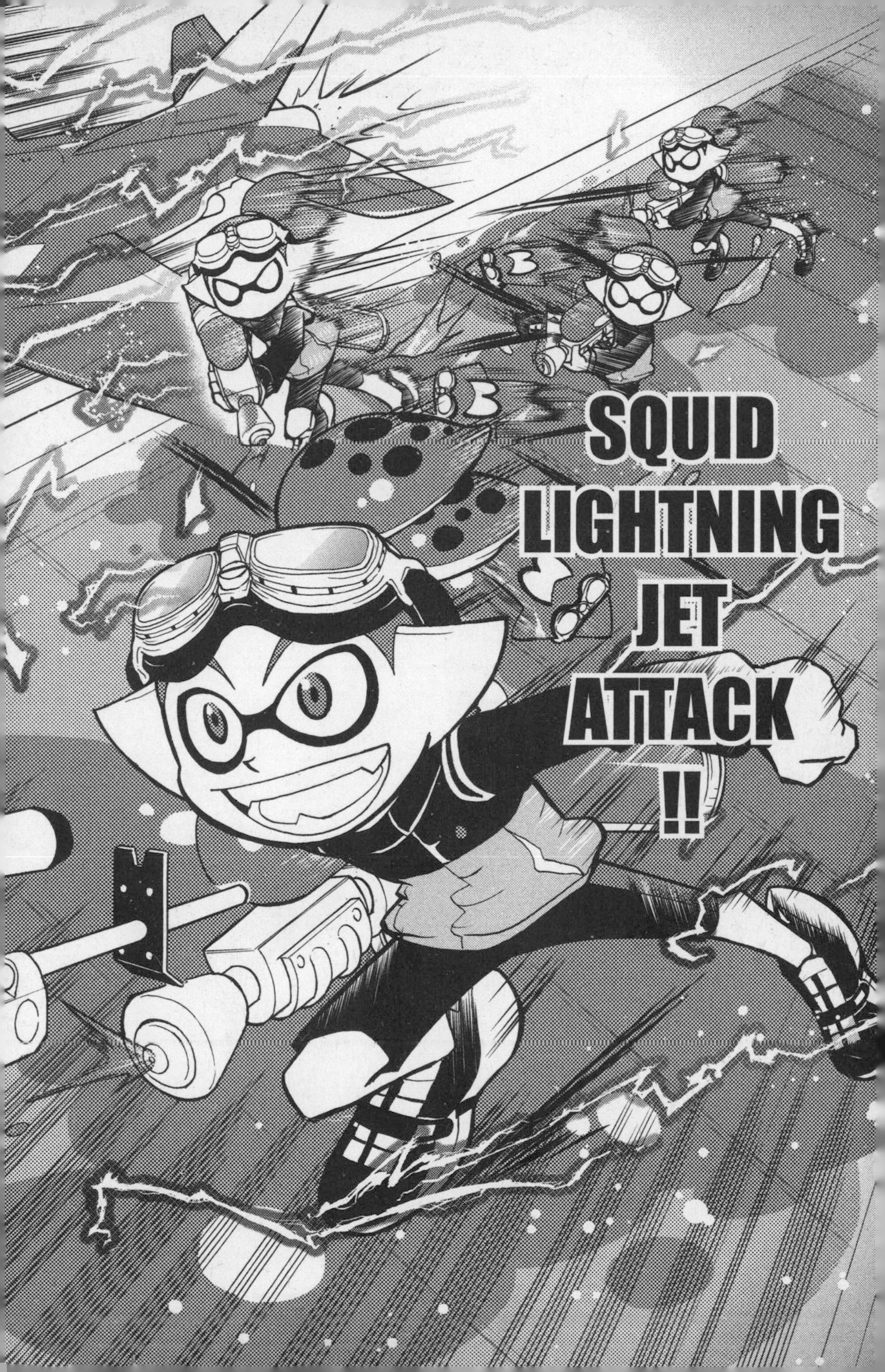
SQUID LIGHTNING JET ATTACK !!

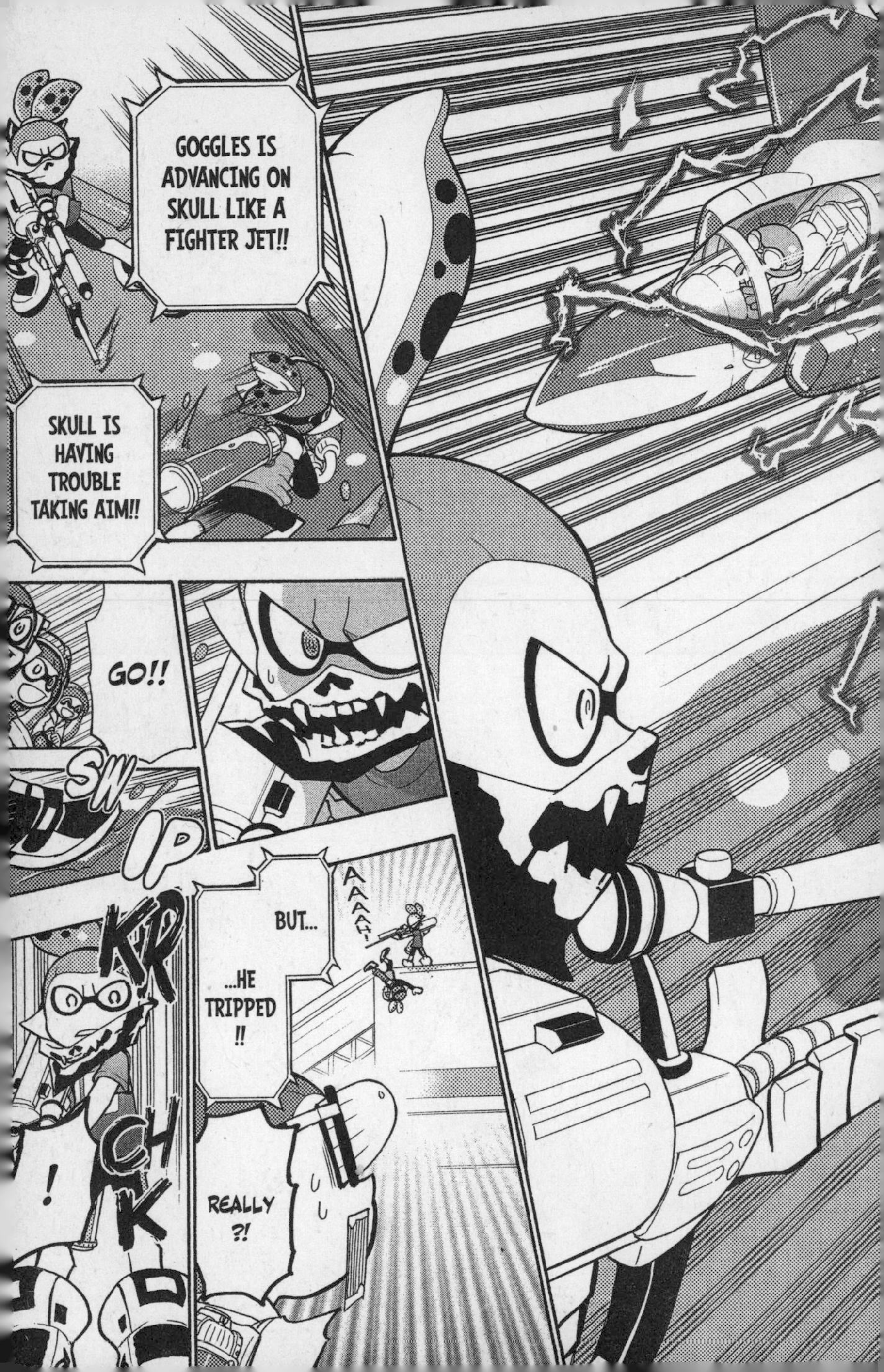
GOGGLES IS ADVANCING ON SKULL LIKE A FIGHTER JET!!
SKULL IS HAVING TROUBLE TAKING AIM!!
GO!!
SWIP
BUT...
AAAAH!
...HE TRIPPED!!
REALLY?!
KRCHK
!

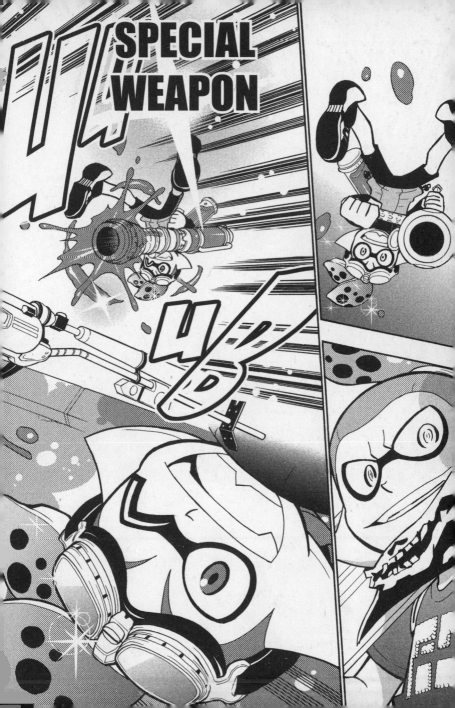

44 SPECIAL WEAPON

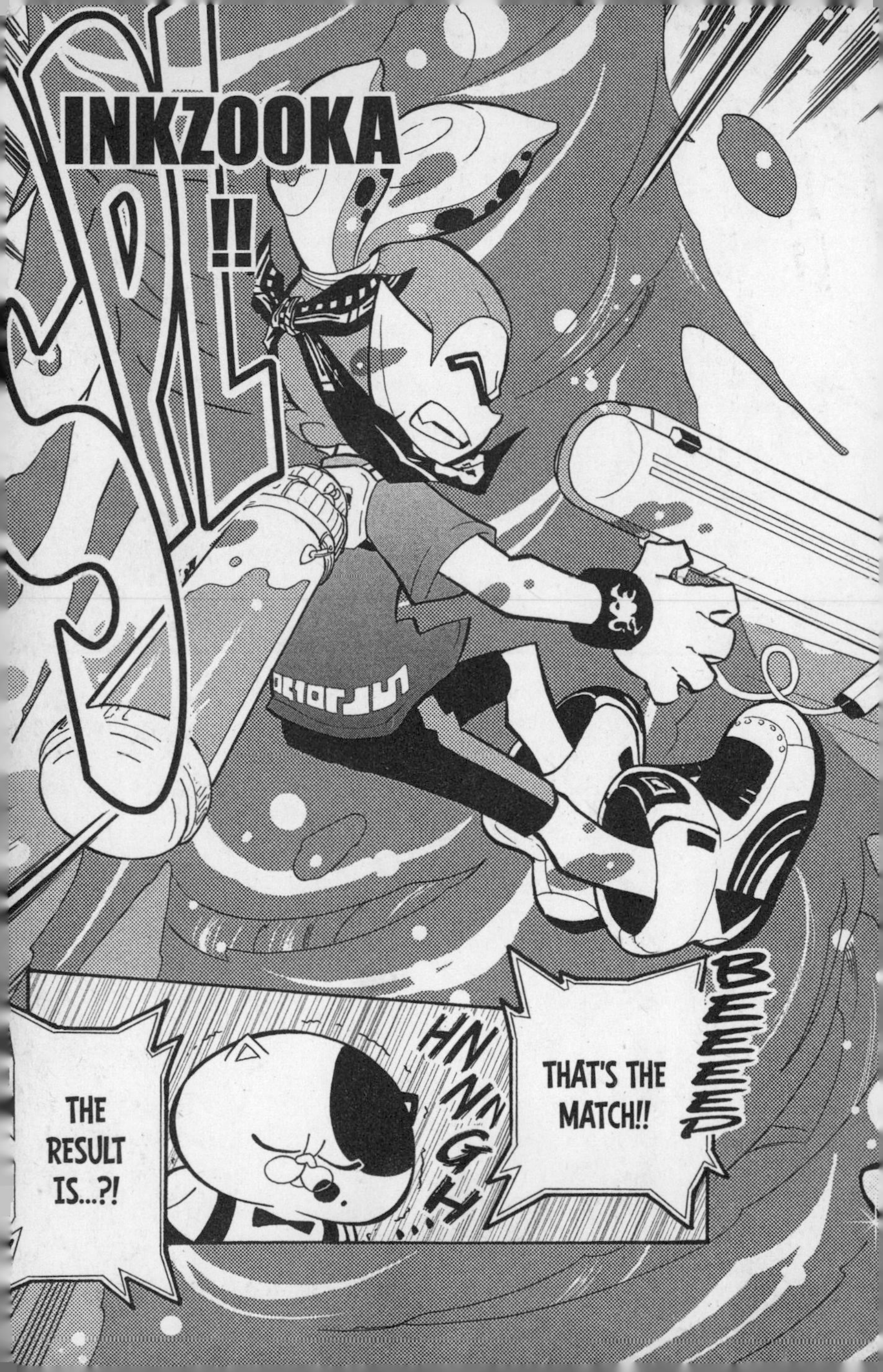
INKZOOKA!!
BEEEED
THAT'S THE MATCH!!
HNNNNGH...!!
THE RESULT IS...?!

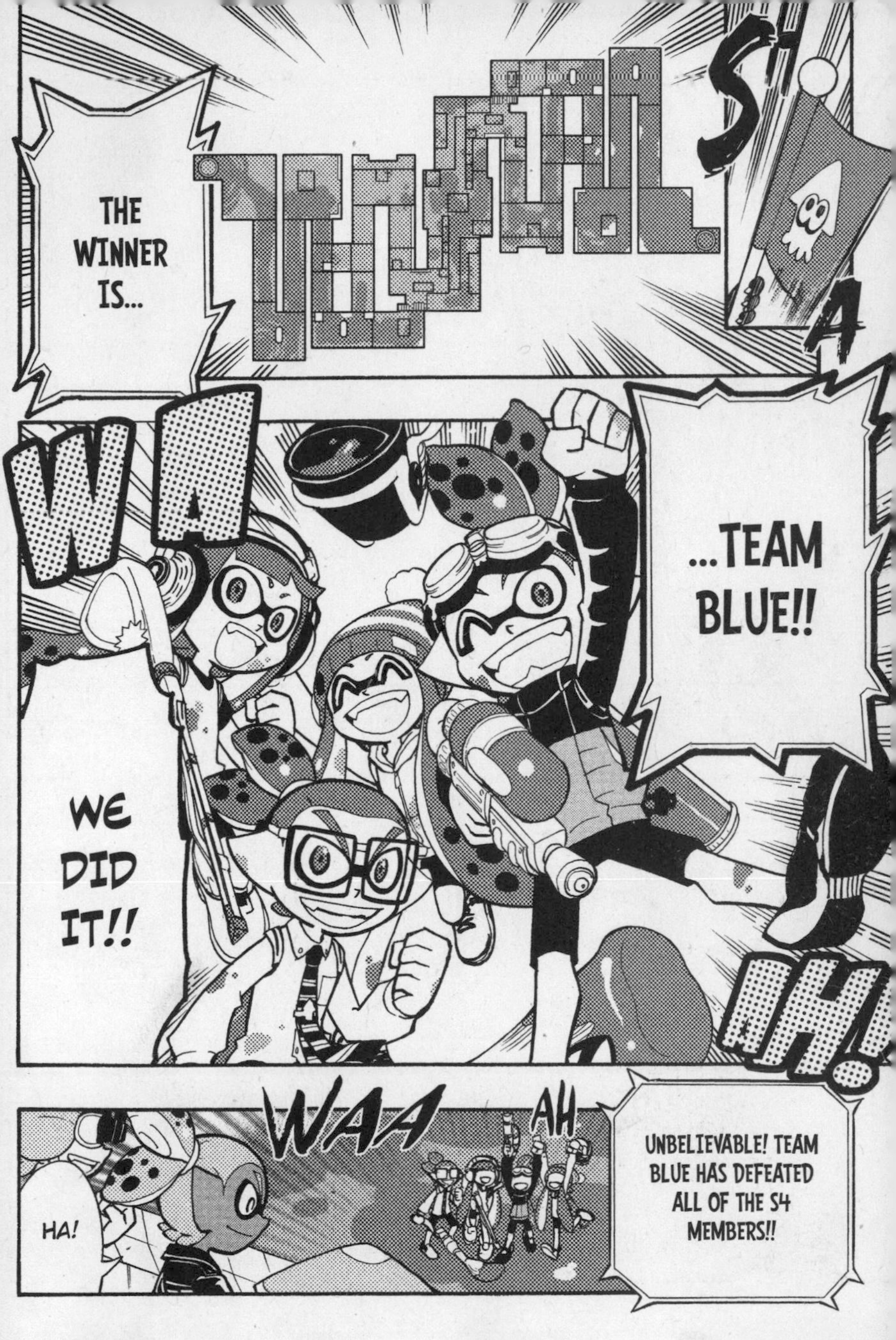
SHA
THE WINNER IS...
...TEAM BLUE!!
WA
AH!
WE DID IT!!
UNBELIEVABLE! TEAM BLUE HAS DEFEATED ALL OF THE S4 MEMBERS!!
AH
WAA
HA!

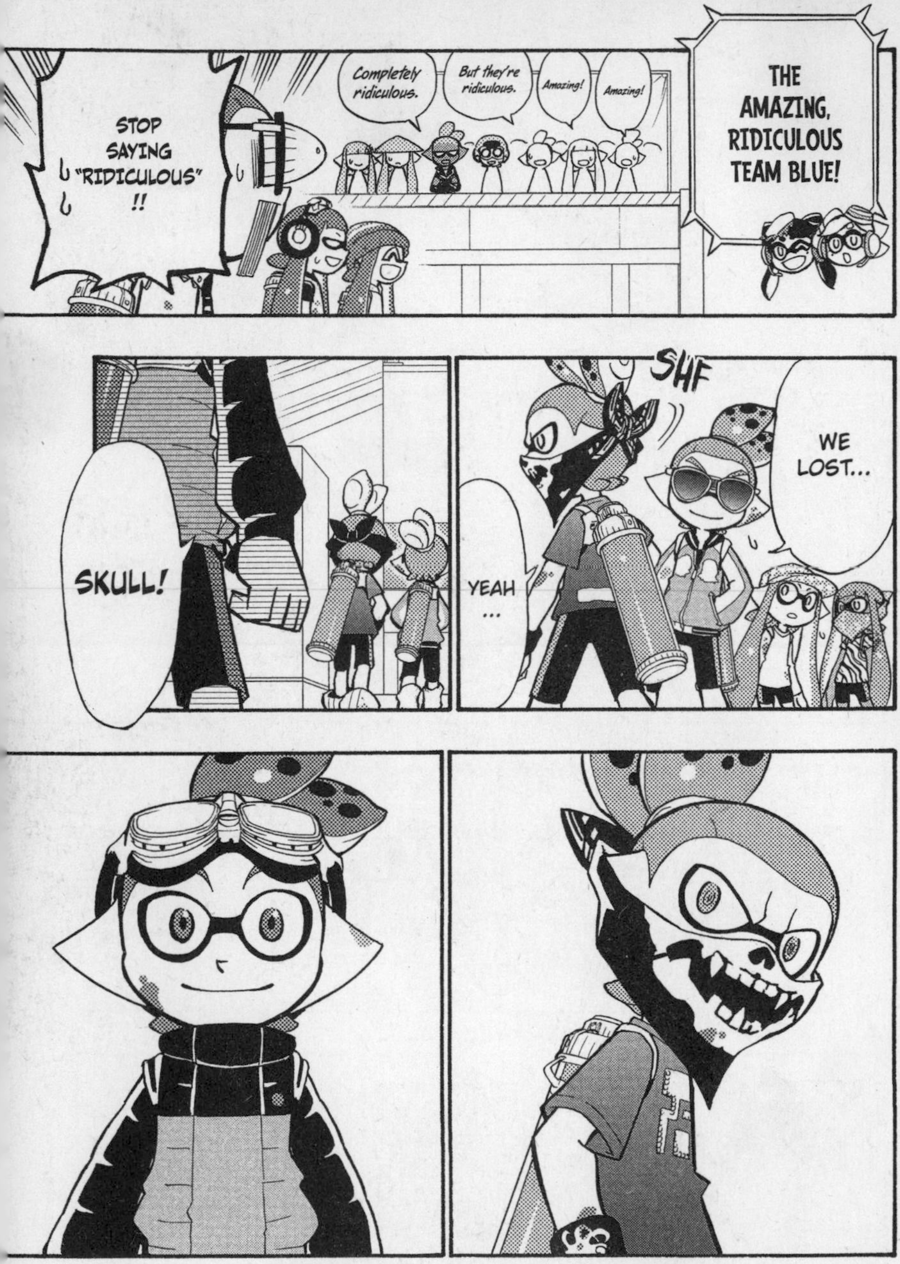
THE AMAZING, RIDICULOUS TEAM BLUE!
Amazing!
Amazing!
But they're ridiculous.
Completely ridiculous.
STOP SAYING "RIDICULOUS" !!
SHF
WE LOST...
YEAH ...
SKULL!

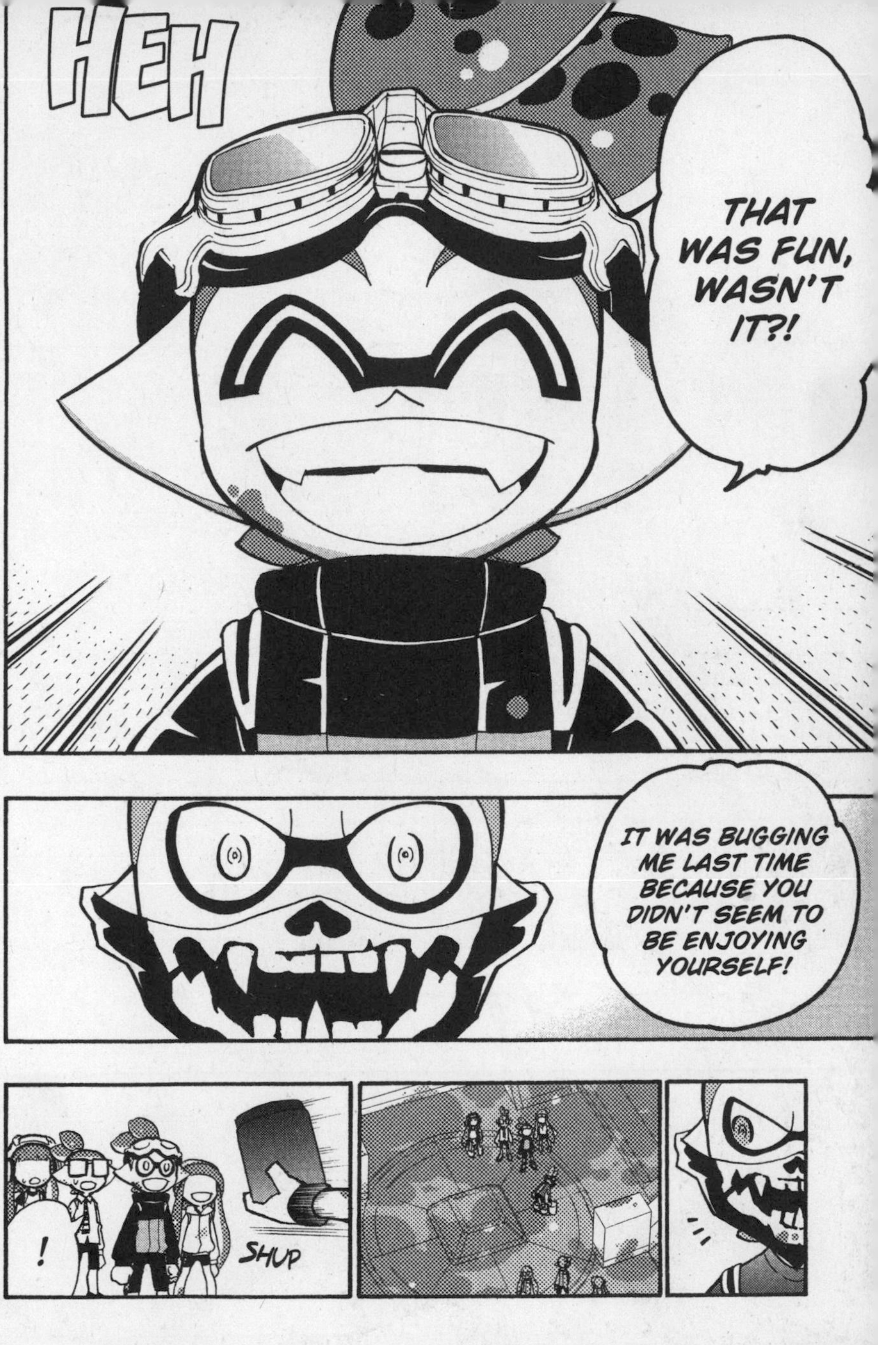
HEH
THAT WAS FUN, WASN'T IT?!
IT WAS BUGGING ME LAST TIME BECAUSE YOU DIDN'T SEEM TO BE ENJOYING YOURSELF!
SHUP
!

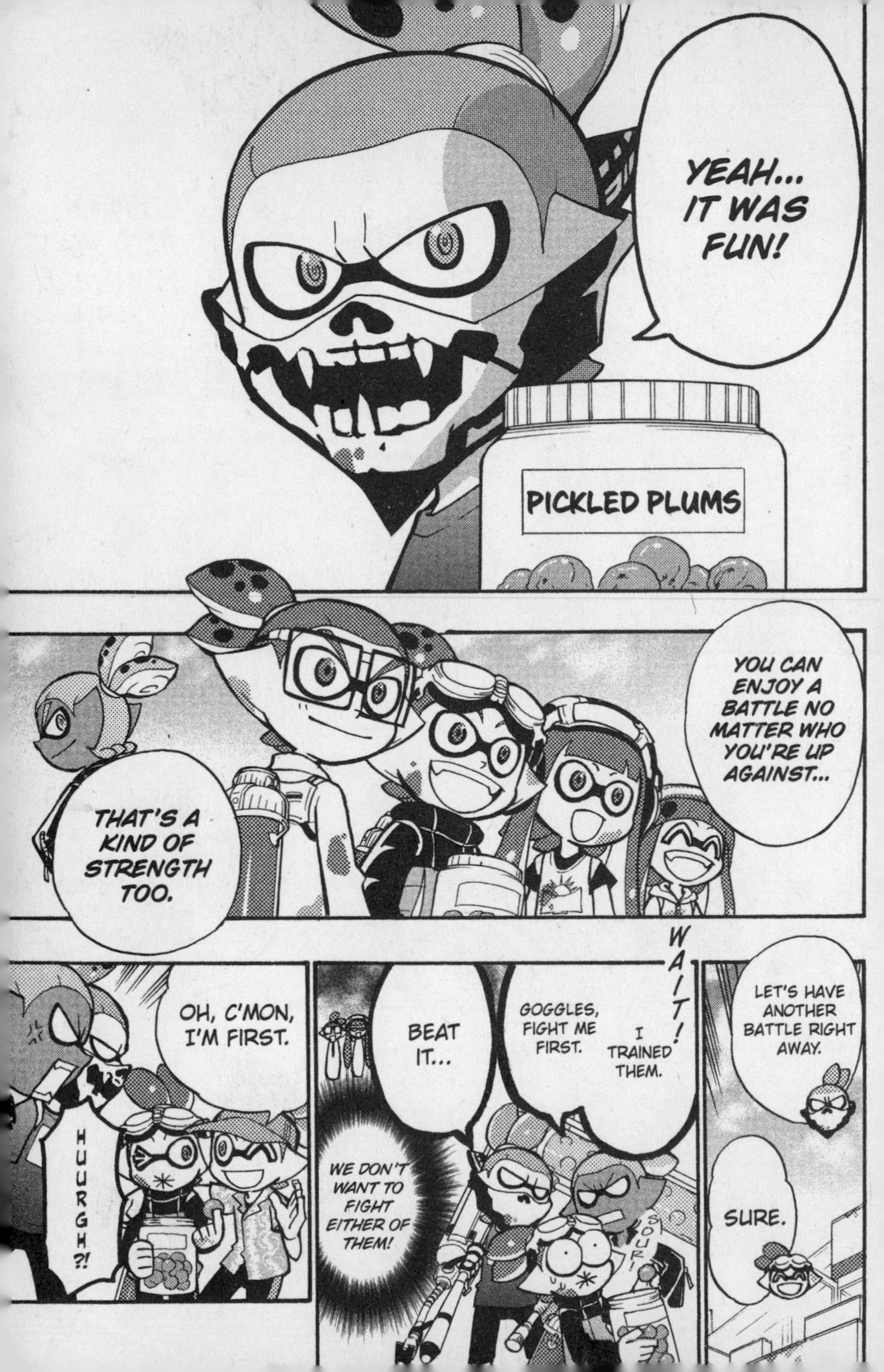
YEAH... IT WAS FUN!
PICKLED PLUMS
YOU CAN ENJOY A BATTLE NO MATTER WHO YOU'RE UP AGAINST...
THAT'S A KIND OF STRENGTH TOO.
LET'S HAVE ANOTHER BATTLE RIGHT AWAY.
SURE.
WAIT!
GOGGLES, FIGHT ME FIRST.
I TRAINED THEM.
BEAT IT...
WE DON'T WANT TO FIGHT EITHER OF THEM!
SOUR!
OH, C'MON, I'M FIRST.
HUURGH?!

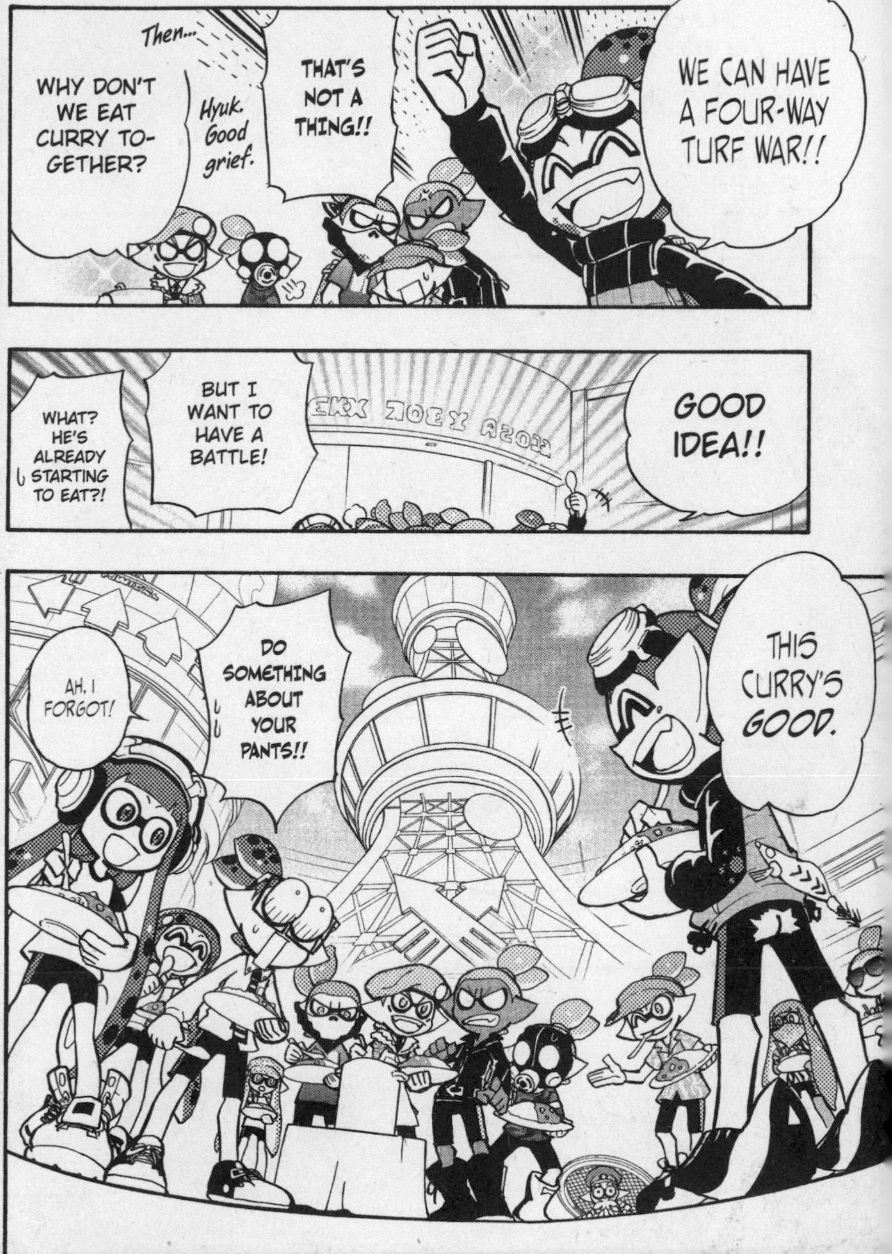
WE CAN HAVE A FOUR-WAY TURF WAR!!
THAT'S NOT A THING!!
Hyuk. Good grief.
Then...
WHY DON'T WE EAT CURRY TO-GETHER?
GOOD IDEA!!
BUT I WANT TO HAVE A BATTLE!
WHAT? HE'S ALREADY STARTING TO EAT?!
THIS CURRY'S GOOD.
DO SOMETHING ABOUT YOUR PANTS!!
AH, I FORGOT!

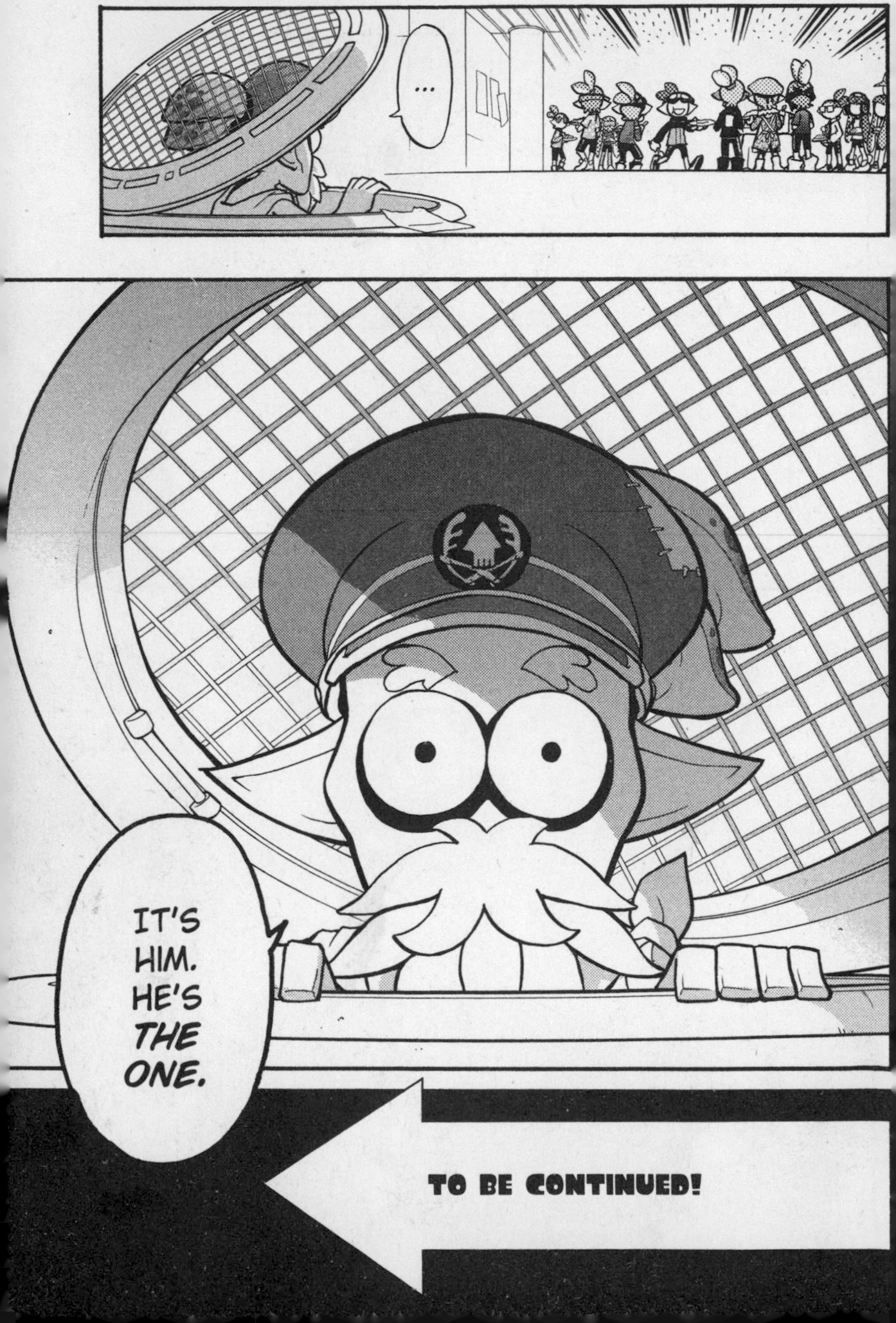
...
IT'S HIM. HE'S THE ONE.
TO BE CONTINUED!

(SPLATOON VOLUME 2 / END)
THIS STORY CONTINUES IN SPLATOON VOLUME 3!

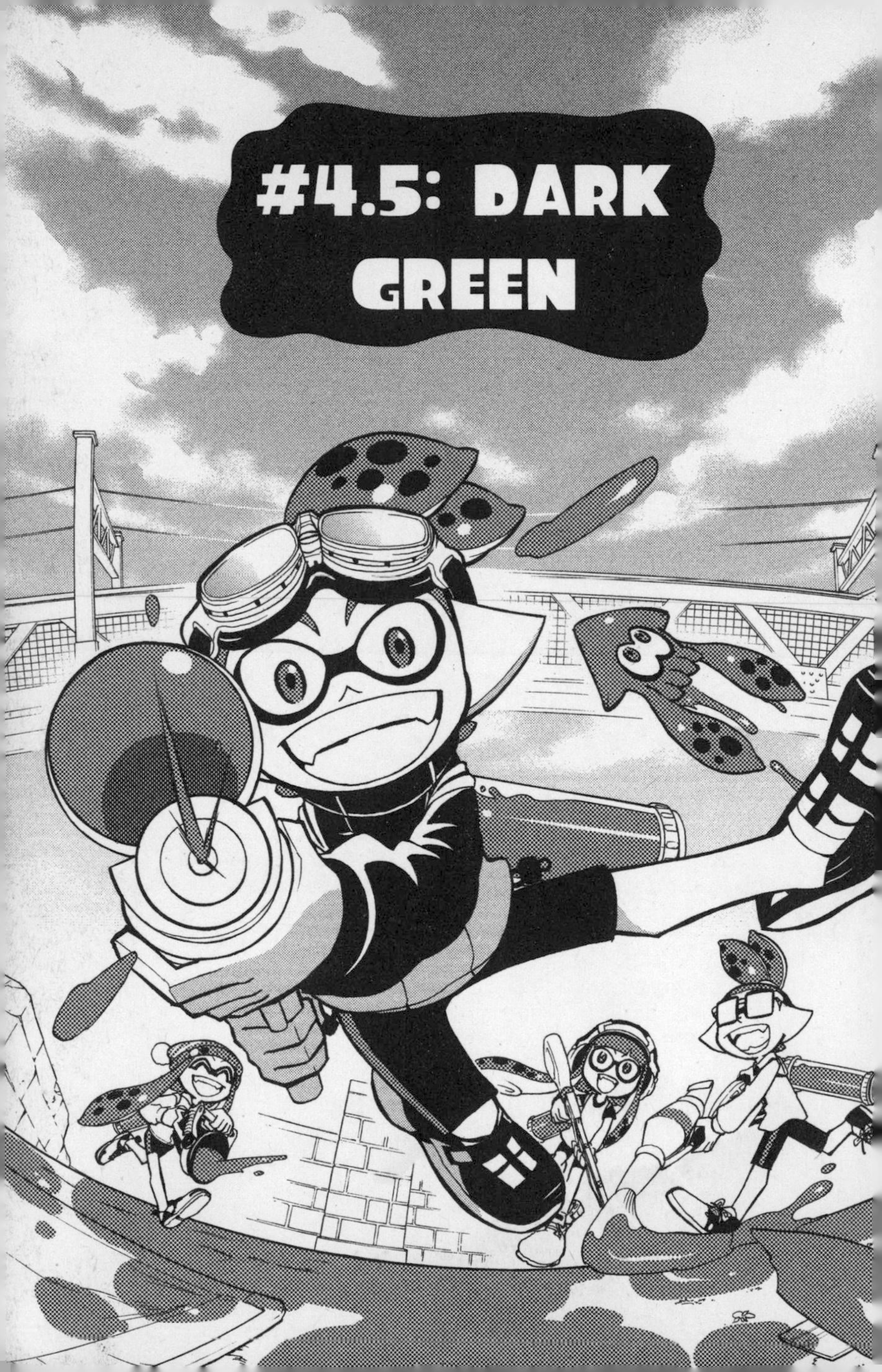
#4.5: DARK GREEN

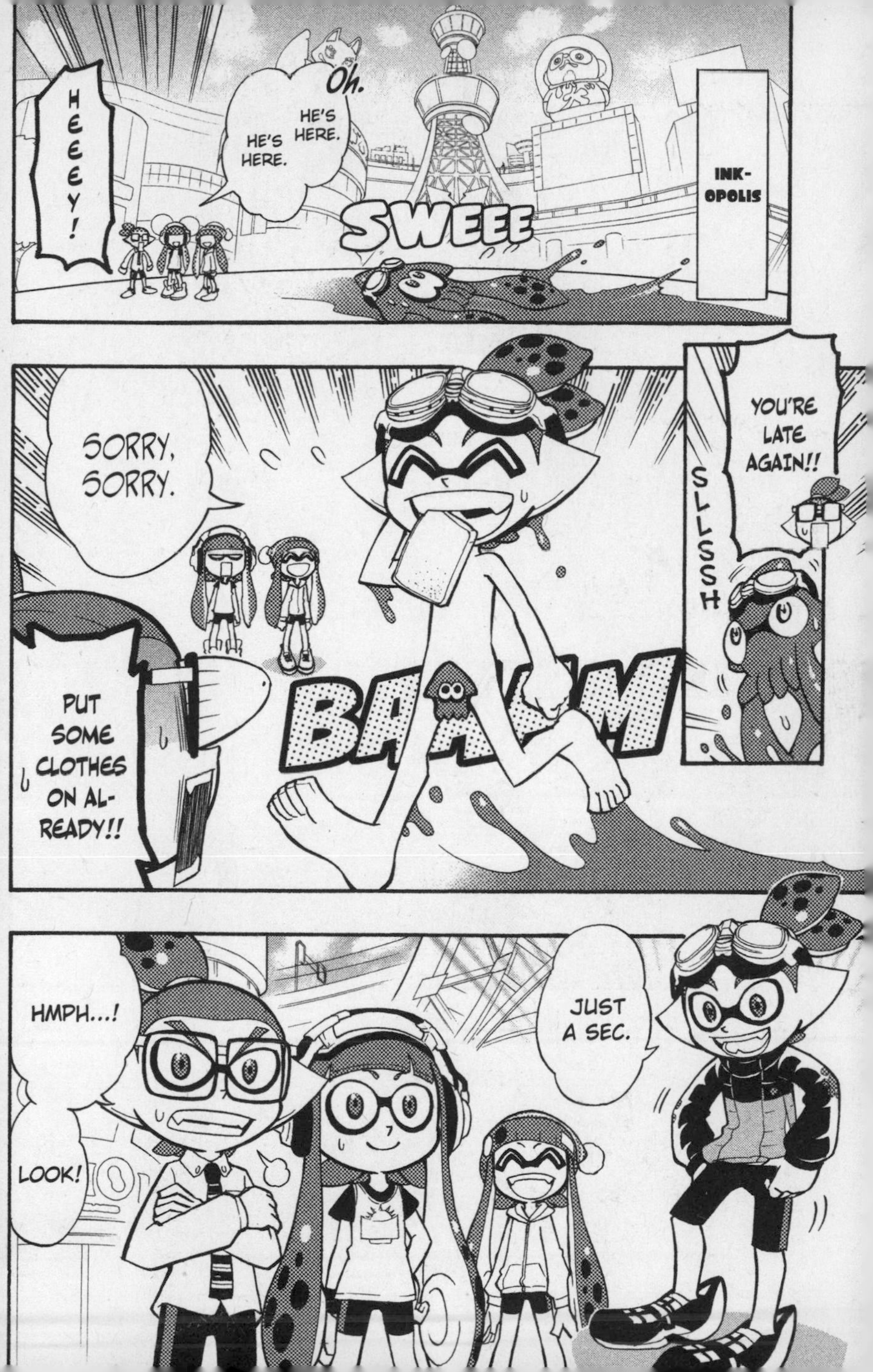
INK-OPOLIS
Oh.
HE'S HERE.
HE'S HERE.
SWEEE
HEEEEY!
YOU'RE LATE AGAIN!!
SLLSSH
SORRY, SORRY.
PUT SOME CLOTHES ON AL-READY!!
JUST A SEC.
HMPH...!
LOOK!

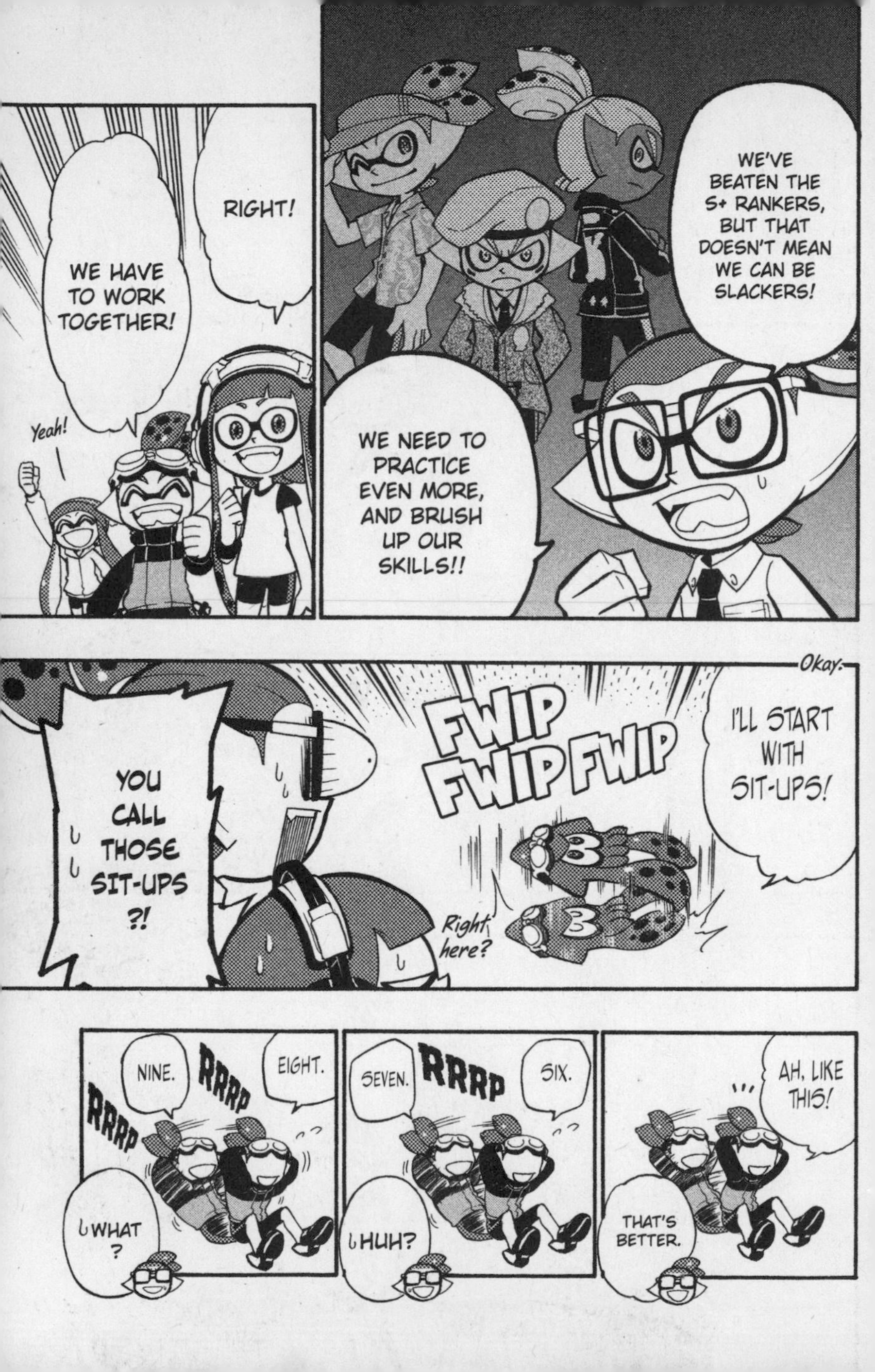
WE'VE BEATEN THE S+ RANKERS, BUT THAT DOESN'T MEAN WE CAN BE SLACKERS!
WE NEED TO PRACTICE EVEN MORE, AND BRUSH UP OUR SKILLS!!
RIGHT!
WE HAVE TO WORK TOGETHER!
Yeah!
Okay-
I'LL START WITH SIT-UPS!
FWIP FWIP FWIP
Right here?
YOU CALL THOSE SIT-UPS?!
AH, LIKE THIS!
THAT'S BETTER.
SIX.
RRRP
SEVEN.
HUH?
EIGHT.
RRRP
NINE.
RRRP
WHAT?

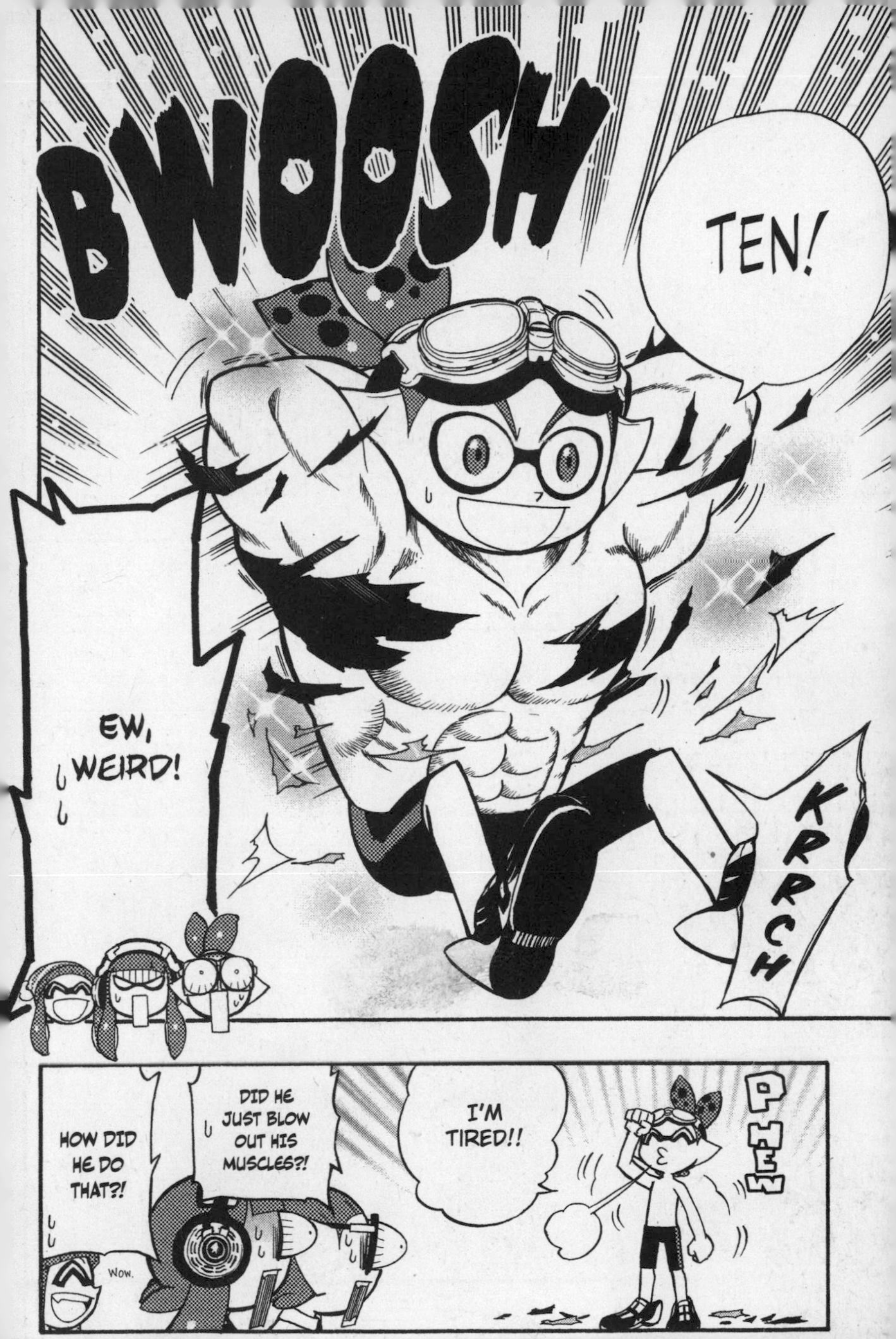
TEN!
BWOOSH
KRRCH
EW, WEIRD!
PHEW
I'M TIRED!!
DID HE JUST BLOW OUT HIS MUSCLES?!
HOW DID HE DO THAT?!
WOW.

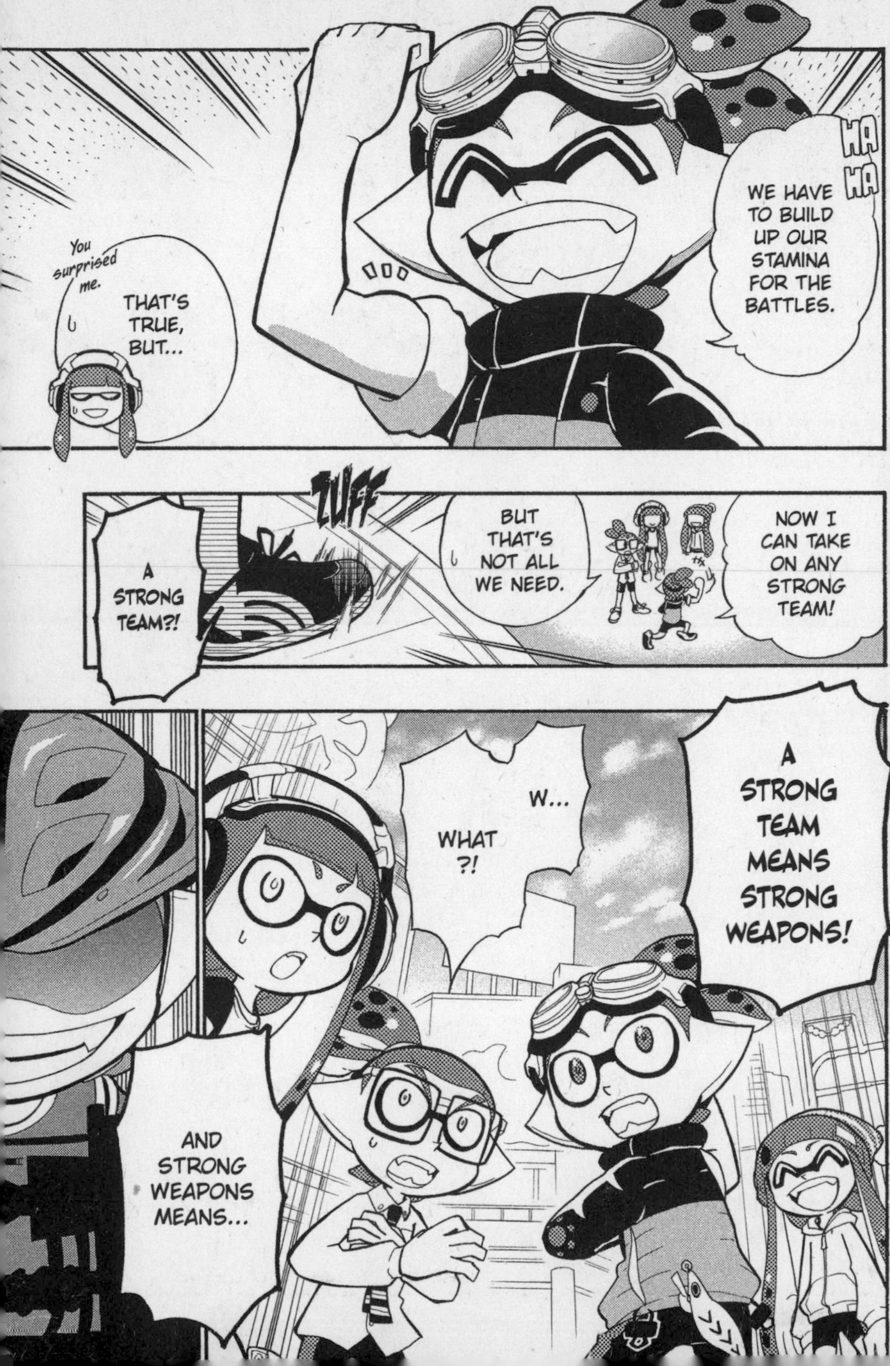
HA HA
WE HAVE TO BUILD UP OUR STAMINA FOR THE BATTLES.
You surprised me.
THAT'S TRUE, BUT...
NOW I CAN TAKE ON ANY STRONG TEAM!
BUT THAT'S NOT ALL WE NEED.
ZUFF
A STRONG TEAM?!
A STRONG TEAM MEANS STRONG WEAPONS!
W... WHAT?!
AND STRONG WEAPONS MEANS...

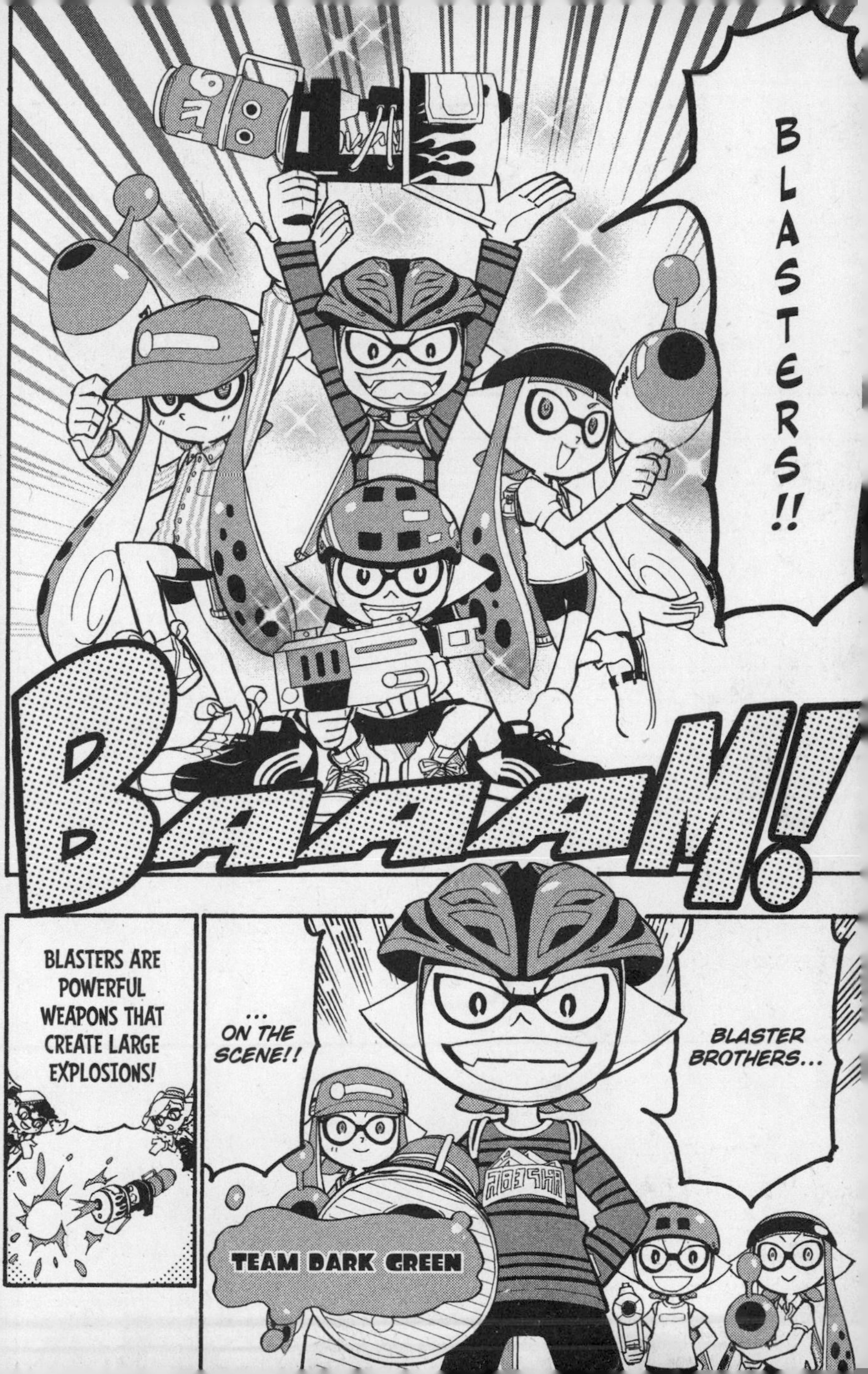
BLASTERS!!
BAAAM!
BLASTER BROTHERS...
... ON THE SCENE!!
TEAM DARK GREEN
BLASTERS ARE POWERFUL WEAPONS THAT CREATE LARGE EXPLOSIONS!

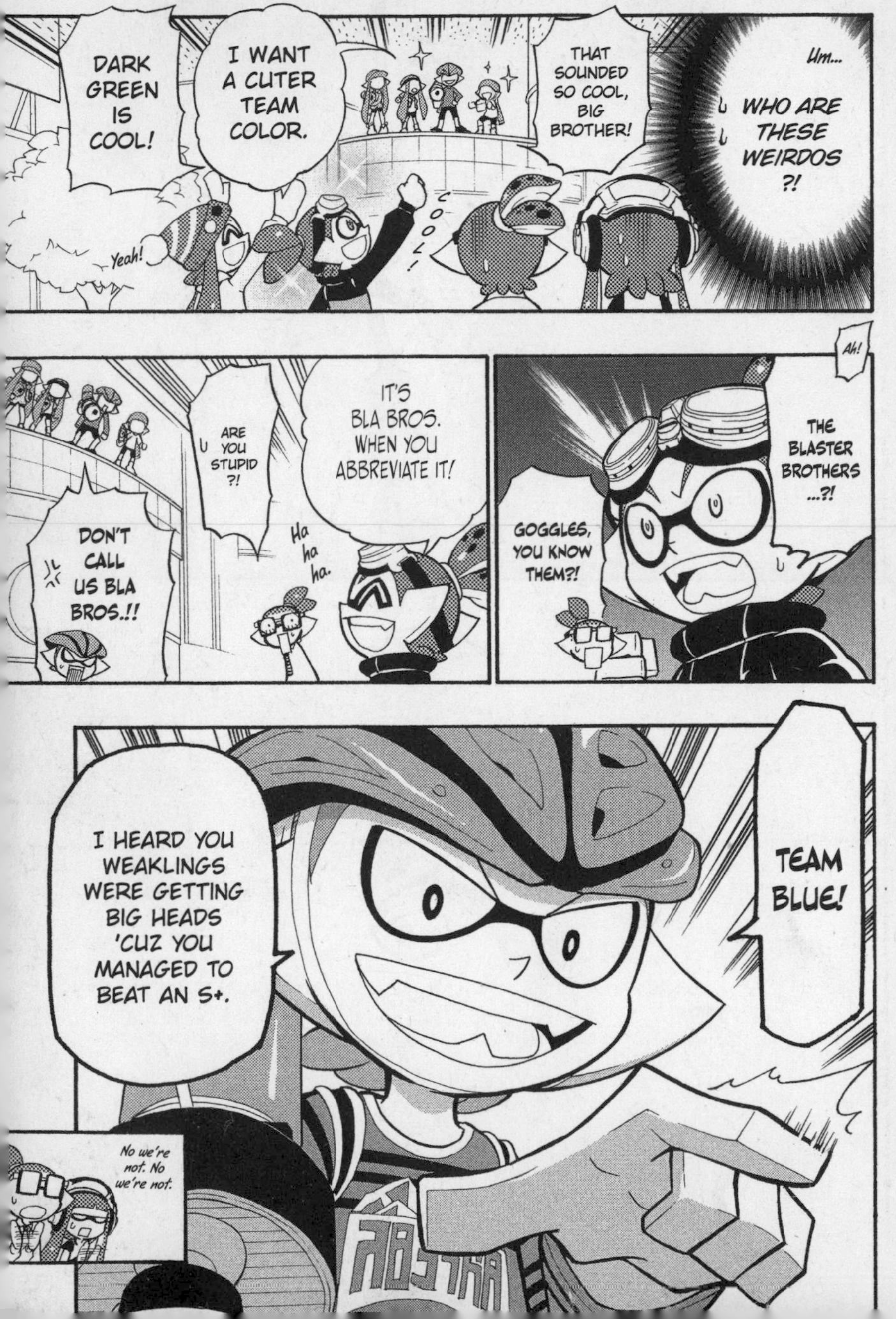

Um...
WHO ARE THESE WEIRDOS?!
THAT SOUNDED SO COOL, BIG BROTHER!
I WANT A CUTER TEAM COLOR.
DARK GREEN IS COOL!
COOL!
Yeah!
Ah!
THE BLASTER BROTHERS...?!
GOGGLES, YOU KNOW THEM?!
IT'S BLA BROS. WHEN YOU ABBREVIATE IT!
ARE YOU STUPID?!
Ha ha ha.
DON'T CALL US BLA BROS.!!
TEAM BLUE!
I HEARD YOU WEAKLINGS WERE GETTING BIG HEADS 'CUZ YOU MANAGED TO BEAT AN S+.
No we're not. No we're not.

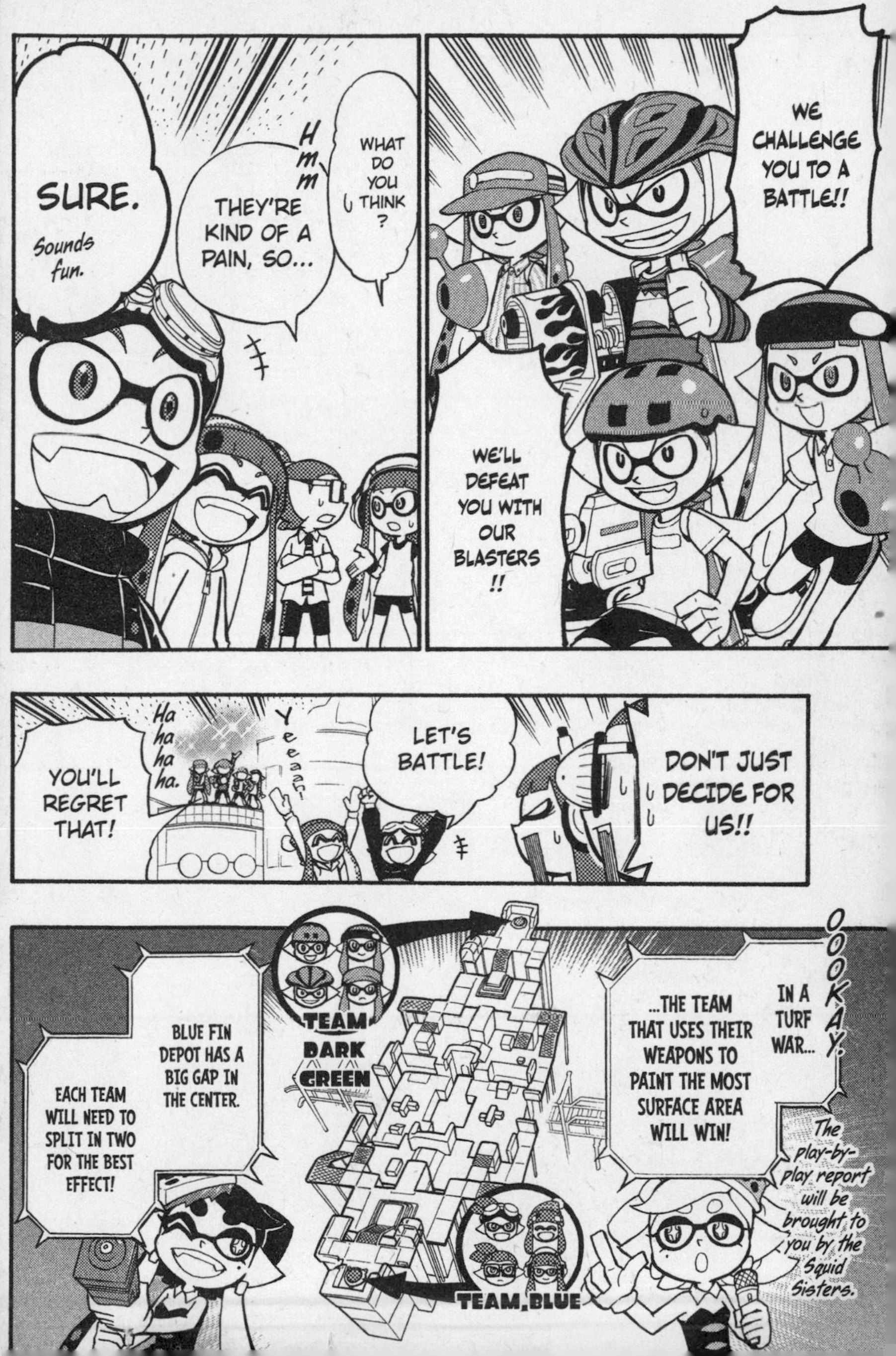
WE CHALLENGE YOU TO A BATTLE!!
WE'LL DEFEAT YOU WITH OUR BLASTERS!!
WHAT DO YOU THINK?
Hmm
THEY'RE KIND OF A PAIN, SO...
SURE.
Sounds fun.
DON'T JUST DECIDE FOR US!!
LET'S BATTLE!
Yeeaah!
Hahahaha.
YOU'LL REGRET THAT!
OOOOKAY.
IN A TURF WAR...
...THE TEAM THAT USES THEIR WEAPONS TO PAINT THE MOST SURFACE AREA WILL WIN!
The play-by-play report will be brought to you by the Squid Sisters.
TEAM DARK GREEN
TEAM BLUE
BLUE FIN DEPOT HAS A BIG GAP IN THE CENTER.
EACH TEAM WILL NEED TO SPLIT IN TWO FOR THE BEST EFFECT!

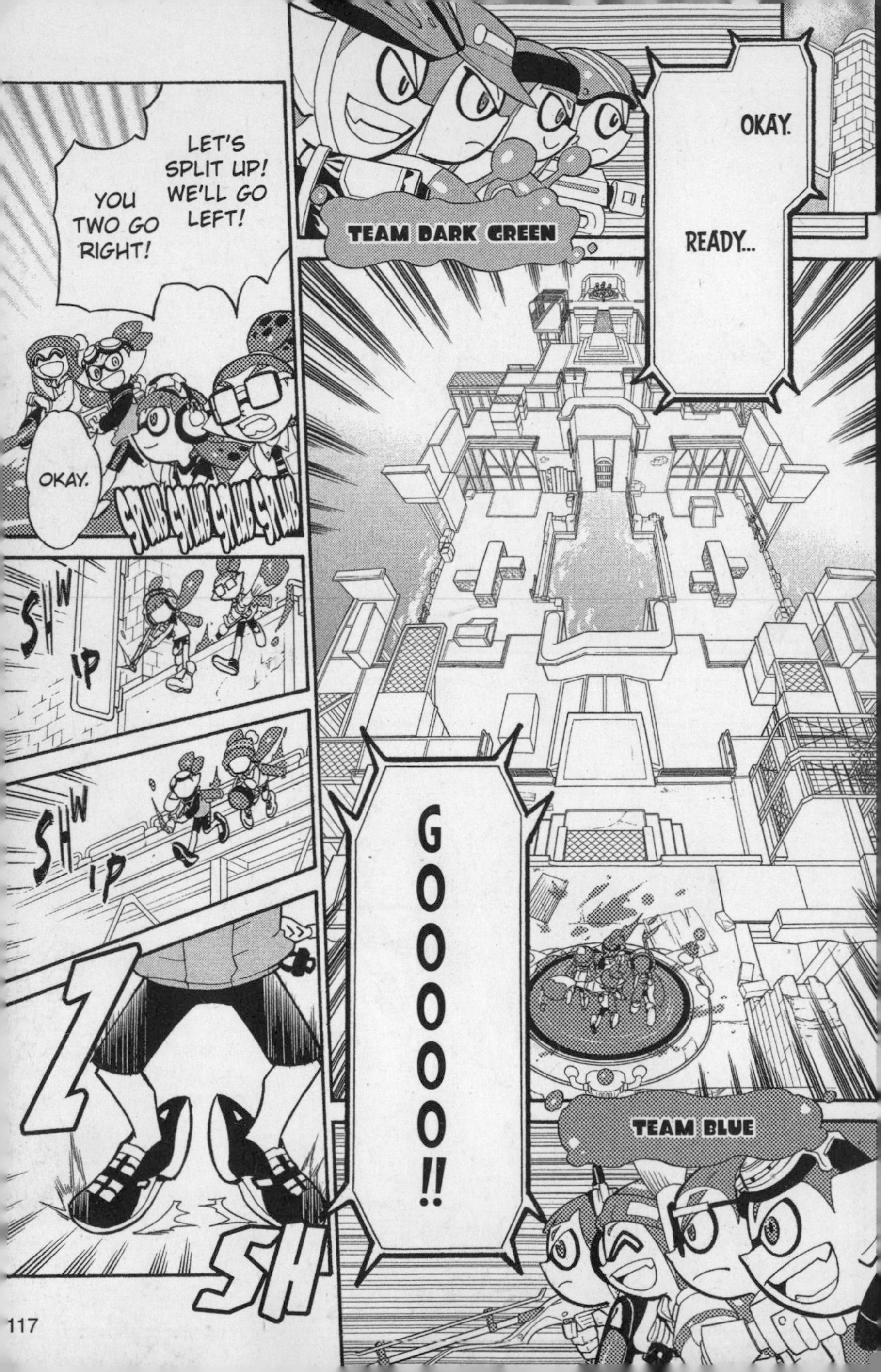
OKAY.
READY...
TEAM DARK GREEN
GOOOOO!!
TEAM BLUE
LET'S SPLIT UP! WE'LL GO LEFT!
YOU TWO GO RIGHT!
OKAY.
SPLUB SPLUB SPLUB SPLUB
SHWIP
SHWIP
Z
SH

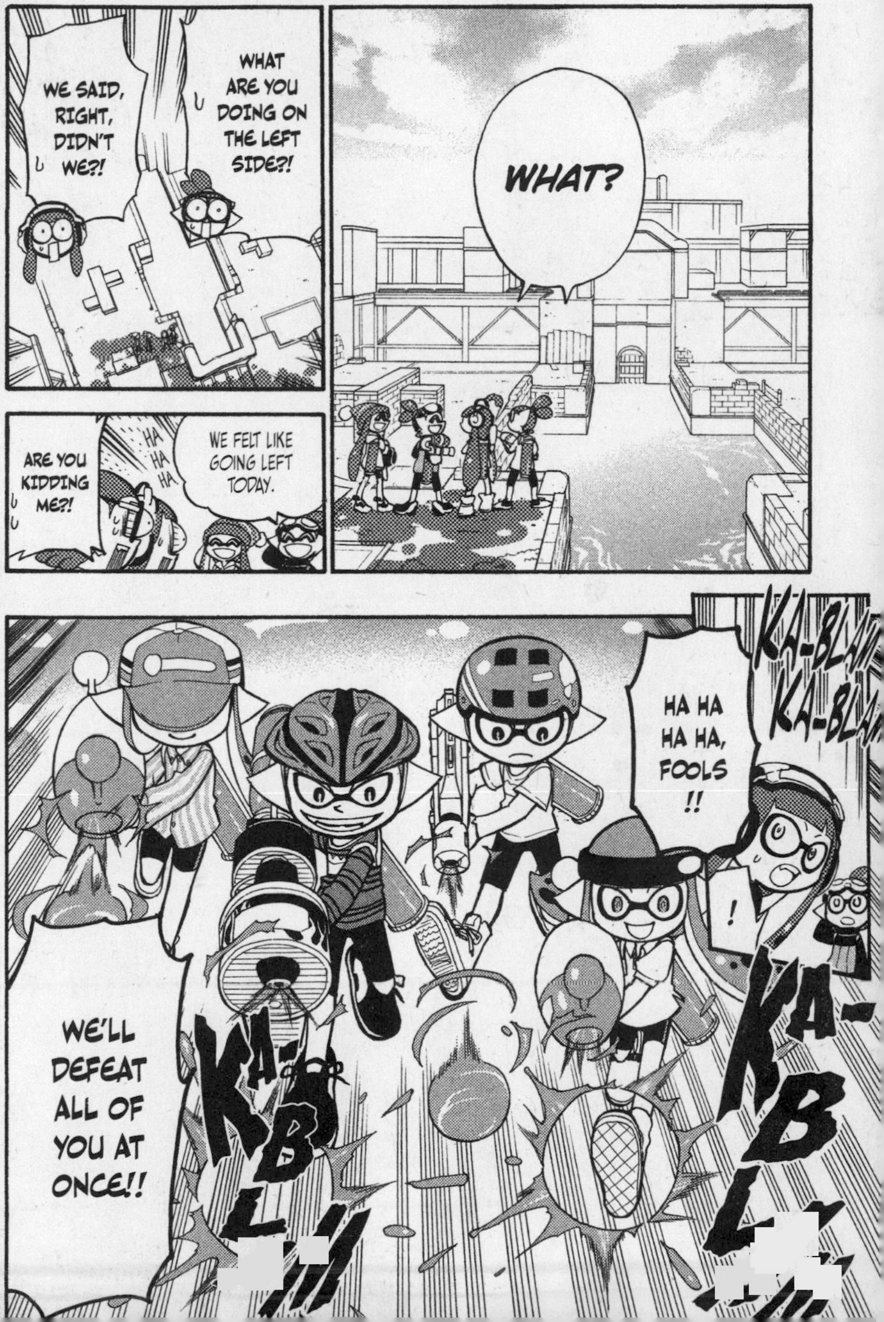
WHAT?
WHAT ARE YOU DOING ON THE LEFT SIDE?!
WE SAID, RIGHT, DIDN'T WE?!
WE FELT LIKE GOING LEFT TODAY.
HA HA HA
ARE YOU KIDDING ME?!
HA HA HA HA, FOOLS !!
!
WE'LL DEFEAT ALL OF YOU AT ONCE!!

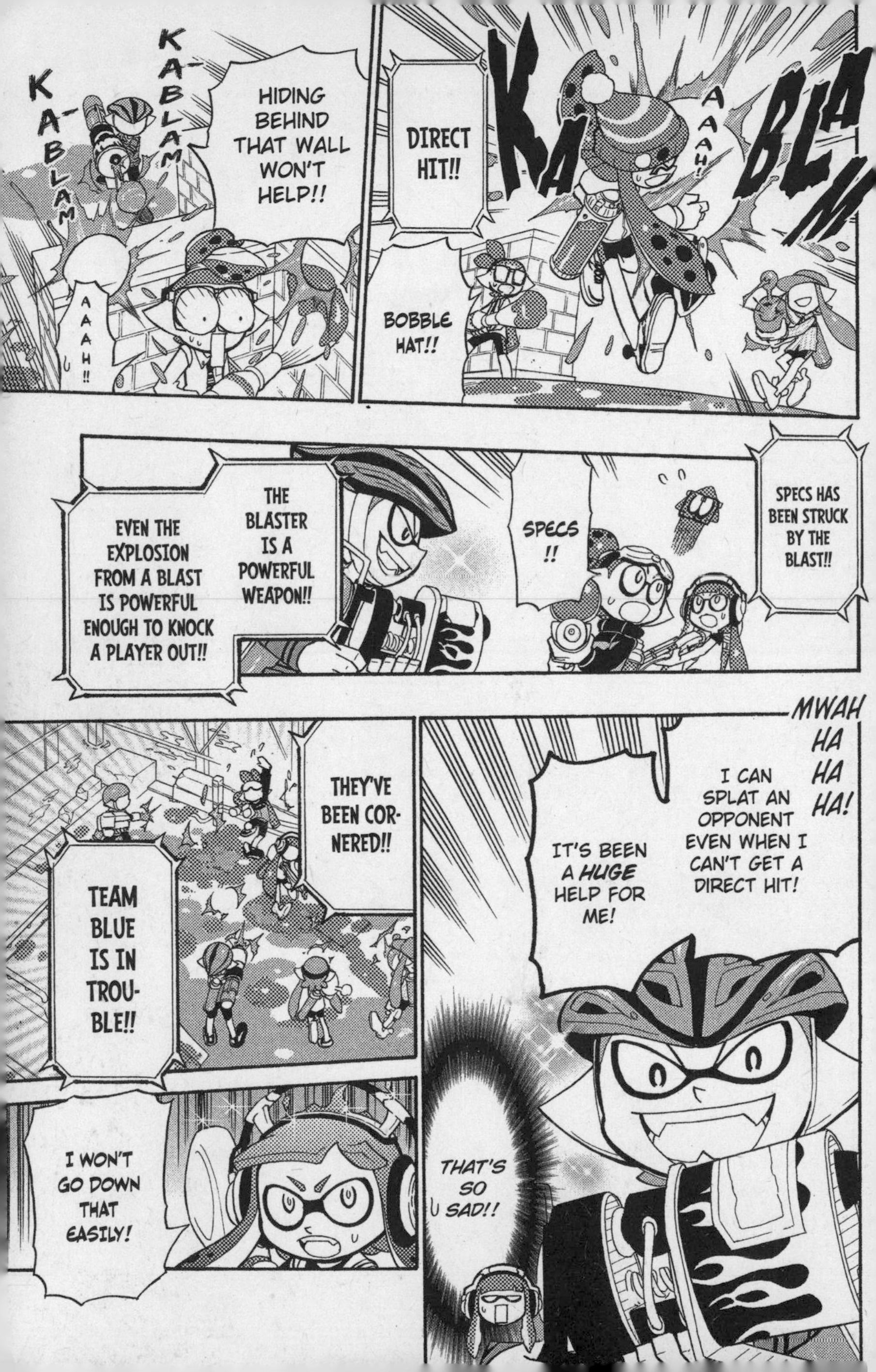
KABLAM
AAAH!
DIRECT HIT!!
BOBBLE HAT!!
KA-BLAM
KA-BLAM
HIDING BEHIND THAT WALL WON'T HELP!!
AAAH!!
SPECS HAS BEEN STRUCK BY THE BLAST!!
SPECS!!
THE BLASTER IS A POWERFUL WEAPON!!
EVEN THE EXPLOSION FROM A BLAST IS POWERFUL ENOUGH TO KNOCK A PLAYER OUT!!
MWAH HA HA HA!
I CAN SPLAT AN OPPONENT EVEN WHEN I CAN'T GET A DIRECT HIT!
IT'S BEEN A *HUGE* HELP FOR ME!
THAT'S SO SAD!!
THEY'VE BEEN COR-NERED!!
TEAM BLUE IS IN TROU-BLE!!
I WON'T GO DOWN THAT EASILY!

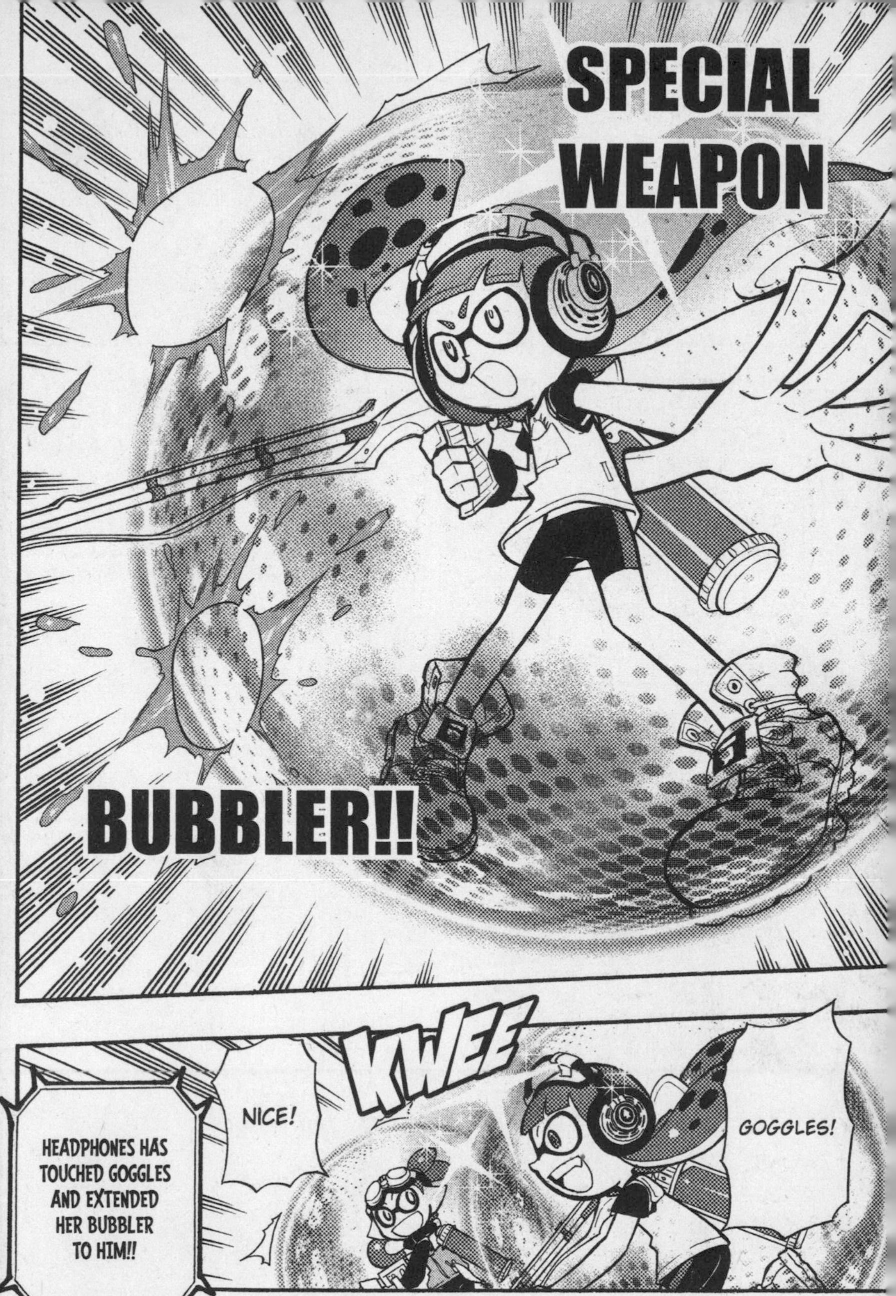
SPECIAL WEAPON
BUBBLER!!
GOGGLES!
KWEE
NICE!
HEADPHONES HAS TOUCHED GOGGLES AND EXTENDED HER BUBBLER TO HIM!!

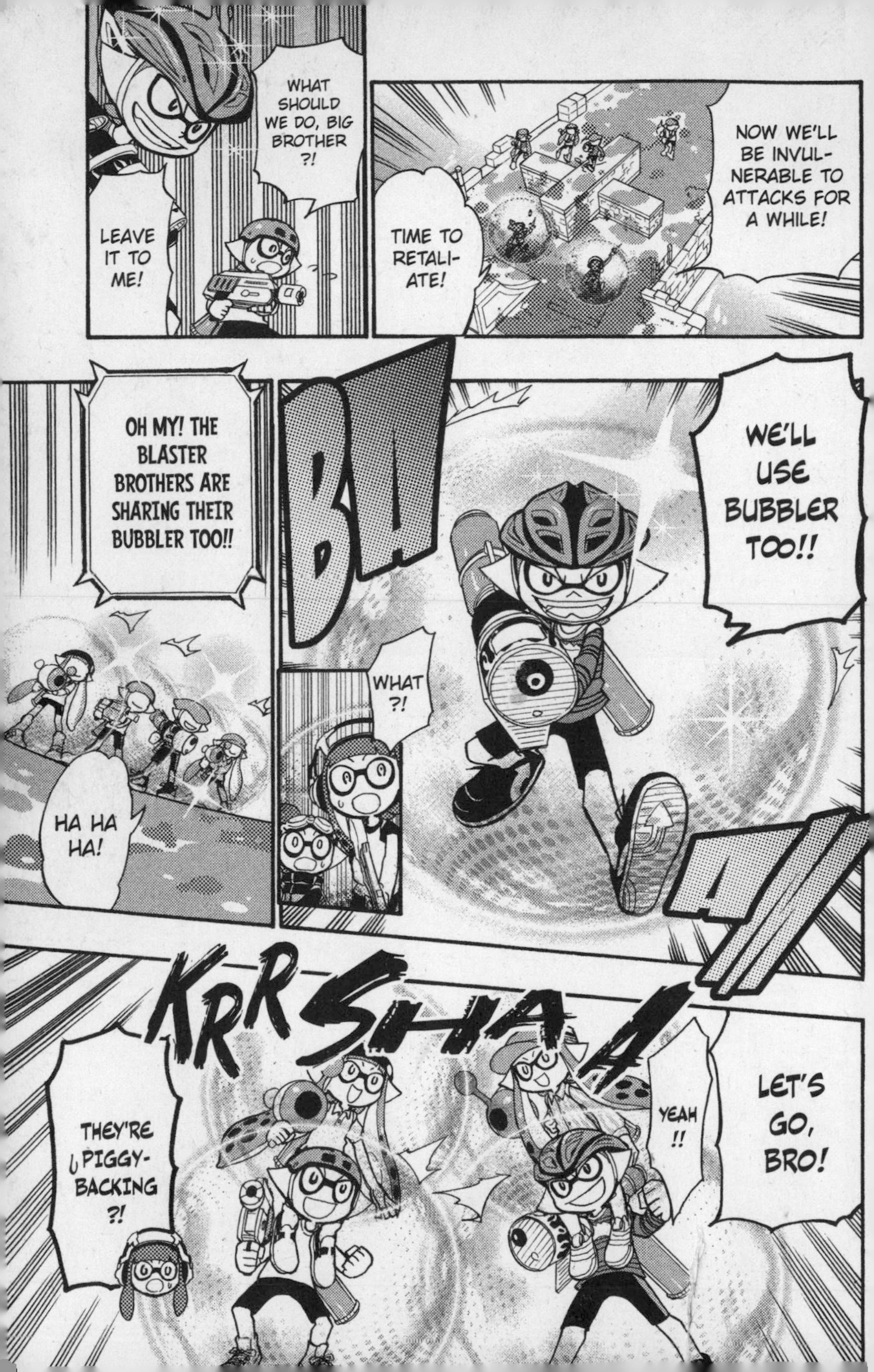
NOW WE'LL BE INVULNERABLE TO ATTACKS FOR A WHILE!
TIME TO RETALIATE!
WHAT SHOULD WE DO, BIG BROTHER ?!
LEAVE IT TO ME!
BA
WE'LL USE BUBBLER TOO!!
WHAT ?!
OH MY! THE BLASTER BROTHERS ARE SHARING THEIR BUBBLER TOO!!
HA HA HA!
KRRSHAA
LET'S GO, BRO!
YEAH !!
THEY'RE PIGGY-BACKING ?!

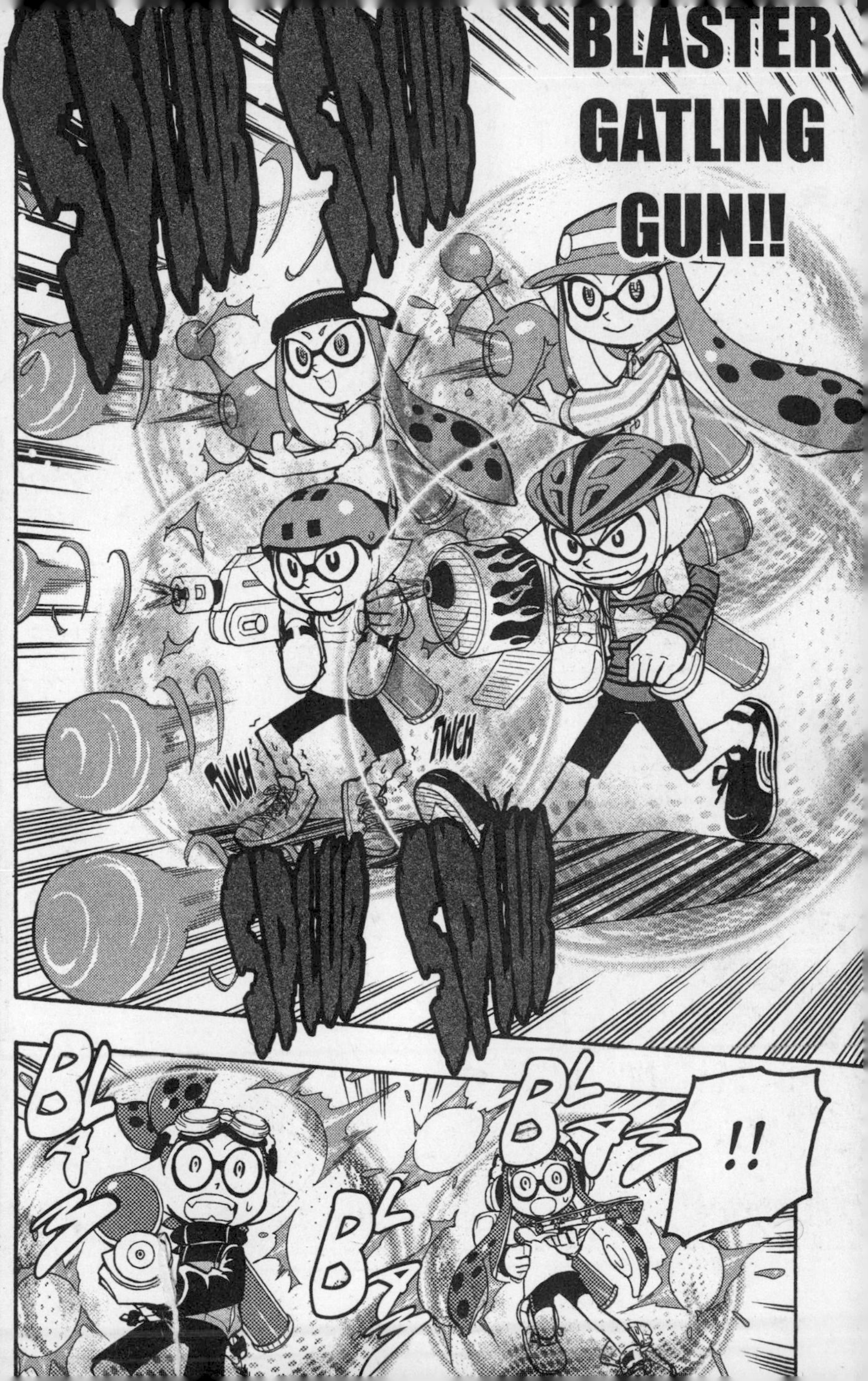

BLASTER GATLING GUN!!
TWCH
TWCH
!!
BLAM
BLAM
BLAM

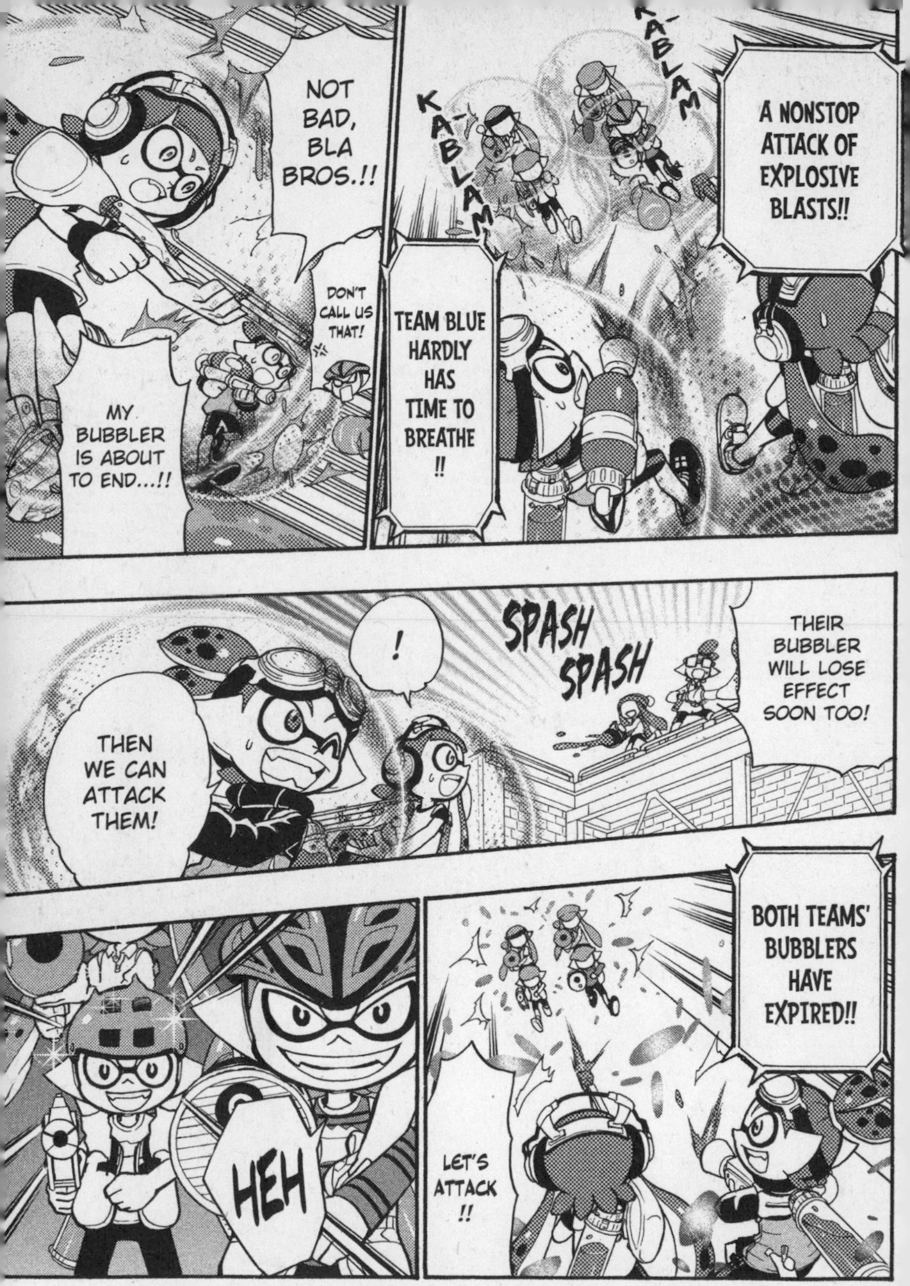
A NONSTOP ATTACK OF EXPLOSIVE BLASTS!!
KA-BLAM
KA-BLAM
TEAM BLUE HARDLY HAS TIME TO BREATHE!!
NOT BAD, BLA BROS..!!
DON'T CALL US THAT!
MY BUBBLER IS ABOUT TO END...!!
THEIR BUBBLER WILL LOSE EFFECT SOON TOO!
SPASH SPASH
!
THEN WE CAN ATTACK THEM!
BOTH TEAMS' BUBBLERS HAVE EXPIRED!!
LET'S ATTACK!!
HEH

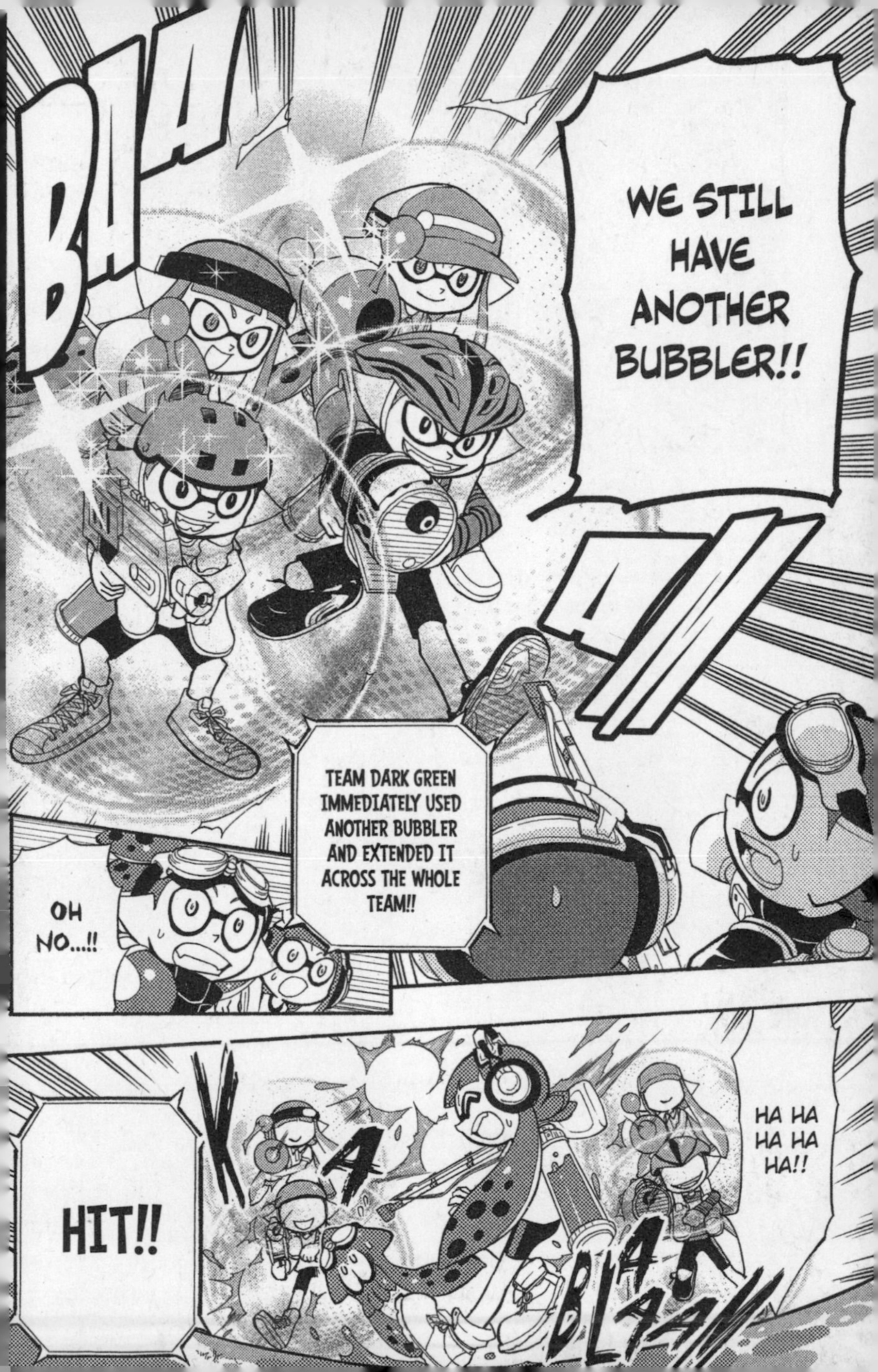
WE STILL HAVE ANOTHER BUBBLER!!
TEAM DARK GREEN IMMEDIATELY USED ANOTHER BUBBLER AND EXTENDED IT ACROSS THE WHOLE TEAM!!
OH NO...!!
HA HA HA HA HA!!
HIT!!

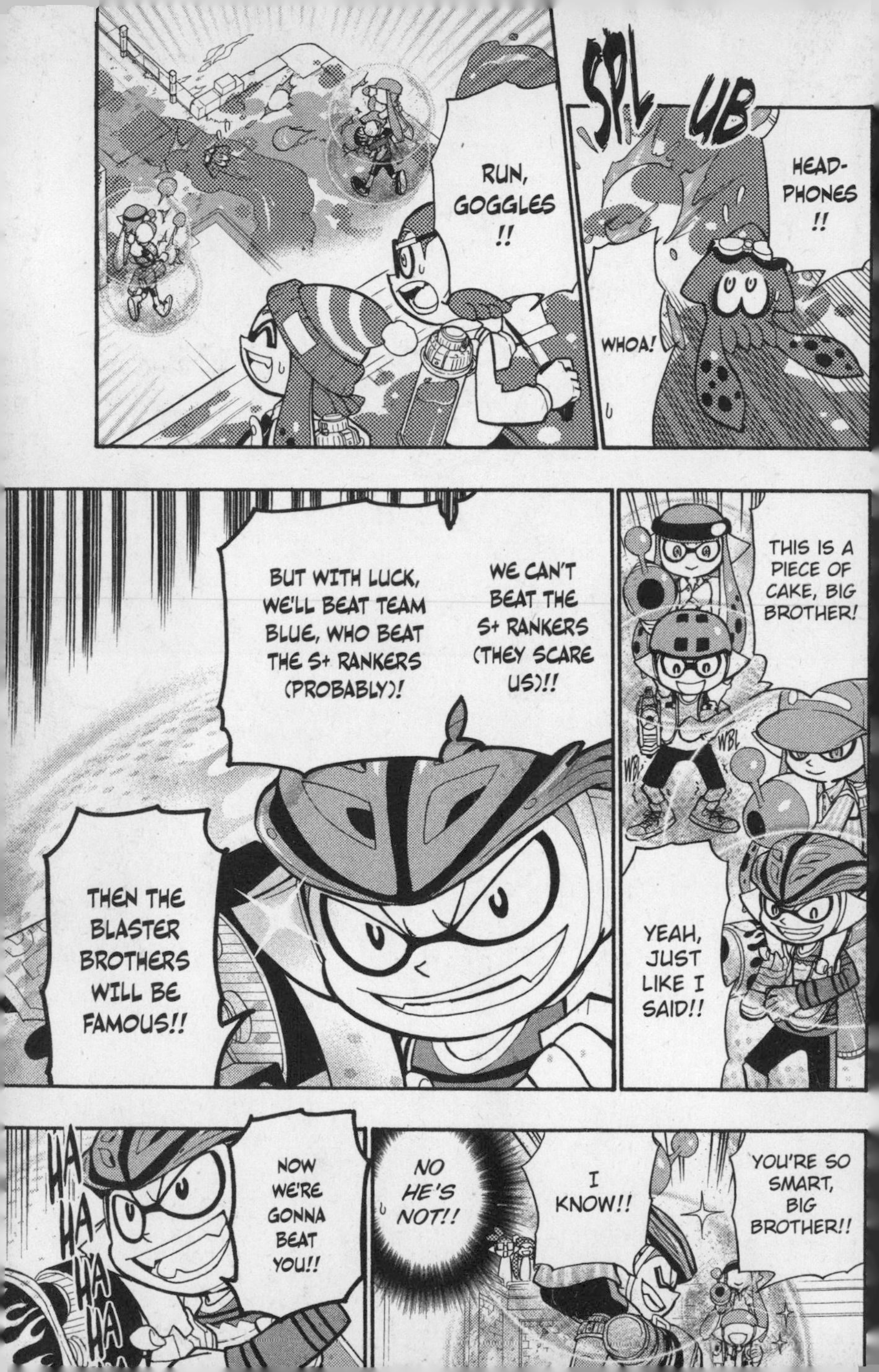
SPLUB
HEAD-PHONES!!
WHOA!
RUN, GOGGLES!!
THIS IS A PIECE OF CAKE, BIG BROTHER!
WBL
WBL
YEAH, JUST LIKE I SAID!!
WE CAN'T BEAT THE S+ RANKERS (THEY SCARE US)!!
BUT WITH LUCK, WE'LL BEAT TEAM BLUE, WHO BEAT THE S+ RANKERS (PROBABLY)!
THEN THE BLASTER BROTHERS WILL BE FAMOUS!!
YOU'RE SO SMART, BIG BROTHER!!
I KNOW!!
NO HE'S NOT!!
NOW WE'RE GONNA BEAT YOU!!
HA HA HA HA HA

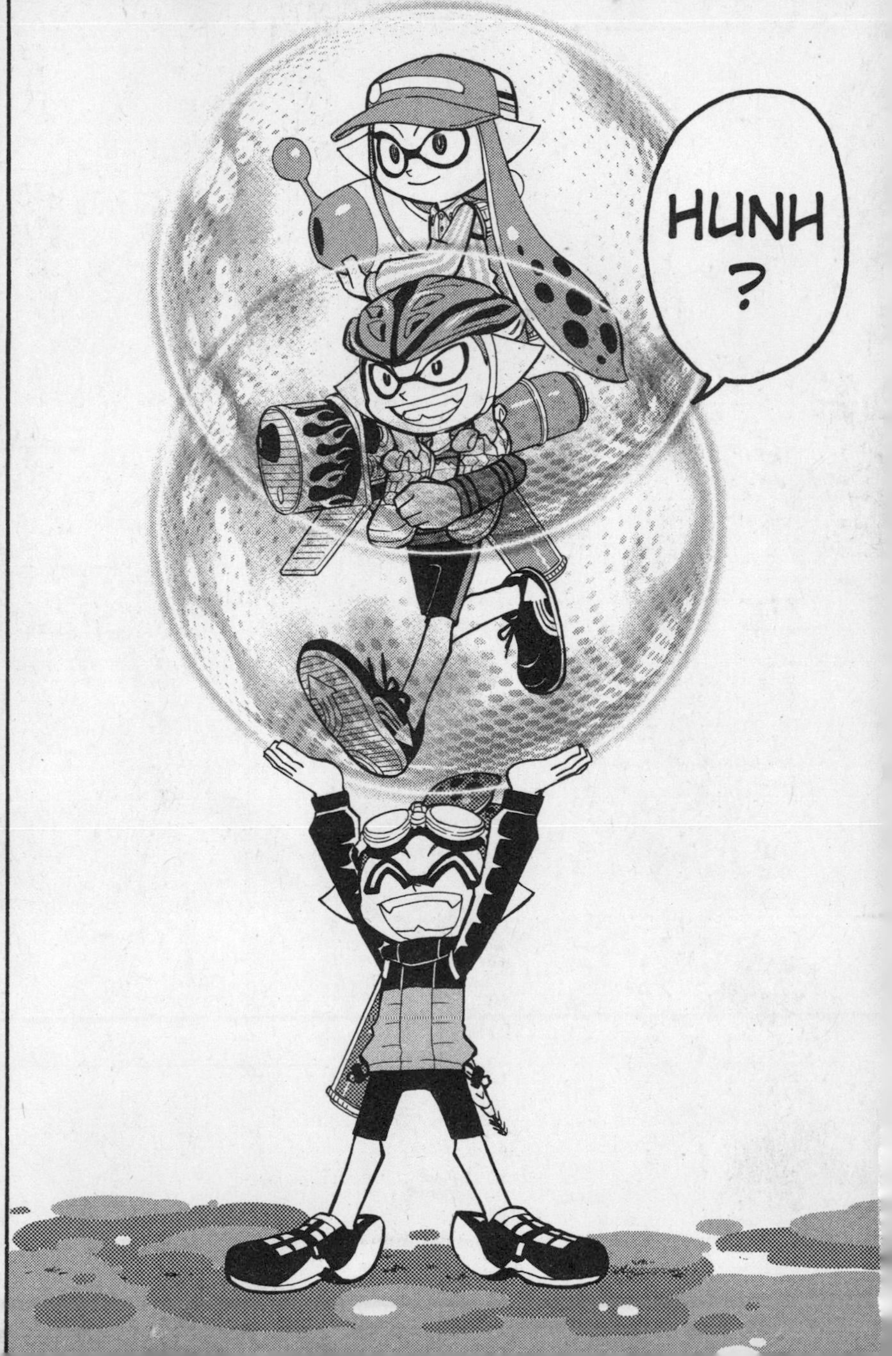
HUNH?

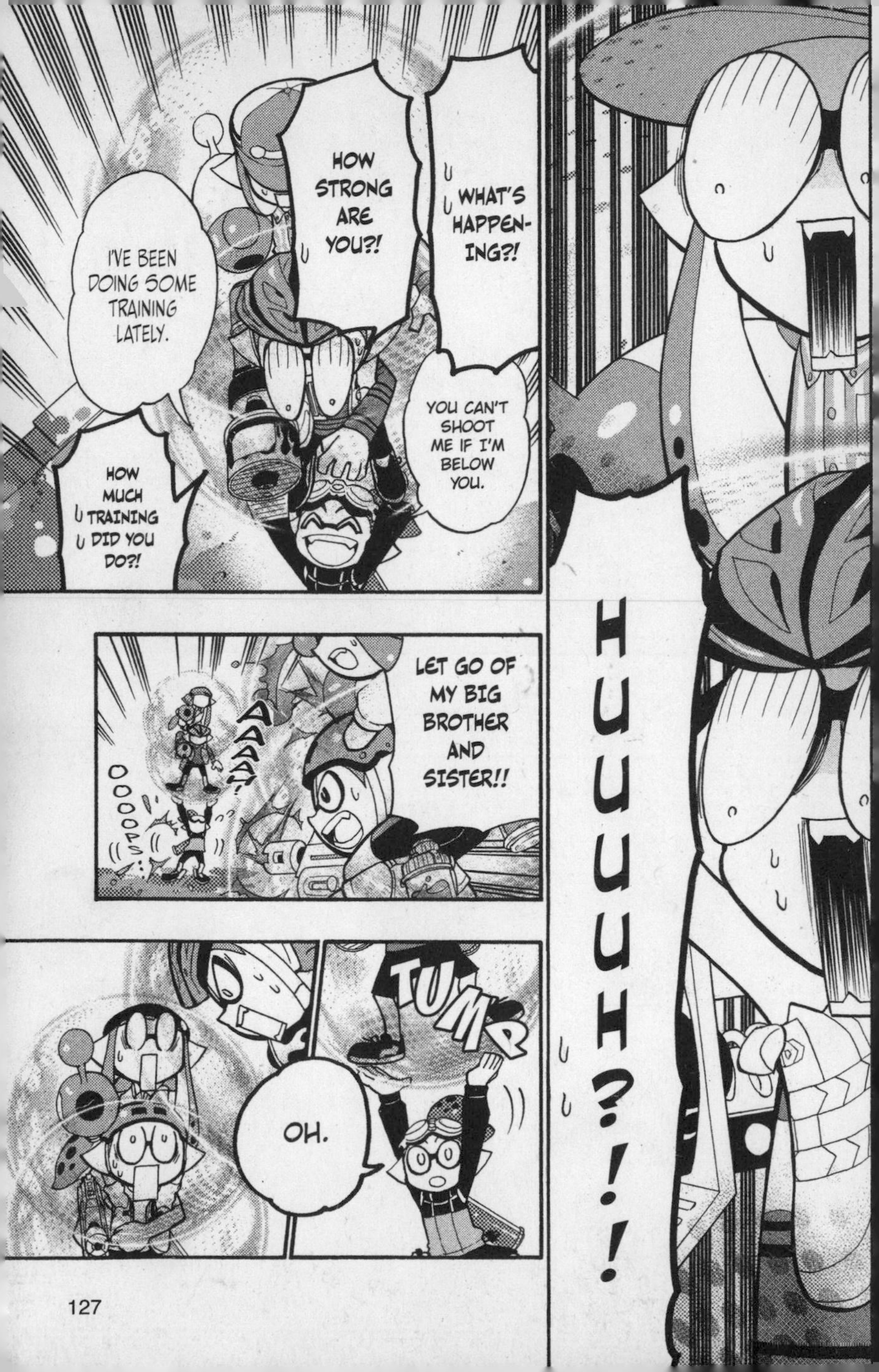
HUUUUH?!!
WHAT'S HAPPEN-ING?!
HOW STRONG ARE YOU?!
I'VE BEEN DOING SOME TRAINING LATELY.
YOU CAN'T SHOOT ME IF I'M BELOW YOU.
HOW MUCH TRAINING DID YOU DO?!
LET GO OF MY BIG BROTHER AND SISTER!!
AAAA!
OOOOOPS...
TUMP
OH.

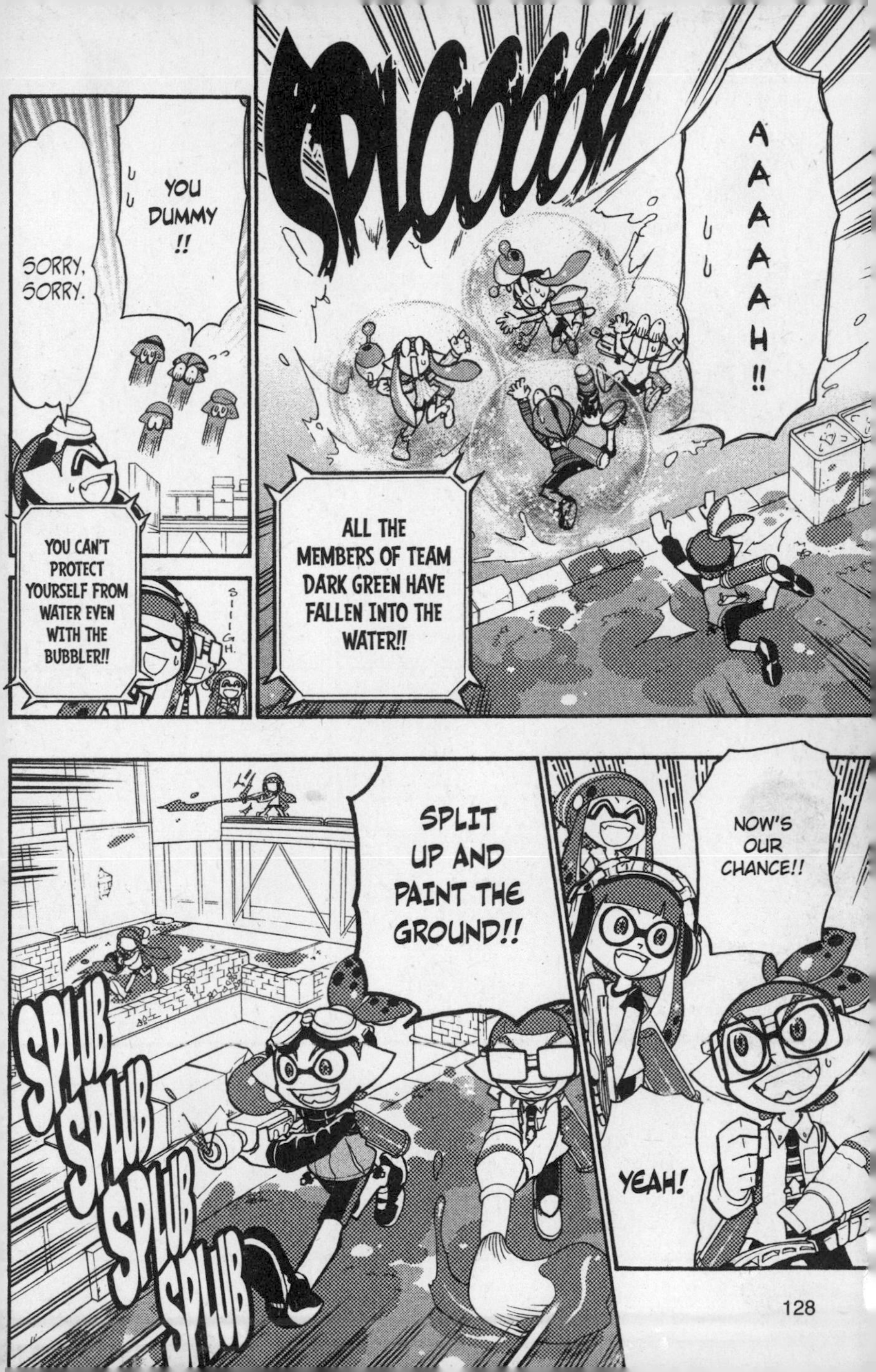
AAAAAH!!
SPLOOOSH
ALL THE MEMBERS OF TEAM DARK GREEN HAVE FALLEN INTO THE WATER!!
YOU DUMMY!!
SORRY, SORRY.
YOU CAN'T PROTECT YOURSELF FROM WATER EVEN WITH THE BUBBLER!!
SIIIGH.
NOW'S OUR CHANCE!!
YEAH!
SPLIT UP AND PAINT THE GROUND!!
SPLUB SPLUB SPLUB SPLUB SPLUB

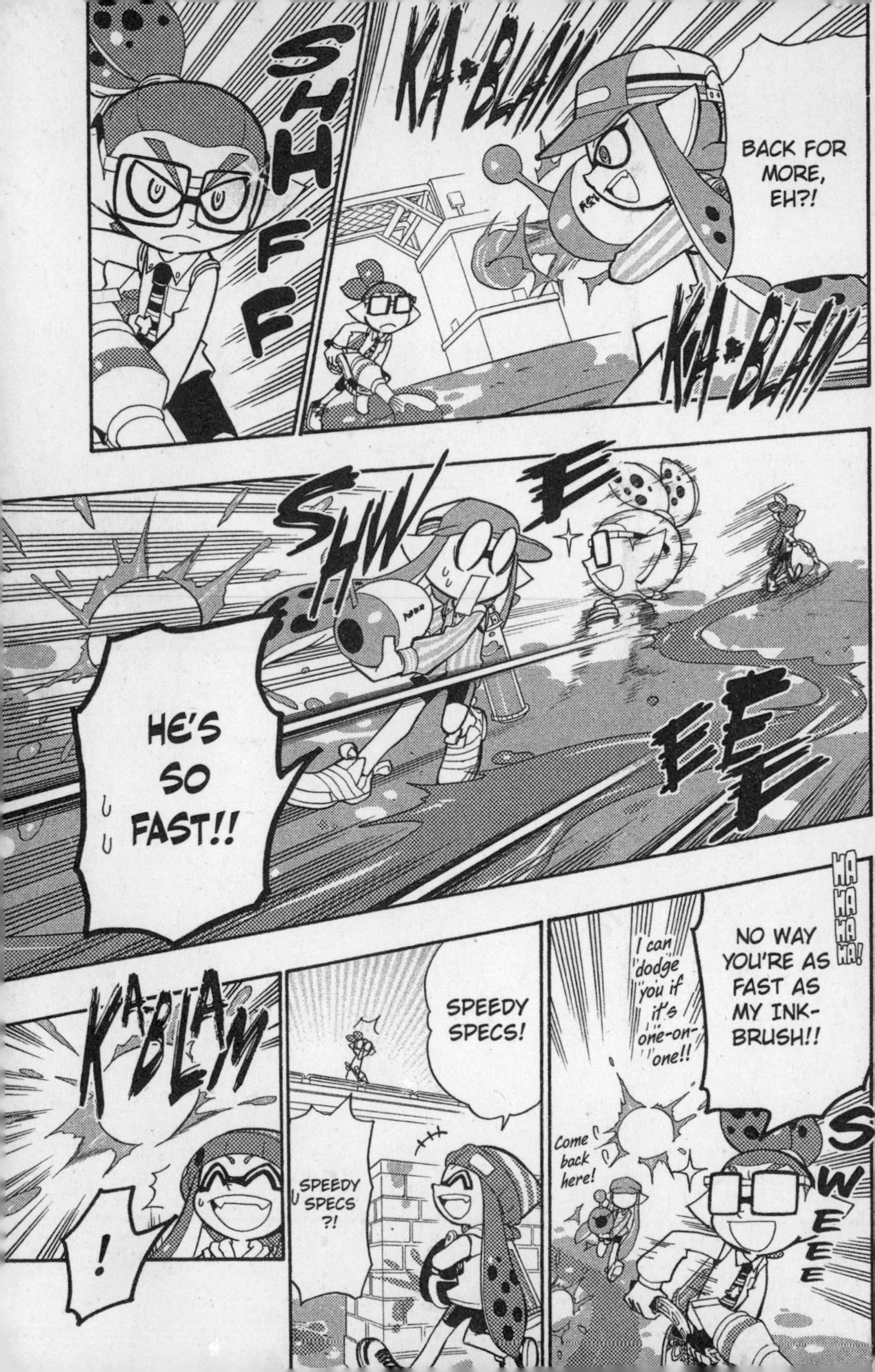
KA-BLAM
BACK FOR MORE, EH?!
KA-BLAM
SHHFFF
SHWEEEE
HE'S SO FAST!!
HAHAHAHAHA!
NO WAY YOU'RE AS FAST AS MY INK-BRUSH!!
I can dodge you if it's one-on-one!!
Come back here!
SWEEEE
SPEEDY SPECS!
SPEEDY SPECS?!
KA-BLAM
!

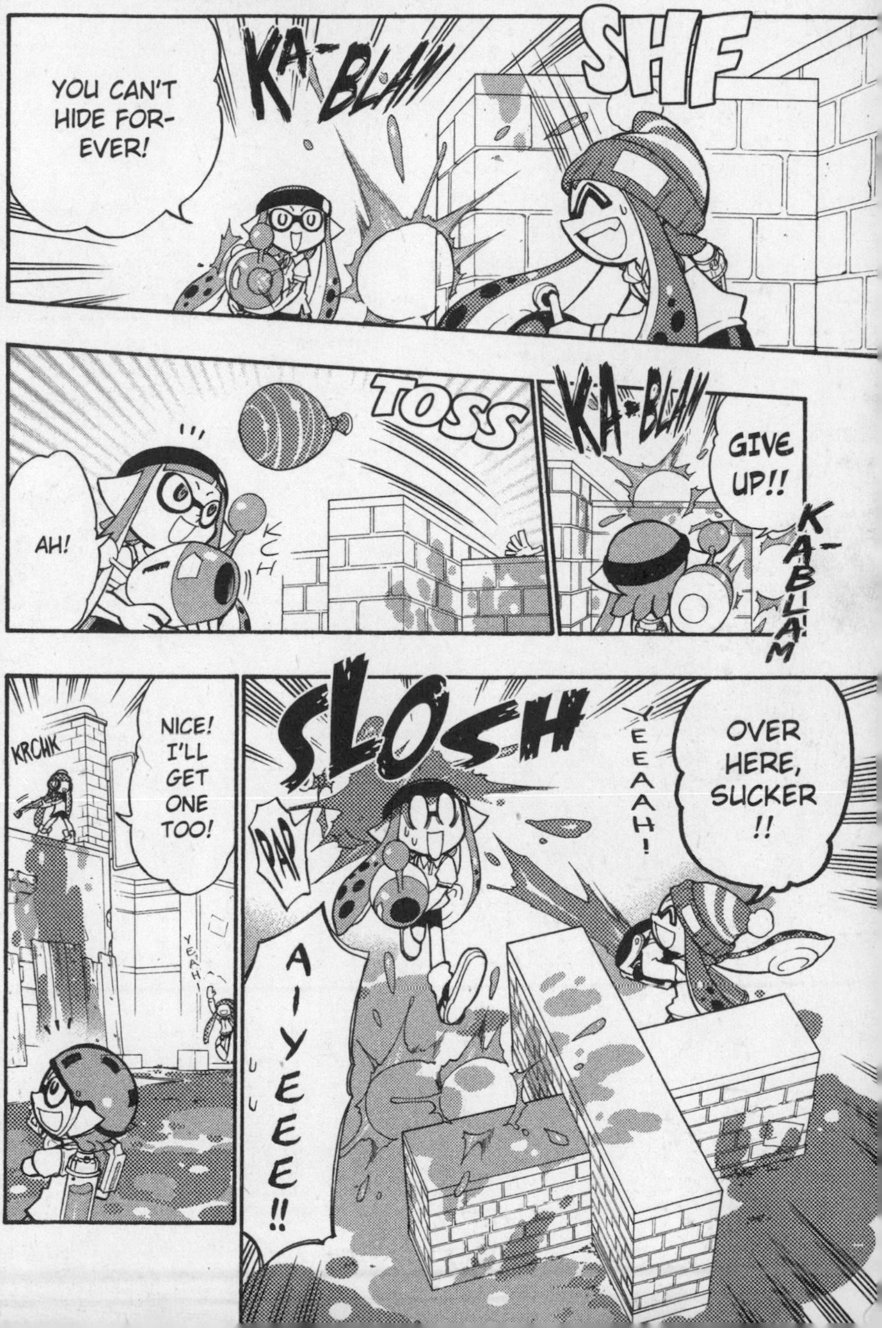
SHF
KA-BLAM
YOU CAN'T HIDE FOR-EVER!
KA-BLAM
GIVE UP!!
KA-BLAM
TOSS
AH!
KCH
OVER HERE, SUCKER!!
YEEEAAAH!
SLOSH
PAP
AIYEEEE!!
NICE! I'LL GET ONE TOO!
KRCHK
YEAH!

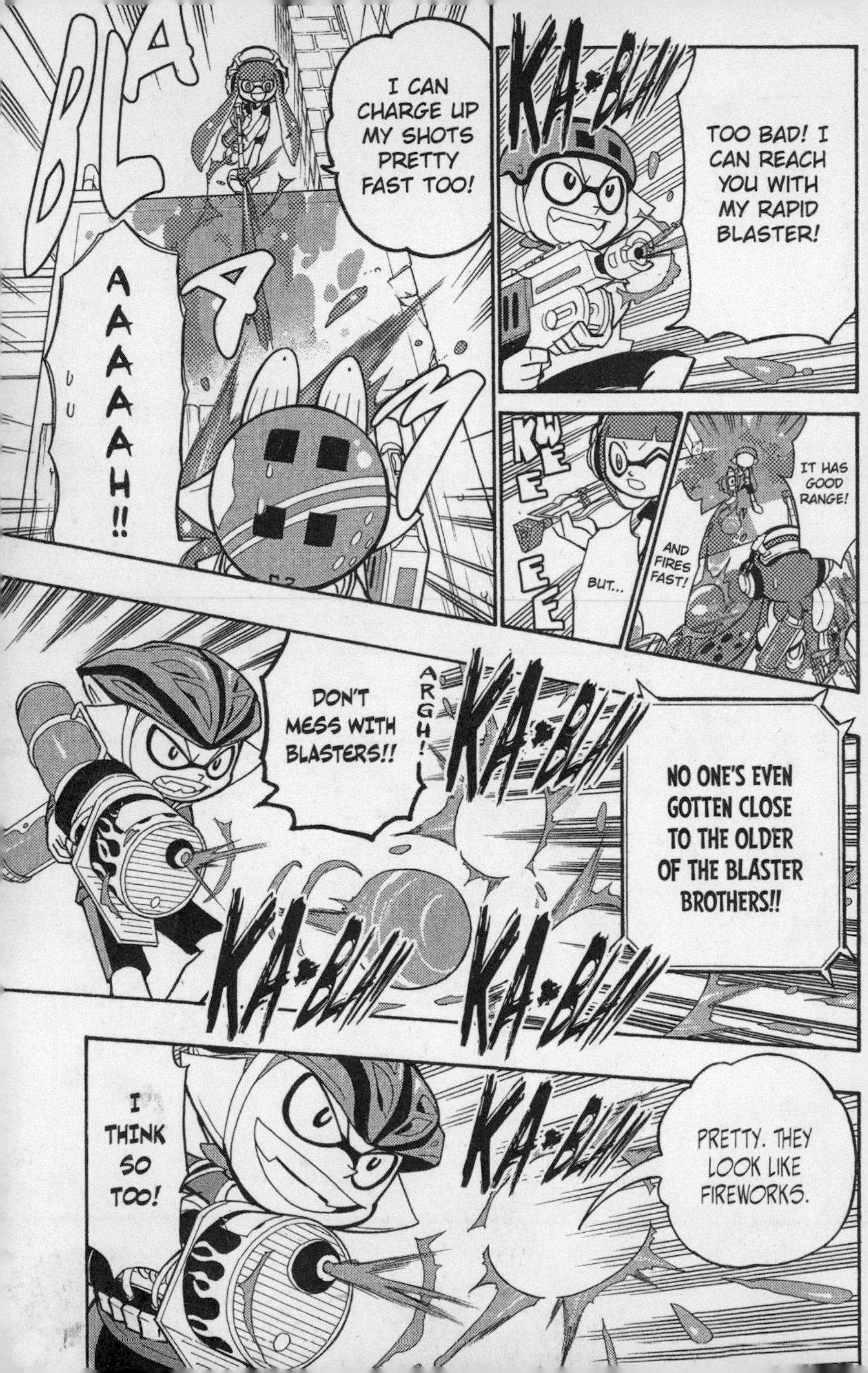
KA-BLAM
TOO BAD! I CAN REACH YOU WITH MY RAPID BLASTER!
IT HAS GOOD RANGE!
AND FIRES FAST!
KWEEEEE
BUT...
BLAM
I CAN CHARGE UP MY SHOTS PRETTY FAST TOO!
AAAAAAH!!
KA-BLAM
NO ONE'S EVEN GOTTEN CLOSE TO THE OLDER OF THE BLASTER BROTHERS!!
ARGH!
DON'T MESS WITH BLASTERS!!
KA-BLAM
KA-BLAM
KA-BLAM
PRETTY. THEY LOOK LIKE FIREWORKS.
I THINK SO TOO!

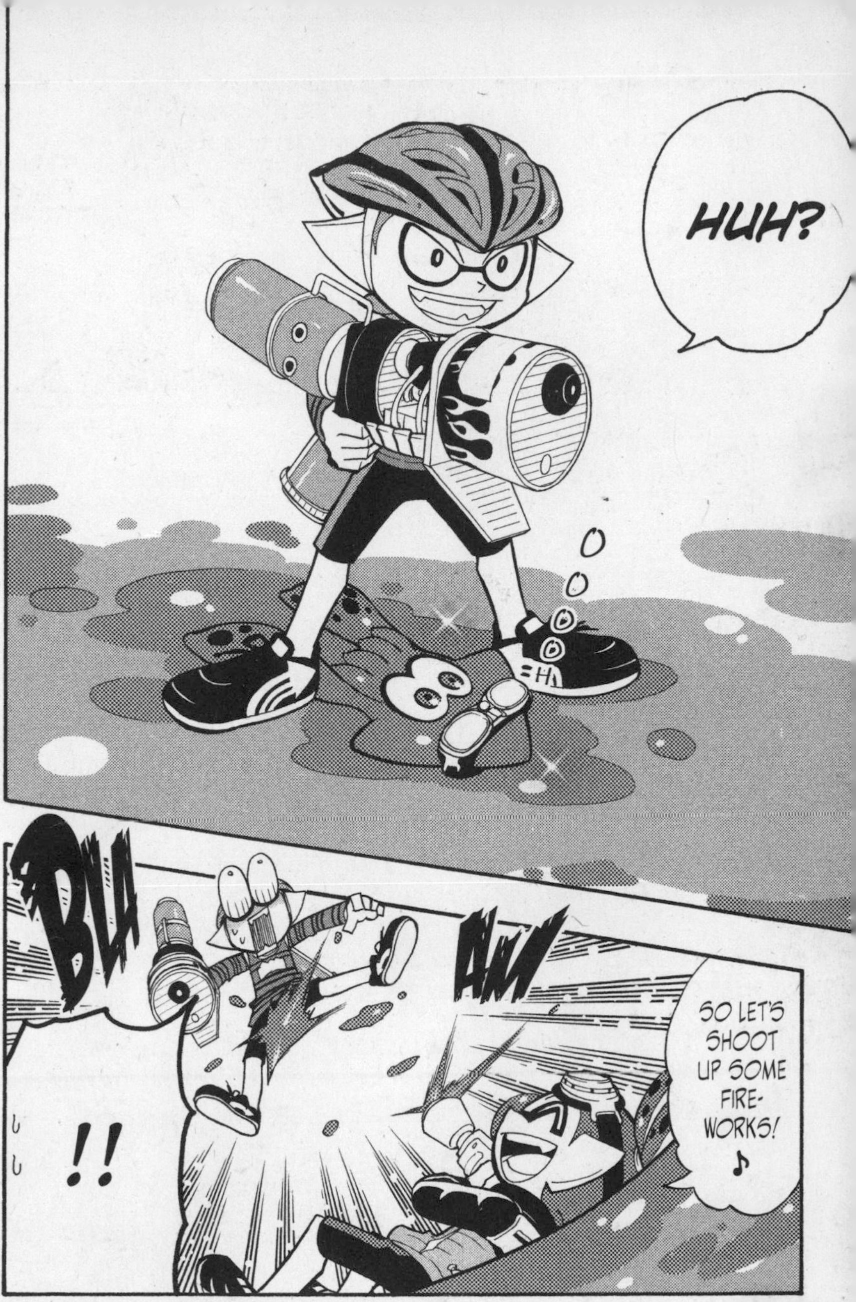
HUH?
SO LET'S SHOOT UP SOME FIRE-WORKS! ♪
BLAAM
!!

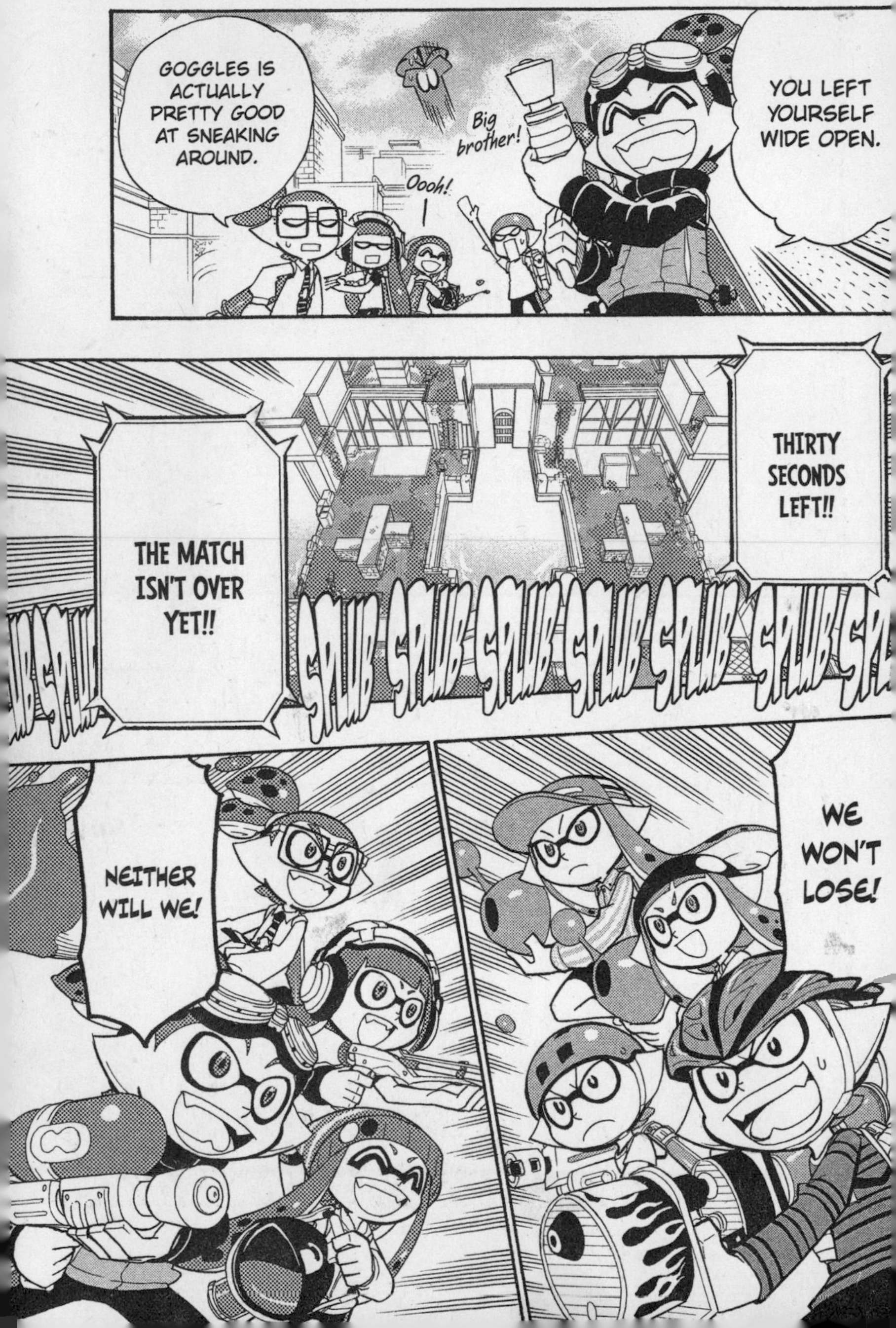
YOU LEFT YOURSELF WIDE OPEN.
Big brother!
Oooh!
GOGGLES IS ACTUALLY PRETTY GOOD AT SNEAKING AROUND.
THIRTY SECONDS LEFT!!
SPLUB SPLUB SPLUB SPLUB SPLUB SPLUB
THE MATCH ISN'T OVER YET!!
WE WON'T LOSE!
NEITHER WILL WE!

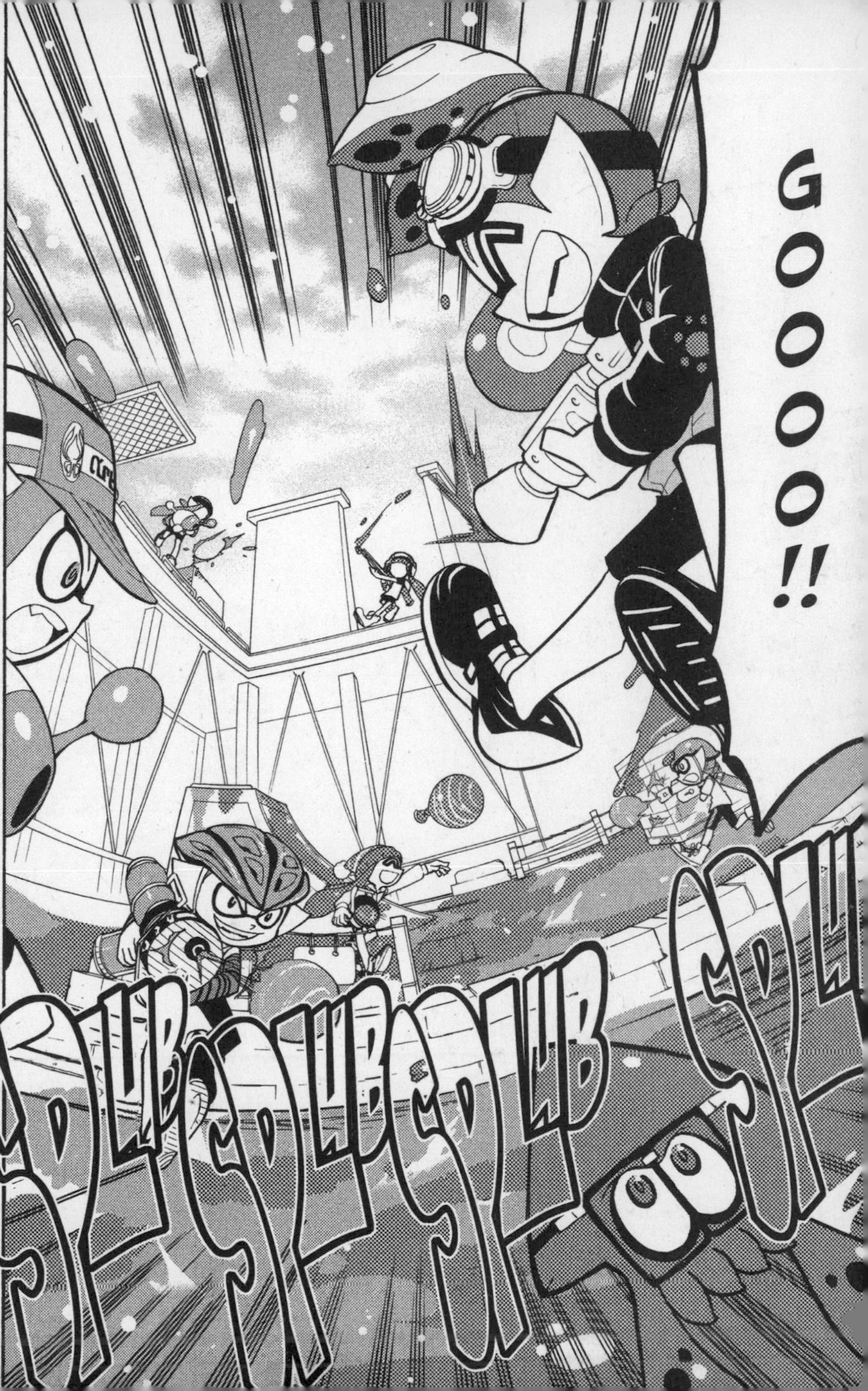
GOOOO!!
SPLUB SPLUB SPLUB SPLU

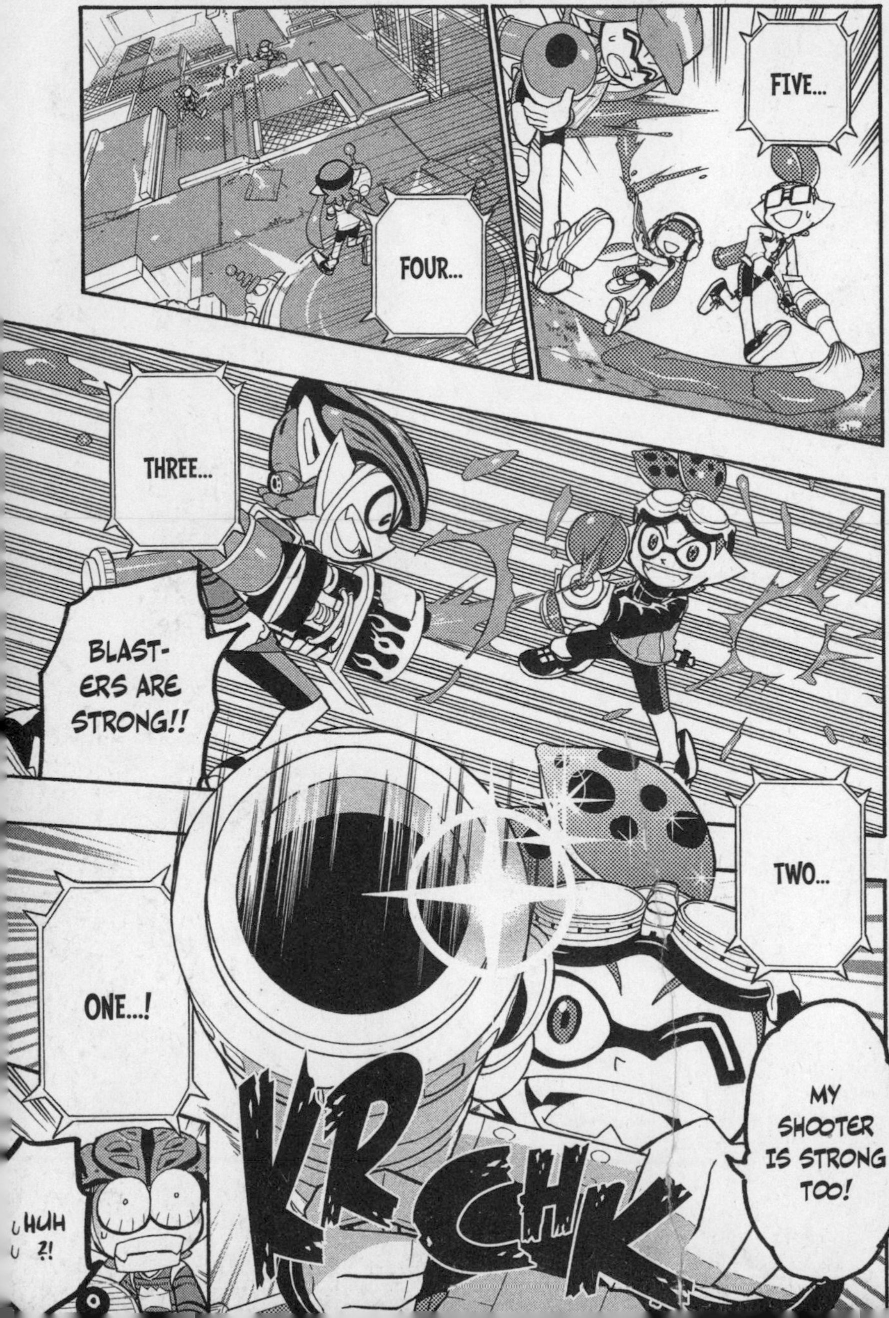
FIVE...
FOUR...
THREE...
BLAST-
ERS ARE
STRONG!!
TWO...
ONE...!
MY
SHOOTER
IS STRONG
TOO!
KRCHK
HUH
?!

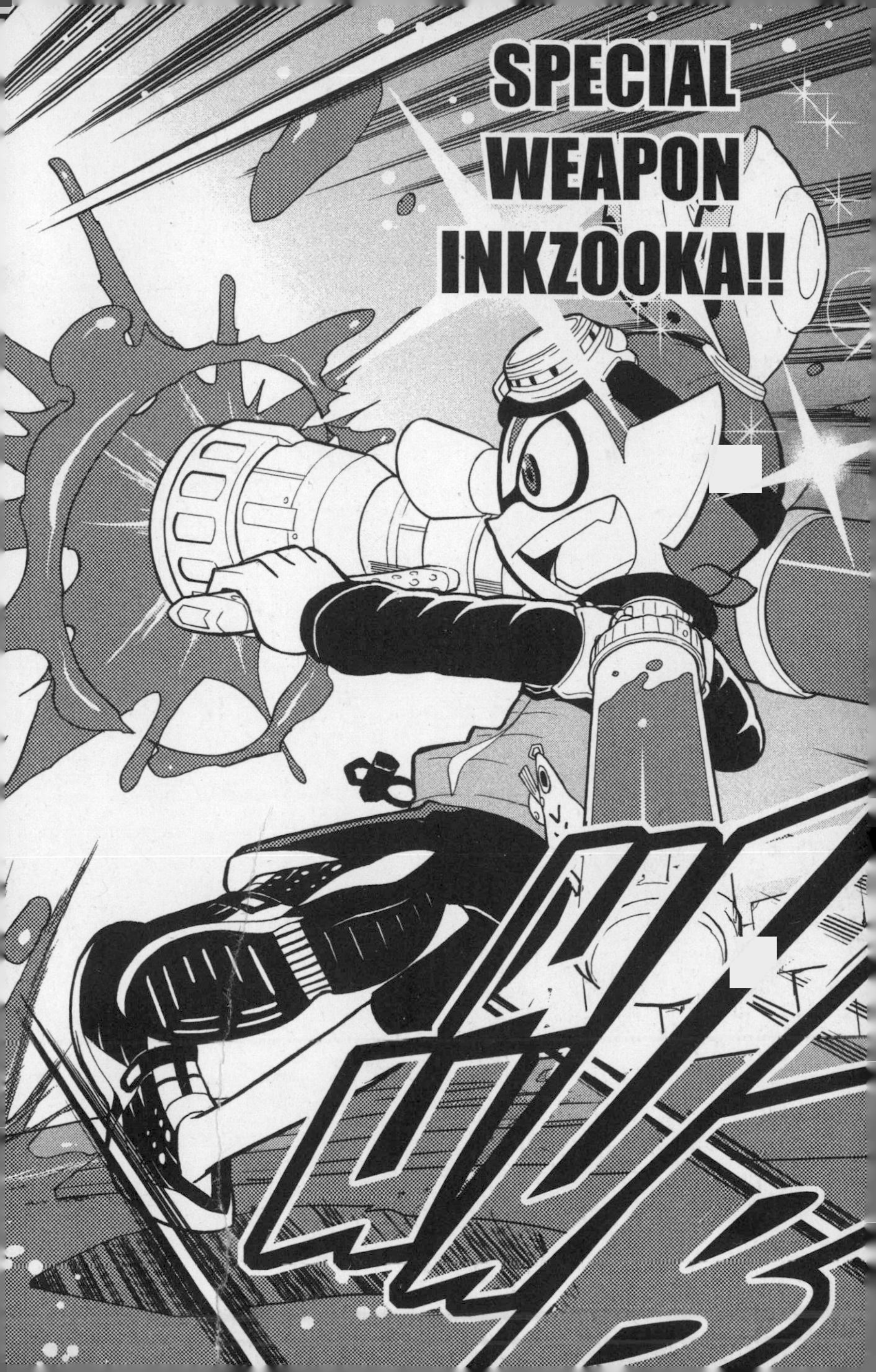
SPECIAL WEAPON INKZOOKA!!

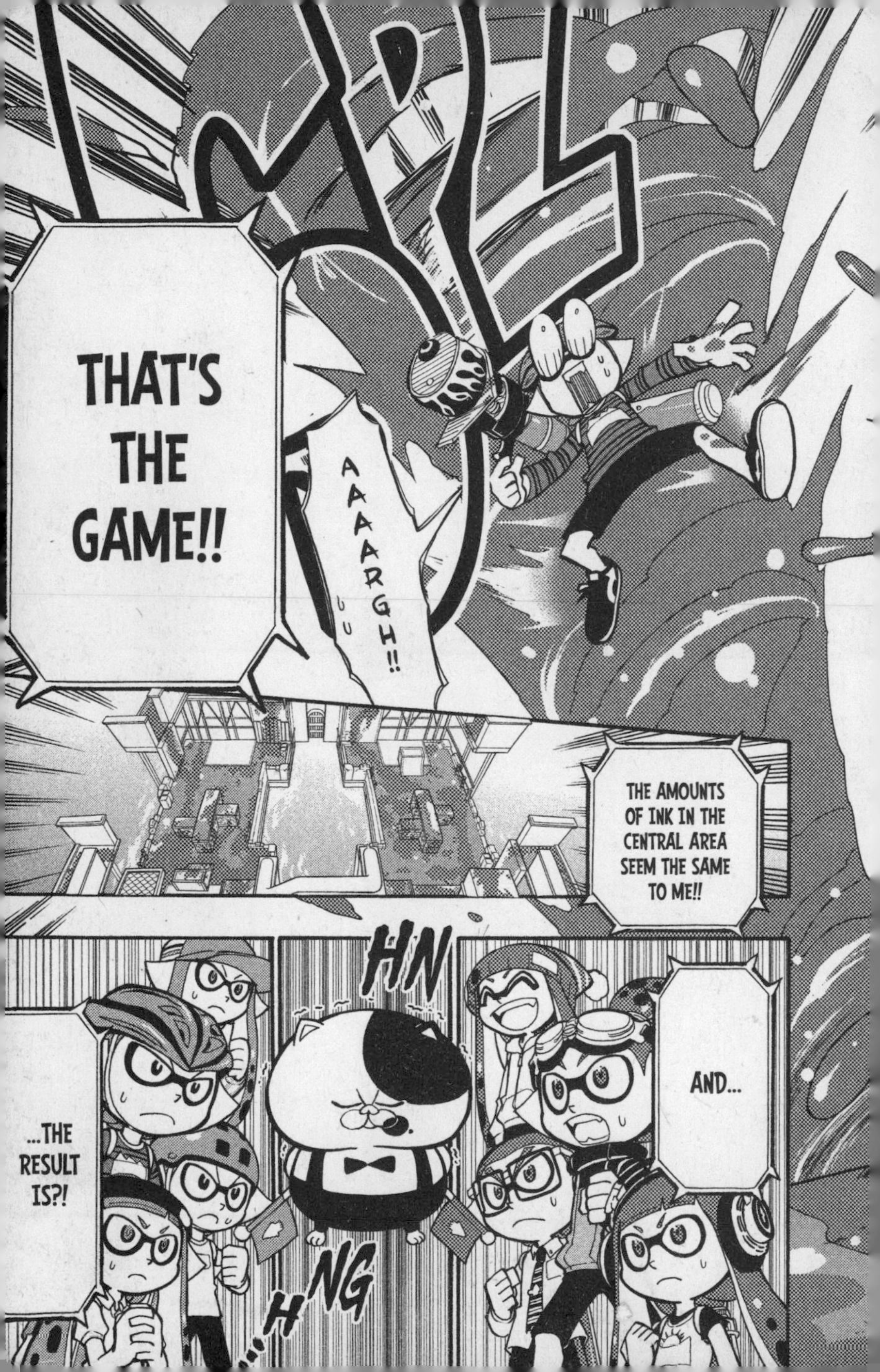
AAAARGH!!
THAT'S THE GAME!!
THE AMOUNTS OF INK IN THE CENTRAL AREA SEEM THE SAME TO ME!!
AND...
HN
HNG
...THE RESULT IS?!

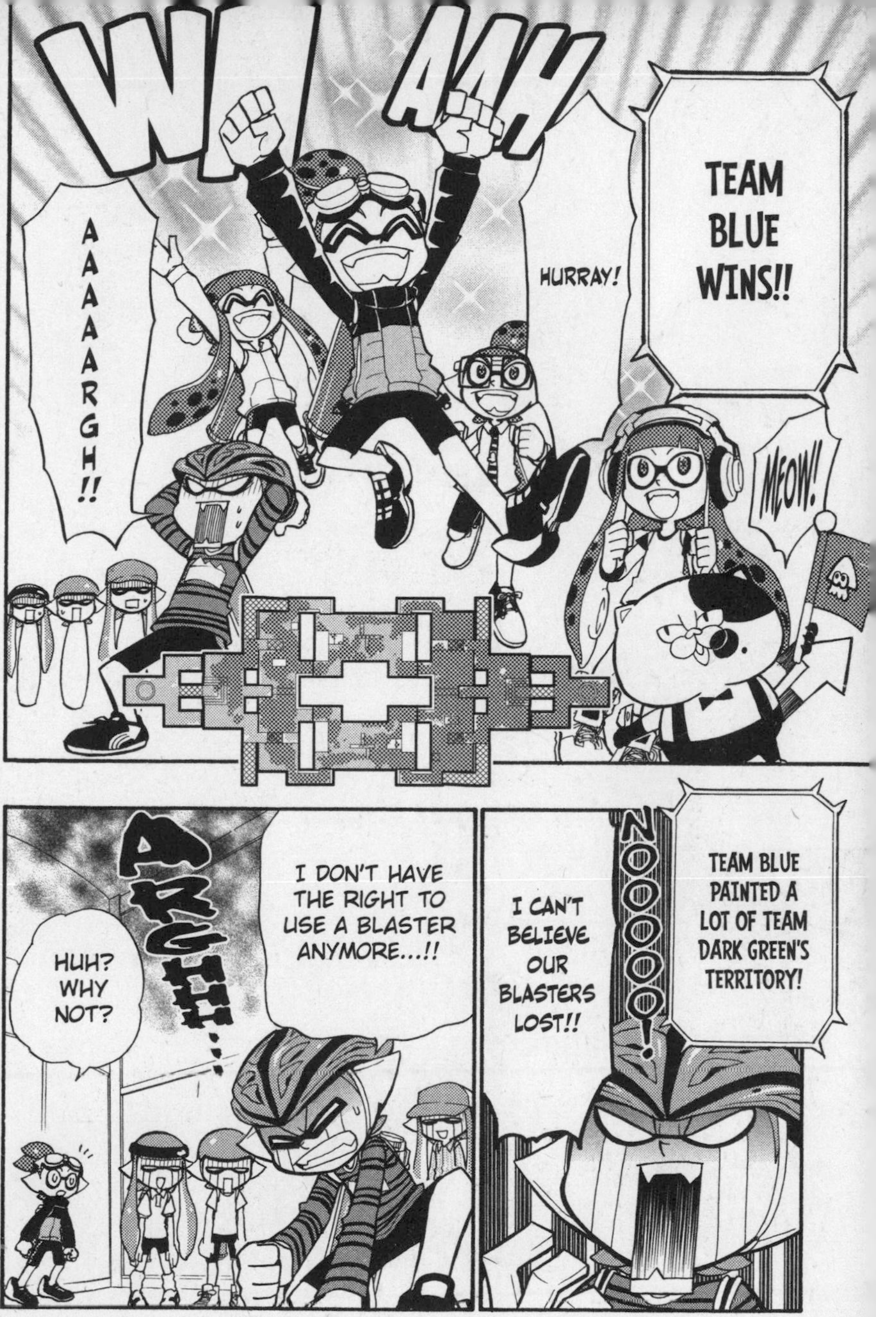
WHAAH
TEAM BLUE WINS!!
HURRAY!
MEOW!
AAAAAAARGH!!
TEAM BLUE PAINTED A LOT OF TEAM DARK GREEN'S TERRITORY!
NOOOOOO!
I CAN'T BELIEVE OUR BLASTERS LOST!!
I DON'T HAVE THE RIGHT TO USE A BLASTER ANYMORE...!!
ARGHHH...
HUH? WHY NOT?

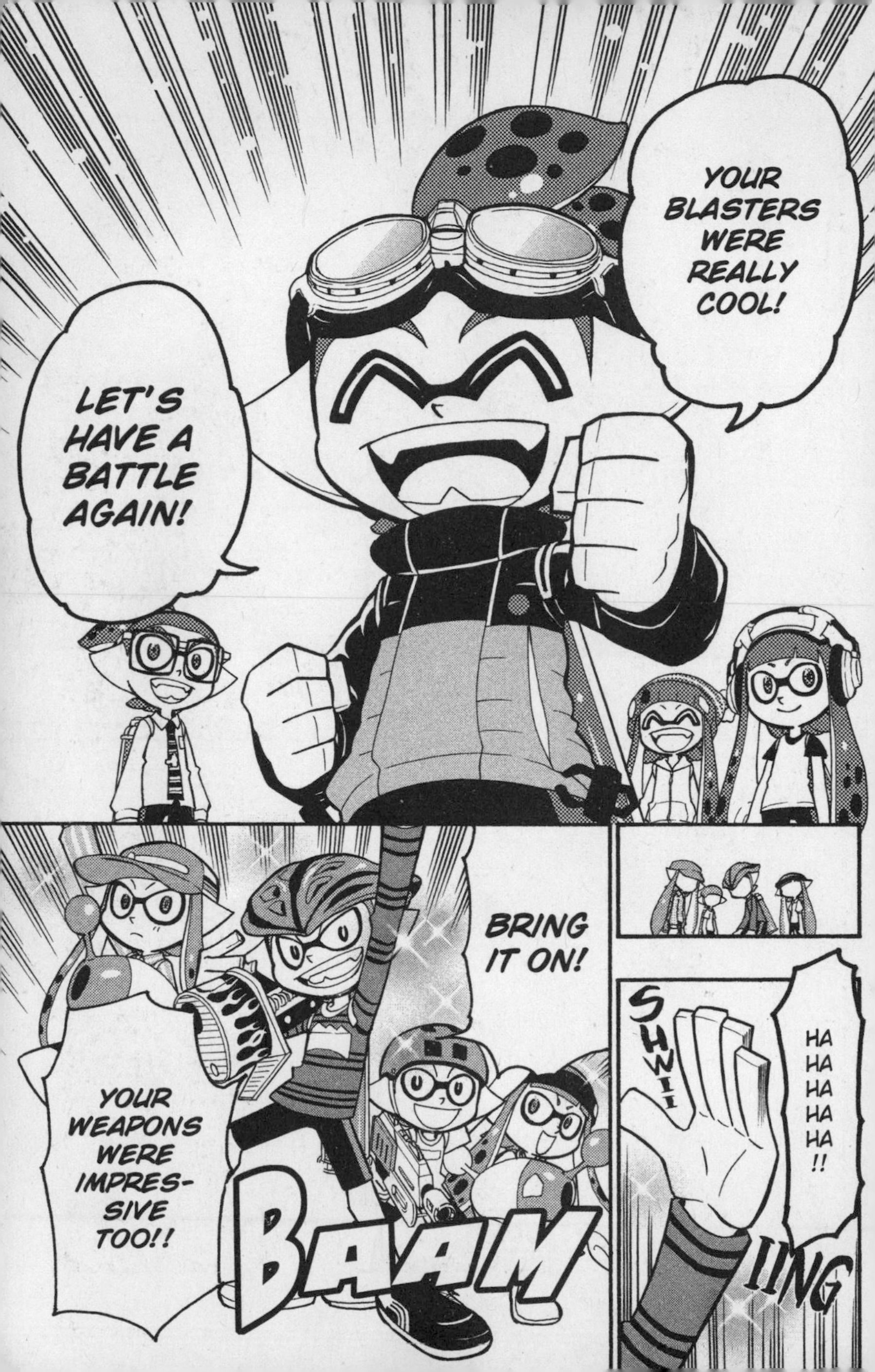
YOUR BLASTERS WERE REALLY COOL!
LET'S HAVE A BATTLE AGAIN!
HA HA HA HA HA!!
SHWII
IING
BRING IT ON!
YOUR WEAPONS WERE IMPRES-SIVE TOO!!
BAAM

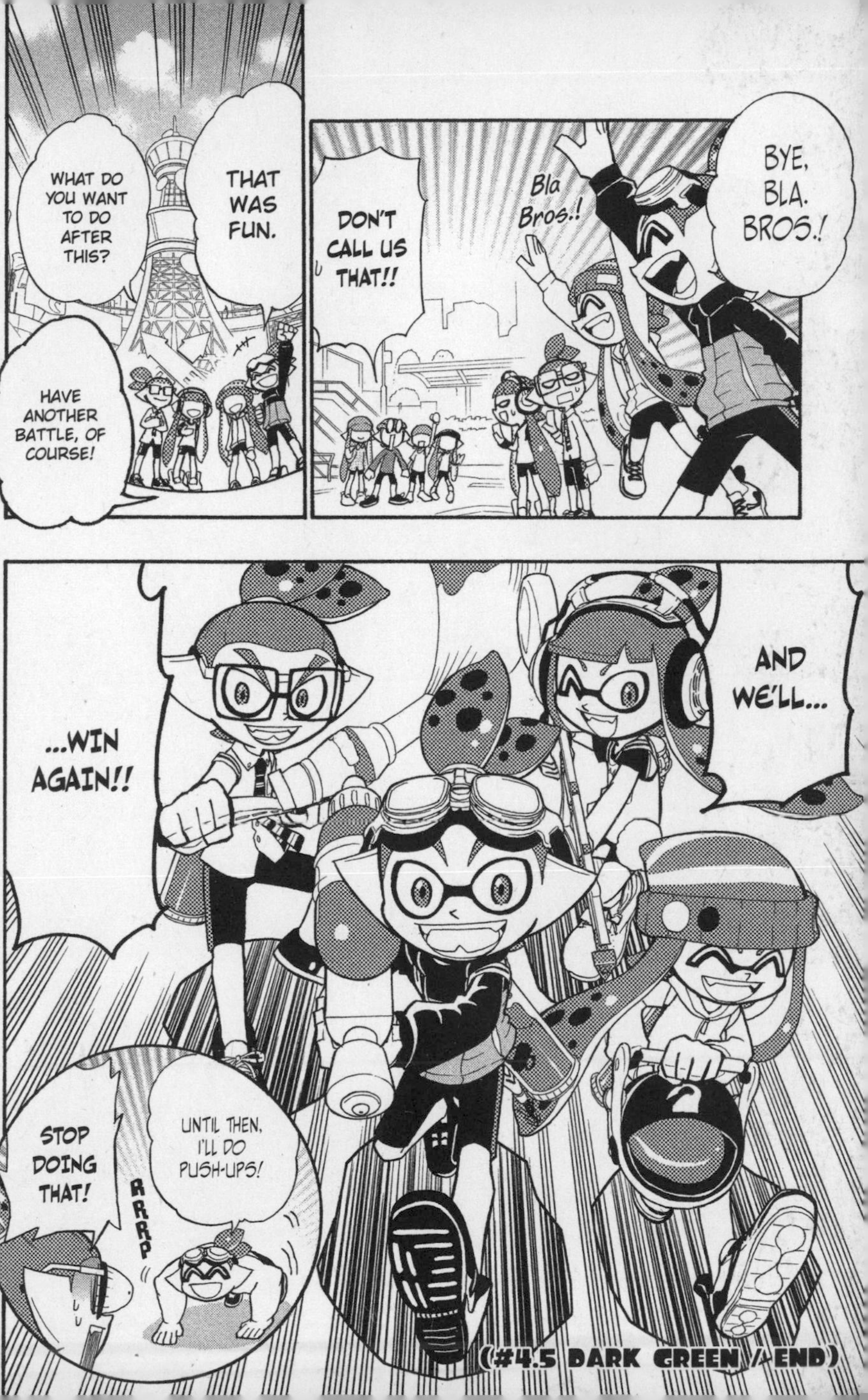
BYE, BLA. BROS.!
Bla Bros.!
DON'T CALL US THAT!!
THAT WAS FUN.
WHAT DO YOU WANT TO DO AFTER THIS?
HAVE ANOTHER BATTLE, OF COURSE!
AND WE'LL...
...WIN AGAIN!!
UNTIL THEN, I'LL DO PUSH-UPS!
RRRP
STOP DOING THAT!
(#4.5 DARK GREEN / END)

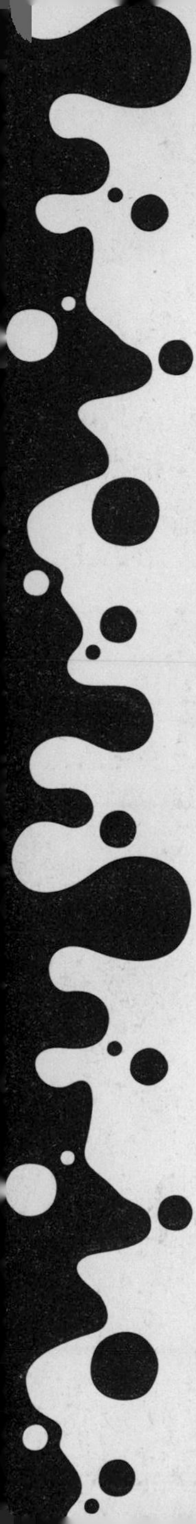

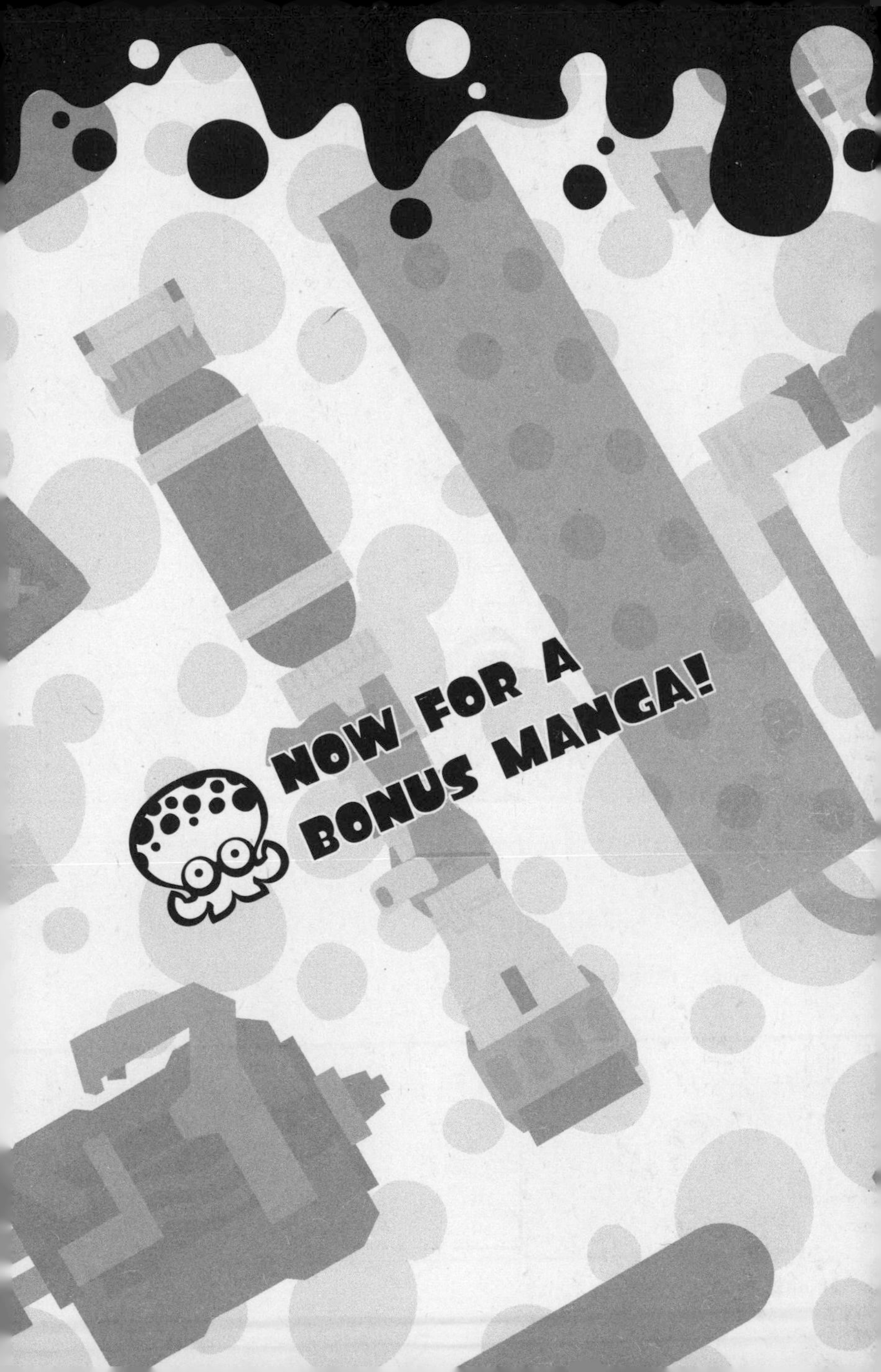
NOW FOR A BONUS MANGA!

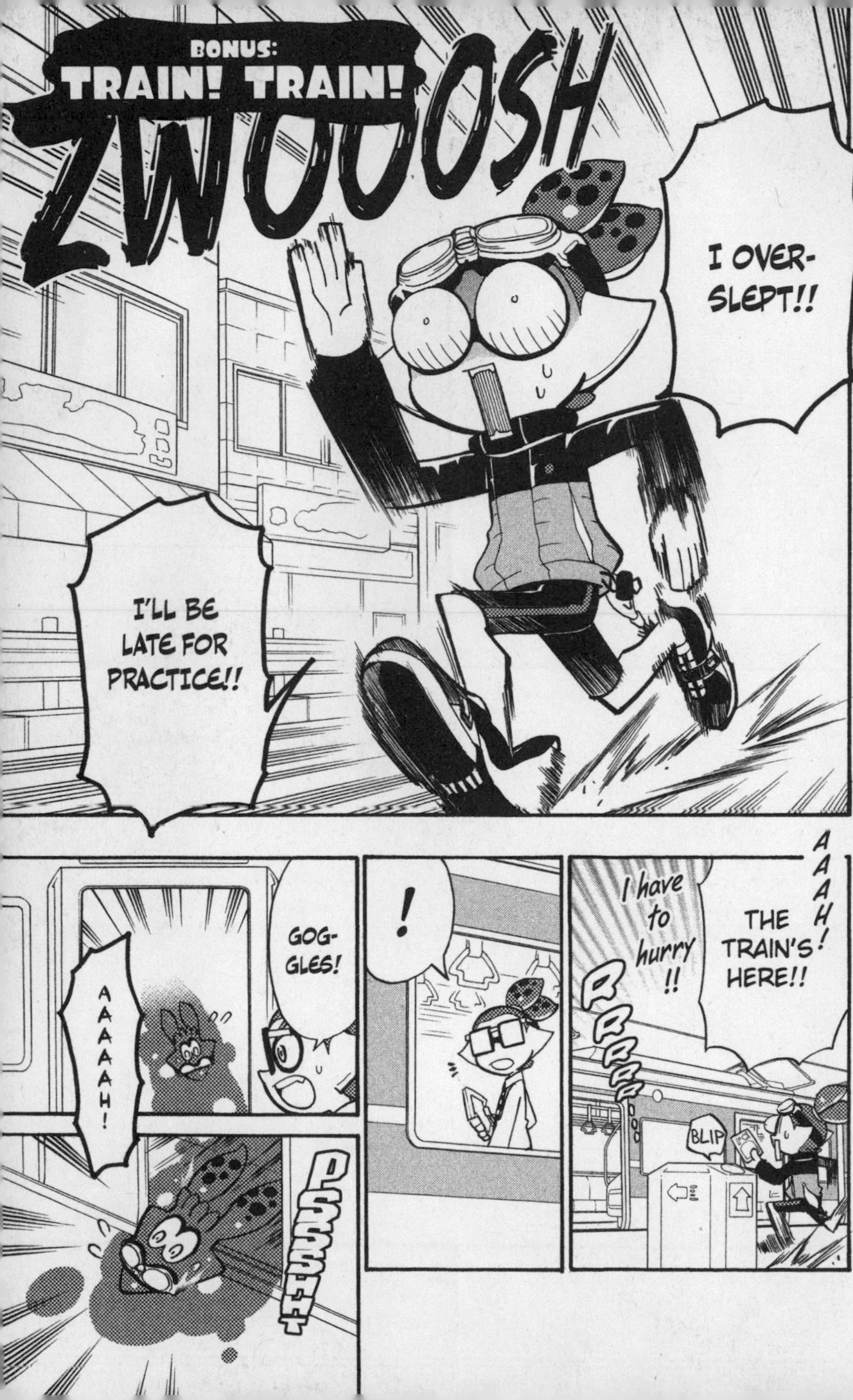
BONUS:
TRAIN! TRAIN!
ZWOOOSH
I OVER-SLEPT!!
I'LL BE LATE FOR PRACTICE!!
AAAAH!
THE TRAIN'S HERE!!
I have to hurry!!
BLIP
!
GOG-GLES!
AAAAAAH!
PSSSHHT

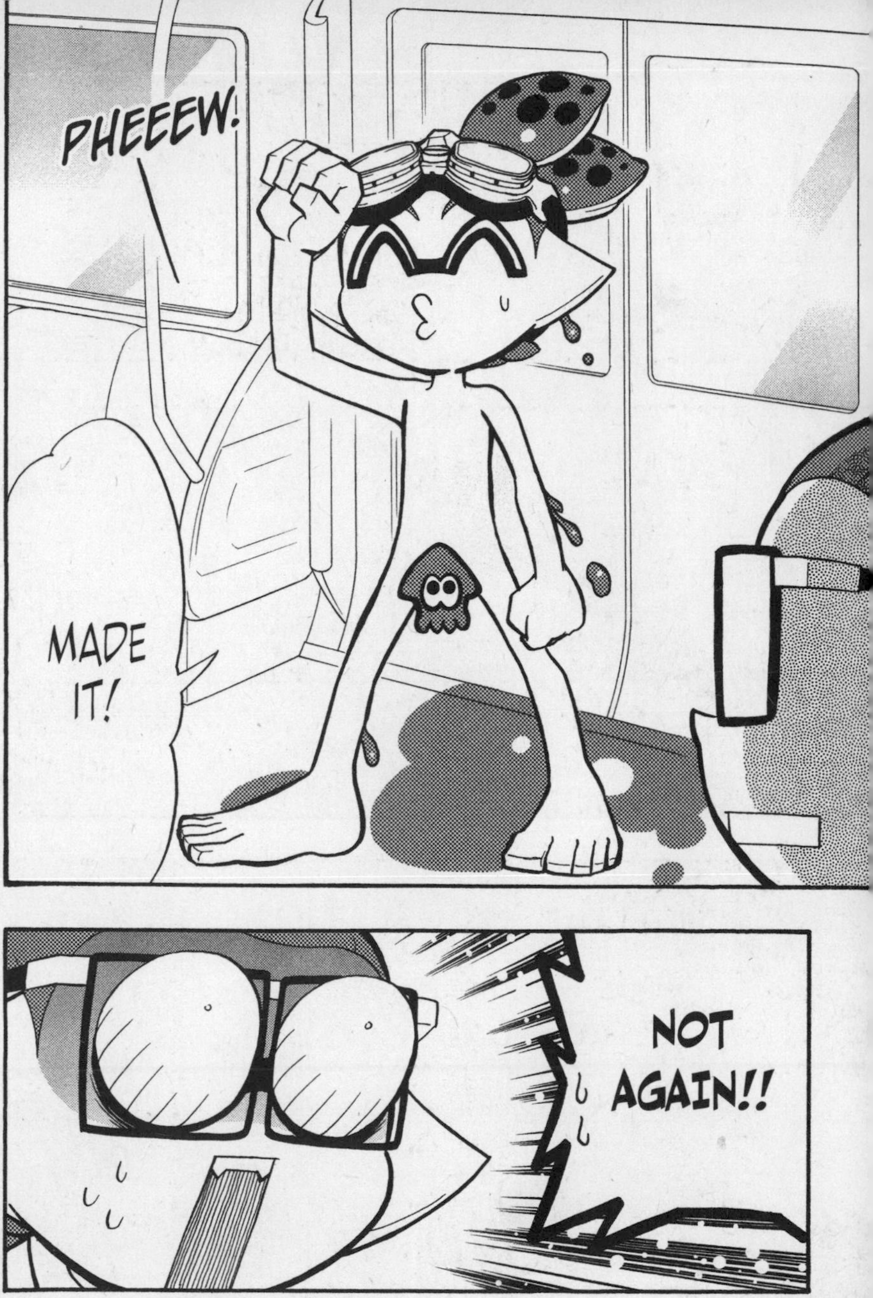
PHEEEW!
MADE IT!
NOT AGAIN!!

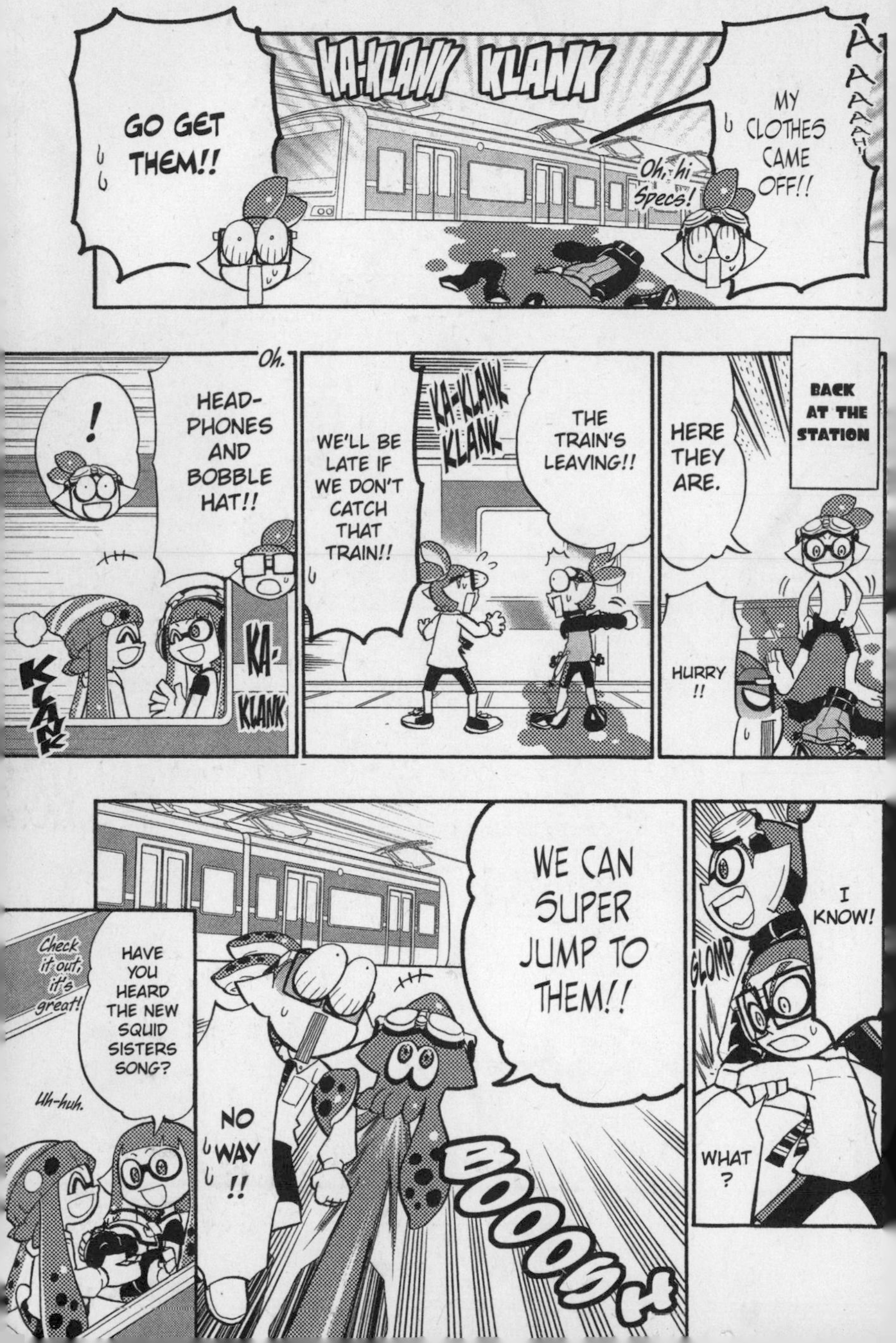
AAAAAH!!
MY CLOTHES CAME OFF!!
KA-KLANK KLANK
Oh, hi Specs!
GO GET THEM!!
BACK AT THE STATION
HERE THEY ARE.
HURRY!!
THE TRAIN'S LEAVING!!
KA-KLANK KLANK
WE'LL BE LATE IF WE DON'T CATCH THAT TRAIN!!
Oh.
HEAD-PHONES AND BOBBLE HAT!!
!
KA-KLANK
KLANK
I KNOW!
GLOMP
WHAT?
WE CAN SUPER JUMP TO THEM!!
NO WAY!!
BOOOOSH
HAVE YOU HEARD THE NEW SQUID SISTERS SONG?
Check it out, it's great!
Uh-huh.

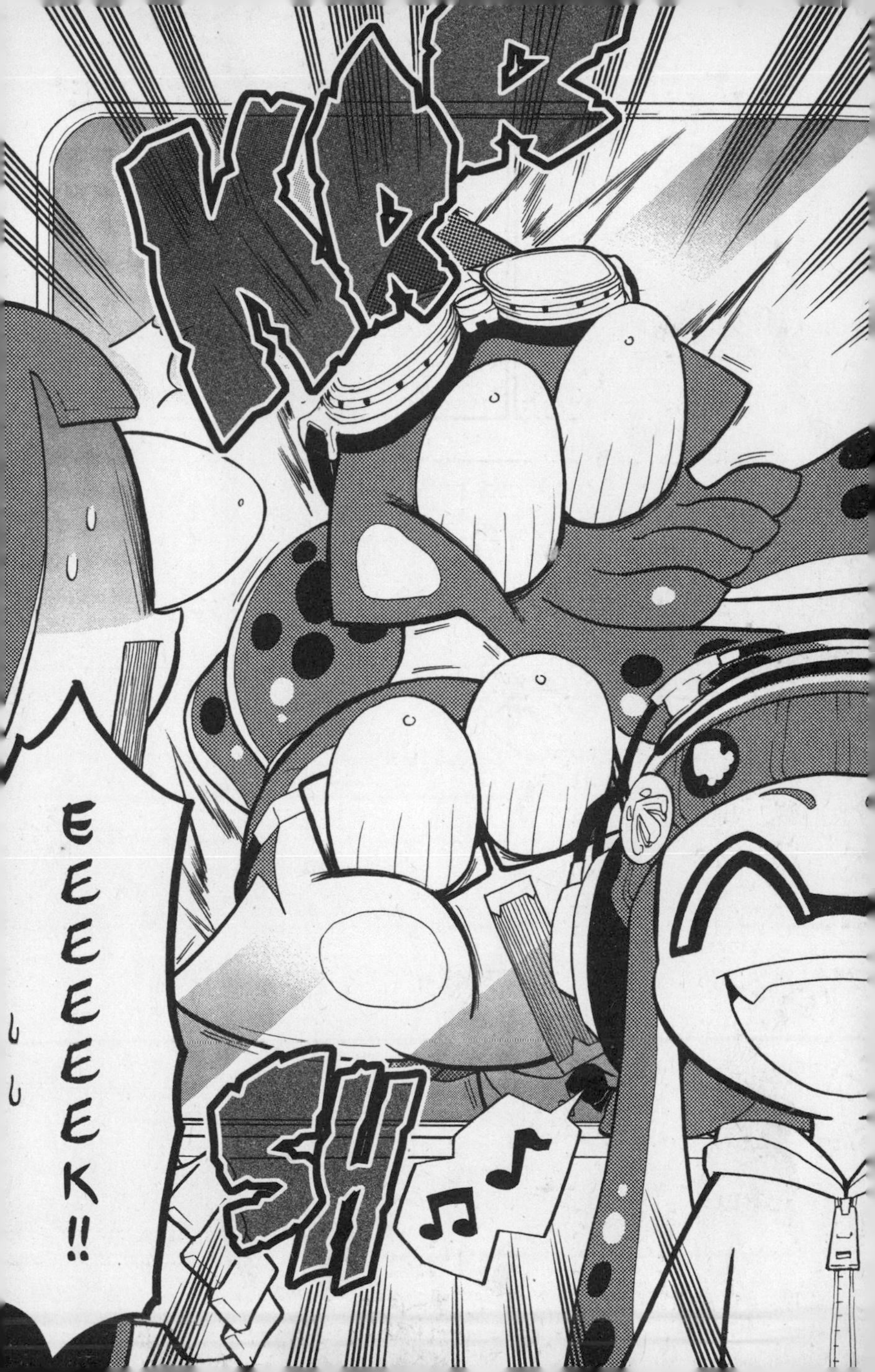
KRA
SH
EEEEEEEK!!

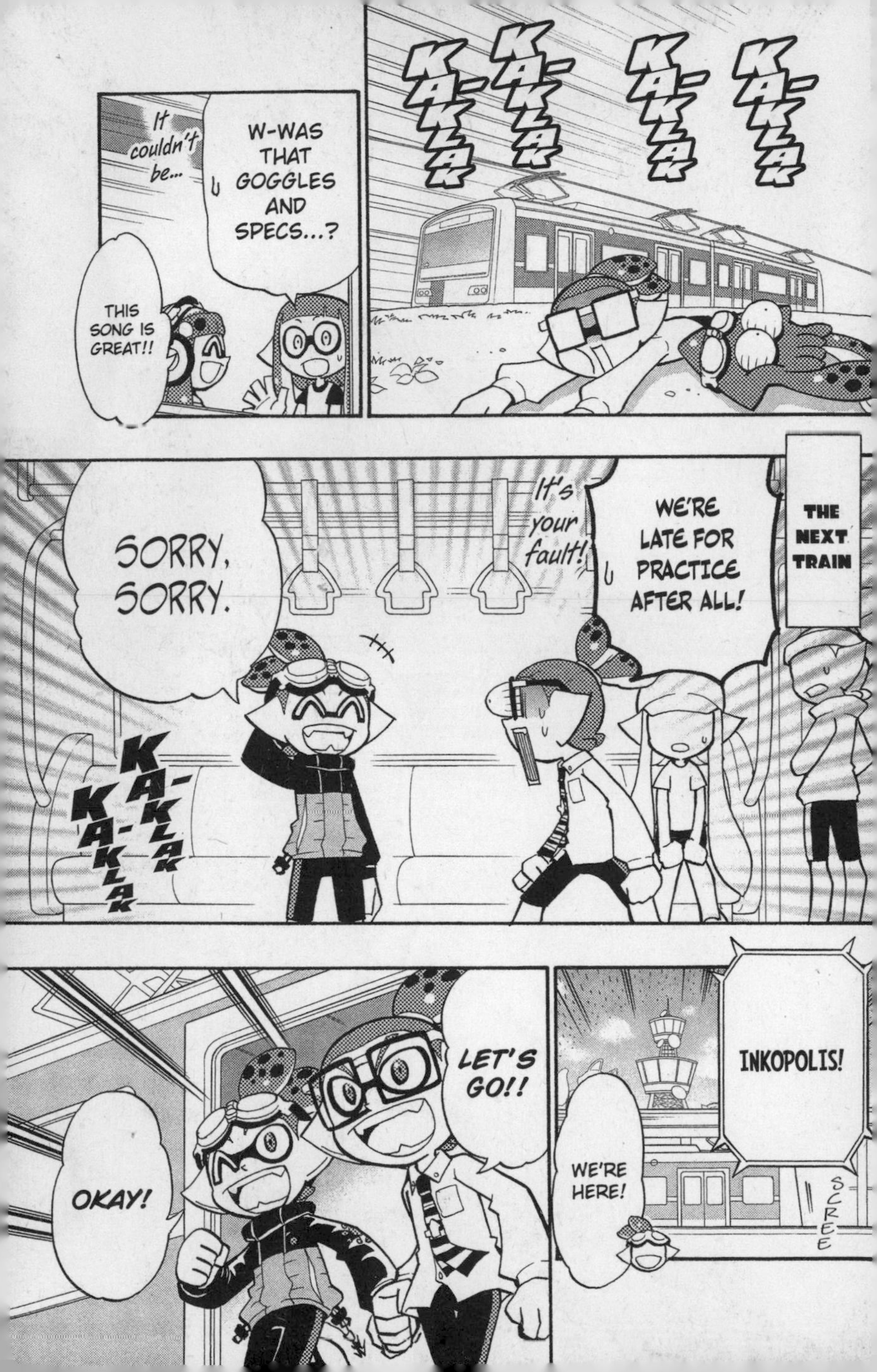

KA-KLAK
KA-KLAK
KA-KLAK
KA-KLAK
W-WAS THAT GOGGLES AND SPECS...?
It couldn't be...
THIS SONG IS GREAT!!
THE NEXT TRAIN
WE'RE LATE FOR PRACTICE AFTER ALL!
It's your fault!
SORRY, SORRY.
KA-KLAK
KA-KLAK
INKOPOLIS!
WE'RE HERE!
SCREE
LET'S GO!!
OKAY!

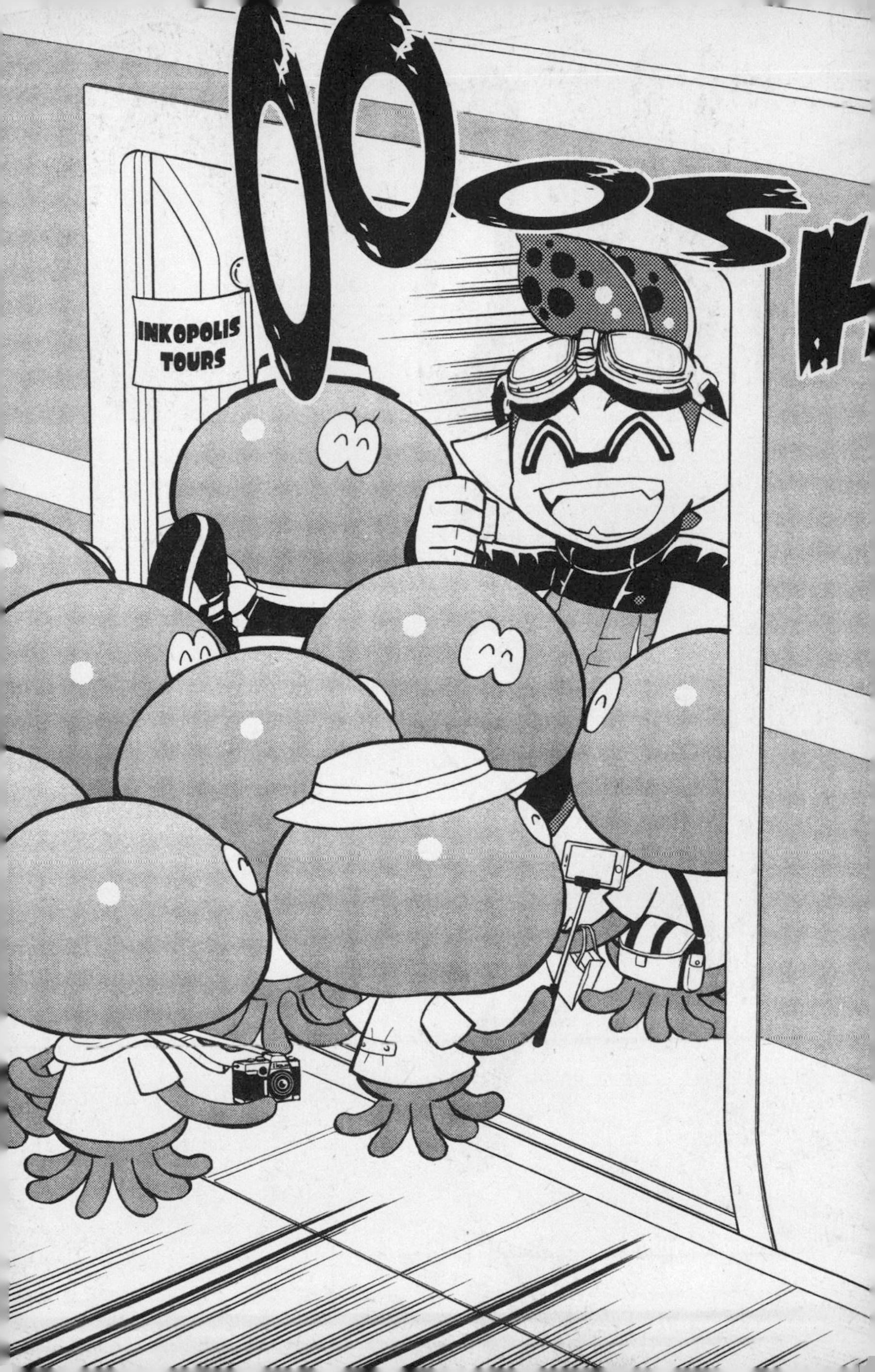
OOOSH
INKOPOLIS TOURS

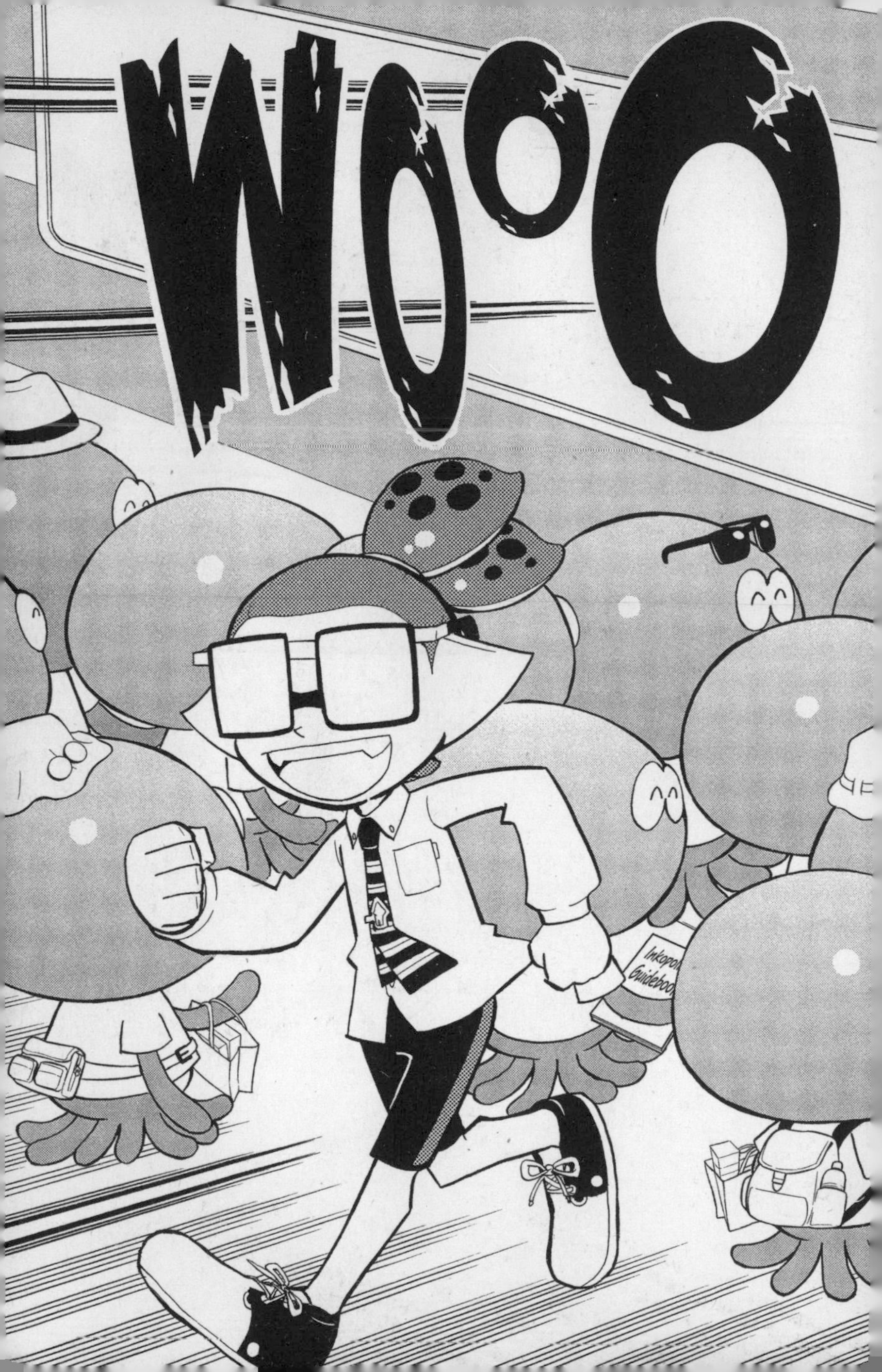
WOOO
Inkopolis Guidebook

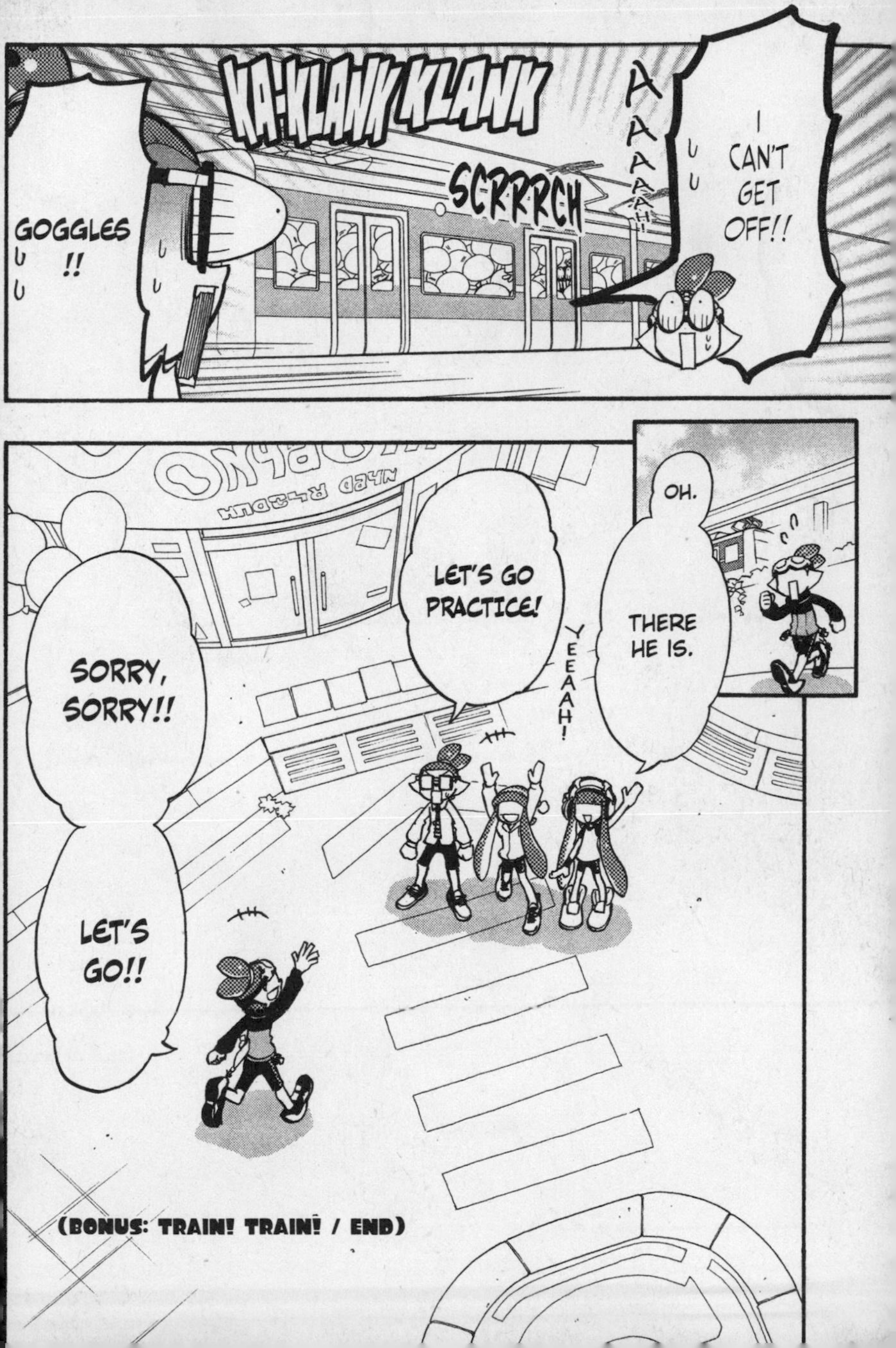
I CAN'T GET OFF!!
AAAAAAH!!
SCRRRCH
KA-KLANK KLANK
GOGGLES!!
OH.
THERE HE IS.
YEEAAAH!
LET'S GO PRACTICE!
SORRY, SORRY!!
LET'S GO!!
(BONUS: TRAIN! TRAIN! / END)

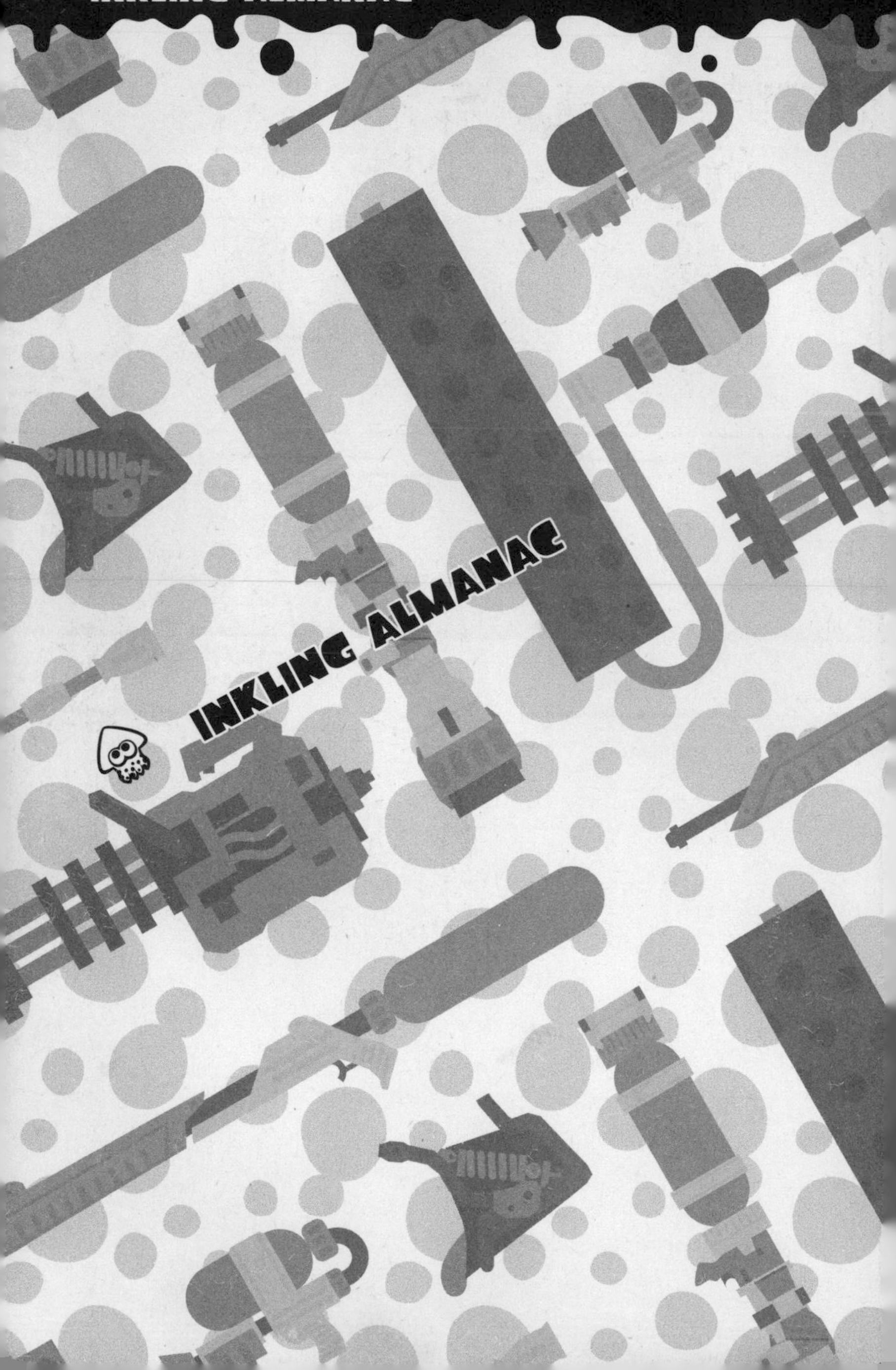
INKLING ALMANAC

H-Hey...

TEAM CYAN

MASK

Weapon: Carbon Roller Deco
Headgear: Gas Mask
Clothing: Purple Camo LS
Shoes: Green Rain Boots

INFO

•He actually has hay fever
(but he's fine thanks to the mask).
•A member of the S4.

SWOO

But he's fine.

Hrak hrak hrak...

JERSEY

FULL MOON GLASSES

DESIGNER HEADPHONES

Weapon:	N-Zap '89
Headgear:	Sun Visor
Clothing:	School Jersey
Shoes:	Blue Lo-Tops

Weapon:	Luna Blaster
Headgear:	Full Moon Glasses
Clothing:	Squidmark Sweat
Shoes:	Punk Yellow

Weapon:	Tri-Slosher
Headgear:	Designer Headphones
Clothing:	Green-Check Shirt
Shoes:	Black Trainer

INFO

•∙∙•°∙ ∙•● ●⁻∙∙●∙ °∙∙⁻∙°∙ •●●°∙ ●● °

•They often get together to play video games and read comic books when they're not practicing.

SKULL

Weapon: Custom E-liter 3K Scope
Headgear: Skull Bandana
Clothing: Octo Tee
Shoes: Gold Hi-Horses

INFO

•Has a wicked sweet tooth.
•A member of the S4.

TEAM PURPLE

PAISLEY

STITCH

AVIATORS

Weapon:	Aerospray RG
Headgear:	Paisley Bandana
Clothing:	Herbivore Tee
Shoes:	Red Slip-Ons

Weapon:	Sploosh-O-Matic 7
Headgear:	Squid-Stitch Cap
Clothing:	White LS
Shoes:	Squink Wingtips

Weapon:	L-3 Nozzlenos
Headgear:	18K Aviators
Clothing:	Squid Satin Jacket
Shoes:	Choco Clogs

INFO

- They don't talk a lot but they get along well.
- Skull and Aviators are childhood friends.

TEAM DARK GREEN

BIKE HELMET

Weapon: Custom Blaster
Headgear: Bike Helmet
Clothing: Striped Peaks LS
Shoes: Black Seahorses

INFO

•He's secretly practicing his shots away from his brothers and sisters.

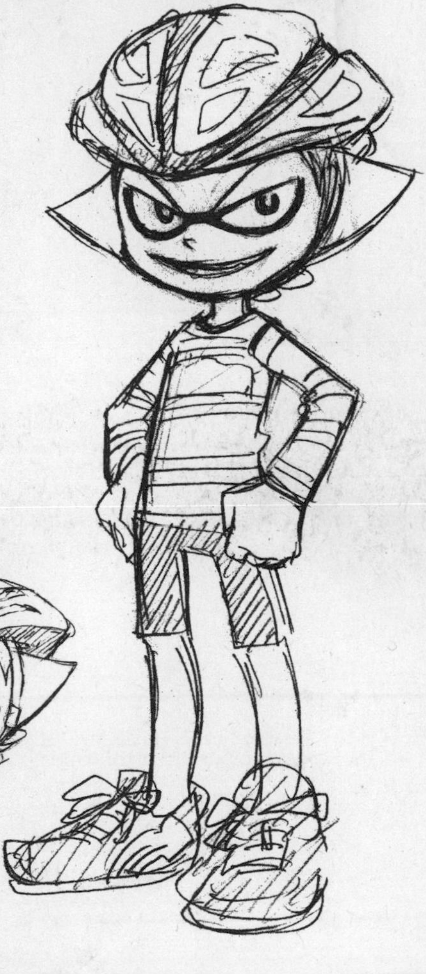

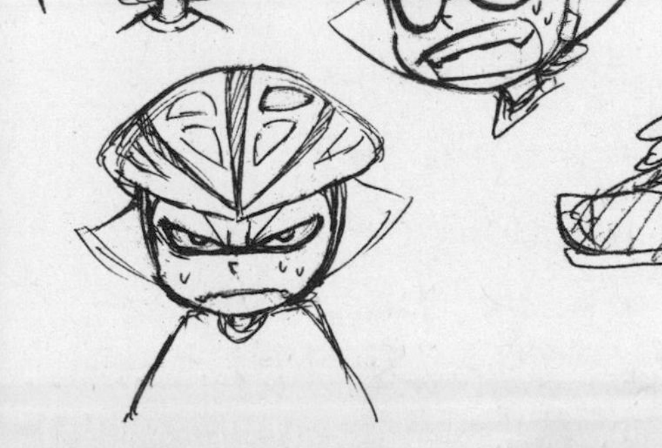

SKATE HELMET

SHRIMP

STRIPE

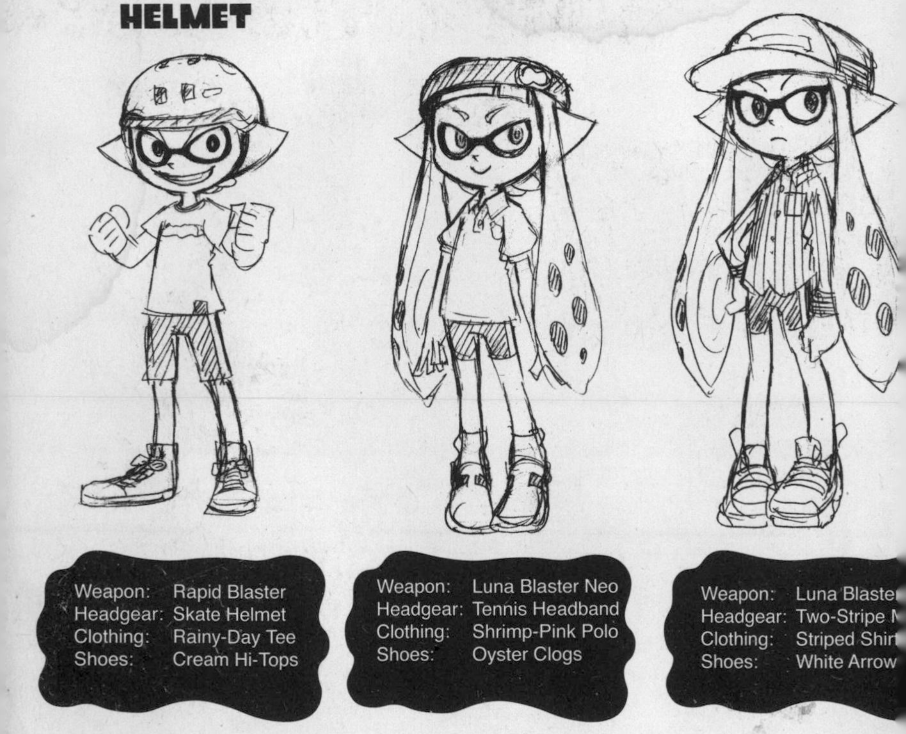

Weapon: Rapid Blaster
Headgear: Skate Helmet
Clothing: Rainy-Day Tee
Shoes: Cream Hi-Tops

Weapon: Luna Blaster Neo
Headgear: Tennis Headband
Clothing: Shrimp-Pink Polo
Shoes: Oyster Clogs

Weapon: Luna Blaste
Headgear: Two-Stripe M
Clothing: Striped Shirt
Shoes: White Arrow

INFO

- They make their own cakes for their birthday gifts. The cakes don't exactly look good, but they taste good.
- The little brother's helmet used to be worn by his big brother.

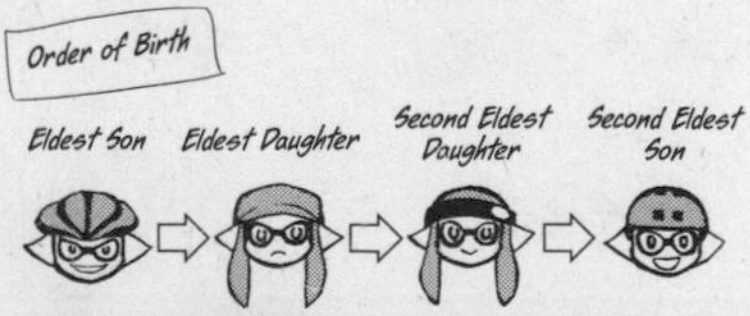
Order of Birth
Eldest Son
Eldest Daughter
Second Eldest Daughter
Second Eldest Son

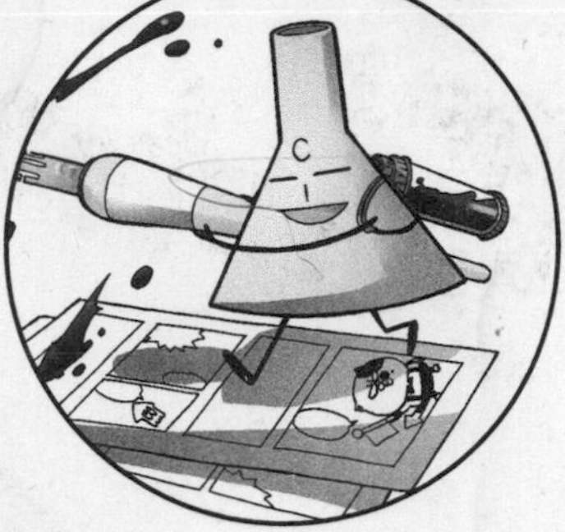

I RECEIVED A WONDERFUL ILLUSTRATION FROM SEITA INOUE, THE GRAPHIC ARTIST OF SPLATOON...! I'M SQUI-DELIGHTED...!

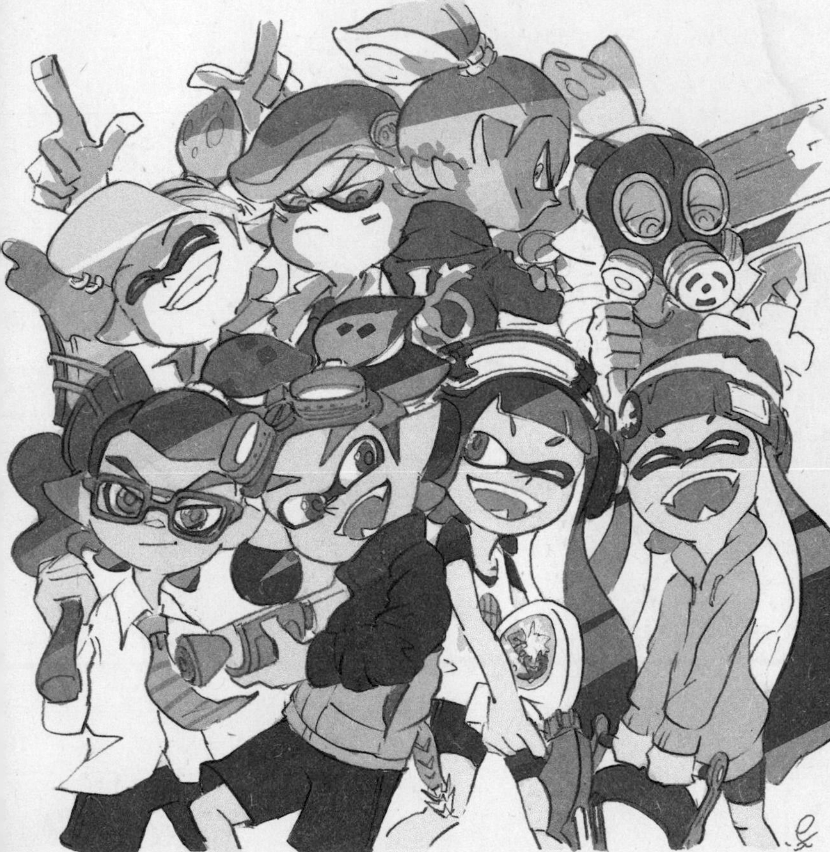

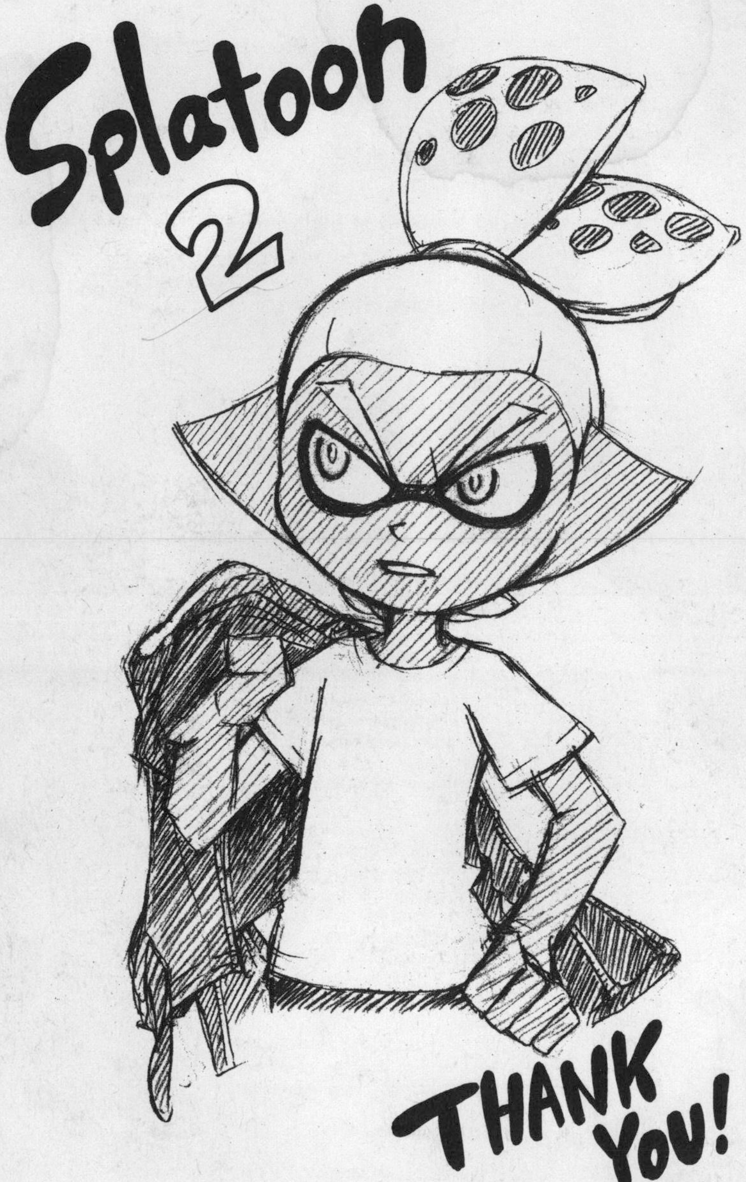
Splatoon 2
THANK YOU!

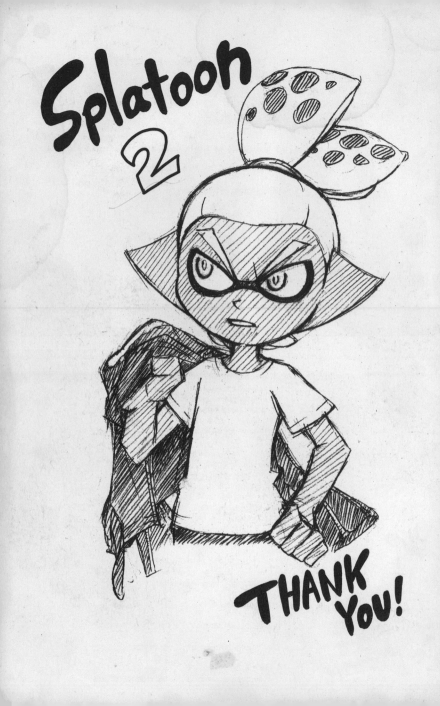

I'm not too fond of high places,
but I wish I could Super Jump.

Sankichi Hinodeya

Volume 2
VIZ Media Edition

Story and Art by
Sankichi Hinodeya

Translation **Tetsuichiro Miyaki**
English Adaptation **Jeremy Haun & Jason A. Hurley**
Lettering **John Hunt**
Design **Shawn Carrico**
Editor **Joel Enos**

TM & © 2018 Nintendo. All rights reserved.

SPLATOON Vol. 2 by Sankichi HINODEYA
© 2016 Sankichi HINODEYA
All rights reserved.
Original Japanese edition published by SHOGAKUKAN.
English translation rights in the United States of America,
Canada, the United Kingdom, Ireland, Australia and
New Zealand arranged with SHOGAKUKAN.

Original Design **100percent**

Printed in the U.S.A.

Published by VIZ Media, LLC
P.O. Box 77010
San Francisco, CA 94107

10 9 8 7 6 5 4 3 2 1
First printing, March 2018

Splatoon
reads from
right to
left!

This is
the end
of this
graphic
novel.

PARENTAL ADVISORY
SPLATOON is rated
A and is suitable for
all ages.
ratings.viz.com